Reid made to go ⬚⬚⬚⬚⬚⬚⬚⬚⬚⬚⬚⬚⬚⬚⬚⬚, but Mia had already climbed down. They walked toward the front of the house, the chirping of crickets punctuating the silence between them. And though the evening was mild and the sky studded with stars, he felt the air crackle with the intensity of an approaching storm. He was too aware of her. Too conscious of the sway of her hips, the fascinating mystery of her body.

Just a few more seconds and he'd be safe from any crazy impulses.

Abruptly tired of the mini pep talks he kept conducting with himself, he bounded up the porch steps and grasped the screen-door handle. Yanking it open, he unlocked the door. Impatience riding him, he took a quick step back. His body slammed into hers.

A high-pitched "oh!" escaped her as she recoiled from the contact. Teetering, Mia windmilled her arms.

He grabbed her before she could tumble off the porch. The banging of the screen door behind them was nothing compared to the slam of his heart as she fell against him. Soft, full breasts pressed against his chest.

Lust annihilated thought. Common sense went up in flames under the searing heat of her body plastered against his.

By Laura Moore

ONCE TASTED

A Silver Creek Novel

LAURA MOORE

BALLANTINE BOOKS • NEW YORK

A Ballantine Books Mass Market Original

Published in the United States by Ballantine Books, an imprint of Random House, a division of Random House LLC, a Penguin Random House Company, New York.

BALLANTINE and the HOUSE colophon are registered trademarks of Random House LLC.

This book contains an excerpt from the forthcoming book *Once Touched* by Laura Moore. This excerpt has been set for this edition only and may not reflect the final content of the forthcoming edition.

ISBN: 978-0-345-53700-3
eBook ISBN: 978-0-345-53701-0

Cover design: Lynn Andreozzi
Cover photograph: George Kerrigan

Printed in the United States of America

www.ballantinebooks.com

9 8 7 6 5 4 3 2 1

Ballantine mass market edition: June 2014

To Elaine Markson, my friend and agent,
who has guided me so wisely these many years.

ONCE TASTED

REID KNOWLES LOVED life's finer pleasures: the feel of a warm, enthusiastic woman moving against him, and the rush of a powerful horse carrying him over the fields in a ground-eating run. Today he was enjoying another: a dawn ride on his Harley, its engine roaring beneath him as he took Route 1's serpentine curves. He'd chosen the coastal route for the simple reason that it was beautiful. The salty bite to the California wind against his face felt great after the weeks he'd spent in the sauna that was South Carolina in early summer.

That he was presently enjoying only item number three on his list of pleasures didn't bother him at all, not when every mile flying beneath his wheels brought him closer to numbers one and two. Acacia, California, had some exceptionally pretty women living in it, and his home, Silver Creek Ranch, had some of the finest Quarter Horses to be found anywhere. In just a few hours, he'd be riding his own, Sirrus, a nine-year-old gelding he'd trained since birth.

No, he had no complaints at all. Life was good. And if there were moments when he recognized that maybe everything in it came to him a little too easily, well, this wasn't one of them.

He was happy.

With a grin into the morning wind, he dropped down a gear on the throttle and leaned into the next curve.

Oh, damn, he must be back.

Mia Bodell didn't need to be a modern-day Sherlock Holmes to guess who'd put the dreamy expression on Tracy Crofta's face at Spillin' the Beans. The barista fairly floated over the wide-planked, unvarnished floors as she took Mia's order, humming to the hissing of the steamer as she prepared her triple-shot latte.

There were other signs, too.

Tracy wasn't the only blissed-out female in the coffee shop. Betty Shales, who was sixty if she was a day, wore a beatific smile. Stationed behind the cash register, she stopped patting her gray dreadlocks only long enough to take Mia's money.

But in case Mia had suffered temporary blindness and failed to notice the women's joyous glow, she'd have had to be wearing earplugs to miss the trills of laughter and excited chatter when, latte in hand, she walked in to the post office—which also housed the local bank, general store, and luncheonette.

Not many towns could boast of having a post office where you could not only pick up your mail but also cash your checks, order a stack of buttermilk pancakes or a burger, pick up a loaf of bread and a bottle of Tide, and get your daily dose of the latest local happenings, too. The post office–general store–luncheonette wasn't just Acacia's hub. It was Gossip Central.

Mia wasn't big on gossip. She'd been the butt of it too often. But as she inserted her key into the metal mailbox and retrieved the mail, dropping half of it into the recycling bin and tucking the rest of it—bills, bills, and more bills—under her arm, the air around her buzzed.

Reid Knowles's name reverberated from all corners of the interior.

There was no escaping it.

The scent of freshly baked goods filled the spacious interior—another reason why the post office was such a popular place. Knowing how much her uncle Thomas loved the luncheonette's blueberry muffins, Mia got in line. And since no good deed went unpunished, she spent the next few minutes breathing in the aroma of melted butter, flour, and sugar while listening to Maebeth Krohner and Nancy Del Ray, who were working the morning shift at the luncheonette, sing Reid Knowles's praises.

"Mm-hmm, yeah, he got back today and dropped in to say hi." Nancy's voice held a wealth of satisfaction. Nancy had two small children and was five years older than Reid, but that didn't stop the divorcée from tracking his comings and goings with the breathlessness of a tween at a One Direction concert.

"Dang." Maebeth shook her head. "I knew I didn't need to fold the clothes sitting in the dryer this morning. I'd have seen Reid otherwise. Was he looking as fine as ever?"

Thirty and single, Maebeth made no bones about how much she liked Reid—really liked Reid. In this she was not alone.

"Could you doubt it? The man rode his motorcycle all the way from South Carolina. He came in here looking windblown and scruffy," Nancy replied.

"Oh Lord." Maebeth made a show of fanning herself.

It was nine A.M.; the luncheonette was busy and would stay that way until around two o'clock. Yet even as the two women dropped slices of multigrain bread into the toaster, set plates filled with steaming scrambled eggs and hash browns in front of hungry customers, and deposited stacks of dirty plates and empty coffee cups into a partially filled black rubber tub, their conversation didn't skip a beat.

"Such a bummer I missed him," Maebeth repeated dolefully. "You think he'll be at The Drop tonight?"

"I expect so," Nancy said.

"His being back sure will liven up the place."

Nancy nodded in agreement. "Mom's already offered to take the kids tonight so I can slip into my boogie shoes."

Mia was tempted to roll her eyes at the women's pre-occupation with Reid Knowles and his limitless appeal. She refrained, reminding herself about casting stones.

Taking a fortifying sip of her latte, which somehow she'd forgotten she was holding while she listened to Nancy and Maebeth, Mia focused her attention on the couple ahead of her, who'd stepped forward to pay. Both wore sturdy walking shoes. A folded map was tucked into the back pocket of the man's chinos.

Tourists, Mia decided. Since they weren't in jeans and cowboy boots, they probably weren't staying at the Knowleses' guest ranch, Silver Creek. There were plenty of other things to do in Acacia, though, such as hiking along the state preserve's trails, kayaking on Silver Lake, or touring the local vineyards. Spotting the *Wine Spectator* sticking out of the woman's canvas tote, she had her answer. Vineyard hopping was on the couple's agenda.

Although less renowned for its vineyards than Napa and Sonoma, Mendocino County produced some ter-rific wines. The carefully selected Dijon and Pommard clones, soil, and microclimate made the Pinot Noirs Mia and her uncle crafted rank among them.

Another vintner might have tapped either wife or hus-band on the shoulder and suggested a stroll over to Good Grapes on Laurel Street, where they could pick up the Bodell Family Vineyard 2011 Pinot Noir. It was delicious and a steal at sixteen dollars. She wished, too, she could have invited them to drive out to the vineyard for a tasting, but her dream of opening a tasting room had yet to materialize.

Besides, while Mia knew wine, she had no talent for self-promotion. Peddling her family's products in front of Nancy and Maebeth, who didn't have a shy bone between them, would only compound her embarrassment. It was all too easy to imagine their expressions at her awkward attempt at a sales pitch.

So she waited in silence while Nancy rang up the couple's items. Transaction complete, they moved aside. Pinning a smile on her face, Mia stepped in front of the register.

Nancy's expression changed from openly friendly to something more reserved. "Hi, Mia."

"Good morning, Nancy. I'd like a blueberry muffin, please." She also wanted to get the hell out of there. Maebeth had been in the same grade as her cousin, Jay, and so knew the stories, which meant that Nancy had heard every one of them, too. Certain tales didn't have an expiration date on piquancy.

But even if she wasn't convinced that both Maebeth and Nancy knew the filth Jay loved to spread about her and her mother, Mia would have felt uncomfortable with the two women who partied their free evenings away at The Drop or at the night spots in Napa. Hers were more often spent in front of the computer, entering moisture, pH, and nutrient levels for the different blocks of their vineyard. Then there was her new pastime of choice: fretting about the distracted look in her uncle's eyes. Something about Thomas had changed over the last few weeks. Was he sick? Was it money again?

"You came just in time. They're still warm." Nancy grabbed a brown paper bag from the stack on the counter and shook it open. Lifting the wire-mesh dome off the platter, she picked up the tongs. "It's for Thomas?"

The tongs hovered in the air. Mia nodded. "Yes."

At her answer, Nancy swooped down and plucked the largest of the batch off the white platter. "How's he doing?"

"He's fine," she said brightly, firmly.

"Your uncle is such a doll. You tell him to come on down for breakfast. We'll make blueberry pancakes to go with his blueberry muffin."

"Heck, we'll put blueberries in anything he wants," Maebeth offered as she picked up two orders of scrambled eggs and home fries for a table.

Everyone at the luncheonette knew Thomas loved blueberries, and they knew why. They'd been Aunt Ellen's favorite fruit. She'd died fourteen years ago, but Thomas never missed an opportunity to order something with blueberries.

Mia's smile lost its stiffness. "I'll tell him," she promised. It'd be fun to watch him gobble down a stack of gold and purple pancakes drowning in maple syrup and butter.

Nancy passed her the paper bag. "Can I get you anything, Mia? A lemon–raspberry muffin? A pecan roll?"

Her hips couldn't afford either. "No thanks, I grabbed a latte."

Nancy looked at the cup with undisguised envy. "I keep telling Charlie to get one of those espresso machines for here, too, but he doesn't want those java junkies over at Spillin' the Beans to go out of business." Charlie Haynes owned both the luncheonette and the building that housed Spillin' the Beans. Diversifying was the name of the game in this economy.

Mia tucked the mail more securely beneath her elbow, ready to say goodbye, just as Maebeth returned with an order. She gave it to Lou behind the grill and then turned to Mia.

"So, did you hear? Reid Knowles is back from South Carolina."

Leaving now would be too obvious, she thought with an inward sigh. "Yes, I caught you and Nancy saying as much."

Maebeth didn't notice her dry-as-dust tone. "You are so lucky to live next door to Silver Creek. I swear, if I were in your shoes, I'd be walking over to the ranch every day."

Nancy snorted. "More like every hour."

Maebeth shrugged off the teasing. "My ma told me a woman should never skip a chance to enjoy the finer things in life. I think most any woman would agree that Reid might very well be one of the finest. Am I right, Mia?"

"Actually, he's not my type."

Maebeth's plucked brows rose. "Really?" she drawled. "My memory must be going."

A blush crawled over Mia's cheeks.

"Honey, it's all right to admit it. That man is *every* woman's type," Maebeth said.

Nancy laughed in agreement.

With some effort, Mia smiled and injected a light tone into her voice. "I guess I'll be the odd man out and leave him to your enjoyment, then."

"Real generous of you." Maebeth's gaze swept over her. Mia knew she was taking in her thick and wildly frizzy hair—hair that Mia, at twenty-seven, still hadn't found styling products capable of taming—her oversize button-down shirt, comfortably baggy linen trousers, and canvas sneakers. Maebeth wasn't overly catty, but her satisfied smile spoke volumes. No woman who looked and dressed like Mia stood a chance at competing for Reid's attention.

True enough. What Maebeth didn't realize was that Mia could strap on a bra to make Madonna envious, squeeze herself into a skintight mini, and jam her feet into punishing dominatrix shoes, and Reid *still* wouldn't notice her.

He would look right through her like he always did, as if she were Saran wrap.

It was true. She, Mia Bodell, had the dubious distinction of being the only female that Reid Knowles, modern-day Don Juan, couldn't bother to check out, let alone flirt with.

Not that she cared.

It wasn't as if she wanted Reid's attention. She wanted more than a too-handsome-for-his-own-good cowboy. She wanted a man who was steady, dependable. Responsible.

"You off to work?" Maebeth asked.

"Yes. The grapes need inspecting." She'd be watching over them like a mother hen until the harvest.

"Things are hopping over in your neck of the woods. Reid said the guest ranch is at full occupancy," Nancy said.

No surprise there.

"And have you heard about the cowgirls' weekend they're holding at Silver Creek?" Maebeth asked.

"Um, no, I haven't—"

"It sounds like such a blast." Maebeth's tone turned wistful. She leaned her hip against the counter, ignoring the customers waiting. "Quinn told me about it. There'll be trail riding—natch—and tons of cowgirl stuff like roping and barrel racing. They'll be offering spa treatments, too—Ava Day and her assistants from the salon are going over on Saturday. At night there'll be entertainment, along with barbecues and karaoke. Nancy and I wanted to sign up—because how often can you go

on a fun-filled, luxury vacation five miles from home?
But Quinn said they're booked."

Quinn was Reid's younger sister and one of the
women Mia liked best in town. By tacit agreement,
Reid's name was rarely mentioned when she and Mia
got together.

"Silver Creek Ranch sure is doing a booming business," Nancy observed. "The Knowleses really know
what they're doing."

Mia flinched inwardly. What Nancy left unsaid was
painfully obvious: The Bodells might be the Knowleses'
closest neighbors, but in terms of financial success, they
were worlds apart.

Even in this tough economy, Silver Creek Ranch was
thriving. And it wasn't simply the guest-lodging part of
the ranch that was turning a profit. A few weeks ago
Mia had been in Wright's, the hardware store, to buy
some hoses, and had overheard two local farmers discussing how smart the Knowleses had been to keep
their Angus cattle grazing this summer rather than
sending them off to the spring sales. They were on track
to fetch a good price at market.

Mia wished she and her uncle Thomas had half the
Knowleses' success. Of course, were that the case,
they'd have to triple their efforts to prevent Jay from
skimming off the profits to support an L.A. lifestyle
that would make even an A-list celebrity blush.

The women were still discussing the upcoming event.
"Maebeth and I are going to try to convince Reid to
offer another cowgirls' weekend later in the fall. Great
idea, don't you think?"

"I'm not sure honing my cowgirl skills would help
me. Grapes don't run, so I hardly need to learn how to
toss a rope."

Maebeth straightened. "We're not talking usefulness,
we're talking fun! Doing something outside the box!"

Mia was pretty sure attending a cowgirls' weekend would be the furthest thing from fun and the closest thing to torture she'd ever find in Acacia. She didn't do the whole "hanging with the girlfriends" thing. She'd always been shy and, since high school, self-conscious. Other women seemed equipped with so much more protective armor. Thanks to years of Jay's cruel taunts, Mia's was riddled with chinks.

Her years at college and the graduate program she'd enrolled in at UC Davis had been easier. There she wasn't a bull's-eye for Jay's spite. But upon receiving her degrees, Mia had come back to Acacia, to the only family she had and the only home she knew.

A small town, Acacia possessed all the virtues and vices—long memories being among them—inherent in that life. Though things were easier now that Jay was gone, Mia was still reclusive. While she enjoyed the occasional get-together with friends like Quinn or with other vintners, the idea of a weekend surrounded by boisterous women living out their cowgirl dreams held scant appeal.

She gave an easy shrug. "I doubt I'd have the time. What with the harvest and the crush, fall's way too busy a period for us."

Maebeth's blue eyes swept over her. "That's a shame. You've got to get out more, girl. There's more to life than work, and it's not like you're getting any younger."

Twenty-seven was not exactly over the hill. "I'll be sure to keep my imminent decrepitude in mind."

Maebeth merely grinned. "You do that." Lou called out her order, and she went over and picked it up, carrying it to her waiting customers.

Mia wished Maebeth's words hadn't struck a nerve. The closest thing she had to a boyfriend these days was Andrew Schroeder. He worked as the cellar manager at Crescent Ridge, a large Napa winery. But with the growing season upon them, they were lucky to schedule a date once a month. Hardly the fast track to a thrilling romance or a sparkling social life.

She decided to call him soon. Otherwise she really would be old and wrinkled before they reached the next stage in their relationship. For some reason she'd been holding back, always calling it quits to the evening and saying good night before he could suggest they take things into the bedroom. A candlelit dinner at Aubergine, a Sonoma restaurant they both loved, would remind her of the reasons she liked him—he was smart, funny, and cute in a Clark Kent nerdy way. Best, he knew a ton about wine. Once she committed to a relationship with Andrew, then surely a blue-eyed cowboy's husky laugh wouldn't make her breath catch.

Maebeth returned and leaned her jeans-clad hip against the counter. "So will you be coming down to The Drop tonight? It's always fun when you do a blind taste test."

Mia decided that Maebeth should consider getting a job on a cruise ship, rounding up the passengers for the night's entertainment.

"And profitable," Nancy chimed in. "I made twenty bucks betting on you last time. I love it when you out-geek the wine geeks, Mia."

"I'm sure I'll be down sometime soon." But she knew she wouldn't be wowing any of The Drop's patrons with her ability to identify a wine with a single sip tonight.

Not if Reid Knowles was holding court.

MIA LEFT THE luncheonette, the mail tucked under her arm and the brown paper bag with Thomas's muffin clutched in her hand, and walked down Main Street to where her truck was parked.

It was summer. The tourist season was in full swing, but Acacia was far enough off the beaten track that parking was never difficult. There was practically always a spot on one of the downtown's four streets.

Many of the out-of-towners who found their way here were guests at Silver Creek Ranch. But at this hour of the morning they would either be enjoying a leisurely breakfast, sunning themselves by the pool, or out on a ride, following the miles of winding trails that covered the ranch. Depending on which trail the wrangler selected, Mia sometimes caught a distant glimpse of horses passing—flashes of copper, gray, and black against the vegetation. If they were loping, a telltale cloud of dust would rise in the wake of the hooves pounding the earth. Once the dust settled, Mia would return to training the vines to the trellis, pruning shoots, or weeding the aisle, while sending a silent prayer to the cosmos. It was a simple one: that when the hungry guests returned from their ride, the ranch's waiters would suggest pairing their food with a Pinot Noir grown less than half a mile away from where they'd ridden earlier that day.

She started the truck, eased out onto Main Street, and headed out of town before turning onto Route 128. With the traffic light and no joggers or cyclists in sight, she was free to enjoy the vibrant greens of the trees that bordered the winding two-lane road.

Her family's home and vineyard was near the end of Bartlett Road, just beyond the turnoff for Silver Creek Road, the private lane that led to the Knowleses' ranch. The Bodells' own drive was much shorter. It only seemed longer because of the ruts that riddled it. Out of habit, she slowed to a crawl. Speeding risked trips to the mechanic, dentist, and chiropractor.

The less-than-perfect drive went nowhere in welcoming visitors or friends, but repairing it was way, way down on the list of budgeting priorities. Although her cousin hadn't struck recently, he was bound to turn up, like a bad penny. When he did, he'd hit up Thomas for money, using lies and guilt to slice open his father's heart and wallet.

Whatever money was left after one of Jay's raids went into the vineyard or toward the crew's salaries. Neither she nor Thomas would have it any other way. And their frugality had paid off, she thought, casting her eye with pride over the acres of neatly trellised grapes, their dewy bright green leaves glistening under the morning sun.

Over the rise, the weathered shingled farmhouse came into view, and her heart clenched. This had been her home since the age of three, when Thomas had brought her to Acacia after her mother's death.

Parking the car in back of the house, she followed the uneven stone path to the front, thinking that she might find Thomas sipping his morning coffee on the porch, one of his favorite ways to start the day. But there was no sign of him.

She opened the door and dropped her keys onto a tray of woven grapevines that she'd made in sixth grade for her aunt Ellen's birthday. The keys jangled as they landed on a pair of pruners and a coil of wire.

"Thomas? Are you up?" she called.

She cocked her ear and heard the thump of footsteps from the master bedroom overhead. Satisfied, she crossed the living room on her way to the kitchen. The house had changed little since Aunt Ellen's death. The furnishings were well loved but, to put it kindly, tired. The green floral-patterned sofa sagged in a shallow "U" in the middle, and its cushions had given up any pretense of being cushiony. Nonetheless, she picked them up and patted them, encouraging them to fluff as best they could.

Time and their cat Vincent's claws had all but destroyed the arms of the beige and dark-pink armchairs, but she ran a hand over them, too, before straightening the magazines and books on the coffee table.

The dining room required no neatening, since it was rarely used in the summer, she and Thomas preferring to bring their dinner onto the porch. And though the wallpaper was a faded memory of what Mia's aunt had chosen, and the trim cried for a fresh coat of paint, the mahogany dining room table still gleamed. It was Aunt Ellen's favorite piece, and Mia dusted it every week, which was more than she did in her own room. There, the dust bunnies under her bed had grown so large they were clamoring for their own Facebook page.

She entered the kitchen, with its red Formica counters and checkerboard linoleum floor. She'd heard Formica was staging a comeback among designers. If true, she and her uncle Thomas were cutting-edge chic.

The white metal cabinet gave its usual squeak of protest when she opened it, took a china plate down, and placed the blueberry muffin on it. The muffin was still warm. She wished she weren't on a perpetual diet, because it smelled divine, too.

Whereas plain Greek yogurt smelled of cold yeast.

Carrying the plate to the small breakfast table nestled underneath the kitchen window, she heard her uncle coming down the hall.

She turned and smiled. "Good morning. I got the mail and the paper as well as a special treat."

"Good morning, Mia. So you've already been to town? I didn't realize it was so late."

"It's not." It was an hour later than her uncle normally rose, but he was sleeping badly these days. She often heard him in the middle of the night. The creaking of his steps on the floorboards followed by the flap of his slippers on the stairs would alert her to the fact that once again he'd gone to fix himself a cup of tea and open his laptop in the small study off the living room. Occasionally, she'd hear his voice and wonder. But it didn't seem right to pry and inquire about his nocturnal conversations when he never mentioned them.

He eyed the muffin and smiled. "That *is* a treat. From the luncheonette?"

She crossed the kitchen to the refrigerator, a martyr to zero percent fat, and plucked a yogurt from the middle shelf with an inward sigh. "Yes, I picked it up along with the mail. Nancy and Maebeth say hi. They're pining for you, Thomas. Nancy picked out the biggest muffin for you."

"They're lovely ladies."

"They think you're lovely, too." Second only to Reid Knowles. "Sit and I'll get your juice and coffee and your pills."

Folding his tall frame into the chair, he rolled up the

sleeves of an ancient plaid shirt. Its faded blue matched his eyes. "You're too good to me, Mia."

"Don't be silly. If I was really good to you, I'd have tried to bake these muffins myself."

"No need to involve the fire department."

She grinned. "Good point. So, you slept okay?"

"Like a baby. I'm as fine as a man my age can be. Don't fret."

"I'm not. I just want to keep you in tip-top shape for the harvest. It'll be here before we know it. Paul and Roberto have already arrived. I saw their trucks by the carriage barn. I'm going to head out and help them. Will you come and look over a few of the blocks with us?"

Thomas picked up his orange juice and drained half of it while Mia swallowed a spoonful of her yogurt and pretended she liked it.

"Perhaps. I need to check the barrels in the cellar," he said, putting the glass down.

"You're still okay with Cork and Cap coming on Monday, right?" To keep expenses down, Thomas hired a mobile bottling company to bottle their wines. The wine from two harvests ago had been aging in medium-toast French Limousin oak barrels for the past twenty-one months. After careful monitoring, Thomas had declared it ready to be bottled.

But ever since Mia called and scheduled the bottling company, Thomas had been checking and rechecking the contents of the barrels. It was odd. He was a master at shaping a wine.

"Yes, Monday should be fine. This wine is going to be special. I want people to remember it."

Mia smiled at the enthusiasm in his voice. "I can't wait until we open our first bottle. So, you'll come out later? It's going to be a beautiful day. A little sunshine would do you good."

"If Vincent doesn't have a better idea. He may decide relaxing on the porch and enjoying the view is in order." Vincent, their tabby cat, was named after Vincent of Saragossa, the patron saint of *vignerons*—winemakers. They'd adopted him from Quinn Knowles, who found the abandoned kitten cowering beneath the gas station's dumpster.

"Vincent might enjoy a stroll down the aisles, too. Bring him along."

He wiped his fingers on the napkin and looked at her steadily. "You don't need me to advise you in the vineyard, Mia. You're more than qualified." Thomas's tone, though gentle, held a hint of exasperation. "Moreover, you should spend some more time in the winery. Your winemaking skills will go fallow," he warned.

She stuck her chin in the air. "They won't."

He raised an eyebrow in silent skepticism but held his tongue—for now. The debate wasn't a new one. But Mia saw no reason for her to fret over the wine fermenting in the stainless steel tanks and aging in the barrels when Thomas was so much more experienced in judging every phase of making superlative Pinot Noir.

Recognizing that she wasn't going to give in, he shook his silver head. "Go take care of our grapes so I can eat my muffin and read the paper in peace."

Relieved he wasn't going to press her, she grinned. "Anyone ever told you you're a grumpy old man?"

"All the time. Now go away." He picked up the muffin and took a big bite.

"Yes, sir." She gave a smart salute, the one she'd been perfecting since the age of four, the first year she'd taken part in the crush.

The memory of that day was still vivid. She could hear the adults' laughter and the anticipation in their voices as they gathered around the mechanical crushers. She could recall her excitement as Aunt Ellen took her hand, steadying her as she climbed into a large tub filled with purple-black grapes. While Mia stood in the center, dressed in dungaree cutoffs, her bare toes curling around the cool, wet fruit, Uncle Thomas explained that she would be recreating the drama of how grapes were crushed long, long ago, before there were cars, trains, or planes.

"Or crushers?" she'd asked.

"Or crushers," he'd confirmed with a solemn nod.

She'd shivered in excitement at the importance of her job as the grapes pressed against her bare calves and ankles.

Then Uncle Thomas looked at her. "Are you ready, Mia?" he'd asked gravely.

Quivering with pride, she raised her right arm and saluted. "Yes, sir!" She'd tried to make her voice as strong as his so the assembled grown-ups could hear.

Uncle Thomas had raised a shiny silver wine goblet high overhead. *"Que le pigeage commence!"*

Those memories—of the thrilling start of the crush coupled with the wet squish of grapes beneath her feet, the sweet, heady scent of their burst skins filling her nostrils, the purple stain marking her legs and feet like a badge of honor—lived inside her as among her happiest, untainted by sorrow.

Though no longer as simple as the barefooted stomp of a little girl mushing grapes in a plastic tub, the pleasure of the crush remained potent. The adult Mia appreciated the more complex emotions that now accompanied it, the anticipation and anxiety of the race against time and the elements to harvest the fruit at its peak moment—a signature part of the winemaking process—and then to crush the juice-filled grapes as gently as possible before transferring the fruit to the fermenting tanks.

Soon it would happen again. Thomas and she would

gather with their crew to celebrate another harvest. With Mia's care, and Lady Luck and Mother Nature's indulgence, Thomas would have yet another excellent wine to fashion and shape.

Everything was on track this year for an exceptional vintage. The niggling sense that something was off when she came upon her uncle lost in reverie, miles away from Acacia, meant nothing. He was fine. And she needed to stop looking for problems.

Chapter

THREE

"Hey, Reid."

Reid glanced over his shoulder, resting the bristle brush on Sirrus's flank. Tess Casari, his brother Ward's fiancée and the guest ranch's events planner, had found him.

After picking up his mail at the post office, grabbing an espresso in town, and exchanging a few "hi"s along the way, he'd come home. There, he'd tossed his backpack at the foot of his bed and grabbed a quick shower so he could make it to the staff meeting on time.

Thankfully, the meeting hadn't been a long one. Even after the round of hugs, kisses, and slaps on the back offered to him, and the barrage of questions about how the grand opening of Aunt Lucy and Uncle Peter's new inn down in Aiken, South Carolina, had gone, they'd wrapped up everything on their agenda within an hour.

Tess had talked for most of the meeting, filling them in on the upcoming event: the cowgirls' weekend. Usually, Reid's mother and father ran the staff meetings, but they were on a conference call with Kent Wallace, their lawyer. The conversation must have been detailed, because they still hadn't put in an appearance by the time the meeting broke up.

No matter. Tess had done a fine job, and Reid could tell how pleased Ward was—though Ward often got that gleam in his eye when he looked at Tess. A better gauge was the satisfied smile on Phil Onofrie's face. In charge of reservations and marketing for Silver Creek, Phil was clearly happy with the way the event was shaping up.

The meeting over, Reid had come down to the corral, eager to see the horses—his in particular. He'd brought Sirrus over to the shade of an oak to groom and tack him. Ward had asked him to ride out and check the cattle in the upper pastures.

Keen as he was to finish grooming Sirrus, saddle him, and head out for a good hard gallop, he gave his future sister-in-law an easy smile. "Hey, beautiful. Aren't you a sight for sore eyes?"

Tess brushed off his compliment with a laugh. "The women of Aiken must be bereft since you roared out of town. Is everything okay, Reid?"

"Sure. Why shouldn't it be?" He wasn't going to reveal to Tess the restlessness that had come over him during the meeting, especially since the feeling wasn't justified or understandable.

"You left the meeting quickly. I kind of wondered."

His brother's fiancée wasn't just beautiful, she was sharp. He shrugged and resumed brushing Sirrus's dapple-gray coat. "No mystery. I wanted to come and say hi to this guy here." He patted the horse lightly. "South Carolina was great, but Aunt Lucy and Uncle Peter don't have horses like him, at least not yet. Glad to see that fiancé of yours took good care of him."

Tess stepped forward and stroked Sirrus's dark-gray muzzle. "Ward rode him almost every day," she told him. "He and your dad also took him and Bilbao out and worked the cattle."

Bilbao was one of the youngsters they were training

as a cutting horse. Ward had been giving him a lot of practice sessions in the corral, working on rundowns and sliding stops and cutting steers from the herd. It would have been neat to see how he performed in the open. "Yeah? How'd he do?"

"Great. Ward's come around to Quinn's point of view."

"What, that Sirrus is teaching Bilbao all his tricks?"

Tess nodded. "Yeah."

From the time Reid's little sister, Quinn, was a baby, she'd been animal crazy. Nothing could get her crawling faster than a cat or dog a few feet away from her. Whenever Quinn had shown signs of fussing, all their mom had to do was bring her to the horse barn or sheep pen. It never failed to calm her.

At twenty-four, Quinn's love of creatures great and small was as strong as ever. Her opinions about them were, too. She'd been the first to notice that whenever Reid rode Sirrus and Ward trained the younger horse, Bilbao seemed to watch Sirrus's nimble hoofwork—fancy enough to have earned him some championships—and to take note of the evil eye Sirrus gave the steer he was cutting from the herd.

Reid and his family often talked about the animals and livestock they raised, discussing their different talents and personalities. It was natural for them. Animals were their livelihood, and they had hundreds of them in their care.

He wondered, though, whether Tess was aware of how comfortable she'd become talking about them. When she'd first arrived at Silver Creek Ranch seven months ago, she avoided the barns and corrals like the plague. Ward had been the one to figure out how to get this animal-shy New Yorker to see that sheep didn't come with fangs and that horses were pretty damned magical creatures.

Tess Casari was more than just a recent convert to the wonders of the animal world. She was also a wiz at events planning. The job description entailed being good at reading people, which was why her next question didn't come as a surprise.

"So, you're sure nothing's wrong?"

Reid wasn't in the mood for reflection. His edginess would pass once he and Sirrus were racing over the meadows. But he could feel Tess's gaze boring into his back as he picked a hind hoof clean. The farrier must have been here recently, for Sirrus's shoes were still shiny.

"Nope." He lowered the hoof, straightened, and then turned around. "It's good to be home and have a moment to relax."

"Relax?" Tess cocked her head. "At last count you had half a dozen different jobs here at the ranch. You care for how many head of cattle and sheep and train how many horses in the fine art of cutting? In your downtime you act as a trail guide for the guests' rides, take the wine nerds on tours of the local vineyards, consult with George, Jeff, and Roo on which vintages to stock in the restaurant's cellar, and brainstorm with Ward and Phil about marketing strategies for the ranch." She paused a beat. "Yeah, I guess there's not much around here to keep you busy."

He shrugged. "Let me put it another way. After helping out with Aunt Lucy and Uncle Peter's inn, everything here seems kind of routine. Silver Creek Ranch functions like a well-oiled machine." Of course, it was good to see the guest ranch running so well, its success the result of years of hard work and an unflagging commitment to excellence on the part of his family and the ranch's staff.

"Then I have good news for you. There's a problem that requires your special skill set."

"Yeah?"

"It's the cowgirls' weekend. You know we're counting on you to do some demos for the ladies—lasso tricks, reining, barrel racing—so the women can admire your, um, skills."

"Skills, my ass," he muttered.

"Oh, your butt will definitely play a key role," she said cheerfully. "Though it's possible a number of the women will swoon just admiring your face."

He shot her a look. "Very funny."

"Sorry." Her tone was wholly unrepentant. "I'm only trying to get into the spirit of the weekend. As the second-best-looking man on the ranch, you should be prepared for a whole lot of that spirit."

"Wait a minute. Are you telling me I'm a notch below Ward in the looks department? Love really is blind."

She didn't take the bait but smiled mistily, doubtless thinking about his older brother's awesome wonderfulness and masculine beauty.

Finished grooming, Reid dropped the hoof pick in the carryall. Not even the clatter of the metal against the molded plastic penetrated Tess's happy fog.

With a sigh, he waved his hand in front of her face. "Earth to my future sister-in-law."

She blinked. "What?"

"I'm on top of the demos I'm supposed to entertain the women with. I'm showing them roping techniques Friday. Saturday morning Quinn and I are going to team up to demonstrate barrel-racing techniques. And Ward, Quinn, and I will also be leading the guests on trail rides. Depending on how busy they are, Pete and Jim may accompany us 'cause they're fine-looking cowboys." He laid his drawl on thick. "So what's the problem?"

"The problem is the wine tasting we've scheduled for

Friday evening. There's a glitch. We don't have anyone to do it."

"It's already arranged. Lana Cruz from Red Leaf Vineyards is handling it." Lana ran the tasting room at Red Leaf and was fun and upbeat. He'd dated her casually for a few months but had called it quits before leaving for South Carolina. She'd been cool about it. Lana liked her relationships free and easy, too.

"Not happening. She just emailed me. One of her staff broke his arm skateboarding. It's his pouring arm, so she has to fill in until he's out of the cast. We need someone else. Adele suggested Mia Bodell."

"Nope." He dismissed the idea calmly as he lowered his tooled saddle onto Sirrus's back, adjusting it and the red-and-black-striped wool blanket beneath it. "How about George? He worked as a sommelier when he lived in Santa Barbara." George Reich managed Silver Creek's restaurant.

"A good idea, but George is already booked. Adele asked him to give a chat with my friend Anna Vecchio about the demands of running a restaurant. People love an insider's look, and what could be better than hearing about a New York City trattoria and an innovative Northern California restaurant?"

"And you'd rather he didn't do two different talks." He picked up Sirrus's bridle. Ward must have cleaned it yesterday. The leather was supple and the snaffle bit sparkled.

"You got it. That's why Adele thought Mia would be a good choice."

He laughed, shaking his head. "I've only been back an hour and she's already at it. Listen, Tess, I know you love your employer and future mother-in-law. So do I— Mom's great. But no way am I asking Mia for anything. So run back and tell Mom to quit while she's ahead in the matchmaking business. She hit one out of the ballpark with you and Ward, but she's punch-drunk if she thinks I'm going to spend more than five minutes in Mia Bodell's company." The woman hated him. Not that Reid could blame her.

"I don't think she's matchmaking, Reid."

"No, she's only been dropping hints that I should invite Mia to such-and-such event for a year now. All perfectly innocent."

"She said Mia knows her wines."

Mia made the widely acclaimed wine critic Robert Parker look like a bum and a slacker. "Listen, Tess, the women who signed up for the cowgirls' weekend are coming to have a good time. Mia would probably expect them to take an exam after her presentation."

"Come on!" she said with a laugh.

"I'm serious. I'll ask Thomas to do it instead."

"Thomas? Oh, you mean her uncle?"

Tess was still learning the locals' names. "Yeah, and the women will love him."

Regardless of how he felt about Mia or how she felt about him—which was at the level of sheep shit on the like meter—Reid considered Thomas Bodell a good friend. "I was already planning to drop by the vineyard to say hi," he continued as he slipped the headstall over Sirrus's ears. "I'll ask him if he wouldn't like to chat about wine with a group of charming ladies. What time have you scheduled the tasting for again?"

"Five o'clock."

"If he's willing to do it, it'll go great and these cowgirls-in-training might actually learn something they can use when they return home. He knows his stuff."

"According to Adele, Mia does, too."

Reid rested a hand on his hip. Time to let Tess in on a few facts. "Listen, Mom's always had a soft spot for Mia, which is fine. It's a free country. But this business of asking her to do the wine talk is moot. Mia won't give me the time of day, let alone—"

Tess's brown eyes widened dramatically. "Stop the presses! You mean there's a woman between here and the Atlantic who can resist your charm?"

"I don't try to charm Mia."

"Huh." Tess was looking at him, amusement dancing in her eyes. "Are you sure we can't get her over here? I'd love to witness the sight of a woman under the age of a hundred not fawning over you."

"Sweetheart, I can tell you've been spending too much time with Ward. Your sense of humor's gotten warped. I'll go over to the vineyard and ask Thomas to give the talk."

"Well, at least we've averted a scheduling crisis," she said. "I'll let Adele know our problem is solved."

"And tell her to quit trying to set me up with Mia. It ain't happening. Not now, not ever."

He watched Tess fight a losing battle with a grin. Good to know someone was entertained by his mom and her matchmaking habit.

"Sure thing, Reid."

Sirrus was happy to stretch his legs in a run as they headed toward the uppermost pastures to check on the cattle that roamed the slopes in the summer months, grazing free. Reid had missed the nine-year-old gelding, which was trained to respond to the subtlest shifts of his body.

The Angus cattle looked good, strong and solid. Just as significant, the pastures looked healthy, and the ponds and tanks that supplied the herd's water were full. As long as a drought or heat wave didn't hit, the cattle destined for market in November would reach a good weight.

He'd have to figure out a good distraction for Quinn come then. Whenever it was time to schedule the cattle for harvesting—the industry's euphemism for slaughter—Quinn, despite being a rancher's daughter, went through a rough patch emotionally. Even though their family raised the cattle in as ethical and humane a way as possible, Quinn hated the thought of them being killed.

Last year Reid had taken her white-water rafting. Maybe a weekend of hang gliding or a trip to a wolf sanctuary would do the job. Knowing Quinn, she'd opt for the wolves.

Sirrus and he had reached the creek for which his family's ranch was named and that wound its way over hundreds of acres. They crossed it. The cool water, scooped by Sirrus's hooves, splashed onto Reid's jeans, and he grinned.

On firm ground again, he moved the gelding into an easy trot. They followed the wide ribbon of water for a ways before angling off to ride the fence line.

Constructed of wood and wire, it, too, was in excellent shape. He spotted no holes along the bottom of the heavy-gauge wire to indicate predators were trying to dig their way in. Once again, a nagging restlessness filled him. It wasn't that he *wanted* anything to be wrong with the ranch. Besides, he knew all too well that soon enough a crisis would arise, either of the animal or human variety. That's the way it was on a guest ranch.

It was just that a part of him craved the challenge of something new, something different. But what it was, he had no clue.

That he felt even an ounce of restlessness or dissatisfaction was ironic since he was the laid-back member of the family, content to drift along with no set agenda. It was his older brother, Ward, who enjoyed taking charge and then charging ahead.

Ward had been the same way with women. Sure, it had taken him awhile to find the right one, but luckily Tess had come along and he'd had the smarts to recognize what an amazing woman she was. Yeah, Ward had definitely lucked out in finding someone like Tess to share his life.

Not that Reid was looking for that kind of commitment himself. He was far too happy enjoying all the different women who came and went. To him, women were like a splendid menu. Why forsake the pleasure of sampling all those delicious creations for one single dish? He wasn't sure he could do it for a month, let alone the rest of his life.

He just didn't see it.

Luckily there was no reason for him to contemplate such a future. Ward was about to tie the knot. Reid was willing to predict he and Tess would soon be producing feisty, pasta-loving cowkids. With the promise of a new generation of Knowleses populating Acacia, California, Reid's mother could surely relax with the matchmaking habits.

His mother was terrific. He loved her. But if she continued with the "Mia Bodell is really a lovely, smart girl" refrain, he was going to enroll her in rehab.

He did like the company of one Bodell, though. And if Reid went to visit Thomas now, Mia would still be tending the vines. He'd gone to the trouble of learning the rhythms of the vineyard to avoid crossing paths with her. On the regrettable occasions when he'd screwed up and run into her either at the vineyard or in town, he'd gotten damned skilled at ignoring her.

The fence's gate was a couple hundred yards away. Reid closed his legs, and Sirrus moved into a flowing extended trot. No time like the present to pay a neighborly call.

Chapter
FOUR

WHILE THE BODELLS' winery shared a property line with his family's ranch, to Reid it was like stepping into a different world, one where regimented rows of grapevines soaking up the California sun replaced fields, live oaks, and fir trees. He might be a cowboy and rancher at heart, taking pride in the grass-fed beef his family raised, the caliber of the wool gathered from their sheep, and the excellence of the Quarter Horses they trained, but he also respected what the Bodells produced with such care and attention to quality.

It was through his friendship with Thomas Bodell that Reid had learned to better appreciate wine and to distinguish the varietals by their color, aroma, and taste. Of course, he would never know as much about wine as someone like Thomas. Or Mia, for that matter. But, unlike her uncle, Mia didn't see the point in sharing her knowledge and educating a cowboy who spent most of his days in the saddle.

At the thought of Mia, he unconsciously pressed his lips in a flat line and swept his gaze over the brilliant green canopy of trellised vines. Her distinctive cloud of gold-brown hair was nowhere in sight. But then he caught a blur of blue. It was Mia. The quick tightening in his gut told him so. She'd wrapped a bandanna around her hair. She was standing deep into a row, her back to him. A good distance separated them.

Excellent. She was busy with her grapes. He'd be able to see Thomas in peace. He drew a deep breath, forcing his muscles to relax.

Sirrus had been walking over the grass that grew along the road to the Bodells' old farmhouse. Approaching the house, Reid guided Sirrus onto the drive. The ring of his hooves on the gravel mingled with the busy cries of the swallows and bluebirds overhead.

A hearty voice called out to him. "Reid! Good to see you, son." Thomas was sitting on the porch with his tabby cat, Vincent, nestled on his lap. By the time Reid and Sirrus reached the farmhouse, Thomas had risen to his feet and descended the porch steps. His cat jumped onto the porch railing, the better to observe the intruders. He stared fixedly, his gray-and-black-striped tail twitching.

"When did you get back?" Thomas asked.

"Rode in this morning." Reid swung his leg over the saddle and dismounted. Grasping the reins in his left hand, he shook Thomas's outstretched one.

"Not on Sirrus, I assume."

Reid returned his smile. "On my Harley."

"Almost as good."

"Yeah."

"Actually, your parents told me you'd be back today. I was hoping you'd drop by. Can you sit awhile? I've got something to share with you."

"A liquid something?"

The older man's eyes twinkled. "That, too, my boy."

Thomas disappeared around the back of the house. Reid took the lasso hanging from his saddle horn and tied a slipknot around the horn, then, making sure there was enough play in the rope, looped another knot around the porch's top rail.

He'd just loosened Sirrus's cinch when Thomas returned, two glasses in hand. "I bring you the nectar of the gods. Sit down and prepare to be transported."

"Ready and willing," he said, accepting the glass. Then he looked more closely at his friend's face. Perhaps it was because Reid had been gone for several weeks, but something looked different about Thomas. His lined cheeks seemed rosier, and there was a bright sheen to his eyes. Was he feverish, Reid wondered with sudden concern. "So how are you feeling?"

"Taste this first. That'll give you one hint as to why I'm smiling."

"It's your latest vintage?"

Thomas nodded, his smile growing broader. *"Salut."* He clinked the rim of his glass to Reid's.

"Salut," he replied. Raising the glass, he paused first to examine the purple-red hue against the midday sun and then to inhale the wine's bouquet. Slowly, he tipped the glass's bowl, letting the wine flow into his mouth and pool, awakening his taste buds. He swallowed.

"It's got a nice, balanced body."

"And the taste?" Thomas prompted.

"Cherries, vanilla, and oak." Reid paused. "There's something else—a lighter note. What is it?"

"You're getting good. Violets," he pronounced proudly.

"Violets?" Reid's brows rose. "Damn, how did those sneak in there? And who knew violets could taste so good?"

Thomas took Reid's teasing with good grace. "Mia did an outstanding job with the grapes. And to think she'd only just graduated from the enology program when this wine was on the vine."

Reid gave a noncommittal "mm-hmm" in reply and

then raised his glass for another sip. "Congratulations on the wine, Thomas. It really is outstanding."

Thomas nodded. "I've had Mia schedule the bottling company."

"I want to order a hundred cases."

Thomas grinned widely. "I'll let Mia know. She'll be delighted."

Reid doubted that. With an effort, he put Mia out of his mind. Few things made him irritable; Mia never failed. "So, how are you feeling, really?"

Thomas reached for his wine, took a sip, and sighed. "Let's just say I'm glad this wine is as superlative as it is, since it'll be the last one I make here."

Reid set his glass down on the table between them with a sharp *clink*. "Thomas, what the hell! Are you ill?"

Thomas slapped a hand on his thigh and barked in laughter. Still grinning, he said, "Good God, man, no! I'm in love."

Reid blinked, feeling stupider and stupider. "In love?" he repeated.

"I've met someone, a wonderful woman. Actually, Pascale Giraud and I have known each other for several years. She and her husband, Michel, owned a small vineyard near Bergerac. I even went and stayed at their vineyard when I was touring the region five years ago. But Michel got sick, and unfortunately we lost touch while he was battling cancer. He died two years ago." He gave a single shake of his silver head. "I saw Pascale again in late May at a conference in Napa, and, well, something clicked between us. We've been emailing and Skyping ever since." The twin spots of color that Reid had noticed on Thomas's cheeks minutes earlier deepened. "She's amazing, Reid. Vibrant, warm, and giving. Pascale's asked me to come and live with her in France. It'll be a new chapter in my life."

Reid looked at his friend. "I'll be damned. I'm happy

for you, Thomas." With a crooked grin, he leaned forward and slapped the bony shoulder beneath Thomas's checked shirt. "Congratulations. When do you leave?"

"A week from Tuesday."

Reid's brows rose in surprise. "That soon?"

"To me it feels like forever. I find I'm as eager as a schoolboy. I want to be with Pascale. At my age it's foolish to let time slip by. I bought the ticket on Priceline. Captain Kirk came through with a good deal."

"A man you can count on. Wow," he said, leaning back in the chair. It was hard to grasp that the days of sitting on the porch with Thomas, sipping Pinot and shooting the breeze, were at a close. "So what'll happen with the vineyard?"

"Mia will take it over. The girl graduated at the top of her class from UC Davis. Time for her to come into her own and make a name for herself." He cleared his throat. "That's the other thing I want to talk to you about."

Still absorbing the news Thomas had delivered, Reid answered automatically. "Sure, what is it?"

"I've offered your family a stake in the winery."

"A stake? Why?"

"That's simple. Money. I'll need substantial funds of my own when I'm in France, and Jay will of course require a sum. That won't leave much of anything in the till for operating costs." His answer was accompanied by an embarrassed grimace.

"What about a bank loan?" Reid asked.

"In this economic climate? It'd be a miracle if I could get one—I haven't exactly been turning a profit on the winery, and Mia doesn't have a proven track record as a winemaker yet. Besides, your parents and I worked out much better terms than any bank would offer." Thomas shifted in his chair, leaning forward. His voice mirrored his eagerness as he continued. "Our lawyers have already drawn up the papers. But Adele and Daniel wanted to make sure you're okay with the plan."

Reid shrugged. "If my parents want to diversify the ranch's investments, I'm not about to object."

"Good," Thomas said with nod. "Because we all agreed this would only succeed if you were willing to work with Mia."

"Whoa. Wait a minute." Reid held up his hand. "Why would I be working with Mia? I'm not a vintner."

"No, but you know more about wine than anyone else in your family, and you know how to run a business—that's what Mia really needs."

Reid was tempted to retort that Thomas could have used a business adviser himself these years; then he might not be in this awkward financial position. But what was the point? What mattered was he had to figure out a way to let his friend down gently. "Thomas, this isn't—"

"A good idea? Sure it is. All you have to do is give Mia a hand to get the business ball rolling, so to speak." Thomas's expression was earnest. "I'm asking you as a friend, Reid. You're a good man and someone I trust. It'll ease any worries I have about leaving if I know you're watching out for her. She hasn't had an easy time of it."

The words were a kick in the gut.

Reid was all too aware how hard Mia's life had been. Her older cousin, Jay—Thomas and Ellen's only child— had seen to that.

Reid was certain Thomas had never learned what happened when Mia, Reid, and Jay were in high school. Reid was equally convinced that if he'd done the right thing that day and confronted Jay, Mia's teen years would have been a whole lot easier. But discovering that Mia had a major crush on him and had even written about him in her diary had embarrassed Reid. Funnily enough, he'd been a late bloomer. At sixteen he was just beginning to think about girls.

What had actually been in Mia's diary—whether the descriptions were like Cinderella fairy tales or far more racy and explicit fantasies—quickly became immaterial once word about the journal spread through school.

Mia had been a freshman. Girls had difficulty shaking certain labels; "slut" stuck like superglue. "Pathetic" was just as hard to shake.

The memory still had the power to make Reid feel like shit. Maybe if he helped her out with the business end of the winery, it would ease the guilt he carried.

"And Mia? Is she okay with our working together?" He had a good imagination. Picturing Mia happy about doing anything with him defied it. Then another thought occurred to Reid. "How did she take the news of your leaving?"

Instead of answering, Thomas stared off in the direction of the vineyard.

"Thomas?"

The older man's gaze shifted to the sage-green floor beneath his canvas sneakers. "She doesn't know yet."

Christ, he thought, rubbing the side of his face. "You mean you haven't told her yet? About any of this?"

"No. No, I haven't." A defensive note entered Thomas's voice. "I haven't wanted to share my relationship with Pascale with anyone. I told your parents only to explain the situation. My feelings are too new and special. I'd almost forgotten what it's like to fall in love. It's the bluest sky, the clearest note, the finest vintage champagne, perfectly chilled and crisp." His blue eyes became dreamy. "When I'm talking to Pascale, everything dances inside me. When I close my eyes, I can feel her in my arms, remember the softness of her skin, the scent of roses and bergamot that clings to her. Surely you of all people understand, Reid. You've had so many women. . . ."

Yeah, he'd had women. But while he adored looking at them and loved having sex with them, none had ever moved him to rhapsodize about blue skies and champagne bubbles. For a second he felt a twinge of something like envy. It passed.

Thomas was still speaking. ". . . so, no, I haven't told Mia. It would be awkward. Besides, I wanted everything settled first. Giving her an incomplete picture would only upset her. I hate scenes."

Reid's brows rose. "You don't think you're going to cause a bigger, messier one this way? What do you expect her to do when she finds out you're decamping half a world away in ten days' time? You're like a father to her, Thomas."

His lips flattened in a grim line. "I know. But the fact is that I'm *not* Mia's father. Not a day passes when I don't wish I knew who he was, so she could have someone else to depend on, another family member to love."

Like everyone else, Reid knew the stories. Serena Bodell, Thomas's little sister by twelve years, had been a wild child, and their elderly parents quite conservative. After one too many blowups, seventeen-year-old Serena had run away. Thomas, apprenticing at a vineyard in Europe, wasn't even informed by their parents that she'd left home. They refused to speak her name.

"You never were able to discover anything about Mia's father?"

"There wasn't a single clue as to his identity. Much as I hate the idea, it's possible Serena didn't know it herself." He sighed. "She and Mia were in Florida when she drowned. The neighbors who'd been watching Mia for the night could only find two documents that held any relevance: Mia's birth certificate—with the father listed as *unknown*—and the telephone number here."

"Nothing else?"

Thomas gave a heavy shrug. "Serena had become a drifter, living on the fringes. Their worldly possessions amounted to little more than some photos of Mia and Serena, a suitcase of clothes, and a few hundred dollars in cash. When we got the call, seven years had passed since she ran away. By then my parents were dead, and Ellen and I were living here. Jay was six. As Ellen and I were Mia's only known family, we brought her home. Then Ellen passed, and I was left to raise Jay and Mia alone. I did the best I could—maybe better with Mia than with Jay."

For a moment Thomas sat lost in memories. Reid, unwilling to cause his friend more pain with his questions, remained silent.

With a shake of his head, Thomas roused himself. "But that's water under the bridge. Both Jay and Mia are grown adults, and I want something for myself now. If that's selfish, so be it. Don't get me wrong, Reid. I love Mia."

"I know you do. But I still think you should tell her as soon as you can."

"I disagree. Holding off will shorten the inevitable unpleasantness."

It always amazed Reid how smart people could be dumb. "Blindsiding her is not the solution, Thomas."

"She'll get over it," he said mulishly. "After all, I'm handing over the vineyard and the winery to her. She'll be busy from dawn to dusk calling the shots from vine to wine. All she needs is a little guidance in the area of marketing and so on." He gave a vague wave of his hand. "With you helping her, she'll have it."

Reid wasn't often angry, but right now he felt like shaking the older man. "You apparently haven't noticed this, but Mia's not too fond of me."

"Oh, she likes you well enough."

The man needed his eyes checked.

A sly grin stole over Thomas's face. "See, Reid, you're doing it already."

"Doing what?" he asked, exasperated.

"Looking out for Mia. Now all you need to do is advise her on how to get our wine into more people's glasses. Simple."

Yeah, right. Sure, he felt as if he owed Mia. And, sure, he'd been feeling a restless itch this morning, as if he needed a challenge, a change from the normal routine. But this was not the solution. Not by any stretch of the imagination.

"So can I count on you, Reid?"

Hearing the worry in Thomas's voice, Reid shifted in the wide-planked chair and wished that, instead of wine, he had a few fingers of whiskey in his glass. He suppressed a sigh. "I'll do what I can."

Thomas stretched out his hand. For a second Reid hesitated. What the hell, he thought, and shook it.

With a relieved grin, Thomas said, "I really appreciate this, Reid. I'll call Daniel and Adele—"

"No, I'll speak to them." He had a few choice words for his parents about springing this deal on him. "I'll go talk to—" His sentence went unfinished, for just then Mia's voice called out.

"Thomas?"

Damn, Reid cursed silently. He didn't want to run into Mia. Not now especially. He wasn't sure he could act as if everything was fine and dandy.

What would shock her more—learning that Thomas was leaving or that he'd fallen in love? And if by some chance she managed to take that news in stride, how would she react, he wondered, when Thomas finally got around to telling her she was going to be working with her least favorite person in the whole world?

MIA HAD WORKED through the morning, moving through the blocks, going from vine to vine and cluster to cluster, inspecting the fruit for any signs of rot or mildew. As she went, she wielded her pruning shears, trimming errant lateral shoots and removing leaves that grew too close to the grapes, stealing the sun from them. Whenever she crossed a weed springing up between the vines, she bent down and tore its roots from the tan dirt.

Growing grapes involved cooperation from Mother Nature: a warm sun to ripen the fruit, and an adequate amount of rain to nourish the vines. Vintners dreaded Mother Nature's nasty temper tantrums. Late-spring frosts wrought terrible damage to the vines' tender buds; heat waves stressed the plants; prolonged or torrential rains waterlogged the grapes and made them rot. Any of these events could bring tears to a winegrower's eyes.

A successful vineyard also required two additional things. First, an excellent site—*terroir*—and, second, a vintner who was moderately to largely obsessive. Like her wildly frizzy hair, this was a trait Mia considered she possessed in spades.

Happily, the grapes were looking healthy this year. The bright green clusters of fruit were full and unblemished. Their leaves showed no sign of being munched on by pests or withered by fungi. As long as Mother Nature continued to cooperate and Mia, Paul Cortez, and Roberto Mora, who helped manage the vineyard, were judicious and vigilant in thinning the vines to give each plant the needed energy to ripen the remaining grapes, they were headed toward a good harvest. Mia refused to say the word "great." She didn't want to jinx the vineyard's chances.

At break time, Roberto and Paul, both of whom had worked with her uncle for years, walked with Mia back up the tractor path toward the outbuildings.

The carriage barn, which now housed far-less-romantic equipment—the small tractor and forklift, the grape bins, the dumper, and the crusher—came into view first. Next came the winery. A long building, its end was built into the slope of a hill to keep the cellar's interior cool. When Thomas and Aunt Ellen had first built it, they'd dreamed of creating a tasting room in the front of the winery. That dream had died with Ellen. Grief had taken root instead.

Though smaller in scale, the staff building, like the other outbuildings, was constructed of redwood. The siding had aged to the color of dark chocolate. The trim and the doors were painted sage green. Climbing roses covered its front.

Ellen had planted the roses when Mia was eleven. Thomas had built the trellises for them, just as he'd constructed the trellises for the first grapes he'd planted in the vineyard, the land inherited from his mother.

Mia had never known her grandmother. She'd died a few years after her only daughter, Serena, ran away. Jay said grief killed her. Jay was skilled at mixing honesty and lies. Mia hated that this was probably one of the occasions when her cousin chose the unadulterated truth.

Pushing her melancholy thoughts away, Mia inhaled deeply, catching the roses' lush scent on the summer breeze. It was too beautiful a day to let anything spoil it.

"I'll see you later, guys."

"We'll be in block five," Paul said, opening the door to the staff quarters.

She nodded. "Maybe I can get Thomas to come down and lend a hand after lunch. I want him to see how nicely the berries are forming."

As the winemaker, Thomas was by temperament more interested in what happened to the grapes—or berries—post-harvest. But this summer he'd stayed away even more than usual, seemingly content to rely on her updates. She couldn't understand his growing detachment.

"The vines should put a smile on his face," Roberto said. "They're looking good, Mia."

Roberto wasn't known for his compliments. Feeling suddenly a little less sweaty and grimy, she waved good-bye and walked up the flagstone path to the back door of the house. Inside the mudroom, she toed off her sneakers and peeled off her socks before padding into the kitchen. The linoleum floor was deliciously cool. A quick glance at the counters showed no new dishes or any other signs of her uncle having foraged for lunch. Surely he was finished in the cellar by now.

"Thomas?"

There was no answer. She moved to the bottom of the stairs and called his name again.

"We're here, Mia."

She turned her head. Her uncle's voice had come from outside. She glanced at the open window. The light wind lifted the linen curtains, making them billow like sails. So her uncle had stuck to his plan and decided to sit on the porch with Vincent.

A second voice reached her. Recognizing the low, relaxed drawl, she stiffened. And here she'd hoped nothing would spoil her day.

Steeling herself, she opened the front door. Unlike the rest of the female population, she didn't intend to go marshmallow soft over the sight of Reid Knowles.

As she stepped onto the wide porch, Reid, handsomer than Adonis and twice as annoying, rose from his chair. She refused to be impressed, knowing he performed the courtesy instinctively. His parents had taught him his manners.

He crossed the porch to lean against the railing. "Mia," he said with a short nod.

"Reid." She spoke his name through clenched molars. No wonder the women at Spillin' the Beans and the luncheonette had been aflutter that their number-one "crushtomer" was back in town. He was tanned, and his gold-blond hair was a little shaggier than usual. His chambray shirt made his blue eyes even more piercing. He must have left his razor behind in South Carolina.

Thank God she didn't like facial hair.

She reminded herself of that fact even as her fingers itched to touch the light-brown stubble covering his lean cheeks in a slow, exploratory drag. Would it feel silky-soft or scratchy?

Stop, her brain commanded. There would be no gawking or fantasizing about what a few days' old beard would feel like against her fingers, her lips, or any other part of her body.

She told herself to look away. Unfortunately, her eyes were as wayward as her itchy fingers, for her gaze landed just below the straight blade of his nose. If she'd had to describe his lips, she'd have said they were normal, of average width and shape. Nothing special. Until he smiled. Then Reid's mouth became a thing of beauty. Outrageously seductive and so very kissable. His smile was like the rest of him: perfect.

A woman would do a lot for a smile from Reid Knowles.

But not her. Her days of dreaming of Reid's smiles, of longing for just one of his kisses, were in the past.

And, besides, Reid didn't smile at her. He didn't even smile *past* her.

He was doing it again, that trick he employed. He'd fixed his electric-blue gaze on a spot just beyond her left earlobe, a neat way of avoiding eye contact with her.

Someday she was going to kick him in the shins, but not today, when her feet were bare. She planned on wearing steel-toed boots when she finally gave in to temptation. She'd had her young heart wounded because of him. No way was she going to break a toe over him.

And no way was she going to start wishing that she wasn't wearing dirt-streaked, shapeless pants and a baggy button-down shirt that was too old even for Thomas to wear. Even with the breeze it had been hot in the vineyard. She was sure that sweat had darkened the faded bandanna she'd tied about her head to keep her hair from going *sproing, sproing,* Slinky-like, in her face while she worked. Her bare feet were in equally dismal shape. She couldn't even remember when she'd applied her current coat of polish.

Why was it a man could look better the scruffier and dirtier he was? Were life fair, she should look smoking hot right now. Yet Reid seemed far from caught in the grip of burning desire.

She reminded herself that she didn't care. She didn't care how she looked, and she didn't care what he thought of her. And she hated the little voice inside her head that screamed, *Liar!*

Thomas was smiling benevolently from his rocker, seemingly unaware that Mia and Reid hadn't moved beyond their one-word greeting—and weren't likely to before the next century.

"Mia, love, Reid and I were just enjoying a chin-wag with Sirrus and Vincent—though Vincent decided he didn't have much to say to a horse and he left. Such a snob, our cat."

Horse? It was only then that Mia noticed the dark-gray animal grazing contentedly on the green grass bordering the house's foundation. As sleek and assured as its owner, the equine hadn't bothered to raise its head at her appearance. She forgave the horse for ignoring her.

How lowering to realize that Reid exerted such a magnetic force on her that she hadn't even seen the large animal tied to her porch rail.

Would she have missed a howdah-strapped elephant, too?

A military tank, perhaps?

It rankled that she couldn't say for sure.

And why was Reid Knowles the only man on earth who could get away with riding his horse over to visit a neighbor? *Normal* people drove cars, rode bikes, or walked. But Reid never did the usual. He did what he pleased.

"Reid's just come back from South Carolina," Thomas said, adding, "he rolled in this very morning."

"Mm-hmm. I heard something to that effect in town."

"Really? You didn't mention it," Thomas said.

She shrugged and allowed herself a small mocking smile. "Not being newsworthy, I guess it slipped my mind."

For a fraction of a second Reid's gaze connected with hers. The jolt seared her. Then his gaze shifted to fix on that damned point beyond her ear. His expression was impossible to decipher.

"Don't tease the man, Mia." Amusement laced her uncle's voice.

"Don't worry about me, Thomas. I think I can handle anything Mia dishes out. I have a bratty sister, after all."

Thomas chuckled. Reid's visit had obviously energized him. He always loved it when Reid came over to discuss winemaking with him and share a glass. And though she had a hard time crediting Reid with much, Mia knew his affection for her uncle was genuine.

She realized that she was still staring at Reid as if he were some masterpiece in a museum. She crossed the porch and sank into the chair he'd vacated.

Unfortunately, that brought her to eye level with his crotch. According to the females in Acacia, and doubtless across the other forty-nine states, the bulge behind the zipper truly was a work of art—a tool worthy of being cast in bronze.

Good Lord, what a thought. She must have had too much sun. That's why her baggy shirt was sticking like flypaper to her back and the curves of her breasts; it wasn't from the thought of what Reid's penis looked like. She forced her gaze to the floor, but of course that involved taking in his casually crossed legs. Drool-worthy muscles stretched the worn denim.

Was there any part of this man that didn't appeal? Oh, yes, his character.

"I should head off." Reid directed his comment to Thomas.

"And you'll talk to Adele and Daniel?"

Because she had yet to tear her gaze away from his jeans-clad legs, Mia saw Reid's thigh muscle jerk. Had he just flinched?

Surprised, she looked up. Twin comma-shaped grooves

bracketed his unsmiling mouth. My God, the ever-relaxed cowboy was *tense*.

She glanced over at her uncle, who was looking at their guest far too intently. Something was going on.

"Yeah, I'll speak to them—" Reid broke off and shook his head. "Damn, I nearly forgot why I rode over. Thomas, would you be willing to come and give a wine talk this Friday? It's for our cowgirls' weekend. After the talk we'll hold a tasting."

"A wine talk. That sounds like fun, don't you agree, Mia?"

She made her shrug careless. "I wouldn't have thought the women who sign up for a cowgirls' weekend would be interested in wine. Shots of whiskey and tequila, perhaps."

"I think you underestimate the sophistication of our guests." Reid's tone had an edge now.

Shame pricked her. She didn't mean to sound condescending toward women she didn't even know. Reid simply brought out the worst in her.

Done with her, Reid switched his attention back to Thomas. "The presentation and tasting will be at five o'clock. It'll be followed by demonstrations in the kitchen from Jeff and Roo."

Now that she'd heard about the other, less typical "cowgirl" activities scheduled, she wished she'd kept silent about the guests' tastes. Jeff Sullivan and Roo Rodgers, the guest ranch's head chef and pastry chef, were incredibly talented. Watching them work would be a treat for anyone.

"Are you sure you're up to giving a presentation, Thomas? It might tire you out. You haven't been sleeping that well."

A flush stole over her uncle's cheeks. She knew he didn't like her fussing over him, yet she couldn't help but be worried about his insomnia and growing distraction.

"I'm fine, Mia. There's nothing wrong with me." But in a sudden imitation of Reid's, Thomas's gaze didn't quite meet hers, leaving her more convinced than ever that something was off with him. Terribly off. The feeling only grew when he said, "But perhaps you're right. Why don't you give the presentation, Mia?"

"What?" Mia squawked. And from the way Reid jerked his shaggy dark-blond head, she knew he was equally surprised and unhappy at the substitution.

Thomas spread his hands as if the idea was self-evident. "Silver Creek's female guests would much rather learn about wine from a woman close to their own age than from an old geezer like me."

"I—I—" she stammered.

"It'll be good for you to address an audience, Mia," he said.

Cod-liver oil was supposed to be good for one, too.

"And, Reid, you're of course fine with having Mia give the talk?"

Reid's tanned throat worked, as if he was forcing something bitter down it. "It's funny—Mom herself suggested Mia."

Thomas's smile looked like Vincent's when he was fed poached chicken. "Did she, now? A smart woman, your mother."

Mia was busy zeroing in on what had been left unsaid. Despite Adele Knowles's vote of confidence, Reid had nixed the idea of Mia giving the wine talk. He'd scratched her off the list even before she'd made the snippy comment about the ranch's guests.

The thought made her stomach churn with embarrassment. She told herself this was nothing new. Reid had never liked her. She still remembered Jay describing how Reid had laughed his head off while Jay read the pages from her diary.

"How about it, Mia? Will you do the Bodell Family Vineyard proud for me?"

She lifted her chin and shot Reid a look of cool dislike. She'd do anything for her uncle. She'd even give a talk to a bunch of strangers. "Of course I will."

"Well, that's settled." Thomas rubbed his hands together in satisfaction, while Mia and Reid each pretended the other didn't exist. "So, what wines will you introduce to the ladies? We'll let them taste our 2009, of course."

"That would be a treat," Reid said.

Thomas nodded. "What other Pinot Noirs could we use to compare?"

"None can compare in terms of quality–price ratio," Mia said.

"Red Leaf Vineyard's 2010 vintage has a nice balance and is priced fairly reasonably," Reid countered.

"Crescent Ridge's is superior," she stated. Moreover, Crescent Ridge Vineyard was where Andrew Schroeder worked. She could get some bottles from him and suggest a date.

"I'd prefer you introduce them to the smaller vineyards located around Mendocino. Sonoma and Napa hardly need the promotion."

"Good point, Reid," Thomas said before Mia could rebut. "It's too bad our 2012 vintage won't be ready." He gestured at the empty glasses. "The wine will need time to recover after bottling. But guess what, Mia? Reid's preordered a hundred cases."

With anyone else, Mia would have flown across the porch and hugged the person. She crossed her arms over her chest. "A smart investment."

"I buy wine to please our restaurant's diners, not as an investment."

"It's a decision you won't regret," Thomas said.

"Of course I won't."

"Well, we can't thank you enough, Reid. For everything."

Everything? Why did Thomas owe Reid gratitude for anything? Sure, Reid had placed an order for a lot of wine, but, then again, he was no stranger to the quality of their grape. And why had Reid's eyes darkened, a storm clouding their vivid blue, when her uncle thanked him? The tension she'd noticed in him earlier—well, it was back.

Something had the laid-back cowboy on edge. And he seemed none too happy about it.

As if aware of her scrutiny, Reid pushed off the railing and straightened. "I've got to go, Thomas. Call me if you need anything."

"I think we've gone over everything I need."

For a moment Reid simply looked at her uncle. "Remember what I said."

Her uncle smiled. "I will."

As Mia frowned in confusion at their exchange, Reid bent and scooped up his hat from where it sat by the leg of her chair. Settling it over his brow, he nodded in her direction. "A pleasure as always, Mia."

He would never be so formal or so quietly cutting toward any of the women who fawned over him. But before Mia could reply with something suitably sarcastic to remind him how little his opinion mattered, he strode past her, giving her a front-row seat to the spectacle of his long legs and tight butt. Any words flew right out of her head.

Then he was down the porch steps and untying his horse, his movements filled with fluid, athletic grace, something she had in woefully short supply.

Placing the toe of his boot in the stirrup, Reid swung himself easily into the saddle and then wheeled his horse in a tight circle, urging him into a trot. Even from the back he was stunning. Tall and proud in the saddle, Reid was a perfect match for the glorious animal moving like quicksilver beneath him.

A weaker woman would have sighed aloud.

REID STOOD OUTSIDE the round pen and watched his sister, Quinn, work with Tucker, a horse she'd adopted this past spring. Quinn had been at the rescue center to pick up another horse—Glory, a sweet-natured gray whose owner had been forced to give him up—but then she'd spotted Tucker.

Few things were as heartbreaking as the neglect and cruelty inflicted on animals by humans. So of course Quinn had come home with two horses. Glory had already begun working as a trail horse for the guest ranch's riders. He was getting rave reviews. Tucker was a different story. When he'd arrived at Silver Creek, the chestnut had been half starved, beaten, and scared out of his equine mind.

The change in him over the course of these last five months was impressive, and all due to Quinn.

Through solid work and endless patience, Quinn had reached the stage where Tucker not only accepted the hackamore, a bitless bridle, he had even allowed her to climb onto his back. For an abused horse like Tucker, his acceptance showed an extraordinary degree of trust. Naturally, he was still skittish. The session today had started with sidestepping, hopping, and breaking—the gelding surging into a nervous run—but Quinn in the saddle was as calm and easy as she was on the ground. She flowed, supple and quiet.

Tucker had slowly settled.

By now only his ears and tail twitched, signaling his hyper-alertness. Quinn's heart must be bursting with pride for the horse's courage. Reid's, too, was full, but for his sister. Earning the trust of another being, especially one that had been badly hurt, was an amazing accomplishment.

Not everyone had Quinn's gift. Reid wondered whether he could succeed even nearly as well. Of course, the creature whose trust he needed to gain was of the two-legged variety.

As had happened all too often this week, Reid's thoughts turned to Mia. He didn't want to be thinking about her. He already felt bad about the tough breaks she'd had in life and regretted his involvement in Jay's public humiliation of her. Now, because of his mother, father, and Thomas Bodell, his conscience was even heavier.

It was Thursday, the day before Mia was due to come and give her wine talk to the guests, and he couldn't stop wondering how she was handling the news Thomas was doubtless delivering with all the subtlety of a one–two punch. Wondering and worrying.

For Christ's sake, Mia thought Thomas was suffering from insomnia, something exercise or a change of diet might cure. How would she react to hearing that his condition required more than a glass of warm milk before bed? That the remedy for love with a capital "L" was to let him follow his heart to the South of France?

Thomas wanted to believe that the prospect of running the vineyard and winery would be enough to make Mia happy.

Reid didn't buy it. If his parents up and announced

their intention to move to New Zealand or Timbuktu, it would come as a hell of a shock. But he would be okay because he had Ward and Quinn to rely on. He had family.

Mia had a royal jackass of a cousin.

And, thanks to his parents' decision to invest in the Bodells' winery, she had Reid.

He didn't think Mia would see that as a bonus. Not in a million years.

He'd spent this week studying the angles, then stepping back to look at the bigger picture. From what he could see, his advising Mia on how to increase the winery's profits and market visibility had the hallmark of a disaster. When she found out he'd been tagged as her business adviser, she'd spit in his eye. An admittedly easy prediction, since that had been her MO every time she got within spitting distance.

The problem was, Reid didn't like failing. At anything. In this he was very much a Knowles. He wasn't the type to walk away from a job, either. So he was going to have to figure out a way to get Mia to agree to follow his advice. To trust him somehow.

"Hey, Reid. How did Roland go for you?" Quinn asked.

He looked up to find that his sister had dismounted and was standing next to Tucker. "Good," he said. "You've done a nice job working with him. His transitions are a lot smoother." Just as Ward had exercised Sirrus for Reid while he was down in South Carolina, Quinn had ridden some of the youngsters Reid was bringing along, among them Roland, a flashy liver chestnut. The four-year-old had the makings of an excellent competition horse.

"Whew." She pushed her straw cowboy hat back and pretended to wipe the sweat from her brow. "From your expression I wouldn't have guessed you were happy about anything."

No surprise that he'd been frowning while he thought about Mia. Few women were as frustrating as she.

"What are you talking about?" he asked as he opened the gate for her, taking care to move slowly and not spook Tucker.

She waited until it was open wide to pass through with the gelding. "Your scowl," she said as he fell in step beside her. "Not that it's new. You've been wearing it most of the week. You've been as much fun as the grim reaper."

"I've been loads of fun," he contradicted.

"Hardly. Even Maebeth Krohner noticed. She cornered me this morning by the mailboxes. She's worried you didn't dance enough at The Drop the other night. What gives? Are you still angry with Mom and Dad? And what's that all about?"

"It's nothing. Just a little disagreement." On Tuesday Adele and Daniel had met with Thomas and their respective lawyers. Papers had been signed to both parties' satisfaction. But until he had word from Thomas that Mia was aware of the deal between the families, Reid was keeping his lips sealed.

"Oh, sure. 'Just a little disagreement.'" Quinn rolled her eyes. "I can't remember when I've seen you storm into Dad's office and slam the door behind you—and on your first day home, too." She made a *tsk*ing sound.

"The wind probably caught the door. I had stuff to say in private."

"And you must've read Mom the riot act. I went in after you'd stomped out. She was standing by the window and didn't turn around, but I could tell she was upset. Her chin was wobbling. . . ."

Oh Jesus, he thought. He'd been good and pissed at both his parents for not giving him at least a heads-up about their negotiations with Thomas, but he hadn't intended to make his mother cry.

They'd apologized, of course, his father explaining that they'd held off finalizing the deal with Thomas Bodell because they'd wanted Reid to be on board with it. He was the logical choice to oversee the management end of the vineyard. Thomas had asked to make the pitch to Reid himself. Since both Daniel and Adele sensed how important it was to Thomas, they'd agreed.

Their explanation had gone some ways toward calming Reid down. He understood why they hadn't wanted to pass up such an investment opportunity. With the proper business strategy, their stake in the winery could open up possibilities for the guest ranch, too. He could already envision them.

Devising ways to increase the winery's profits while preserving its quirky boutique charm would be a challenge for him but one he thought he had a successful shot at. If he could figure out a way to work with Mia.

And that was a big if.

With a start, he realized his sister was still talking.

". . . but then the next time I peeked into Dad's office, Mom and he were smooching. Then they left, saying they were heading up to the house—most likely to indulge in some afternoon delight—so all's well that ends well. Which means you can stop looking so guilty."

"Do you ever shut up?"

"Not if it means missing a chance to bug you or Ward," Quinn replied with an angelic smile.

They walked toward the corral, Reid careful to maintain his distance from the horse. Tucker still trusted only Quinn. Men in particular frightened him. Easy to guess what gender of shithead had taken a whip to him.

"I've been thinking—" he began.

"No!" At the look he shot her, she shrugged. "Okay. Spill. What were you thinking about?"

"Stuff."

They'd reached the far end of the corral, away from the barns and the mill of ranch hands and guests coming to inquire about trail rides and private lessons. It was where Quinn liked to groom and tack Tucker.

"Stuff, huh? That's deep."

He bit back a smile. Damn, he liked his kid sister. "Yeah. Listen." He hooked his booted foot on the bottom rail and swept his gaze over Harper and Bristol, the two geldings Quinn had selected as Tucker's pasture buddies. Good choices. Bristol and Harper could make a pair of sloths look hyper. He glanced back at his sister. "Be nice to Mia, okay?"

She turned, and the look on her face implied that he was a few cells short of a brain. "I *am* nice to Mia. She's a friend and one of the more sensible women in Acacia. Oh, wait! It's all becoming clear. This sudden need to chew the cud has to do with her. Are you worried about the wine tasting tomorrow?"

That, and a few dozen other problems looming on the horizon. "We have some forty-odd women coming to have a good time. Mia's not exactly known for being a barrel of laughs."

"Not true."

He raised his brows.

"Okay," she admitted. "She's not Tina Fey, but Mia's a really good egg. And she's a freakin' encyclopedia when it comes to wine, which is kind of relevant. I heard Mom telling Tess she hoped Mia would want to do the talk. Once she recovered from the tongue-lashing you gave her, I could see she was really happy that Mia had agreed. Have you noticed she's been singing Julio Iglesias songs?"

"Always a bad sign. And that's not singing when Mom does it." She had lousy taste in music. The schmaltzier, the better. Since telling his parents what he thought of their negotiating deals that involved him without bothering to let him in on the details, Reid had been keeping his distance by staying in the saddle and steering clear of the main lodge and its back offices. The upshot was that he'd missed his mother's happy warbling—so, yes, there was a God.

There was another positive to consider. He realized that the reason his mother had been pushing Mia had more to do with their financial investment than with her matchmaking habit. Her chirping wasn't the omen signaling the end of his prized bachelor days.

But none of this solved the Mia problem, he thought. "Mom's an eternal optimist. Of course she thinks everything's going to go swimmingly tomorrow. I'm a little more realistic. So help Mia out if you see she's having problems."

"Yeah, 'cause I'm such a wine expert," Quinn drawled. "I'm the one who buys a bottle based on the label's design, remember? You're the one in the family who can tell the difference between a maligned Merlot and a princely Pinot."

That had been his parents' line of argument for choosing him to be the one to help manage the winery, too. Neither Ward nor Quinn cared much about what went into making a fine wine.

Lifting the fender on her saddle, Quinn loosened Tucker's cinch and slipped the saddle and blanket off his back, revealing a sweat-darkened coat. Even a short training session was stressful for the gelding, the equivalent of a two-hour ride for Sirrus.

Quinn propped her saddle against the rail of the corral at a safe distance from Tucker's hooves, grabbed a hand towel from the plastic carryall, and began to rub him dry. "Here's an idea: Why don't you help Mia out if our wannabe cowgirls' eyes start rolling? Who knows, if you save her butt, Mia might even smile at you." The idea was entertaining enough to make Quinn snigger.

Reid shook his head in mild disgust. "You really are an alien, aren't you? Let me explain human psychology to you. Mia's not going to smile at me if I help her out with her talk. She'll just resent me more."

"Yeah, that's possible. But it isn't as if she's ever been a fan—which, by the way, shows astoundingly good taste on her part—so why should you care now?"

Good question, and one he wasn't about to answer. Locking his jaw, he felt the muscle along his cheek jump.

Sharp-eyed Quinn noticed. She sighed. "I can't believe I'm saying this to you, but you need to relax, dude. It'll all be good with Mia."

"Just trying not to blow our cowgirls' weekend. Tess wants those ladies happy."

"Yeah. So does Phil Onofrie. He's fantasizing about every one of them booking a return stay—with all their girlfriends and kin."

"I'm all for a guy having his fantasies fulfilled."

"Eww. I don't want to even contemplate Phil's fantasies—or yours. I shudder to think which are pervier." She looked at him and her eyes narrowed. "Yours, probably."

"You have no idea." He grinned. But as he walked away, an image of Mia's naked feet flashed in his mind, and his grin faded.

Her feet were long and slender.

It wasn't often he got a glimpse of Mia's skin. She covered a lot of herself up. Her clothes, shapeless and drab, were only marginally more stylish than a nun's habit. He thought of that saying—how certain women could wear sackcloth and still look beautiful. Mia was the proof. She dressed like crap, hardly ever wore makeup, yet he was still obsessed, hungering for every glimpse of her he could get.

It explained why the sight of her bare feet had affected him so strongly the other day, jolting him with an erotic charge strong enough to make sweat bead and then trickle down the length of his spine. Powerful enough to make his fingers bite into the painted wood of the porch railing behind him.

A damned good thing Thomas had been there to prevent him from doing something insane, like pouncing on Mia and stripping her of every god-awful piece of clothing she wore and taking a good long look at the rest of the body she hid so ruthlessly.

Even now his mouth went dry at the thought of freeing her of those criminally baggy clothes.

But damned if he was going to let Quinn or anyone know what fantasies Mia's bare feet engendered.

Mia the last of all.

MIA COULDN'T UNDERSTAND what was wrong.

The bottling company had come as scheduled, and the day had been celebratory. Thomas had chosen a favorite, Bizet's *Carmen,* for the background music. The opera's soaring notes were the perfect accompaniment to the percussive and deeply satisfying clink of glass as the sanitized bottles moved in a regimental line along the narrow conveyer belt to the fillers. There, a thrilling stream of wine flowed from barrel into bottle. The fill line reached, the bottle was then inched forward to the next automated station, the corker, where a presoaked cork was driven into the neck.

Next came the wrap and crimp of the maroon-colored tin cap over the mouth and neck, adding a protective layer to preserve the wine. Then the final touch before the bottles were packed into cardboard cases: the affixing of the glue-backed labels.

The sight of that first bottle, its label sporting the words BODELL FAMILY VINEYARD, never failed to raise a cheer.

Everything had gone perfectly, without a glitch.

And even after the bottling company's truck had left, rattling down the road, the celebratory atmosphere had continued. Mia had gone into the house to put the finishing touches on the pesto pasta and the equally large radicchio salad with Manchego vinaigrette she'd prepared, and she'd warmed two sourdough loaves in the oven.

Thomas had plucked six bottles of their 2010 Pinot Noir from the cellar to pair with the meal. Tired from the long day but beaming nonetheless, Roberto and Paul, along with their wives, Anita and Sue, and Leo and Johnny, who worked at the winery as Thomas's cellar rats—apprentices—gathered around the two picnic tables Mia had pushed together.

As the sun disappeared behind the lavender-hued mountains, the early-evening air had been full of laughter and reminiscences. Over coffee and a dessert of rich, gooey brownies that Sue had baked, they'd watched the bats come out for their nocturnal hunt, their pointy wings beating jerkily against the sapphire sky.

Bats were good.

Life was good.

By all rights, Thomas should be happy. The cases of the newly bottled wine were now safe in the climate-controlled warehouse, where they would rest and bottle-age until they were shipped to the local retailers and restaurants.

Yet he wasn't. Over the next few days he seemed more distracted than ever. No, that wasn't quite it, Mia thought. He wasn't so much distracted as *withdrawn*. He spent hours holed up in his room. When he did venture out, it was to announce he was going for a walk or a drive—with no invitation to accompany him extended. Her own suggestion that they go into Acacia for a blueberry binge of pancakes and muffins at the luncheonette was met with a vague "We'll see."

Now it was Friday afternoon and Mia was at her wits' end trying to figure out if she'd done something wrong and disappointed her uncle somehow. Worry gnawed.

It didn't help that her stomach was already aching with the fluttering of a thousand nervous butterflies at the prospect of giving a talk at Silver Creek Ranch.

Thinking that maybe she could go over her talk with Thomas—a kind of dress rehearsal—as a way to calm herself and clear the air between them, she left Roberto and Paul thinning leaves in the vineyard and walked up to the house.

The truck was back—Thomas had taken it on one of his undisclosed errands, skipping lunch. Entering by the back door, she slipped off her shoes and gulped down a glass of water at the sink. It had grown hotter today.

She heard his footsteps above her, moving along the upstairs hall in the direction of his bedroom. She opened the fridge and pulled out a pitcher of home-brewed iced tea and poured a tall glass, adding some ice cubes to it.

Drawing a deep breath, she hurried up the stairs with the tea, her peace offering. She knocked on the half-closed door and peered around it, a determinedly bright smile pinned on her face. "Hi, I thought you might like some tea."

Thomas spun around from where he'd been bent over the bed. "Mia," he said uneasily. "This isn't a good time—"

She saw two open suitcases behind him on the bed. Clothes covered the remaining space. "What are the suitcases for?"

In the short silence that followed, something awful crawled through her. It left her as cold and sweaty as the glass in her hand.

"I'm going to France."

"Oh." She relaxed. Of course. Thomas loved France and adored tooling through Burgundy. And, really, this was the perfect time for him to leave. He'd come back refreshed for the harvest. "Well, I'm happy to look after the cellar while you're away. I promise I won't break too many pipettes or glasses."

"No, Mia." His voice was gentle. "I'm going to live there. I'm leaving on Tuesday."

"How could you not tell me?" It seemed to Mia that she'd been repeating these six words for hours now. She was trying to keep her voice steady. She was failing.

What if she hadn't gone upstairs? Would Thomas have waited until he was asking her for a ride to the airport? The muscles in her throat clenched.

"I didn't know how," Thomas answered. "Listen, I understand you're upset, but what I'm doing isn't just the best for me—though it is—it's the best for *you*."

She fought the panic. "But, Thomas, we're a *team*—"

He shook his head. "You need a chance to come into your own. If I stay here, you're never going to believe in your abilities as a winemaker. I want to still be alive to enjoy your wines. I want to be able to crow with pride when you begin winning awards. But you know what I also want? A chance to live out the rest of my days with the woman who's made me remember what it is to love. Would you deny me any of those things?"

"No, of course not." She swallowed the lump of pain that was lodged in her throat. "I'm happy you've found someone. You deserve it. It's only—" Didn't he understand how she felt? "France is so far away."

"Well, there's email and Skype. Pascale and I have gotten very savvy at Skyping. You and I can, too."

Skype? Email? As if those things could ever replace her uncle's presence. Once again, she was losing someone she loved. Her mother. Aunt Ellen. And now Thomas. She hadn't really thought about her future or what would happen if she found someone to love. But Thomas had been a given. A constant. She'd thought that she would care for him as he aged, her way of thanking him for taking her in and raising her like a daughter. But now he was leaving her. . . .

"And with Reid advising you—"

"What?" She scrambled to recall what Thomas had been saying just now. "What does any of this have to do with Reid?" The awful, crawling sensation was back.

Thomas looked surprised. "As I explained, the Knowleses have invested in the winery. A very sizable stake. It goes without saying they'd like to see a return on their investment. Adele, Daniel, and I have decided Reid is the best person to oversee the business end of the operation."

"Reid? No." She shook her head. "I don't need, I don't *want*—" For a second her mind went blank, over-whelmed by an avalanche of things she didn't want. How could she have been so happy on Monday, so optimistic? Now her life was falling apart. And how could Thomas stand by his nearly packed suitcases and offer up Reid Knowles as the answer to her misery?

"Mia, we both know the winery needs help. Badly. This arrangement will allow you to make something of this place. You'll be able to make great wine and have it actually reach consumers. Reid will make—"

"Thomas." She fought to keep her panic at bay. "I'll grant that the Knowleses are talented businesspeople. Adele and Daniel are smart. Ward, too. But Reid? He doesn't really do much except ride and have fun and—"

"Reid's talented."

She snorted. "In many areas, I'm sure. But not in the winemaking business."

"I'm surprised at you, Mia." Thomas's tone was un-characteristically severe. "I thought you were a better judge of character."

When she remained silent, he sighed and glanced at his watch. "It's a little after three o'clock. Why don't you go over to Silver Creek now? Perhaps Reid will be free and you two can have a chin-wag. Break the ice, so to speak."

Right, she thought. That would happen when grapes ripened on a willow.

She arrived at Silver Creek Ranch's main lodge at ten minutes before five, her uncle's suggestion that Reid and she enjoy a "chin-wag" be damned, but found not a single cowgirl, real or aspiring, in sight. Reid wasn't around, either. No great surprise. Why would he be at the main lodge just because she was due to give her talk in a few short minutes?

The guest ranch was impressive in any season. But Mia loved it in summertime especially, when the shrubs and gardens were in bloom, their blossoms vivid and fragrant. The landscaping was brilliant. It pleased the eye and fooled it, effectively camouflaging the cabins behind the plantings. A person could wander along the bluestone and gravel walkways that wound through the property and hardly notice the guests' lodgings. It made for a private and peaceful atmosphere.

She paused a moment to appreciate the gardens in the front of the main lodge, which held the reception area, restaurant, bar, and lounge, as well as the back offices where the Knowleses and their staff ran the business. The flower beds were filled with perennials. Daylilies, delphiniums, and roses welcomed the visitor with a riot of warm color. The lodge's pale stone and cedar façade was the perfect backdrop.

Perfection. It was hard to think of the Knowleses' ranch linked with the Bodells' much smaller and, with the exception of the vineyard and the winery, far more ramshackle property. It was equally hard to imagine her family, rife with dysfunction and heartache, allied with theirs.

As she approached the carved wood door to the lodge, a voice called to her. "Mia!"

She turned. Adele Knowles was walking up the gravel road that led to the corrals and barns. She wore jeans and a button-down Liberty print shirt covered in pale-blue flowers that matched her eyes. Her cowboy boots were an equally stunning color of deep blue.

The boots were incredible. But there was no point in being envious. Mia knew she would never be able to pull off a look like Adele's. Of course, it helped that in addition to being tall, blond, and a successful business-woman, Adele was a cowgirl, too. She'd ridden all her life. According to Quinn, her mother had won numer-ous reining competitions before she and Daniel mar-ried.

Mia's throat was still raw from her conversation with Thomas. Even attempting a "Hi, Adele" was painful.

"Mia, I'm so pleased to see you!" Adele clasped Mia's hands in hers. "Thank you for agreeing to give the talk today—" Her eyes, so similar to Reid's, scanned Mia's face. A worried frown replaced her smile. "Are you all right, dear?"

The sympathy only made Mia's throat ache more.

"Yes, of course," she replied tightly. "I'm sorry I didn't arrive earlier. Do I have enough time to make sure the wines for my presentation are ready?"

"Oh, don't worry about that. Everything's set up. Reid gave George Reich the list. The bottles have been opened to allow the wines to breathe. Why don't you head down to the corral? Reid, Ward, and our fore-man, Pete, are giving our guests roping lessons. The women have been having such a good time, they're still practicing—"

"That's okay, I can wait up here—"

"Go on down," she urged. "You can meet the guests and join the fun, Mia. And it'll give the men the perfect excuse to let you take center stage."

Center stage, where she least liked to be.

"Woo-hoo!"

Mia cringed. She wanted nothing more than to turn around and march back up the drive to the main lodge's parking lot, where she'd left her pickup truck. But she had too much pride to pull a disappearing act now that Adele had seen her.

Another round of whoops pierced the air, this one followed by laughter and applause. A crowd of women—many more than she'd expected—had congregated in the corral nearest the horse barn. In the center of them, three men—Reid, Ward, and Pete Williams, the ranch's foreman—worked their lassos. The ropes danced, twirled, and jumped like live things.

At a signal from Reid, the three ropes came together, each twirling, one directly below the other. Mia had no idea how the men kept them from becoming entangled. The "oohs" from the guests showed she was not alone in being impressed. Pete reeled in his rope first, Ward followed next, while Reid kept his in the air. Then, with a flick of his wrist, he caught the loop. Applause erupted. The three doffed their Stetsons.

Settling his dark-beige hat on his head, Ward addressed the audience. "Thank you, ladies. Now, we've gone over the basics of roping, and tomorrow we'll practice some more both on the ground and in the saddle, but we thought we'd end our session with one last demo by Reid here. You ready, Reid?"

With a nod, Reid sent the rope into the air again. It circled above him like a spinning wheel.

"So this next trick is in honor of my fiancée, Tess, and her friend Anna, who's come here from New York City. Say hi, Anna," Ward instructed with a grin.

A woman stepped forward and waved. "Hi, everybody," she called cheerfully.

Cheerful "hi"s echoed back.

Ward resumed speaking. "Now, there's a story behind how my lovely Tess came to Silver Creek Ranch. It involves a blindfold Anna tied over her eyes before Tess placed her finger on a map of California. Anna made Tess promise that wherever her finger landed would be her destination." He grinned at the "aww"s that resounded. "So you all can imagine how pleased I was when Anna presented me with the very scarf she'd used on Tess." From his back pocket, Ward pulled a black-and-white-patterned silk scarf.

"So how about we put this blindfold over my little brother's eyes and see how well his roping skills hold up. Do you mind, Reid?"

"I'd say I stand a better chance than you of roping something, Ward," Reid replied, adding with the supreme cockiness Mia knew so well, "blindfolded and with both hands tied behind my back."

Ward flashed a smile, and Mia bet most of the women wished this tall, dark, and handsome cowboy wasn't engaged to be married. Of course, with Reid standing next to Ward and looking like a sun-kissed god, their disappointment was probably short-lived.

"Strong words, bro. Let's see whether you can back

them up." Ward quickly folded the scarf over itself until it was a wide band. "Ready?"

Reid looked at Ward and flashed a grin. "Always."

Placing the scarf over Reid's eyes, Ward made a show of knotting it behind his head. "Can you see anything?" he asked.

"Not a damned thing."

The words were a catalyst. Despite how hostile Mia felt toward Reid and his new role in her life, knowing that he couldn't catch her staring was too great a temptation. She looked her fill.

He stood easily and confidently, a smile playing over his lips, as if it didn't matter that he was blindfolded in the middle of a corral, surrounded by a group of women, all of whom were staring as avidly as she. The wind toyed with the ends of his hair, causing them to brush against the collar of his light-tan shirt. He was still twirling the lasso in the air, and she saw the corded muscles beneath his sun-burnished skin flex and jump. The rest of him was just as leanly and beautifully sculpted, she thought, her gaze traveling down the length of his body.

Ward's voice startled Mia out of her absorption. "Ladies," he said. "We'll need four volunteers for this demonstration. That's right. Don't be shy. Want to round 'em up for us, Pete?"

Pete Williams was someone Mia knew from perusing the wire selection at Wright's Hardware, from waiting in line at the bank, and from their shared love of Spillin' the Beans's Colombian roast. Pete walked over to the semicircle of women, every last one of them waving her hand in the air, eager to volunteer for anything that included Reid.

With the skin around his brown eyes creased with devilish mirth, Pete took care to prolong the communal excitement by spacing his selections out. He hadn't even gotten to "three" by the time he reached the far end of the horseshoe formation, where Mia waited for the demonstration and for the entire blasted evening to end.

"And how about you, miss?" he asked a woman standing a few yards from her.

The woman's response was identical to that of the two others Pete had selected: unfettered glee. After hopping up and down like a game-show contestant—a hop that made her truly impressive breasts bounce beneath her rhinestone-studded shirt—the woman sashayed into the inner circle of the corral, in jeans so tight Mia wondered how she could breathe, let alone sit in a saddle.

Preoccupied with observing the woman's progress, Mia didn't realize that Pete had moved closer. "And how about you for number four?"

Mia looked around and then realized with horror that he meant her. "No, I really don't—"

A chorus of women's voices went up, drowning her out. "Come on, it'll be fun!" And "You go, girl!" A hand even gave her an encouraging shove.

A stunned Mia found herself stumbling forward. Then Pete was herding her into the center of the ring as if she were a wayward sheep. Pete had always seemed like a nice guy, ready to shoot the breeze about the week's weather forecast as they waited for their java fix, so this struck her as an unexpected betrayal.

There was a lot of that going around today.

Ward acknowledged her presence with a grin and a nod. But before she could plead to be returned to the audience, he spoke to Pete. "Let's get the ladies in position."

Since Mia was closest to Pete, she was the first to be escorted—or, rather, marched—to her designated spot. Hers was directly behind Reid. She had no idea what this game entailed, but she figured that hers might be the best place to be. The thought made her breathe a little easier.

Reid's nose had begun to tickle, but he wasn't about to scratch it. He had his dignity to consider. He felt foolish enough already. What the hell was Ward thinking, egging these women on with some last-minute trick involving him and a blindfold? They hardly needed encouragement. A number had already taken pains to let him know which cabin they were staying in—as if he or anyone in his family would ever get involved with a guest. That path led to a manure pile the size of Mount Everest.

Tomorrow he'd figure out a way to sic the women on Ward. It'd be satisfying to turn the tables on his brother and see how much he enjoyed being chased around the guest ranch by females looking for a roll in the hay with a cowboy. Of course, Ward had cleverly preempted any overenthusiastic overtures by mentioning his fiancée a couple of hundred times.

From the bursts of high-pitched giggles, he figured Pete and Ward were having a fine time with the women. He didn't know what Ward had planned. Didn't care at this point. He only wished they'd pick up the pace. Mia would be arriving soon. He didn't want to look like an idiot standing with an Italian scarf wrapped around his head.

"All right, Reid. The ladies are in their places."

It took you long enough, Reid retorted silently.

"You're a lucky guy to be surrounded by such beauty. Now, Pete and I have placed the ladies at twelve, three, six, and nine on the clock. Each one is standing about twenty feet away from you. Your job is to see whether you can lasso one blindfolded."

Tricky but doable. Sometimes Reid, Ward, and their

father would get into competitions—pissing contests, really—with the ranch hands. They'd used bandannas on occasions to up the ante. But it had been ages since he'd last tried to lasso anything blindfolded. Luckily, he was good with a rope.

"So, Reid, what's your favorite hour?"

He caught a giggle in front of him and equally annoying titters to his left and right. Behind him, though, nothing, just blessed silence, even when he strained his ears. Yet somehow he sensed the woman's presence more strongly than that of the others. Interesting.

"You know, I've always been partial to the midnight hour. Crazy magic happens then." The words were no sooner out of his mouth than Reid spun on his heels and, picturing the distance in his mind's eye, let the lasso fly. He felt the weight of the rope in his hand as it descended and waited an extra millisecond—damned if he was going to catch the woman by the neck—before giving a quick jerk of his wrist.

He was met with solid resistance. Oh, yeah, that was a body caught snug in his rope. Satisfaction pierced him as a round of hearty applause went up. With a grin, he pulled off the blindfold, all set to make an extravagant bow to the captured lady.

Instead, he froze. *Oh, fuck.*

Pete had had the bad judgment to include *Mia,* of all the women in attendance, in this roping stunt? Of those four, Reid had had the atrocious luck to pick *her*? Usually he was the kind of guy who rolled with it, able to see the humor in life's little jokes. He wasn't laughing.

Neither was Mia.

Torso and arms bound by the lariat, she stood as stiff as a board and half as fun. If looks could kill, he'd be dead and buried. And if Mia had her way, she'd see that he spent an eternity rotting in hell.

He was accustomed to her looking down her nose at

him with her nostrils pinched, as if he'd stepped in a cow patty. She wore that signature look now. It was no surprise she was annoyed that he'd had the lousy luck to catch her in his lasso. The feeling was mutual. But there was something else, more than just condescension or even outrage in her expression.

Her face was drawn and pale.

Damn. So Thomas had delivered the news that he was leaving Acacia for France.

He didn't want to feel sorry for her.

Aware that there were far too many pairs of eyes on them, he forced a grin. "Mia," he said loudly. "So nice to see you."

He was met with stony silence. Oh, man, this didn't bode well. Any longer with her standing there looking like a grim priss in her tan skirt and olive top and clogs—Mia was the only woman he knew who would wear *clogs* to a cowgirl event—and these paying guests would be demanding their money back.

Best get this over with. He resurrected his grin—a miracle—and kept his gaze fixed on her chin. This was not the time to be caught checking out her breasts. A pity. With the rope tight about her, this was a rare opportunity to actually *see* them.

Determined to turn an awkward moment into an entertaining one, he gave the rope a yank and began to reel her in. Mia, being Mia, performed perfectly and predictably. She resisted him every step of the way.

A complex dance ensued. Reid forced Mia to yield to his superior strength without causing her to trip or fall as he drew her in, inch by inch, foot by foot.

"And this, ladies, is how we catch a wild one!" His voice rang with forced joviality. "May I introduce you all to Mia Bodell? Mia's family owns the vineyard next door. She's going to be telling you about some really great local wines and her family's approach to wine-making. That is, if I can bear to free her."

It didn't say much for the intelligence of the assembled cowgirls that they seemed to eat this last bit up. Their applause grew louder with every reluctant step that Mia took. Of course, Reid was the only one close enough to see the fury burning in her eyes.

"Listen," he said, knowing that the other women wouldn't hear him over their whoops and hollers.

She cut him off. "You knew," she accused through gritted teeth. "You knew about Thomas's plan back when you came to visit. You just love humiliating me, don't you?"

They both knew the last accusation encompassed far more than Thomas's confiding in Reid. "What could I have done? Blurt out the news? Like that would have gone over well. Listen, you're upset. I understand—"

"You don't understand anything about me."

"I think I do. Thomas has thrown you for a loop." He winced. Bad choice of words. "I'm sorry about it, but it's not my fault."

"Of course not. You never take responsibility."

The words cut deep. Had she guessed that comment would hurt more than any other? "Now who doesn't know what she's talking about?"

"I know enough not to like what I see," she replied flatly.

Abruptly, he realized that they were standing virtually nose-to-nose as they exchanged barbs. A part of him wanted to grab her shoulders and shake her for her obstinacy; another part wanted to haul her into his arms and let her cry out the rest of her shock and hurt over the blow Thomas had dealt. From the bright sheen in her red-rimmed eyes, he figured the tears were about to breach the dam. And he *did* know Mia. Knew her well enough to guess how much she would hate to let even a single tear fall in his presence.

He made a final attempt to reason with her. "Will you just listen? You don't have to give this wine talk. I'll—"

"What? Replace me?" She sniffed scornfully. "So now that your parents have invested in the winery, you're an expert?"

"For Christ's sake, I didn't—"

"You may think you know something about wine. You've certainly fooled Thomas into believing you know enough to help advise us on how to promote our winery. But you know what I think? That I'm going to be stuck working with a shallow playboy cowboy whose knowledge of wine couldn't fill a spit cup."

Fury could carry Mia only so far before stage fright took hold. Resentment could last only so long before chagrin set in. As angry as she was at Thomas for dropping his bombshell on her, and as much as she disagreed with his plan to form a partnership with the Knowleses, it was unfair to lash out at Reid. Yet so far he'd been the sole target of her bitterness.

He didn't deserve the words she'd hurled at him in the corral, didn't deserve to be treated like a verbal punching bag. Her excuse—that this was one of the worst afternoons of her life and, after being lassoed and hauled across a dirt-filled corral like a stubborn heifer, one of the more embarrassing ones—didn't hold water.

She hated being in the wrong. But apologizing to Reid was impossible when she was in the middle of a talk—or, rather, when she was in the middle of screwing up a talk that she should be able to give in her sleep, and probably had.

She should have been telling the women clustered around the teak tables on the flagstone patio how much fun it was to grow Pinot Noir grapes, the most challenging varietal of all. She should have told them how Pinot was referred to as "the heartbreak grape," as its delicate skin made it particularly vulnerable to frost and rot, two enemies of vintners.

She should have talked about how rewarding it was when her diligence in the vineyard's blocks and Mother Nature's indulgence came together to make a perfect black and sweetly juicy grape.

She should have talked about Thomas's and her efforts to grow grapes in a responsible, sustainable manner. She could have told them about the birds they'd encouraged to live on the twenty-five-acre property—songbirds and owls—by building houses and nests. They welcomed bats, too, since they, like the birds, ate the pests that gorged on grapes and destroyed vines. Filling the sky with the soar and dip of winged creatures was far preferable to filling the soil with chemicals.

She should have talked about the joy and excitement of the harvest, from the picking to the de-stemming to the press. She could have told them about the expensive French oak barrels they imported because of the unique flavor, with hints of vanilla and spice, they gave to the wine aging inside.

She supposed she did actually speak about all these points. Kind of, sort of. The thing was, whenever she mentioned the vineyard and the vision Mia and her uncle shared for it and the winery, a sadness as heavy as wet cement weighed upon her. It made her lose track of her thoughts, exacerbating her stage fright. Her recourse was reflexive. She relied on the technical terms of graduate school seminars and presentations. Arid words like "Brix" and "malolactic fermentation" and "active acidity" and "pH scales" began to litter her sentences.

The worst wasn't how badly she was flubbing the talk; it was her listeners' politeness. They were so courteous and respectful. These women who'd been laughing boisterously and having such a good time just minutes ago in the corral now sat with the blank-faced tolerance reserved for visits to one's crotchety ninety-year-old aunt.

It was possible that on another day she might have been able to switch gears and save the talk from mind-numbing tediousness. But not today. Fortunately for the women gathered around the tables with their hydrangea and calla lily centerpieces, Tess Casari and her friend and scarf-lender Anna Vecchio came to Mia's rescue.

Just as Mia was about to launch into an explanation of what tests were run to determine a wine's readiness—because these ladies were clearly *dying* for a chemistry refresher—Tess raised her hand.

"Mia, my friend Anna and I are eager to hear more about the vineyards around Mendocino, and I'm sure these ladies, too, would love to have an insider's guide. And while you're telling us about the wines you've picked out, we could all begin tasting them."

"Oh—of course!" Caught up in the miserable hash she was making of her presentation, she hadn't recognized the easiest solution to her dilemma: to let everyone enjoy the grape.

The bottles were aligned in neat rows in front of her on a long table. "Well, we have one wine here that's made less than a mile away: It's our Bodell Family Vineyard Pinot Noir. Then this is a very nice Merlot, an excellent Cabernet Sauvignon, and a Petite Sirah that's a really lovely summer wine."

She moved down the table to where the white wine sat chilling in miniature-sized oak barrels—such a nice touch and utterly in keeping with everything the Knowleses did at the guest ranch—and continued. "And for you white-wine lovers, we have a Chardonnay, a Sauvignon Blanc, and a Viognier. Viognier is a less well-known varietal but one I think you all will enjoy."

She paused, aware how easily the words had come, and became determined that her next ones should flow as smoothly. "Reid, who you know already from his impressive roping skills, is also pretty savvy when it comes to wine. It was his idea to feature varietals from Mendocino so that you could enjoy the local flavors. Let's give him a round of applause, ladies."

Although Reid was standing at the other end of the patio, about as far from her as he could get, Mia saw the surprise that crossed his face at her acknowledgment. After the mean-spirited things she'd said to him in the corral, he certainly wouldn't have been expecting it.

For a second their eyes met, and he gave her a slight nod. The tight knot in her stomach eased a little.

Barely any wine remained, and the level of enthusiasm along with the cowgirls' laughter had returned in full. Mia was also pleasantly surprised when a number of the women came up and thanked her for the talk and complimented her on the Pinot Noir. That Anna Vecchio and Tess Casari were among them was an even greater surprise.

"Oh, hi!" she said as they stepped forward.

"Thanks for the great talk, Mia. I learned a lot," Tess said.

"Maybe more than you wanted to," she answered.

"Not true." Tess shook her dark head. "I'm loving what I'm discovering about the regional wines here. Mia, I'd like to introduce you to my friend Anna. She's opening a restaurant in New York City this fall. It'll be the hot spot for real Italian food."

Anna elbowed Tess affectionately. "I'm hoping that's the case—and maybe it will be if Tess keeps promoting

Lucia's to anyone with ears. Admit it, Tess, you've even been talking to your lambs about me."

"Angie, Arlo, and I talk about lots of stuff," Tess said. "They're happy your dream of owning a restaurant is coming true. All they care about is not ending up on any of your plates. Or in a ragù."

"Oh my God, she's going to turn vegan on me and start wearing hemp," Anna exclaimed with a dramatic roll of her eyes. "Still, coming to Acacia's obviously been good for her. And, as Ward said, it's all thanks to my Nonna Lucia's favorite scarf. Nonna always claimed it brought her luck. I'm figuring you may be the next in line to benefit from its positive magic, Mia."

Mia blinked. What did one say to someone who announced that her grandmother's silk scarf held supernatural properties? Despite Anna's countrified outfit of jeans and a poppy-red button-down shirt decorated with black stitching, she had the air of a sophisticated New Yorker. Tess Casari looked normal, too. Neither seemed like the type to go for palm readings or such. Mia settled for a lame "Uh, that would be nice."

"Of course, the good luck would have to extend to Reid, wouldn't it, Anna? After all, he was the one who was blindfolded," Tess observed.

Mia wondered whether she could take back the "that would be nice" bit now that Reid was involved. Did someone like him really need any more good fortune?

"It would have to," Anna agreed, as if this were a perfectly normal conversation. Maybe it was for them. They both looked pleased as punch at the idea of a magic scarf sprinkling joy, happiness, and serendipity. Unfortunately, Mia was living through one of the worst days of her life and was skeptical that a scarf had any power to improve it.

Mia gave silent thanks when Anna changed the topic. "I wanted to tell you how much I enjoyed your family's

Pinot Noir. What are the prospects for this year's harvest? Do you think you'll be able to make as good a wine as the one you offered us today?"

"I hope to. But my uncle's moving to France, so I'll be taking over the role of winemaker. I've got big shoes to fill," she said in a massive understatement. The thought had her stomach clenching once more.

"Your uncle's moving to France?" Tess's surprise was obvious.

So the small town of Acacia hadn't guessed what she herself had been unable to figure out. That was a relief of sorts. "Yes," she said. "Thomas has fallen in love with a French vintner."

"He's fallen in love? That's great!"

Affianced to a gorgeous man, Tess might well think so. "He's very happy." And Mia was happy for him. She only wished he'd fallen for a Napa winemaker.

"So you'll be running the business on your own?"

"Actually, I'll stick to growing the grapes and making wine. Reid will be—"

She got no further. Tess's attention had suddenly been diverted. Mia turned her head, following Tess's gaze, and the reason for the distraction became clear. Reid and Ward were walking toward them.

The brothers were undeniably stunning. Ward had the tall, dark, and handsome thing thoroughly covered. He took after his father, Daniel. Reid was whipcordlean, and his eyes shone brilliant blue in his tanned face. He still hadn't trimmed his shaggy gold-blond hair. The casual, tousled look suited him. Everything suited him.

Mia had known them both for years. She'd always admired Ward. He was serious and responsible—just the sort of man Mia always told herself she was looking for. Why, then, was it Reid who made her heart thump until it hurt? Why did he cause everything to melt inside her when she wasn't even sure she liked him and when she knew *he* didn't like *her*? She hadn't missed his horrified expression when he removed the supposedly lucky scarf and saw exactly who was caught in his lasso.

Ward went straight to Tess. Wrapping an arm about her waist, he kissed her on the lips. Mia heard the collective sigh that escaped the women who'd observed the embrace.

Ward released Tess from his kiss. "Jeff is wondering whether Anna is ready to make the zucchini pizzas," he said, still holding her close.

"Oh, yes," Anna replied, then turned to Mia. "This was one of my Nonna Lucia's recipes. It's incredible."

"We were telling Mia about Lucia's lucky scarf," Tess said. "Isn't it interesting, Reid, how you ended up roping Mia?"

"I think that would depend on your definition of interesting," Reid said.

His brother Ward smiled, which Mia assumed meant he, too, had heard the irritation lacing Reid's voice. "It would be nice if that scarf brought you both some luck," he said. "Reid just told me that he'll be working with Mia on building the winery's business." He transferred his smile to Mia and it warmed, reaching his eyes. "Welcome to the family, Mia."

Perversely, Ward's remark only made Mia feel forlorn. Here he was, welcoming her into the "family," but he was doing so only because her own, real family was deserting her. And would the Knowleses be as gracious and generous if she failed to produce good wines?

Swamped by a wave of loneliness and anxiety, she managed only a weak smile when Ward, Tess, and Anna excused themselves to go make culinary magic with Jeff.

"That was a good talk."

Reid's words startled her out of her depressing

thoughts. She raised an eyebrow, grateful for the spurt of irritation she felt. "No need to lie."

The corner of his mouth rose. "Okay, it wasn't a good talk. But at least it got better at the end."

"Only after everyone had consumed three glasses apiece and discovered that one can drink a fine red with barbecue," she said drily. As soon as the ladies began to sample, the wait staff had passed platters filled with bite-sized morsels of grilled and barbecued meats. Cheese puffs and miniature fritters had followed.

"Exactly." Reid nodded. The ghost of a smile played across his lips.

Perhaps it was the smile that prompted her. Perhaps it was the guilt festering inside. Either way, she found herself blurting out, "I'm sorry about what I said earlier."

It was his turn to raise an eyebrow in mocking disbelief. "No need to lie."

"Okay," she said. "So I meant most of it. I don't think you know a whole lot about wine."

"Ah, vintage Mia," he said. "You're right. Compared to you and Thomas, I know next to nothing. I don't pretend to. But I bet I know a whole lot more about what it takes to run a successful business. Can you say the same?"

He had her there. She gave a shrug. "I'm aware your family knows how to run one. I've no proof you can."

"Well, that puts us on even footing, doesn't it, since I've yet to taste any wine you've made." For a second their eyes met. He was looking at her—for once really looking at her—and the effect was just as powerful as she'd imagined. She found herself lost in the dazzling blue, as deep as any sea.

Her heart began to hammer against the walls of her chest.

A stranger's voice broke the spell Reid had cast so effortlessly. " 'Scuse me."

Mia jerked her gaze away from Reid's. The speaker was one of the women who'd been in the corral with her when Reid had done his rope trick, the one with the scarily tight jeans and improbably large breasts.

The woman reached out and grabbed Reid's arm. The tips of her fingers ended in bright-red claws. "I hate to butt in," she said with a smile as aggressive as her talons, "but you've been gettin' a lot of attention from this here cowboy. It's our turn now."

From across the room Mia heard the now familiar "Woo-hoo!" as a group of women cheered on their friend. A glance at Reid's face showed that his easy grin was in place. He didn't look at all upset to be leaving her.

So maybe Reid and she had reached some kind of détente. So maybe he had actually looked her in the eye for once. So maybe a smile had flitted across his face. That didn't change the essentials. He was still a womanizing cowboy.

Chapter
TEN

THOMAS HAD PROTESTED. Mia had insisted, arguing that the drive was nothing, a straight two-hour shot. For once Mia got her way. But, as if to rub her nose in it, the traffic to San Francisco International Airport, was, as Thomas had predicted, as unmoving as a clogged drain.

The conversation between them eked out in fits and spurts, with as much being quashed by Mia as voiced. Thomas burbled with excitement.

"Reaching me might be tricky for the next few weeks. Pascale has some friends with a yacht, and we're going to cruise around the Mediterranean and explore Corsica. There are wild pigs in the hills. At night we'll dine on board on grilled sardines, olives, tomatoes, peasant bread, and Corsican rosé. Then we'll continue to the Greek Isles."

"And if there's an emergency?"

"I suppose you can try my cell. I just don't know how good the reception will be. The best bet is the Knowleses."

Tightening her fingers around the steering wheel, she glanced sideways at Thomas. She understood he was in love. But did he realize how easily he was cutting his ties to the vineyard, to her, and how much that hurt?

Thomas was still talking, saying something about his complete faith in Roberto and Paul and how Leo and Johnny were good, responsible kids and meticulous about keeping the winery clean as a whistle. They were young, but they loved the wine they helped make. His tone changed, however, becoming tinged with brittle cynicism, when he mentioned her cousin. "If you ever hear from Jay, do let him know my whereabouts."

She took her eyes off the road, even though other drivers were doing wild and crazy things on I-380. "I thought you'd called him."

"I did. I left three messages on his cell. Four seemed a shade superfluous. None of my calls were returned. It's possible he didn't understand that I was leaving today— more likely he saw no reason to get in touch, since I'd already arranged the money transfer. I should have insisted he contact me so I could outline the terms of the financial settlement and only then deposit his share. But old habits die hard."

She thought back to the trip Thomas and she had made to Ukiah yesterday to visit Donald Polk, Thomas's accountant and lawyer. They'd needed her signature on the four copies of the contract Thomas and the Knowleses had negotiated.

The pages of legalese outlining the terms had made her head swim. But Don Polk had answered her questions, so she now knew the basics of the partnership. She was manager of the vineyard and winemaker, Reid its marketing and administrative director. In return for the money the Knowleses invested in the winery, they would receive 40 percent of its profits. Mia would earn a salary in addition to a 30 percent share. Thomas would receive 20 and Jay 10 percent. Thanks to the Knowleses, Thomas had been able to withdraw a lump capital sum in order to live comfortably in France and a slightly smaller one—but still princely—for Jay.

Mia hoped the cash infusion and the 10 percent cut would satisfy him. She preferred to avoid her cousin. Contact with him left her feeling dirty.

The exit off I-380 with its sign for SFO was approaching, and as they drove the next couple of miles she stared ahead, hating the signs directing travelers to the different terminals.

She flicked the turn signal and eased into the exit lane for the parking garage.

"What are you doing, Mia? You need to go straight."

"The exit for the garage is—"

"We don't have time to search for a parking space. The flight leaves in two hours, and I have bags to check. Drive to the international terminal and drop me off. I'll get a skycap to help me with the bags."

Mia jerked the wheel to get out of the exit lane and was rewarded with an angry blare of a horn. The driver whizzed by her and gave her the finger. Charming.

"Careful, Mia," Thomas cautioned. "I don't want to miss my flight."

She drew a breath and debated pointing out a tiny fact to her uncle: She'd never been in an accident in her life. But then she decided that silence was golden.

She pulled up to the curb at departures and jumped out of the truck. Thomas was already at the back, unloading his cases. "I'll go park and meet you at the check-in."

"No need for that, Mia. Let me say farewell here, my girl, so you can get on your way." He lined up his suitcases in a row and enfolded her in a hearty hug.

"Thomas, I *want* to come in with you."

"But why? You have another two-and-a-half-hour drive back. Maybe longer. It's rush hour now."

"I'll be fine. It doesn't matter."

"But don't you have a date tonight? It's with Andrew, right?"

Dreading the prospect of returning to an empty house and eating dinner alone, she'd called Andrew Schroeder on Sunday and suggested they get together. They were to meet at Aubergine, the restaurant in Sonoma they both liked. The reservation was for eight o'clock, which gave her ample time to get there. Now she wished she hadn't made the date or mentioned it to Thomas. "Yes, I'm seeing him," she admitted reluctantly.

"Well, then," Thomas said, "go have fun before you're both too busy with your harvests to have any at all." He hugged her again and kissed both her cheeks. Then he stepped back and gave her a tender smile. "I love you, Mia."

Her own smile was fierce, beating back her sadness. "I love you, too. Have a safe trip. Call me when you can. And, Thomas—" She paused and swallowed her pain. "Be happy."

"Thank you, darling." With a jaunty wave, he picked up his bags and deposited them onto the metal cart. "Air France," he said to the porter, before turning to Mia with a final smile. *"Au revoir, ma belle."*

"Au revoir," she echoed hollowly.

Mia sat toying with the wax drippings at the base of the candlestick. She'd begun fiddling with the wax as a way to keep herself from finishing the bowl of roasted chickpeas the waitress had placed at her table, or from drinking her glass of Zinfandel too quickly, or, worse yet, from checking her watch again.

Andrew was almost thirty minutes late. She'd called as soon as she arrived and left a message on his voice mail that she was at the restaurant. Her cell was on the table, set to vibrate, but it had yet to come alive and shiver across the polished dark wood. Perhaps he'd received her message just as he was starting out and hadn't wanted to answer it while he was driving.

Cheered by the thought, she plucked a roasted chickpea from the bowl and munched on it while she cast an eye about the crowded interior. It was a good thing she'd reserved. Aubergine was hopping. The bar was jammed with diners waiting for a free table. She hoped Andrew showed up before the hungry patrons began to complain that she'd been seated before her companion had arrived. When it came to nabbing a table at a hot eating spot, people lost their California cool awfully quickly.

She'd been right to suggest the dinner date. She'd be able to tell Andrew all that had happened, knowing he'd appreciate what she was going through. Looking across the table into his steady brown eyes, magnified by his square horn-rimmed glasses, would banish the image of Thomas's final wave before he'd followed the porter into the terminal. The sliding glass doors had closed all too quickly, leaving her on the curb, her fixed smile crumbling to dust.

She was sure Andrew would understand how heartbroken she was to have lost her uncle. And being as unadulterated a wine geek as one could find in Sonoma, Napa, or Mendocino, he would totally get the stress of having been handed an entire vineyard and winery to run.

Their dinner would soothe her, and hopefully he'd ease her apprehension about stepping into Thomas's shoes. If they lingered at the table long enough, she might even stop worrying about the fact that tomorrow she'd have to start dealing with Reid—on a regular basis.

She took a gulp of her wine.

Mia had no idea what Reid had in mind in terms of

promotion and marketing—she'd never liked any aspect of winemaking that didn't involve the grapes—but Andrew surely would. Sometimes Mia wondered if Andrew ever thought about anything other than how to make, sell, and distribute wine.

Mia's server had passed her table several times, her glance at the empty chair opposite Mia increasingly harried. This time she stopped. "Can I get you anything else while you're waiting?"

"No, thank you. I'm good for the moment."

The phone that she'd set on the table began to hum like a swarm of bees. She picked it up hastily and glanced at the screen. She gave the waitress a quick, apologetic smile. "Sorry—this is my date calling." Pressing the ACCEPT button, she said, "Hello?"

"Mia, it's me."

"Hi, Andrew. Where are you?"

"I'm at Jake's. We're hanging out with Sonya."

"Sonya?"

"Sonya Ortiz, our distributor. So I saw you called. What's up?" The question sounded perfunctory.

"I called because we have a dinner date tonight. You were supposed to meet me at Aubergine at eight. Did you forget?"

"Crap. That's this week?"

"Yes, it's this week. Andrew, we spoke only a couple of days ago. You said you were hoping they'd have fried zucchini flowers as a special on the menu. They do. I asked."

"Sorry, Mia. I forgot. Work's been insane and then I've been showing Sonya around the vineyard. We're branching out in our exports. Sales are going to go through the roof. So we're having a little celebration. You know."

She didn't, actually. What she did know was that when she made a date with someone, she remembered and kept it. "I've got our table. If you leave now, you can be here in fifteen minutes. I'll order the zucchini and a plate of—"

"Uh, Mia. I'm not up to dinner out. Jake's got a fish stew on. We're just going to sit around and chill and play video games. Can you believe it, Sonya rocks at Mass Effect Three?"

She didn't know exactly when in Andrew's reply she reached the tipping point. Whether it was his admission that he'd forgotten their dinner date, or his obvious enthusiasm for Sonya, the ace gamer who was going to distribute Crescent Ridge wines far and wide, or when it became clear that the guy she was dating preferred to slump on a sofa playing a gratuitously violent video game to having dinner with her, it was irrelevant. It was suddenly all too much.

She was damned tired of being treated like so much flooring.

"Andrew, I'd really like it if you joined me. It's been a rotten day—several days, actually—and I could use your company."

"Uh, I don't—" Whatever Andrew was about to say was cut off by the sound of an explosion, a triumphant yell, and female laughter.

"Andrew?"

"What? Oh, yeah. Listen, I'm beat, Mia. Maybe we can hang out together next week or sometime after that?"

The. Last. Damn. Straw. "You know what, Andrew, I don't think so. In fact, I think we should stop dating."

"Oh."

She waited. "'Oh'? That's it? That's all you have to say?"

"Well." He cleared his throat. "I'm just kind of surprised. I hadn't realized we were going out."

She took her cell away from her ear to glare at it.

"What did you think our dates were? What did you think when you put your tongue down my throat and your hands on my breasts?"

That must have gotten through the fog of Mass Effect 3. "Gee, I don't know," he snapped. "That maybe you'd finally put out?"

A red haze descended over her vision. "Have a great time with your video game." She clicked the phone off and lowered her head to the palm of her hand.

"A no-show?"

Mia straightened with a jerk. The waitress was still there and must have caught enough on Mia's end to deduce the outcome. Well, what was one more humiliation? "Hard to compete with an Xbox and global destruction."

"Especially if he has high-def," the waitress said drily. "How about another glass of Zin? It sounds like you could use one."

"No, thanks. Just the check, please." She opened her purse to fish out her wallet.

The waitress stopped her with a wave of her hand. "Nope, no charge. Any sister who gets stood up by a loser drinks free here."

Mia slumped in her chair. "Wow. I knew I loved Aubergine for more than its gazpacho. Thanks," she said, dredging up a smile.

"Want some advice?"

After being given a free glass of very superior Zinfandel, she could hardly refuse. "Please."

"Go somewhere fun and forget all about the dude. You'll feel loads better in the morning."

Fun, huh? Not a bad idea. She certainly didn't have a better one, and she was sick and tired of being the good girl, the model citizen, the pillar of respectability. The person everyone could count on and then forget about.

Her smile grew grimly determined. "You know, you may be onto something."

"No question about it. Been there, done that, got the T-shirt. Now, do you mind clearing the table so I can make some money on it?"

THE BOPPING RHYTHM of Buckwheat Zydeco's "On a Night Like This" poured out the open windows of The Drop as Mia walked up the path to the converted wood-and-stone barn that now housed Acacia's favorite watering hole. Beau and Nell Duchamp, The Drop's owners, originally hailed from Louisiana, and so music from the bayous often made it into the evening's playlist.

It was a good place to unwind. Nell and Beau had installed a pool table at one end of the spacious interior; at the other end was a dance floor that was just the right size to accommodate people in the mood to boogie the night away. Best of all, they'd preserved the rustic barn-like feel, keeping the exposed rafters and roughly scraped plaster walls.

Mia stepped inside. Her sweeping glance picked out familiar faces, acquaintances as well as friends. Some were twirling on the dance floor, some relaxing on the Chesterfield sofas and upholstered chairs that Nell had picked up at antiques shops and estate sales. On one sofa, Quinn was sitting with Ward and Tess. Quinn noticed her and waved, then made a wide gesture with her hands on either side of her head before giving Mia two thumbs-up and a huge grin.

For a second Mia was baffled. Then she realized Quinn approved of her having yanked off the three scrunchies required to control her hair. The tangled coils bounced about her. She probably looked like Medusa, but she didn't care.

Her eyes scanned the far corners of the bar. She realized that if this many of the younger Knowleses were present, it was a safe bet Reid was, too. A man of action, he'd be doing something, shooting the breeze with whoever was tending bar tonight or perhaps making some woman divinely happy with a turn on the dance floor. Oh, there he was. Hunkered over the pool table like a pro, of course.

One of his fan groups—Maebeth, Nancy, Tracy Crofta, and Pru Savage, a whippet-lean lifestyle coach who ran ultra-marathons for the hell of it—was clustered near him, looking on hungrily as he leaned over the green felt and executed his shot.

The music ended just in time for Mia to hear the *clack* of the balls striking one another and then the *thud* as one of them rolled into the pocket. Typical, she thought. Reid was like the guy in the Carly Simon song "You're So Vain." Sublimely irritating.

It was as if she'd shouted the snarky observation at the top of her lungs. Reid straightened abruptly, his gaze colliding with hers.

She tamped down the surge of satisfaction that he'd acknowledged her at all. Because of course he *had* to pay attention to her now, didn't he? His family had a financial stake in the winery. His newfound interest wasn't personal.

The thought made the anger that had been simmering inside her for days come to a boil.

Reid had best steer clear of her tonight, she thought,

as she shot him a narrow-eyed glance. She was so not in the mood.

Beau was tending bar. "Evening, Mia. Nice to see you," he said in his Louisiana drawl.

"Thank you. It's busy tonight." In addition to the familiar faces, there were lots she didn't recognize.

"Tourists and such. More and more seem to find us." Beau didn't make it sound as though that was really a good thing, and she liked him all the more for it. She could relate to a bartender who was an introvert.

"What can I pour you?" He turned to the row of local wines lined up against the wall behind the bar. They had a nice selection. She loved that Beau and Nell stocked her family's wine. It was always a thrill to watch whoever was tending bar pour a glass for a customer.

She usually ordered a red—a Cabernet or a Petite Sirah—but not tonight. She refused to be predictable—in any way, in any how. "A pomegranate martini, please. And, Beau? Don't hold back on the vodka."

His lips twitched, and for a second his dark eyes regarded her searchingly. Then he scratched the black scruff covering his cheek and nodded. "Coming right up, *ma chère*."

She watched him fix her drink. Finished, he set it before her with a deliberate solemnity totally at odds with the amused smile curving his lips. "*Santé,*" he said.

Raising her glass, she admired the cocktail's violet-red hue. It didn't look anything like the wines she sampled and judged. Good. Saluting him, she took a sip. And then a second, longer one. "Mmmm. This is delicious."

"Thomas get off to the airport okay?"

Of course the news had spread that Thomas was leaving. "Indeed he did."

"And you're okay?"

"Just peachy," she drawled. "And you?"

"Fine and dandy."

"So glad all is right in the world," she said, and tipped her martini glass, letting the cold alcohol fill her mouth. She closed her eyes in appreciation. She swallowed, then observed, "There's something to be said for the directness of distilled liquor, Beau. A no-nonsense, cut-the-bullshit quality to the drinking experience—"

"Better still, it's medicinal," a voice said.

She opened her eyes and turned her head. The man had thick red hair and was smiling at her. She put him at thirty or so but only because of the faint lines fanning out from the corners of his brown eyes. Thanks to the smattering of freckles across his face, he'd look youthful well into his AARP years.

"Medicinal? Is that right?"

He nodded and gestured to the stool next to her. "May I?"

"Sure," she said. She could always walk away and huddle in a corner with Quinn if he began to bore her. She hadn't seen Quinn at the tasting. No surprise there. Wine tastings weren't exactly Quinn's cup of tea. A chat would be good. They needed to catch up.

The man sat and ordered a shot of Wyborowa vodka from Beau. "My Polish grandfather swore by vodka's virtues. He claimed a shot of *wódka*"—he pronounced the word with a double "o"—"would cure whatever ailed a body. Hiccups, achy joints, a touch of flu, you name it." He propped an elbow on the counter. "Fortunately, you appear quite healthy."

He grinned as if they'd known each other for ages.

She decided to be charmed. "Thank you for noticing."

"Impossible not to. My name's Will. Will O'Shea."

"I'm Mia Bodell." She shook his hand and found the

grasp firm, with only a touch of sweat. "O'Shea. That doesn't sound exactly Polish."

"My dad's Irish. So I got the easier name to spell but I also got the red hair. Can't have everything."

She thought of the pictures of her mother, faded snapshots. At Serena's death, Thomas had gathered the photos from the two-room apartment in Florida where she and Mia had been living and put them into a shoe box, so Mia might have some memories. Her mother had been tall, like Thomas. Mia assumed her own height had come from the Bodell side of the family. The rest—her impossibly dense curls, the shape and greenish-brown color of her eyes—well, the rest must come from her father.

Or maybe she was a freak of nature, as her cousin Jay had so often jeered.

She pushed the thought away. "You're right. You can't have everything."

Will O'Shea didn't seem to note the change in her voice. "On the other hand, it's a beautiful summer night, and despite my carrot top I've been lucky enough to wander into a friendly bar and meet an attractive and interesting lady. So cheers." He clinked his shot glass against her raised martini.

"Cheers," she replied, and watched as he downed the vodka in a single swallow. Impressive, she thought, and deciding she could do no less, downed the rest of hers.

Setting his glass on the bar, Will signaled Beau over. "I'm in a celebratory mood tonight. May I buy you another?" He pointed at the empty martini glass. "And perhaps entice you onto the dance floor later?"

Despite her reckless mood, Mia instinctively paused to inspect him a little more carefully. He gazed back at her in an open and non-pushy manner. After the men she'd been dealing with, he seemed positively charming.

She put some warmth in her smile. "You know what? I think that's a fine idea."

Will O'Shea was in sales. Nut harvesters, specifically. At least she knew enough about the local almond and walnut growers to discuss the preferred ways of harvesting their product. If he was disappointed by the fact that she grew grapes—and hired extra crew come harvest time so they could be picked by hand in the time-honored tradition—Will didn't show it.

Will also liked golf. Born in Indiana, he currently lived in Santa Rosa. He liked California. The winters here were a hell of a lot more pleasant than back home. He wasn't married.

"I'm going to be in the area for the rest of the week," he said. "How about I come by and take a tour of your vineyard? I've heard the Pinots in Mendocino are the hot buy right now."

No one should buy a wine simply because it was the current fad. Wine was about taste, and thus deeply personal. It spoke to you or it didn't. Reid might not be a wine connoisseur, but she knew he understood that crucial point.

Except she wasn't going to think about Reid. She was going to concentrate on Will O'Shea, who seemed pleasant enough. She drew an aimless circle on the zinc bar. "Sure, come over whenever." Though it will probably break the axle on your car, she added silently.

"I'll do that."

He smiled and leaned closer. After his second shot of vodka, twin red spots had bloomed on his cheeks, making him look even more boyish. His brown eyes seemed a little out of focus, but his words sounded crisp enough when he announced abruptly, "I need to go to the gents'.

Then how about you and I take a spin on the dance floor?"

"Okay."

He looked delighted, which was darn gratifying. Gesturing to her half-full glass, he said, "Drink up. Can't have you falling behind." Perhaps thinking he needed to set the pace, Will signaled to Beau for another vodka before wandering off.

Now that Mia was alone, the sounds of the bar—the buzz of conversation and bursts of laughter, the bluesy vocals of Buddy Guy, the sharp *clack* of striking billiard balls—became more distinct. She was debating going over to Quinn's table and saying hi to her and Tess when an all-too-familiar voice addressed her.

"You might want to slow down on those martinis." Reid's tone held a mixture of irritation and something else that she didn't immediately recognize. Whatever it was, it lent a rough rasp to his voice.

She shifted on her stool to study him. He looked as irritatingly handsome as ever. Holding his gaze, she gave him her sweetest smile, picked up her martini, and drained it. Then she had to stifle a gag, the cocktail suddenly possessing the cloying heaviness of cough syrup. It settled uncomfortably in a stomach that was empty save for six chickpeas, a glass of Zinfandel, and her last, much more delicious martini. Drawing upon whatever acting skills she possessed, she kept her smile in place and set the glass down.

Will returned. "I'm back." His announcement was accompanied by a wide grin. "Miss me?"

"Loads." It was painful to look at him beside Reid. No need to detail why he appeared abruptly softer, blurrier, and infinitely duller. And he was grinning far too much. Moreover, he'd done something funny to his hair. It stood up in short, straight spikes, making him look like . . . well, for some perverse reason, the only thing that came to mind was a red hedgehog.

She wasn't sure hedgehogs came in red.

But, unfortunately, Mia suspected that Will could have magically transformed from his present likeness into George Clooney and she still would have found him lacking.

She really should have her head examined.

Will scooped up his newly refilled shot glass and tossed the liquor back. "So, Mia, ready to shake your delicious booty on the dance floor with me?"

She winced inwardly. "I'd love to."

Reid hadn't moved from the bar since Mia sailed past him. He could see the dance floor from where he was. A Train song was playing—Beau's temporary concession to the fact that they were in California rather than Louisiana—and it wasn't particularly danceable.

Perhaps Mia would get sick of the guy rocking from side to side with a goofball smirk on his face while he pumped his elbows at her, and she'd walk off the floor. Then again, Mia's stubbornness knew no end—just as Reid's idiocy was boundless.

"You look like you could use another beer."

Reid didn't turn around. "No thanks, Beau. I rode the Harley here."

"A good night for it. Saw you talking to Mia just now. Didn't seem to go well."

When did it ever? "You know anything about the guy she's with?"

"Heard him say he was in sales. Harvesters of some sort. He had some pickup line about vodka's healing properties. So far he seems harmless. Lousy dancer." Reid didn't have to look across the bar to know Beau had lifted his shoulders in a heavy shrug. "Mia's looking good tonight. Different."

"Yeah." She'd freed her hair, for one thing. It moved as she swayed to the beat, the gold-brown curls taking on a life of their own. She was dressed differently, too, in a dark purple top and a long white skirt with a purple and navy blotchy print. The outfit didn't show anything, draping with frustrating looseness, but it was pretty.

The fact that she'd dressed up bugged him to no end, because she hadn't done it for him. Even worse, she was dancing with an equipment salesman, someone Reid ordinarily would have no problem sharing a beer with while discussing capacities and the different attachments that came with the models he hawked. But tonight all Reid wanted was to run him out of town. Five minutes ago.

What kind of goony Neanderthal did that make him? A jealous one, that's what kind.

It was the damnedest thing. He hadn't initially been attracted to Mia in high school. She hadn't even been a blip on his radar. Then after the crap Jay pulled, making all the guys in the locker room listen to Mia's fantasies about Reid, his former obliviousness toward her became . . . well, complicated. A messy mix of embarrassment, attraction, and self-consciousness. The combination was too confusing for his sixteen-year-old self to handle. His bungled attempt to apologize for her cousin's cruelty—he winced to remember how he'd stumbled over the words—had only made things worse. And any chance of getting past the awkwardness and asking her out—which would doubtless have opened the door to even more snide gossip and humiliation for them both—became impossible.

Avoidance had been the obvious solution.

Dodging her hadn't been hard, since she'd been even

more embarrassed about the diary thing than he. When they happened to pass in the hall at school, she invariably turned a scary shade of red. But then, after a month or so, things had changed. Her cheeks no longer flamed. Instead, he was treated to white-pursed lips, pinched nostrils in a nose stuck high in the air, and a narrowed critical gaze. And that had been Mia's fixed expression for pretty much the last twelve years.

Given their history, he shouldn't be experiencing the telltale tightening of his gut whenever she was near. And he certainly shouldn't be tormented by the thought of what Mia would look like naked. He shouldn't wonder what she enjoyed in bed, whether he'd be able to please her.

What was human nature if not perverse? For some insane reason, he wanted to know the answer to all those questions.

There was just something about Mia.

Hell, maybe it was because she'd written about him in her diary, had spun those fragile teenage dreams about him. Whatever it was, it made him *possessive*.

He didn't like the emotion, and he really didn't like that it was becoming harder to control around her. It turned him into someone he didn't recognize.

The song ended. He watched Mia's thick mane flow and shift across her back and around her shoulders as she shook her head, refusing the guy's attempt to convince her to stay for a second dance. As Mia made to walk away, Reid's hopes rose, only to plummet when the guy stepped in front of her and put his hands together as if saying *pretty please*.

Christ almighty, she wasn't going to fall for that, was she?

Damn it all, he cursed in disbelief when she relented. And *of course* the next song was slow enough to justify the guy crowding her and wrapping his arms about her waist.

"Hey, Beau?"

"Yeah?"

"If Mia orders another drink, make sure to give her some pretzels and a glass of water, too. And don't let her leave the bar without my knowing."

"Gotcha."

He'd told himself he wouldn't watch. But when he dropped into the chair beside Ward, Reid angled his body so he had a clear view of the couples on the floor.

"Having fun?" Ward asked.

"A blast." He drummed his fingers against his thighs, the tempo much faster than the music coming out in surround sound. At least Beau didn't play extended tracks.

"Why don't you dance? There are several women who appear quite eager to take a spin on the floor with you."

"Don't feel like it."

"Oh. You'd rather watch?"

Reid dragged his attention away from the dance floor for a second to shoot his brother a clear message about what he could do with himself and then shifted his gaze back to the couple shuffling slowly on the dance floor. "Jesus, did you *see* that?"

"What? You mean his hand? It does seem a touch friendly. Ah, that's the way to discourage him, Mia." Ward's voice was warm with approval. "I think it's a safe bet Mia's dance partner will be limping for several hours."

Reid stood, his eyes never leaving her. "He's lucky she only decided to stomp on his foot. I'll take her back to her house."

"On your bike?"

Right. The Harley wasn't an option if she was looped. She hadn't seemed drunk earlier, but vodka and sugar had a way of ambushing a body. He wasn't going to risk her falling off his motorcycle. "I'll take her truck and come back in the morning for the Harley."

"No need. I'll ride it back to the ranch. Tess and Quinn can follow in the Jeep."

"Thanks." He dug his keys out of his pocket and tossed them to Ward.

"You're welcome. And, Reid? Don't break the guy's arm."

AMAZINGLY, DESPITE HAVING his foot crushed by an annoyed Mia, the guy who'd been dancing with her was still hanging on, perhaps too rocked from groping her ass to feel the broken bones or to recognize how close he was to acquiring a few more.

Any sane or sober man would have taken a good look around and known better than to mess with Mia in Beau's watering hole. Beau Duchamp was not someone to rile, and he was staring like a hawk at the red-haired man, more than ready to jump over the bar and rescue Mia. But it was clear from the sloppy grin on the guy's face that he was too damned happy to read the scene. Whether that was from drink or a Mia rush was immaterial. His night of boogying down and feeling up was over.

On his way to the dance floor, Reid caught Beau's eye. "Call Ralph Cummings, would you, and have him take this bozo wherever he belongs?" Ralph Cummings was the sole taxi driver in the area. Since Ward had told him he couldn't break the guy's arm, Reid figured sticking him in the back of Ralph's car—far from the most pleasant ride in Mendocino County—would suffice as punishment. And the roads would be safe.

"Consider it done," Beau replied.

As he neared the dancers, Reid saw that Mia was none too pleased with her new friend. She was pushing at his shoulder. He kept squeezing.

"Time to head home, Mia," Reid said.

She turned at the sound of his voice. Naturally her expression only grew darker. Why be grateful that he was saving her from Octopaw?

"And who are you to be telling her anything?" The guy looked at Reid and puffed out his chest, a bantam preparing to fight.

Reid smiled. He only hoped the man was stupid enough to throw a punch at him.

Instead, the guy turned to Mia. "Who's he?"

"This is Reid. He's—"

"I'm her partner," Reid said, before she could offer her own scathing characterization. With a tender smile he said, "Isn't that right, *darling*?"

She scowled but remained blessedly silent.

"Partner?" the guy repeated. "She didn't tell me—"

"I'm telling you. Loud and clear. So beat it, pal."

Mia shook off his grip as soon as they stepped outside the bar.

"That was totally unnecessary," she informed him as she marched toward her truck. "I did not need your intervention."

He kept stride with her. "You sure did. He was all over you. Not even the threat of a second mangled foot was stopping him. What were you doing with him, anyway—what happened to you and Andrew Schroeder?" He couldn't believe he'd asked that.

The question obviously surprised her, too. She faltered, tripping on a stone, but when he reached out to steady her, she flapped her arm like an angry bird.

"How did you know I was going out tonight with Andrew?"

"I know lots. Answer the question."

"Thomas told you, huh? Andrew and I came to a parting of ways. He needs more time to play video games."

Her breezy tone didn't fool him. "Schroeder's a moron."

That stopped her in her tracks. She even looked at him sort of pleasantly. "You know, that's the nicest thing I've ever heard you say."

Was that true? Probably. Funny, he knew exactly what to say to a woman—if her name wasn't Mia Bodell.

"But actually I should thank Andrew," Mia said as she resumed her military march. "He showed me what a jerk he was before I made the mistake of sleeping with him."

Reid's jaw nearly hit the ground.

Blithely unaware, she continued. "He also helped me realize how sick and tired I am of being me. That's why I went to The Drop."

"To guzzle martinis like they're Gatorade and pick up guys? Brilliant plan."

"Ha. Very funny. I didn't pick up Will; I merely didn't discourage him. And he was perfectly nice until that third shot of vodka."

"A prince among men." Thank God this Will person was taking a cab to wherever he was staying. Reid hoped the fare was astronomical.

"Again, your wit dazzles. And for your information, I did not guzzle. Not really. And I'm not drunk."

"Not really," he replied, but his sarcasm was lost on her. He could tell she wasn't drunk—her clearly articulated sentences proved that. But she had to be a little buzzed. Otherwise she'd have never shared that information about her and Andrew. And she was still babbling—ranting—away.

"I'll tell you what I am," she said. "I'm pissed. *Angry.* And I'm not going to take any more crap from anyone." With her hair loose and riotous, he couldn't see much of her face, only the tip of her nose. It was making its way skyward. Some things had to remain constant.

"Bully for you," he said.

"And that includes you, buster."

"Mia, you've never taken any crap from me."

"I'm not going to, either."

It was his turn to stop in his tracks. "So you had to go on a booze binge and manhunt to work that one out?" He shook his head in disbelief.

The nose looked down on him. "I hardly think a cowboy with a harem should be giving me life lessons."

They'd reached her pickup. Taking the keys from her, he unlocked it and yanked open the passenger door. "You're mixing your cultures. I do not have a harem."

"Oh, excuse me. Your traveling groupies, then."

"For Christ's sake, I don't have groupies, stationary or otherwise."

She snickered. "Oh, *please.*"

"Right. Whatever. Just get in the truck, Your Royal Pain in the Assness."

"This is the passenger side."

"Astounding powers of observation. You drink, you don't drive. Get in," he repeated.

She cast him a withering glare but, thankfully, she didn't argue as she climbed into the seat. He made sure to shut her door before she could change her mind. Then, he circled around the hood, slid behind the steering wheel, glanced over to make sure she'd fastened her seat belt, and tried not to ogle her breasts in the process. He started the engine with a roar.

* * *

Eight seconds later, the truck's interior had shrunk to the size of a shoe box, and her scent had wrapped itself around him. It reminded him of the beach in summer, of hot sun mixed with ocean spray, salty and delicious. She smelled of lemon, too, and something else that made him dizzy when he breathed.

He opened the window, but that didn't help. The wind caught the soft tendrils of her hair so they flew about and teased his forearm—"brush" would be too heavy a word. His head spun from something far more potent than alcohol.

In all the time Reid had known Mia, they'd never been alone in such a confined space. The intimacy heightened his perceptions until he swore he could hear her pulse beating and see the rise and fall of her breasts, even though he kept his eyes glued on the dark road ahead.

What he couldn't divine was the taste of her.

Would she be tangy and salty and unexpectedly fiery, or succulent and sweet like a perfectly ripe peach?

The desire he battled so often around her renewed its attack.

He stepped on the gas.

They arrived at Bartlett Road in record time. If Mia noticed that he'd gotten them there at warp speed, she kept it to herself. She'd been silent during the short trip.

He wasn't going to tempt fate by initiating a conversation.

He passed the gates marking his family's ranch and half a mile on turned right at the Bodells' drive.

He'd barely straightened the steering wheel when the front tires went into a rut the size of the Grand Canyon. The jolt of the suspension nearly concussed him.

But it was Mia's jouncing off the seat and then landing close—far too close—that had him hissing in pain and the muscles of his thighs hardening in readiness.

Fortunately, she scooted back to her side of the cab a millisecond before he hit the next crater.

"What the hell?" he said.

"Surely you know our driveway." Her hands were splayed against the dashboard. "You come over to see Thomas all the time."

"Why drive when I can cut across the property on foot or ride Sirrus?" He spoke through gritted teeth so he wouldn't bite his tongue off on the next pothole. "How long's it been like this?"

She made an airy gesture with her hand, nearly swatting him in the face when the wheels went over a log-sized bump. "Awhile."

"Has it ever occurred to anyone that the road could be repaired?"

"Really? Wow. That's pure genius. Here's a news flash for you: Fixing a road this long costs thousands. My family has barely two pennies to rub together. That's where you come into the picture, remember? Besides, our road is a good test of skills. If you know how to drive at all, the ruts are easy to avoid."

Deciding it might be the only way to shut her up, he aimed for the biggest one he could find.

The porch light was on, and a yellow glow from a single lamp shone in an upstairs room.

It was simple, he told himself as he cut the engine. All he had to do was to escort her up the front steps, unlock the door, watch her step inside, and wait to hear the lock slide home. Then he could do what he did best in Mia's company. Turn around and get the hell away from her.

Reid made to go around to her side of the truck, but

Mia had already climbed down. They walked toward the front of the house, the chirping of crickets punctuating the silence between them. And though the evening was mild and the sky studded with stars, he felt the air crackle with the intensity of an approaching storm. He was too aware of her. Too conscious of the sway of her hips, the fascinating mystery of her body.

Just a few more seconds and he'd be safe from any crazy impulses.

Abruptly tired of the mini pep talks he kept conducting with himself, he bounded up the porch steps and grasped the screen-door handle. Yanking it open, he unlocked the door. Impatience riding him, he took a quick step back. His body slammed into hers.

A high-pitched "oh!" escaped her as she recoiled from the contact. Teetering, Mia windmilled her arms.

He grabbed her before she could tumble off the porch. The banging of the screen door behind them was nothing compared to the slam of his heart as she fell against him. Soft, full breasts pressed against his chest.

Lust annihilated thought. Common sense went up in flames under the searing heat of her body plastered against his.

He may have groaned and she may have gasped. The roaring in his ears was too loud for him to be certain, and any sounds were short-lived as their mouths found each other and fused. They kissed in a desperate mash of lips, clicking teeth, and tangled tongues.

His hands closed around curves deliciously lush. His hunger spiked, desperate to uncover all she'd camouflaged for years under layers of god-awful clothing.

Her breasts were just right, amply filling his large hands. He fondled their exquisite softness with his palms, exulting when her nipples turned pebble hard. He plucked them with his fingers, massaged them with his palms, and caught her moan in his mouth as he kissed her feverishly.

God, he wanted her so badly. He raised his head, his lips hovering over hers. He needed to be sure.

"Mia?" His voice was rough with arousal.

"Mm-hmm."

"One more time. You broke up with Andrew, right?"

"Mm-hmm."

"And you're not drunk?"

She opened heavy-lidded eyes. "No. Stupid maybe," she whispered.

"Yeah?" He let out a low laugh. "Me, too."

Her arms were about his neck. She clung to him as if he were a lifeline. It was damned fine with him. He caught her around the waist, kissed her again, and the heat between them flared like an inferno.

"Up. Stairs. Bed. Room." He managed between frenzied kisses.

A hazy few seconds later, his heart pounding as loudly as the thud of their sprinting feet on the stairs, they were in Mia's bedroom. He stretched out his arm, feeling for a wall light switch.

She caught the movement and stopped him with an urgent "Don't. Leave it dark."

He let her have her way. There was a moon tonight, and its beam stole through the open window, casting the interior in a gray-blue light. It'd be enough. For now.

He moved, before he could think, before *she* could think, before either of them could wise up enough to put a stop to this insane need claiming them. He took her in his arms and kissed her, slanting his mouth across hers, sweeping his hands from her waist to her ribs to the sweet full globes of her breasts, learning her as they crossed the room. With every step, he touched, tasted, and burned.

They reached her bed. He gave silent thanks. He didn't have time for finesse, not the way the blood was pumping in his veins, and his cock was stiff and pulsing.

Urgency fueling him, his hands now moved with a rough efficiency that would have ordinarily appalled him. At the moment he couldn't give a damn. He felt like he'd go blind if he didn't get her naked and him inside her.

There was one good thing about Mia's clothes: They were blessedly easy to remove. A hook, a zip, and her skirt dropped in an obliging cascade. Her blouse was loose enough to bunch as he kissed her, dragging it up while his knuckles grazed satin skin. He released her soft lips long enough to pull the top over her head and past her thick halo of hair.

And then he had to gasp for air, suck in lungfuls of the stuff, as he caught his first glimpse of Mia in the moonlight.

Holy fuck. Even in a plain white bra and undies, she was gorgeous: generous curves and long, strong limbs, and hair—all that glorious, crazy corkscrew hair that fell down her back. It was as wild and lush as the rest of her. He spared a thought for all those too-skinny women with sparrow bones and knew he was probably grinning like a fool, a happy fool. He only hoped his tongue wasn't hanging out like a dog anticipating a yummy treat.

"Take 'em off, Mia."

Her eyes widened. "I'm not sure—"

Damn. She was already thinking too much, revving up for an argument. "I want to watch. Do it, Mia."

Maybe it was the rasping need in his voice; maybe it was the sight of his hands moving to his shirt buttons, his fingers working quickly; maybe, just maybe, she was as crazily aroused as he. But for once in their rocky relationship, she actually did as he asked.

And, man, did he appreciate it.

She wasn't practiced. She didn't strike a pose that mimicked some porn starlet's or that showed him she was up on the top-ten moves money-back-guaranteed to drive a man wild. Good thing, too. His control was hanging by a thread as fine as a spider's web.

She reached up and brought her hands to the middle of her back so her elbows stuck out at sharp angles. She fumbled with the bra's catch. Her breasts jiggled. And, truly, that was all the erotic come-on he needed.

The bra slid off. Okay, he hadn't expected perfection. But there it was: generously rounded globes, puckered aureoles, and tight, tempting nipples begging for his touch. He swallowed and yanked the shirt off his shoulders.

He caught her looking. Her gaze roamed over his chest, down his heaving ribs, to his navel, then followed the narrow line of hair that led past his belt buckle. Then she saw the part of him that was begging, too. Big time.

Her eyes locked on the bulge near his fly and her mouth formed a silent "oh."

"Panties," he growled the command. Fuck finesse, fuck politesse.

It did the trick. Her fingers moved to the elastic waistband. While he still had a few functioning brain cells, he dug his wallet from the back pocket of his jeans, flipped it open, and tossed a foil packet onto the bed.

He returned his wallet and reached for his belt buckle just as Mia's sweet triangle of curls was revealed. And then it did feel as if he'd gone a little blind, as a blast of lust seared his retinas.

He shucked off his boots and socks, jeans, and knit

boxers in a blur of motion. There was no grace involved but probably a fair amount of comedy. He was too aroused for laughter, though.

As for Mia, she was staring at his erection as if her eyes were going to pop out. He hoped that was a good sign. Because he was desperate to be inside her, the instinct as all-powerful as the one driving a stallion to claim and mount a mare.

He fought the urge to tackle her, but he couldn't stop himself from crowding her until she sank down on the mattress as if her knees had turned to water. He followed, his body bowing over her.

"Mia." He nudged her legs apart.

She let him.

Was that enough? No, damn it, it wasn't. He had to make sure. He could still stop, turn around, dress, and walk out of here. His cock wouldn't shatter in a million pieces. "You want this to happen between us?"

He saw the column of her throat work as she gulped. "Yes."

Thank God. "Okay, then." Part of him registered that he was not going to win the smooth-lover-of-the-night award, but words were getting hard to string together, let alone formulate. He spared another second to take her in: Her hair spread out in a thick fan, some of the strands resting on her torso, brushing the tips of her breasts. His gaze traveled down the flat of her tummy, the hollow of her navel, the sweet curve of her hips, the triangular thatch of hair marking the entrance to where he most wanted—most needed—to be. There, inside that magic heat, that delicious wetness, that incredible tightness. Inside Mia.

Was she ready for him?

He sank to his knees. He ran his palms up the length of her smooth thighs, urging her legs to open even wider. Beneath him, her muscles leapt and quivered, and, as his fingers moved closer and closer to the apex of her thighs, the heat that was Mia built.

He brushed his fingers against her dark curls. They were damp. He closed his eyes briefly as a wave of male satisfaction swamped him. Opening them, he locked his gaze on hers. Slowly, deliberately, he parted her slick folds, slid one and then a second finger inside her, exulting at the tight squeeze of her muscles gripping them and the hot moisture coating them. He set a rhythm, moving in and out in a slow thrust and drag, and watched her eyes widen and then her lids become heavy, weighted with pleasure. His cock lengthened, growing harder still.

Feeling her muscles begin to spasm, he brushed his thumb over her clit, smiling as she moaned and arched against him, urging his fingers to slide deeper. She was close, he knew.

He had to taste her, drink her pleasure as he took her over the edge.

While his thumb slowly circled, he lowered his mouth to the straining nub and gave a slow lick as he thrust his fingers home.

She came with a scream, arching off the bed and clamping his fingers in a velvet vise. As her hips bucked, he licked and kissed her, savoring her tangy essence. While the contractions continued to rock her, he kept his fingers deep inside her, withdrawing only when her harsh pants quieted.

His own heart was pounding, his body shaking with a need as intense as any he'd ever felt. Blindly, he reached for the condom, brought the foil wrapper to his mouth, and tore it open with his teeth. Sitting back on his haunches, he slid the latex over his erection and shuddered. Mia stared at him, her breasts rising and falling. His hunger spiked threefold. Locking his gaze on her, he looped her long legs about his hips and guided his cock to her center. His muscles tensed in anticipation, he drove deep, sheathing himself to the hilt.

She came in a second loud scream.

Holy fucking hell was his last coherent thought.

Consumed by desire, mad with need, Reid moved inside Mia in a fevered dance. His hands stroked, hers clutched. At times they urged him on, at others they clung as she rode the storm of their passion. Throughout, his hips pumped and ground against hers with a barely restrained violence.

Sweat slicked their bodies.

He dove his fingers into her thick mane, wrapping it around his wrists like a silken anchor, mooring himself to her as they strained against each other. Their mouths hungry, their teeth scoring, raking and nipping quivering flesh. The torture was exquisite.

Arousal wound them ever tighter, propelled them ever higher. Once again Reid felt Mia stiffen beneath him, moving more urgently as she reached for that sweet release. He slid his hand between them and dragged his finger over her slick nub, rubbing it. She cried out his name as she came, her body clenching around him, milking him exquisitely, triggering his own climax. With a deep, savage groan, he surged into her and, joined, came with a rush that stunned.

So very right, he thought, once he could think again.

That was the biggest surprise of the night, how flawlessly he and Mia fit together. Moved together. Came together. It was fucking incredible, actually.

Spent, beyond replete, Reid collapsed onto the bed beside her, one of his hands still wrapped in the thick silk of her hair. He was too tired to move it. He had only energy enough to smile when her breath tickled his damp chest. His smile widened as he heard a delicate yet distinct snore escape her.

So the wild-haired witch who'd blown his mind had fallen asleep on him. Who'd have ever imagined such a thing, and he shifted his head to press a kiss against her brow. Still marveling, he closed his eyes and succumbed, too.

Chapter

THIRTEEN

MIA NEEDED TO pee. She needed to open her eyes, too. But her lids were as heavy as cinder blocks. She swallowed, and all the sand of the Sahara slid down her throat.

She felt awful, kind of like overstretched taffy, and though her head didn't pound, she couldn't move it. It was stuck somehow. Never, ever again would she drink pomegranate martinis.

The cries of the awakening birds came through the open window. Then she heard something else. The sound was low-pitched and reached her right ear in a warm blast. Someone was breathing.

Suddenly she became aware of a heavy, solid presence near her. Mere inches away.

It was a body. A quietly snoring body.

Panicked, she wrenched her lids open to stare at the ceiling. She knew those cracks as well as she knew the lines of her palms. She was awake, she was in her room; this wasn't some terrible nightmare. This was far worse: reality. *Oh God,* what had she done?

A rush of memories flooded her, far more vivid than the purplish-red martinis she'd drunk.

Her heart thudding, she cautiously looked sideways.

And the very worst suspicion was confirmed. Horrified shock had her jackknifing—or trying to. The attempt ended in a howl of pain.

"Ow!" She went to clutch her head. Instead, her elbow slammed into Reid. Hard. Her second "Ow!" was answered by his "*Shit!* Damn it all to hell, that *hurt*."

His stream of curses continued. She ignored them, concentrating on the excruciating spot at the back of her head and trying not to hyperventilate because Reid was buck-naked next to her in bed. Trying not to pass out because she was equally so.

Her head was throbbing in pain. It felt like a large hank of hair had been ripped out by its roots. Her fingers searched for the spot and found his hand instead. She swatted it. "Get away!"

"I can't," he growled, obviously no happier than she. "My watch is caught in your hair."

She turned to glare at him and winced as pain stabbed her. "Well, get *uncaught*."

"Nothing I'd like better, believe me," he said. His right hand was cupped over the side of his face. He lowered it and she saw exactly what part of him her elbow had rammed. While his fingers probed the area around his bleary eye, a surge of guilt welled up inside her.

But embarrassment topped it.

Last night had been so—she had no words to describe the feelings, the oceans of sensation that had swept over her when Reid had touched her, kissed her, and then entered her. She'd never experienced sex like that and was sure she never would again. Because who could compare to Reid? No one. And now? The damage was done.

What wouldn't she give to have five minutes alone to cry and release some of the emotions flooding her? Instead, she was trapped with the man who now occupied an even bigger role in her life than he had before. She'd had difficulty enough putting her high school infatuation behind her. How in the world was she to forget that Reid had been everything she'd ever imagined in a lover—and far more?

And after a night like the one he'd given her, now this, a mortification-filled morning after. Actually, this was a far more believable scenario, especially one in which Reid costarred. She was feeling stupidly groggy, had a mouth that probably smelled like a swamp, and her hair was doing its freshly electrocuted thing. Even worse, its manacled thing.

And she still hadn't peed.

Even in the predawn light, even with bed head and a sleep-creased face, Reid was breathtakingly handsome: all smooth, bronzed skin and sculpted muscles. She wanted to drag the covers over her head and hide. But of course she couldn't, not when his wristwatch was caught in the overgrown thicket that passed for her hair.

She spoke through gritted teeth. "Would you kindly get on with extricating yourself?"

"I'm trying my best." His voice was as tense as hers.

He scooted closer, six-foot-two inches of glorious male beauty.

Remembering the weight of his body pressing down on her, of his hard length moving inside her, she dropped her forehead to her upraised knees, hiding cheeks that burned. What was he doing here in her bed? Was he even now regretting their night together?

"Damn, your hair is thick."

"Tell me something I don't know," she muttered. Like why you decided to sleep with me, she added silently.

"Okay, how about this? I've seen jungle vines tamer than this."

She squeezed her eyes shut. She bet most of Reid's

women got at least a good-morning kiss. She got insults about her hair. "And where have you ever seen a jungle vine?"

"On those wild-animal programs on TV. Quinn loves them. They take you into a jungle like this." He tugged, gently enough. But, rattled by his presence and the heat of him and the male muskiness of him, she jumped.

"Ow," she said, extra crossly. Raising her hand to the spot, she brushed his fingers.

For several beats there was silence, as electric as the rush of desire through her veins from that accidental touch.

Then he batted her hand away with a gruff command. "Stop crowding me. It's difficult enough to see what I'm doing here. And quit squirming, or you'll be wearing a hat for the next six months."

She hunched defensively, trying not to think about everything they'd done on this bed together, that she'd climaxed three times and that he probably gave every woman he slept with that kind of epic pleasure. She failed. Miserably.

He leaned closer. She could only assume she alone felt the heat building between them as his fingers carefully sifted through her tangles. The gentleness of his fingers unnerved her as much as the presence of his naked body, inches away.

Her heart banged painfully in her chest. Oh God, oh God.

He shifted, his skin grazing hers, and she caught her breath.

She was dizzy from holding it by the time he gave a grunt of satisfaction. "Free at last," he said, lowering his hands.

Before she could form a coherent reply, he'd jumped off the bed as though she had a communicable disease.

She raised her head and caught sight of his naked butt. The twin globes were pale, as were the topmost portion of his legs. His skin darkened abruptly where his swim trunks must end. She watched his muscles clench as he pulled on his dark-gray knit boxers and then jammed his feet into his jeans. She heard the rasp of his zipper and then saw his arms move as he buckled his belt.

He scooped his shirt off the floor and turned back to the bed. She only just managed to avert her gaze, lowering it to the rumpled cotton coverlet.

"We should talk about this," he said.

The words sounded forced to her ears. She could guess how much he wanted any kind of conversation. She kept her eyes fixed on the white appliqué pattern, staring until her vision blurred. "What's there to talk about? We had sex. No big deal. Besides, it's not like it's going to happen again. Ever."

He must have descended the stairs at warp speed. Seconds later she heard the front door slam.

Well, at least she could cry now.

It was early, not even six o'clock, when Reid reached the barns and the corrals, on his way to a hot shower, a fortifying cup of black coffee, and an ice pack for his throbbing eye. It stung like a bitch.

His good eye spotted Ward inside the enclosure. He was currying Gomez, one of their trail horses, while the white gelding nibbled on his breakfast flakes of hay. In the summer, the morning trail rides started earlier, to save both riders and equines from baking under the sun at its zenith. Ward, Quinn, and Jim, one of their wranglers, were taking the morning group out. It would be Reid's turn tomorrow.

The sound of his booted feet on the gravel had Ward looking up. "You're back."

"Yeah."

"A little later than I expected."

Reid cocked his head. "You keeping tabs on me?"

"Nope, I just want this business deal between us and the Bodells to work out."

"Interestingly enough, that's my plan, too. After I get some coffee inside me, I'm taking one of Dad's tractors and a grading rake over to their place. I don't think Thomas's tractor has enough horsepower." He was also going to put in a call to Howie Briggs. Howie owned a gravel company outside Ukiah and rode Quarter Horses competitively on the weekends. It just so happened he'd bought one trained by Reid. According to Howie, Condor was the best horse he'd ever had. Reid figured that was worth an express shipment of gravel at cost.

If Ward was surprised that Reid was taking farm equipment over to Mia's, he didn't show it. "Okay," he said. "Will you be done with the tractor by the afternoon?"

"We're vaccinating the calves today, right? Yeah. Count me in." Sirrus would enjoy the work.

Ward nodded. "Good. Did you sleep with her?"

"None of your goddamned business."

"I'll take that as a 'yes.' So that's probably a first for you."

"What do you mean?" he asked, thinking he really needed that coffee. And the ice. And about four aspirin.

"Spending the night with a beautiful woman and coming home with a black eye."

He hadn't realized Ward thought she was beautiful. Probably because Mia didn't scowl at him.

Instead of replying, Reid ducked through the wooden railing, picked up a bristle brush, and began to groom Felix, who was tied next to Gomez. The gelding had found some mud to roll in. Every vigorous stroke sent brown clouds into the air.

"So where does the shiner come into all this?" Ward asked.

Not pausing in his brushing, Reid raised his left hand and probed the bruise gingerly. "My wristwatch got caught in her hair. I guess she was a little disoriented when she woke up and she winged me with her elbow. It was an accident—although she's certainly been itching to give me a black eye for a while."

"Mia?" Ward said in disbelief. "I know she's never been a card-carrying member of your fan club, but I didn't know she longed to do you bodily harm. Care to share?"

Older brothers with a sense of humor early in the morning left something to be desired. But he figured he might as well tell Ward, since his brother wasn't likely to let it rest.

"Remember when you were recovering from the knife wound you got when that gang ambushed Brian Nash?"

"Yeah. After I got out of the hospital, I had to stay home and have Mom fuss over me."

"Well, I had an adventure of my own that week, only I didn't come off quite so heroically. The opposite, in fact."

Ward let the currycomb rest on top of Gomez's rump. "What are you talking about?"

"You know Jay, Mia's older cousin?"

Ward's mouth turned down at the corners as if he'd tasted something vile. "Yeah."

"He got hold of a diary Mia was keeping and brought it to the locker room for show-and-tell."

"Always was a jerk."

"An understatement. He's slime. Anyway, Mia'd written stuff about me. I should have decked Jay when he started reading—"

"If memory serves," Ward interjected, "he had about fifty pounds on you. He played football, right?"

"Defensive tackle. He got off sacking quarterbacks."

"That's right. He used to gloat at the lunch table whenever he'd sidelined another player. Asshole."

"The point of this story is, it doesn't matter that Jay was a pumped-up goon in high school and that I was still a scrawny runt. I didn't stick up for Mia when he began entertaining the other guys with story hour. I didn't do anything. Actually, I did." And Reid felt that familiar wave of self-disgust wash over him. "I hit the showers and pretended I didn't care that he was humiliating his cousin."

"Ah." Ward took his sweet time following up on that insightful comment. "And you still feel guilty because Jay was a shithead to Mia? I guess that explains it."

"Okay, I'll bite. Explains what exactly?"

"Why you're always so jumpy around her."

"I'm only jumpy because she hates my guts." But, damn, their bodies had liked each other just fine. He still couldn't believe how explosive the sex had been between them and how responsive she'd been. Or how easily she'd brushed him off this morning. So she never wanted to have sex again with him?

Remembering her categorical statement ticked him off all over again.

"You think she hates your guts?" Ward asked, interrupting his thoughts. Trading the currycomb for a mane brush, he circled around to Gomez's face and began to comb out his long white forelock.

"She's given a damned good impression of it for more than a decade now." She hadn't been exactly lovey-dovey this morning, either.

Ward smiled and shook his head. "I don't think it's hate she's feeling."

"You don't, huh?" Okay, maybe her body didn't hate

him, but her mind wasn't any too crazy about him. He ducked under Felix's neck and was grateful to find the other side of the gelding free of caked dirt. He resumed brushing. "So, Ward, when did you become such a flippin' expert on the female psyche?"

"Funny, isn't it? That's supposed to be your area of expertise. You've got women staring at their cellphones, hoping your number will flash on their screen. Hell, they adore you even when you *don't* call."

Reid shrugged. "I like women, women like me. It's not a complicated equation. The reason they continue to like me is equally simple. I don't make promises I won't keep."

"Only proves my point," Ward said, nodding. "You've got the opposite sex pretty well figured out. Which means you're smarter than the rest of us guys."

"Glad you finally noticed."

Ward continued as if he hadn't spoken. "So I think the question is, if you're so smart about women, why are you so dumb about one in particular?"

WITH THE SLAM of the front door still reverberating, Mia had realized she needed to do something even more urgently than having a good cry. She'd raced to the bathroom and, after seeing to vital needs, showered, scrubbing herself pink. Afterward, she dressed in an old button-down shirt of Thomas's and jeans she would have given to Goodwill if they'd accepted them.

In the kitchen she downed two Advil and, as added penance, ate her yogurt spartanly unadorned. It tasted as yucky as she felt.

Her head ached. It would be nice to blame it on alcohol. But it was mortification that made her temples throb. That, and the countless pins she'd stuck in her hair. She'd been ruthless with it, going for her severest style, one that involved tying, twisting, and pinning, something right out of a BDSM fantasy.

After the excruciating scene in her bedroom, awkward minutes ticking away while Reid extricated himself from the "jungle" of her hair and while she wished her bed would swallow her whole, she'd been tempted to take a machete—or her pruning shears—and hack off every last one of her curls. But the only period she could remember when her hair had been short was when Jay coated her head with Gorilla Glue while her aunt and uncle were out running errands.

Upon their return, Jay had been punished in the usual way: sent to his room without supper. Hardly a deprivation, since he had eaten the entire banana nut loaf Aunt Ellen had baked that morning. Distraught, her aunt had scoured the shelves at Wright's Hardware for a product to remove the glue. Nothing worked. Mia's fifth-grade school picture showed her with a buzz cut and a wobbly smile.

The memory of that early-October day extinguished what little appetite Mia had. Dumping the remains of her yogurt, she put the bowl and spoon in the dishwasher, absently wondering how long it would take before the machine was full enough to justify running it.

The dishwasher was too empty, the house too quiet. Vincent didn't even meow when she fed him his breakfast. He simply regarded her as if she were a stranger, ate a few bites, and then, crooking his tail haughtily, padded over to his cat door and leapt through it with the elegance of a circus lion navigating a suspended ring.

There went another male all too willing to desert her. She tried to take it in stride, reminding herself that only yesterday, before the martinis led her to a series of disastrous choices ending with Mr. Terribly Wrong in her bed—and, no, she couldn't truly blame the alcohol for what happened with Reid, but what was the harm in indulging in a brief pity fest—she had made one good decision. She'd resolved to be less like herself, at least less like the Mia she was sick and tired of, the one gripped by fears and insecurities.

She needed to act on that resolution.

On an ordinary day, she would have gone directly into the vineyard and walked among the rows of grapes, checking them and their verdant canopy. Simply picturing how the vines would shortly be heavy with black-purple fruit never failed to calm and center her.

Today, she instead followed her feckless cat outside and crossed the yard, pointing her feet in the direction of the winery. Thomas had pulled its sage-green doors shut after taking a farewell tour of the stainless-steel fermenting tanks and the rows of oak barrels lining the cellar.

At present, some of those barrels were filled with wine still aging and developing. She'd be responsible for finishing and shaping it, judging which barrels from which lots needed blending, and determining when the wine was ready for bottling.

She needed to become acquainted with the barrels' contents and know them as well as she did the grapes growing in the vineyard.

That was one challenge. The other that loomed was overseeing the *vendange*—the fall harvest. Every stage involved in turning the selected grapes into a nuanced and delicious wine would depend upon her ability to mix craft, science, and artistry.

She'd studied enology, had been an excellent student, but very soon she would actually have to put her learning into practice. For all intents and purposes, she was a rank rookie and just a little terrified.

So many things could go wrong. And it would matter if they did. Paul, Roberto, Johnny, and Leo were salaried employees. To up the stakes, the winery now had an investor. As Thomas had pointed out, the Knowleses weren't in the business of throwing away money. They expected a return. A 40 percent share of the profits, to be precise.

Her stomach knotted.

But her worries weren't centered solely on money. Being able to fashion a wine that came close to what a Pinot Noir could taste and smell like—an extraordinary bouquet of fruits and flowers—was also about identity. Her identity. Mia didn't know her father's name. Her mother was a memory supplied by others' stories, her face little more than a blurry vision from faded snapshots. But if Mia could make wine, really good wine, then she had an identity, a solid link to her uncle Thomas that went beyond the sharing of a name and DNA strands. It would justify her having been taken in by him and Ellen. It would say to the world that, yes, she was a Bodell and deserved to live and work on this beautiful parcel of land.

Even though she couldn't help but feel hurt by the careless way Thomas had given himself over to his new love and life with Pascale, Mia still craved his approval, wanted him to boast to every vintner in France about how smart he'd been to leave the vineyard and winery to her stewardship.

And maybe this was totally out of left field and utterly irrational, but even more than a nod of approval from Thomas or a glowing write-up from the likes of Robert Parker, Mia wanted to knock Reid's boots off when he took his first sip of her wine.

But could she do it, could she make a wine that good? And if she failed? Who then would she be?

Squaring her shoulders, she pulled open the heavy doors and stepped inside.

The tractor rumbled beneath Reid, its massive wheels rolling down Silver Creek Road to its destination: the rut-gouged lane that led to the Bodells' winery. The tractor's crushing noise was the perfect soundtrack to his mood, a mood soured by his conviction that once again he'd blown it with Mia.

Who had a playbook for what to say or do after the kind of night they'd shared? With anyone else, he would have turned on the charm and parlayed it into some brand-new-day sex.

Not with Mia. For his efforts he'd received a beaut of a black eye. Good thing the forecast was for sunshine and lots of it. He could justify wearing his aviators well into the evening. Unintentional as it had been, Mia's elbow slam had set the tone for their first in-bed conversation. It hadn't helped his own mood that she was appalled at finding them still entangled—kind of funny when he considered just how wrapped up in each other they'd been only a few short hours before. Apparently the only dewy-eyed one in the bed had been him.

So he had fought the urge to flip Mia onto her back and find out what she looked like bathed in the soft dawn light, to discover how big and what color her nipples were and whether the skin between her thighs was as satiny smooth as he remembered.

His restraint hadn't ended there. He hadn't even attempted to caress the pale nape of her neck, exposed when he pushed back her thick curtain of hair to free his watch. He hadn't pressed his lips against the knobby bone of her spine bumping her sweetly scented skin. He'd wanted to do all those things and more, but he'd been right to deny his need.

Ward might think that being an engaged man meant he was ready for the afternoon talk shows on the Oxygen channel, but when it came to analyzing Mia and him, Reid's brother was way off the mark.

Reid wasn't dumb where Mia was concerned. He was wary. And with very good reason. It wasn't simply the awkward history between them that made him extra cautious. Mia was different from the women he dated. Take Lana Cruz. She knew the score and was as determined to retain her independence as he. She had plans, a future that didn't include him. And he was more than fine with that.

With Lana, things had been safe, contained. If he were to text her and suggest they get together, their evening wouldn't lead to her dreaming of mutual exclusivity and setting up house. He could rest easy.

He hadn't been bullshitting when he told Ward that the reason women liked him was because he kept his promises. He slept with women like Lana, who were fun; he danced and shot a few games of pool with women like Maebeth Krohner and Nancy Del Ray, making sure never to lead them to believe he wanted a "relationship"; he stayed the hell away from women like Mia.

Usually.

And though she'd left him dumbfounded with her cavalier claim that they didn't need to have one of those "Discussions," with a capital "D," and annoyed him, too, because who the hell wouldn't want a repeat of sex that was as stellar as what they'd shared, Reid knew he should be dropping to his knees and giving thanks for his reprieve.

He reached the end of the ranch's private road, downshifted, braked, and then pulled out onto a deserted Bartlett Road. The tractor's tires were quieter on the asphalt, but he noted the decrease in volume only absently.

He couldn't get Mia out of his thoughts—which was further proof that he needed to keep his distance. A woman like Mia represented serious, heavy-duty promises. Even sitting with her on the bed had been dangerous—his self-control had almost spun off into the stratosphere at the thought of her mouth opening under his and her body melting under his as he deepened the kiss. He'd wanted to devour her. Every frowning amazon inch of her.

The best thing he could do was to behave as always and avoid occupying the same space as she did. Since they were supposed to be working together, that would be a challenge, but he figured he'd perfected the art of dodging her.

But if he knew what he needed to do for his self-preservation, why in the hell was he making his way back to her place on a big green 150-horsepower chugging giant when he could simply have asked Howie Briggs to repair the blasted road by himself?

The easy answer came first. Over the last few days he'd realized that the task of boosting the winery's profits excited him. The winery and his family's guest ranch shared certain similarities. Both businesses straddled the hospitality and agriculture industries. From his work in the back offices at the guest ranch, Reid had learned a fair amount about building a solid and loyal customer base. It'd be interesting to see whether he could take that knowledge and apply it to the winery.

It wouldn't be easy, because there was one important difference between the guest ranch and Mia's winery. No one in Mendocino, Napa, or Sonoma had an enterprise that could compare to Silver Creek Ranch. In Mia's case, the competition was all around her. Literally.

These days it seemed as if every other property owner in this part of California was plunking grapevines into the soil with the intent to make fermented grape juice come the fall. Those were the mom-and-pop hobbyists. Then there were the huge, fancy wineries and vineyards—temples to the grape—where entire hillsides and sun-kissed tracts were covered in trellised vines and the wineries looked like châteaux on steroids. These were the super wine producers, whose labels could be found in liquor stores and restaurants around the world.

The Bodells' boutique winery fit in between those two extremes. But even here the playing field was crowded. It meant Reid would have to come up with a multipronged approach to raise the winery's profile. He'd have to be creative, and that could be kind of fun.

An easy way to increase the winery's profile and generate new devotees was to make it so people could actually *get* to the winery. Hence the tractor and Howie Briggs.

But Reid knew that the other reason he was perched on one of his father's beloved tractors—his dad, talented horseman and cattleman, was like a needy six-year-old when he browsed a John Deere catalog—had to do with Mia alone. And that made her even more dangerous.

He spied Howie up ahead, leaning against the door of his dusty dump truck. Good man, Reid thought. He'd driven the load over personally.

Reid waved and, easing up on the pedal, slowed down to a crawl as he pulled alongside him.

"Good to see you." Reid braked and leaned over to shake Howie's hand. "Thanks for coming out."

Like Reid, Howie wore shades and a cowboy hat. "I had an estimate on another job scheduled out this way. Figured I could kill two birds with one stone. How's it going, Reid?"

"No complaints."

"Glad to hear it. And the horses? Got any nice prospects for sale?"

"Yeah. You in the market?"

"Sure," Howie replied with an easy nod. "My son's joined the business, so I have more free time on my hands. Might as well enjoy it before I need a cherry picker to hoist me into the saddle."

"No argument there," he said. "We're vaccinating the calves this afternoon, but if you come by early evening— say five-thirty or six—I can show you a couple of them." Even though Roland was still green, the four-year-old might suit Howie.

"It's a date. So, where do you want this gravel? This one of your properties?" Howie asked, hitching his thumb in the direction of the Bodells' drive.

"No, it belongs to friends of ours. How about you dump the gravel as you go up—you'll understand real quick why I called you—I'll follow." After rolling over the first crater, Howie wouldn't be traveling any faster than Reid on the tractor. "I'll lower the rake attachment on the tractor once I turn into the drive," he said.

"Sounds like a plan. Let's get to work."

Mia was reading Thomas's notes on the wine presently aging in the oak barrels. It had been racked four months earlier. Racking involved transferring the wine from one barrel to an empty one so that it didn't rest too long on the lees, the sediment that collected at the bottom and could affect the wine's taste if contact was too prolonged. The procedure also allowed the wine to aerate briefly, encouraging its flavors to develop and deepen.

Thomas was meticulous when it came to planning the shaping of a wine. But when Mia looked at his desk calendar to her right and flipped to the next month to see if he'd marked a date for the next racking, the entire month was blank, as were the following ones.

The reason was clear. Thomas had purposely left the future of the next vintage in her hands. She knew she should be pleased at his tacit confidence in her ability to take over as winemaker, but those blank squares mirrored the emptiness she'd felt in the house. Less than twenty-four hours had passed, and she missed her uncle so.

She wished she could telephone him and ask his advice, perhaps engage in one of their many debates about wine. Even more, she longed to hear his voice and assure herself that he was happy with the decision to leave Acacia.

She wanted him to be happy. How could she not, when finding love was so rare? If Thomas had a second chance at happiness with Pascale, it would be marvelous. Amazing.

If only his newfound love hadn't taken him so far away, and if only walking into the cellar didn't cause a lump of sadness to lodge in her throat.

A noise reached her, a loud one. It penetrated the enclosed glass wall of the temperature-controlled cellar. For a second, she reacted like any Californian, wondering whether a quake had struck. But there were no distinctive tremors. A violent storm, perhaps? Always concerned about her acres of grapes, Mia was a National-Weather-Service junkie, so she knew the answer to that. The forecast had predicted nothing but clear skies.

The rumble came again.

She pushed back the webbed office chair, which she'd gotten for Thomas two Christmases ago when he'd complained of an aching back, and hurried outside.

The din and the dust were unbelievable, a scene straight from one of those monster-truck shows, with gnashing and crashing and brown-gray clouds filling the air. It made it impossible to see who was in the infernal machines, but she had an idea who must be driving one of them.

The Knowleses had a number of tractors, but only one member of the family would be so high-handed as to overhaul her road without even asking.

A heavy-duty steel-toothed rake was attached to the back of the tractor. When the anonymous truck driver disgorged a small mountain of gravel, Reid went into action. Maneuvering the tractor this way and that, he raked the gravel over the area in front of the winery, the carriage barn, and the smaller outbuilding used by the staff, filling in the craters and potholes.

She nearly jumped out of her skin when the truck driver leaned on his horn, a blare loud enough to wake the dead. Then he stuck his arm out the window to wave goodbye before heading down the drive.

Reid continued his work, crisscrossing the lot and spreading the crushed stones until the area was smoother than Mia had ever seen it. At last he stopped the tractor, turned off its engine, jumped down, and approached.

His walk had always screamed "male." Now she knew just what those hips, legs, and what lay between them could do for a woman. She crossed her arms about her middle.

"So, what do you think?" He looked as pleased as punch. "Great, huh?"

"Not," she uttered through clenched teeth. "Not great at all."

He looked at her as if she were insane. "And that would be because you like trashing your suspension every time you venture up or down your drive?"

"No, that would be because I like being asked before things are done to my property. You didn't."

"I assumed this would be a welcome change. And I seem to recall you wanting me to prove my chops. Well, Mia, this here is Marketing 101. Real basic stuff. A lot of wine buffs these days like to visit wineries. No one's going to come and taste your wine and buy a bottle, let alone a case, if the customer can't make it up the road without blowing a tire. And here's a tip from Marketing 201: You'll make more money selling wine directly to customers who visit your tasting room."

"We don't have a tasting room."

"Another thing to rectify."

"And what other unilateral decisions are you going to make?" she demanded, angry enough now to forget how weak-kneed he made her. Angry enough to over-come the sheer bizarreness of the situation. She'd slept with him! "Will I come back from a trip into town to collect my mail and find you building the damned tast-ing room?"

"I repaired the driveway, Mia, that's all. Don't make a federal case out of it."

Of course that was exactly what she was doing—blowing a desperately needed repair way out of propor-tion. It didn't help that he was right. She drew a breath. "I know your family's invested in the winery," she said. "But it still belongs to us. So I get a say in everything that happens. Understood?"

In a gesture of frustration, Reid swept off his Stetson, raked his fingers through his gold-streaked hair, and resettled his hat. "Fine. I apologize for fixing your dri—" He left the sentence unfinished. "What? What are you looking at?"

"Your eye." She swallowed a lump of horror at the sight of the purple bruise lurking behind the curved lens of his sunglasses. She hadn't noticed it until he'd re-moved his hat.

"My eye? Oh, yeah." He removed the aviators.

Her gasp was involuntary. "My God."

Bizarrely, her reaction seemed to alter his mood with lightning speed. His frustration vanished, replaced by a teasing grin. His blue eye—the one that wasn't swollen shut and surrounded by a ghastly blue-black bruise—twinkled.

"Does it hurt very much?" she asked.

"Like a bi—like the devil," he finished with contrary good cheer.

"I'm—I'm so sorry," she said. She couldn't get past the fact that she'd done that to him—after everything they'd done to each other.

He stepped closer. "Feel like kissing it and making it better?"

"I . . ." Distracted by his nearness, it took a minute for his words to penetrate. ". . . What?" They'd had sex and now Reid was flirting with her? Had she entered some alternate universe?

"You've got a vicious right elbow, Bodell. I figure I deserve at least a couple of kisses for the unimaginable pain I suffered." His grin widened.

The man could make her dizzier than a dozen cocktails. Incapable of speech, Mia stared at his handsome face, and she might as well have been fourteen and tongue-tied with love.

"Come on, Mia, I dare you." He lowered his head, angling it so his mouth would fit perfectly over hers. The world went still as she waited for the touch of his lips. Her eyes drifted shut.

"Hey, Mia, the road totally rocks!" Leo's cheerful call had her jumping halfway to Sacramento.

With a soft curse, Reid straightened and put his shades back on, hiding his black eye and shielding his expression.

Leo dismounted from his bike. Thomas's winery assistant was into living off the grid and traveled everywhere on his bike. Except when he bummed rides off others. "Hey, Reid," he said, nodding his bandanna-covered head in greeting. "You responsible for the sweet repair job?"

"Yeah. Glad you appreciate it."

"What's not to appreciate?" Leo replied good-naturedly. "Fixing the road has been high on Mia and Thomas's wish list for, like, months. Right, Mia?"

She felt the weight of Reid's gaze on her. "Yes," she admitted.

Reid could have won this last round in their ongoing battle of wills with a single sarcastic comment about how that was news to him. Instead, he said, "I'm hoping it will bring more wine lovers this way."

"Cool."

Reid turned to her. "I have to tend to some things at the ranch. I'll be by tomorrow. Maybe you'd like to write a list of things—a wish list—you think would help the winery. I'll do the same. We can see whether any of our ideas mesh."

She hated the polite formality that infused his tone. "Okay. And, Reid?" She paused to clear her throat. "Thanks for fixing the driveway."

Even with his hat obscuring his expression, she could tell he was surprised. She guessed he hadn't been expecting her to agree with his proposal and certainly not to thank him, however belatedly. Because what kind of relationship did they have but an adversarial one?

But their last almost-kiss had left her confused, off-kilter. It had been broad daylight, with no alcohol in either of their systems, and she'd wanted nothing more than to feel his mouth on hers. She still did. Was it possible that after all these years of pretending that she was invisible to him, he wanted her, too? Could she believe it, or believe in him?

She wasn't sure.

"Bye, Leo," Reid said.

"Take it easy."

She watched Reid climb back onto the tractor. It didn't seem to matter what he rode—motorcycle, horse, or mammoth machine. He looked amazing doing it.

The tractor rolled off. She listened to its rumble long after it disappeared from sight. Finally Mia drew her gaze away from the rut-free road and told herself it was time to stop wondering what would have happened if Leo hadn't interrupted Reid and her. She should simply be grateful he had.

A tall order.

MIA SPENT THE rest of the morning in the wine cellar with Leo and Johnny, who'd arrived shortly after Reid departed. Johnny, too, exclaimed over the "wicked smoothness" of the repaired drive. The two assistants were die-hard Thomas acolytes—Frodo and Samwise to Thomas's Gandalf—but surprisingly they didn't seem unhappy about her taking their beloved wine wizard's place. They'd been helpful, drawing samples from the different barrel lots and recording the pH and Brix levels.

After last night's vodka fest, she decided to hold off on any taste tests: Her taste buds, indeed her entire system, needed a chance to recover. She suspected, however, that even had she spent the previous night drinking only the purest artesian-well water, she'd have shied away from sampling the wine aging in the barrels.

She kept her suspicion to herself. It wouldn't exactly inspire Leo or Johnny if she were to admit she was too chicken to trust her own palate and nose.

Mia left Thomas's—no, she corrected—*her*—assistants scrubbing and sanitizing the equipment and drove into town. Today was the farmers' market, with vendors selling vegetables, fruits, cheeses, meats, and everything else grown and made under the Mendocino sun. She hoped that if she wandered past the stalls set up in the elementary school's parking lot, it might inspire her to cook dinner for herself.

She settled on a carton of farm-raised eggs, an avocado, some wildly misshapen heirloom tomatoes, and a cantaloupe melon that smelled divine. Scrambling eggs constituted cooking, right?

Thomas's name was on everyone's lips. Her own grew tired from the smile she pinned on them as she responded to their questions. Yes, he'd gotten off fine. No, first he was going on a vacation to Corsica and Greece with friends. Yes, that did sound absolutely lovely. Yes, she missed him already. Yes, she certainly had her work cut out for her. . . .

She climbed into her sunbaked truck with a sigh of relief.

With the farmers' market in full swing, the post office and luncheonette were quiet, making it impossible to escape the notice of Maebeth and Nancy.

Maebeth paused in the midst of wiping down the tables to greet her. "So you decided to cut loose last night. I hardly recognized you."

"Wasn't it you who told me I should get out and have fun? Just following your advice," she replied lightly.

"She's got you there, Mae," Nancy said.

"Well, you sure know how to switch gears, don'tcha? Next time come shoot pool with us. We'll team you up with Tracy."

Tracy Crofta was an even worse pool player than she, which was saying something. "Sounds like lots of fun."

"So Reid took you home?" Maebeth asked.

Ah, now they were getting to the meat of it. "Yes, he volunteered to be my designated driver," she said brightly. No way would she talk about what other services Reid had provided—she wanted to live to twenty-eight.

"That was good of him. Real neighborly." Nancy nodded her approval as she carried a grilled cheese sandwich to a man sitting at the table by the window. "Ralph gave the red-haired guy a ride."

"He had to be poured into the taxi," Maebeth told her with a disapproving sniff. "So what's this I hear about you and the Knowleses entering into a partnership?"

"Great, isn't it?" No matter what she thought privately or expressed to Reid, Mia wasn't going to reveal a single reservation in public. "We're still working out the details—"

"Who? You and Reid?"

She swallowed. "That's right."

Maebeth's expression dimmed just a little, and Mia felt a pang of sympathy, a sisterly bond. She understood what was behind the crestfallen expression, what it was to spin dreams around Reid, to hope he'd see her, recognize that she was the *one*.

Even though Reid and she had slept together, Mia knew there were lots of women just waiting to take her place. A night of incredible orgasmic sex didn't mean the same to Reid as it did to her. Actually, she was convinced the only reason they'd had sex was because they'd both temporarily lost their minds. And the almost-kiss this morning? She'd had time and space to analyze that one. It was just Reid testing her, seeing whether he could ruffle her feathers. It didn't mean he was truly interested in her. Or in love with her—no matter how much she dreamed and hoped.

She needed to remember that.

* * *

In the end, Mia found she couldn't summon the enthusiasm to scramble eggs, so instead she fixed a plate of sliced tomatoes and half of the avocado, and brought it, along with a large glass of water, onto the porch and sat down on the top step. After her quasi-dinner, she watched the wind stir the branches of the old oak that shaded the southern end of the house.

She was always glad to see Quinn, so when she spied her friend's red truck coming up the drive, the heaviness that had pressed upon her lifted.

The truck disappeared momentarily from sight, but seconds later Mia heard the metallic slamming of a door. Then Quinn appeared, carrying a plate with something on it—something that looked like a chocolate-frosted cake.

"Howdy, partner," Quinn said cheerfully. "Nice repair job on the road. Now I understand what Reid was doing with the tractor and rake. Of course, he wouldn't tell me anything about it. Never does."

"Is that what I think it is?" Mia eyed the cake, a huge mouthwatering creation. "Get thee behind me, Satan. You know I'm on a lifelong diet."

"Which, as I've told you a hundred times, is the stupidest thing in an already seriously messed-up world. You don't need to lose weight."

"So says the skinny girl from the genetically blessed family."

"Knock it off," Quinn said. And the great thing about Quinn was, she meant it. Quinn's total disinterest in her beauty was just one of the many reasons Mia liked her.

Wearing jeans and a fitted long-sleeve T-shirt with the words BE KIND TO ANIMALS OR I'LL KILL YOU emblazoned on the front, Quinn dropped down onto the step beside her. No sooner had she settled than, as if by magic, Vincent appeared, brushing back and forth against her shins like a love-drunk tomcat.

"It's amazing how he remembers you," Mia said.

Trading cake for cat, Quinn placed the plate between her and Mia and scooped Vincent up onto her lap; he began a full-throated purr. "He's a smart cat," Quinn said. Abruptly, she wriggled and grimaced. "Oops. I forgot." With a flourish, she produced two forks from her back pocket.

Shaking her head in amusement, Mia accepted one. "So what's the occasion?" she asked. The scent of chocolate was already teasing her.

Quinn removed her straw cowboy hat and dropped it by her booted feet. "The cake? It's your prize for being the first woman to blacken my brother's eye. But here's the thing. Unless you offer a blow-by-blow account, I'm going to eat every last crumb in front of you."

"Ah, well, not much to tell." Or, rather, that Mia could tell.

Quinn's fork was poised over the chocolate cake. "In case you need further incentive, Roo baked this."

Roo Rodgers, the multipierced, tattooed Australian pastry chef at Silver Creek, was a true artist. It'd be stupid to pass up one of her creations.

"You are so evil. But, really, there's not much to share. I, um, had a few too many last night."

"I noticed. Not your usual style, Mia. I kept waiting for you to tear yourself away from the bar, but you were too busy making a new friend."

"Sorry about that. I was a little out of sorts. I broke up with Andrew. And I missed dinner. I guess I ended up drinking it," she said.

"Missing dinner sucks. Breaking up with Andrew, well, I don't know why you bothered to date him in the first place."

"Quinn, that's what you say about men in general."

She grinned. "Yeah, pretty much. Who has the time

for them and all their expectations? So what did Andrew say when you told him you were finished?"

"Well, apparently Andrew hadn't even realized we were dating." She smiled when Quinn snorted in disgust. "So my calling it quits had significantly less impact than I would've liked—I doubt it put him off his video game." And she recounted how he'd been playing Mass Effect 3 while she sat waiting for him at Aubergine.

"See?" Quinn said, poking the air with her fork. "I told you guys are a waste of time. Still, what a moron. Good riddance."

"Yeah, good riddance."

Mia must have looked as depressed as she felt. Quinn waved a hand in the direction of the frosted cake. "Okay, first bite allowed."

"Don't we need a knife to cut it first?"

"Don't tell me you're going to get civilized on me? What's the point of living here on your own if you can't wage an all-out attack on a cake?"

"Quinn, think of Roo."

She sighed. "Fine. We'll be boring adults and slice it."

"I'll get a knife while you and Vincent catch up." The cat was now lying on his back, legs extended in bliss as Quinn stroked his belly.

Picking up her used plate and half-empty glass, Mia went into the house, stowed the plate in the dishwasher, and rooted around in the drawer until she found a cake knife. She grabbed two dessert plates, a glass of water for Quinn and a refill of her own, and rejoined her friend.

"Here you go."

"Thanks." Quinn plucked the water and the knife off the plates. She waited until Mia was seated, then sliced two enormous pieces.

"So, back to last night and my brother, who is many

things but not, thank God, an idiot like Andrew Schroeder," she said, and passed Mia her plate. "How'd you manage to give him a black eye?"

"Well, basically, I slammed him with my elbow. The details are kind of fuzzy." And that wasn't really a lie. No way was she going to divulge precisely *where* they'd been when her elbow connected with Reid's eye. Omitting the fact that they were naked and that they'd spent the night having the best sex of Mia's life seemed wise, too. "I didn't intend to hurt him, exasperating as he is." She took a bite of the cake and moaned. "Lord, this is amazing."

"Yeah. Roo does have a way with all things chocolate," Quinn said, shoving a forkful into her mouth. "So why is it that Reid rubs you the wrong way?"

Three years younger than Mia, Quinn wouldn't have heard the stories flying through high school after Jay's public reading of her diary.

Mia couldn't bring herself to tell the tale or admit how long it had taken—years—to get over her puppy love for Quinn's brother. Now, because of her colossal foolishness the night before, she was terrified she might fall right back in love with him.

"It's like this," she offered instead. "Your brother—suppose he was a woman."

Quinn blinked. "Okay, it's a bit of stretch, but I'll give it a try for novelty's sake. So Reid's a Rita. Go on."

"Well, Rita is the type of woman who can eat all the chocolate desserts she wants, every day if she feels like it. And she never gets fat, never breaks out, never feels sick to her stomach, even after the brownie pan's been scraped clean of every gooey crumb. She's impervious."

"Ooh. I hate Rita." Quinn forked up a huge piece of cake. She chewed busily. About to plunge her fork in again, she paused. "Quick question, Mia. What in hell does this have to do with Reid?"

"My point is, Reid's like Rita with her chocolate desserts. Only he's that way with women. He can have as many doe-eyed Barbie dolls as he wants, with no repercussions. No heartbreaks."

"Huh." Quinn twirled her fork meditatively. "Do you really think so?"

"Think about it. Have you ever seen him down in the dumps or acting in any way brokenhearted after he and a woman part ways?"

Quinn was silent as she stroked Vincent's belly. "No, I suppose not," she said at last. "Wow, if that's really how you see Reid, I totally get your hostility."

Mia had eaten only a couple of bites of cake, but, thanks to the discussion, they felt as heavy as bricks in her stomach. She put her fork down and pushed her plate away. "Quinn?"

"Yeah?"

"Be honest, okay?"

"Nothing but."

"Am I sounding like a total witch? Bitter and shriveled?" she asked.

"You? God, no. You may be a bit tangy—tart, even—but not vinegary bitter. I get where you're coming from, Mia. Reid can be annoying. You should have seen him and Sirrus this afternoon, working the cattle. He put Domino and me to shame—and let me tell you, my gelding and I are *good*. Right now he's showing a couple of our horses to Howie Briggs, who must have provided all the gravel for your now super-smooth driveway. He'll probably sell Roland or Jagger to Howie, and because Reid's trained them, he'll get top dollar. And tonight, after we have dinner at Mom and Dad's, he'll probably go hang out at The Drop and, in spite of the fact that he's sporting a seriously ugly shiner, he'll charm half a dozen ladies." She broke off to slice another piece of cake for herself. "Yeah, it's pretty galling to watch him in action sometimes."

Mia remained silent. What was there to say? She only wished being right about Reid felt better.

Quinn lapsed into silence for a moment, too. But then suddenly she shifted, leaning forward with a kind of urgency as she spoke. "But here's the thing about Reid. All that stuff I just said about him? It's an accurate description and thus supremely aggravating. He's got a lot of talent, and for all his mellow attitude, he's pretty driven, which means he's successful at most everything he does. But when it comes to women, I think your take on him is wrong."

"Really? How so?" she asked.

"Well, first of all, he doesn't pursue them. He doesn't have to, because they swarm him. Or, to use your cake analogy, I'd say they treat him as if *he's* the cake."

"True enough." Mia tried not to sound miserable. Or guilty. Because when she looked at Reid, didn't she do exactly the same? Fantasize about the touch of his lips, the taste of his kiss? Oh God, she thought with sudden despair, as it occurred to her that she now knew for a fact that he was more delicious than any chocolate on earth.

"There's another thing you may not see about Reid, but I do, being his sister."

There was no way Mia was going to admit to Quinn how close a study she'd made of Reid all these years, so she opted for "What's that?"

"You made it sound like Reid's immune to love. I don't agree. I think the truth has more to do with him not having found the right woman yet. Or maybe he has and that right woman won't give him a chance."

Quinn couldn't be referring to her, could she? The idea was laughable—if only it weren't so depressing. Reid had made no sign he cared a fig about her. "Quinn,

I know how much you adore Reid, but I just don't see him pining for any—"

"Hey, who could that be?" Quinn interrupted.

Mia turned to look where Quinn was pointing. A silver sedan was speeding up the road. The sight of it made the cake in her stomach turn to acid sludge. "It's my cousin Jay."

MIA COULD NO longer remember a time when Jay's presence hadn't caused her mouth to go paper dry even as her skin turned clammy with cold sweat. He hadn't pinched her, tripped her, or viciously pranked her in years, but the fear lingered, a toxin in her system.

He'd changed, at least outwardly. Gone was the faux-homeboy look he'd sported at the end of high school. He now favored sharkskin suits and shiny shirts—today's was gangster black—unbuttoned past his sternum to show off his deeply tanned, bulked-up chest. While the tanning-bed, steroid-pumped look wasn't uncommon in California, Acacia was far enough removed from L.A. and Venice Beach for Jay to stand out like a sore thumb.

But, somehow, her older cousin always succeeded in making her feel as though she were the freak. Actually, he made her feel worse than a mere freak or an outcast. He made her feel dirty and scared.

She did her best to push away the fear and the choking sense of inadequacy and shame he always instilled in her. She rose to her feet, ridiculously grateful when Quinn, in a silent show of support, did the same.

Vincent, no fool, slunk across the porch and leapt

onto the railing, keeping a safe distance from the toe of Jay's polished shoe.

There was no point in exchanging civilities. "What are you doing here, Jay?"

"Last I heard, this was my childhood home, the site of many fond memories. Are you telling me I'm not going to be welcomed with open arms?" he asked mildly.

He'd always enjoyed sick jokes. His pretending to be pleasant was his latest one.

"Thomas left yesterday," she said.

"I didn't come to see dear old Dad. I had some business in the area. And of course I wanted to check up on you."

The idea made Mia's skin crawl.

His gaze slid from her to Quinn. When it lingered, Mia felt her go rigid. "You're Quinn Knowles, right?" he asked.

"That's right." Quinn's tone could have frosted glass.

Jay smiled as if he hadn't noticed her hostility. "How are your brothers?"

"Fine."

"Glad to hear it. I wish that we'd stayed in touch after I left Acacia," he said, perhaps thinking that because Quinn was younger she wouldn't have known her brothers' high school friends and that he wasn't among them. "Tell Reid and Ward how happy I am that we're partners now."

"Thomas is the one who's partners with the Knowleses," Mia said. "Not you."

He shrugged off her remark. "I'm his son. His only child. Don't think to exclude me so easily, Mia. Or deprive me of profits that should be mine."

What a joke. The principal reason the winery wasn't showing a profit was standing six feet away. But she was relieved to have the Jay of old, always concerned about his due, reappear. "Thomas has settled everything between him and the Knowleses. You got your cut. Any questions you have should be directed to Don Polk—"

"Who I'm meeting tomorrow. I was thinking that afterward you and I could have dinner and talk."

She was stunned speechless. Jay couldn't stand her. Having dinner would be almost as unpleasant for him as for her.

"Mia's busy tomorrow. She's having dinner with us."

Grateful for her friend's lie, Mia said nothing to contradict Quinn.

Amazingly, Jay's smile didn't falter. Mia knew well how much he disliked being thwarted. "Ain't that neighborly? Well, I'm not leaving the area for a while yet. We can get together another time. We're family, after all."

She felt like she was in *The Twilight Zone*. He was going to stick around in the place he'd always considered the sticks? "Where are you staying?" she asked.

"Here, of course." Then he laughed heartily. "Just joking. I wouldn't want to cramp your style, Mia." His upper lip lifted in a familiar smirk. "I'm crashing at a friend's in Mendocino. But I am serious about talking to you so we're straight on a couple of things."

"Why don't you tell me now, Jay? That way I won't waste your time." And I won't have to see you again, she added silently.

"How could meeting someone like Quinn be classified as a waste of time? By the way, I like animals." He let his gaze rest on the front of Quinn's shirt and its warning to be kind to animals. "Pussies especially," he added.

Could he be any more obvious? Any more odious? Determined to draw his attention away from Quinn, Mia said, "Fine. Let's meet the day after tomorrow."

He shifted his gaze back to her, and his smile was knowing. "I'll come by and pick you up."

"No." She shook her head. She didn't like having him

here. But the prospect of sitting across a restaurant table from Jay made her mind go momentarily blank. She wouldn't last past the appetizer. Knowing she had to say something, she blurted, "Let's meet at The Drop."

"Whatever you say, cuz."

The triumphant expression on his thick features belied his easy tone. Jay had gotten what he came for. Mia would find out all too soon what else he wanted and how far he was prepared to go to obtain it.

The cold beer sliding down Reid's throat was almost as satisfying as the sale he'd just negotiated with Howie Briggs. It wasn't only the hefty chunk of change that would be coming Reid's way once Howie's vet examined Roland and gave him a clean bill of health that made him happy. It was also knowing that Roland would be with an owner who would treat him right and enjoy bringing him along. It was nice, too, that the gelding would be staying in the area, where Reid could keep tabs on him.

He chugged down another few gulps before lowering the bottle. "The steaks look good, Dad. They smell even better."

"They do, don't they? Tell your mom that she and Tess have three minutes left to gush over the wedding dresses Tess is considering."

"I'll do it," Ward volunteered, setting his own beer onto the long patio table that was already set for dinner. "If Reid goes, they'll need to show him every design Tess has bookmarked, to get his expert opinion. However, if Tess catches me anywhere close to peeking distance, she'll close her iPad faster than Usain Bolt runs."

"Good point. I've got to tell you, Ward, January cannot come soon enough."

"I'm right there with you, Dad."

"Somehow I'm guessing Ward's reasons may not center solely on Mom and Tess's current obsession with all things bridal," Reid said.

Daniel put down the tongs. "Oh, you mean your brother might be thinking about the two-week honeymoon he's planned?"

"Reid's got me there," Ward confessed with a happy grin. "Back in a few."

Alone with his father, Reid took another pull of beer, then almost spewed it across the patio when Daniel said, apropos of nothing, "I trust things are going better between you and Mia than that black eye would indicate."

He swiped his mouth with the back of his hand. "Things are fine." Considering.

"Good. Your mother and I don't want to see Mia hurt."

Wait. Wasn't he the one with the black eye?

"I had my doubts about this arrangement, but your mom and Thomas convinced me the two of you would work well together. Were they wrong?"

"We're meeting tomorrow to discuss what the winery needs by way of improvements. I'm starting to get some ideas about how to heighten the vineyard's visibility and increase sales."

"Good to hear" was his father's response, but Reid guessed more was coming. He waited while his father picked up the grilling fork and turned off the grill. "Thomas's numbers were pretty soft. Grab that platter, would you?"

Reid picked up the large porcelain platter and held it at the ready. "I don't think the business side of the winery interested Thomas very much."

"I agree with you. I'm hoping Mia has a better business head on her shoulders. It would be nice if this venture didn't become a giant financial sinkhole for us."

"I'll do my best to turn things around."

"Good." He lowered the first of the steaks onto the platter. "And, Reid?"

"Yeah?"

"Try to avoid getting a second black eye in the process."

Ward returned to the patio, armed with two more beers and accompanied by Adele and Tess, who carried serving bowls filled with summer salads. Besides the steak there was also a platter of grilled vegetables.

Reid nabbed a slice of zucchini and popped it in his mouth. After the day he'd had, his stomach felt as empty as a cave.

He wasn't surprised to find his father equally impatient to take his knife and carving fork to the steak.

"Anyone know where Quinn is? That girl should remember when we have dinner," he grumbled.

"I heard her say she was going to see Mia," Adele replied. "Maybe they were catching up and lost track of time. Let's sit down and begin. Quinn won't mind, as long as we save her a plateful of veggies and salad." Quinn didn't eat meat. And, because they loved her, they didn't tease her about it.

"And three-quarters of the dessert," Ward said, holding out a chair for Tess and then sitting in the one beside her.

Reid was wondering what topics Mia and Quinn might cover as they "were catching up" when his mother said with a bright smile, "Come and sit by me, Reid. I want to hear how things are going."

He did as requested and sat, his muscles tensing,

while he waited for the inevitable question about his eye.

None came. No comment at all. Which was hilarious since it looked garishly psychedelic—the purplish-black bruise now had an additional smear of yellow-green.

What was doubly hilarious was that his mother was known for her eagle eye. During room checks in the cabins or inspections of the public rooms in the main lodge, she was invariably the first to spot a smudge, rip, stain, or crack. Therefore, he knew her cheerful loading of his plate with potato-cucumber-and-dill salad and tomato-and-basil salad didn't mean she'd gone blind.

It meant she was playing a deep game.

Helping Tess and Ward with their wedding preparations must have juiced her matchmaking instincts. So much for being in the clear, he thought.

His mother was doomed to disappointment in his case. He didn't want to get married, and Mia didn't even want to have sex with him again, though he was more than willing to try his hand—along with his mouth, lips, teeth, and any other body part—at convincing her to rethink her stated position.

He decided to let his mother understand loud and clear that the relationship between Mia and him was strictly professional. "I repaired the Bodells' drive this morning. Tomorrow we're going to discuss other improvements. Hey, Tess." He looked across the table. "What do you think about getting those artists over to the vineyard? It'd be a really pretty spot to paint." Tess and an amateur artist named Madlon Glenn had organized an artists' weekend at the guest ranch. It was the next big event on Silver Creek's calendar.

"That might go over well," Tess said with a nod. "I'll see what I can do."

"Thanks." He made a note to himself to make sure

Tess approached Mia with the idea. He didn't want Mia to accuse him of riding roughshod over her.

"Is there a tasting room?" Tess asked. "I could tweet about tasting events for you guys."

He smiled. "I have a feeling a tasting room will be at the top of Mia's wish list."

"I'm glad to hear you and Mia are already getting down to work," his mother said, as she piled potato salad onto Ward's plate. "That reminds me, Daniel. I think we should advertise for another ranch hand, since Reid will be devoting time to the winery and Ward will have to take time off for the wedding and then his honeymoon."

"Didn't Quinn say she'd step up her hours in the saddle?" Reid asked. "She's as good as any wrangler you'll find."

His mother nodded. "Yes, but she'll be in New York for the wedding, too, and you know it's pointless to have her around the ranch when the cattle are driven to market."

"She's a basket case," Ward said. He took his plate from Adele.

"Yes, that's why having someone in place is the best option. Can you ask Pete Williams to spread the word that we're looking for an experienced wrangler, Daniel? Once we have some names, I'll pass them along to Grant," she said.

Grant Hayes was the head of security at the guest ranch. For obvious reasons, no one got a job at Silver Creek Ranch without a thorough background check, to ensure that the guests, who ranged from ordinary folk to über-rich to movie-star celebrities, enjoyed privacy and safety.

"It just so happens I already talked to Pete today," Daniel replied.

"You did?" Adele said.

"I did. I have my own reasons for wanting to hire another ranch hand, seeing as how I'm planning on whisking you away for a vacation of our own after Ward and Tess return from their honey—"

"You've already reached the honeymoon stage of discussing the wedding of the century?" Quinn asked by way of announcing her arrival. "Sorry I'm late for dinner," she continued, circling the table and kissing her mother's and father's cheeks before dropping into the empty chair beside Reid. "I was at Mia's and had to stay later than planned when Jay showed up. I don't need food so much as a delousing after fifteen minutes in his company."

"Jay Bodell showed up?" Reid asked sharply.

Quinn nodded, unfolded her napkin on her lap, and passed her plate to him so their mother could load it with salads. "Yeah. In a shiny car, a shiny suit, and shiny shoes. All that shine gave me the creeps, let me tell you."

"And Mia? Is she—"

"Mia's okay, Reid. You can sit down," Quinn said.

He hadn't even realized he'd pushed his chair back or that he'd risen to his feet.

Luckily, everyone's attention was focused on his sister. He dropped back into his chair and said, "Jay is bad news."

"No kidding. He made my flesh crawl."

This time Reid forced himself to remain seated. "What did he do?" he asked.

"Other than eyeball me like a lecherous creep and act all aggressive toward Mia?"

"Aggressive? How?" If he'd touched one hair on her head . . .

"You know, puffed up and territorial, talking about

his home, *his* father, *his* percentage, blah, blah, blah. But then, when Mia stood up for herself—and, man, was I proud of her for not taking any of his BS—he changed tactics, going all smiley and pleasant. Way too smiley," she muttered.

"I can't ever remember Jay being a pleasant young man," Adele said.

Quinn nodded. "It seemed as fake as his tan. He even suggested he and Mia get together tomorrow night to discuss the particulars of our partnership with the Bodells. I told him she was having dinner over here."

"Good thinking, Quinn," Daniel said.

"I try, Dad, I really do," she replied with a teasing grin. "Tess, I thought you might join us so we could leave Ward and Reid to FaceTime with Brian about the bachelor party." Brian Nash was Ward's best friend and would be in the wedding party, along with his wife, Carrie. It was Carrie and Brian's wedding at Silver Creek that had brought Ward and Tess together.

Tess smiled in pleasure. "I'd like that. I think Mia's interesting. She impressed Anna, too. It's not easy being a woman vintner."

"I'm glad you like her. She needs friends who understand what she's all about," Quinn said, helping herself to the grilled eggplant and zucchini and digging into her mountain of salad and vegetables.

There were times when his kid sister really showed what she was made of, and this was one of them, Reid thought, elbowing her affectionately in the ribs. Typical Quinn, she elbowed him right back and twice as hard.

Finished with her mouthful of food, she spoke again. "Oh, and guess what I've decided Mia needs. A dog. A big one. He can be a cream puff at heart, but at least he'll be there, standing by her side with lots of muscle and teeth." She shifted in her chair and flashed him a wicked smile. "Kind of like you, Reid, only with a brain."

The family didn't even bother to stifle their mirth.

He gave an exaggerated sigh. "You do realize they're just laughing to make you feel better about the calf that ran you and Domino ragged." Quinn had actually done a great job, but the calf had been wily as hell.

Quinn scowled and then waved off the taunt with a breezy "whatever."

"So back to Jay," said Ward, who liked to have all the facts. "Did he stick around long?"

"Long enough for me to realize a big dog would have been excellent company right then. Mia and I only had Vincent—you remember the cat I gave her and Thomas, don't you, Dad—and a cake knife to fend him off. I was *not* happy."

"I'm not sure I'm happy about Mia being all alone at the vineyard, either," Daniel said.

"Until Quinn locates a suitable dog for Mia, we could ask Grant to go over and . . ." his mother began.

Okay, he'd had enough. Grant Hayes did not need to start patrolling Mia's house, as his mother well knew. Mia didn't know Grant, and it would spook the hell out of her to have a stranger knock on her door.

And what would Mia do if Reid showed up? Give him another black eye? At least then he'd have a matching pair. "I'll make sure everything's secure at Mia's. But why don't we have Grant check into what Jay's been doing down in L.A? I, for one, would like to know."

"Go ahead, son," his father said.

His mother merely smiled serenely.

Reid tried to tell himself that wasn't a really bad sign.

Rather than risk Mia's sneaking up behind him and braining him with a cast-iron skillet as he circled the house to check that her windows and doors were locked, Reid decided to knock on the front door.

He wanted to know she was okay, a perfectly normal need considering that less than twenty-four hours ago she'd been in his arms and he'd been deep inside her. It didn't represent anything more than basic kindness and neighborly concern.

He lifted a brass knocker molded in the shape of a cluster of grapes and let it fall. It took two more raps for her to answer—and half that time for him to realize that the worry nibbling at him was at odds with his usual attitude.

One glance told him his concern was justified. Her hazel eyes were enormous in her drawn face. The lashes framing them were dark and clumped from recently shed tears. Her nose, that snooty organ so often angled skyward in his company, was red from too many encounters with a tissue.

She was dressed in a white T and a pair of gray cotton drawstring bottoms decorated with navy-blue polka dots. Her sleepwear was a far cry from sexy, but that didn't matter to Reid's libido or his imagination. After all, her arms and feet were bare and, judging from the voluptuous swell resting against her crossed arms, she was braless.

Oh, yeah, those details were more than enough for him to picture the two of them on her bed, his fingers tugging on the drawstring's looped bow, loosening the waist to allow his hand to slip past and skim over soft, quivering flesh to the curls and moist heat waiting for him. His other hand would be just as busy traveling north to explore the twin mounds and their exquisitely sensitive peaks. . . .

"Do you want something?"

She had to ask? "I heard Jay came by today."

"Yes, it was . . . unexpected, though now that I've

had time to think about it, I'm not surprised he decided to pay a visit."

"Money?"

"Of course. With Jay it's always a question of money. He'd have enjoyed the chance to rattle me, too."

"Are you all right?"

"I'm fine." She hugged her middle even more tightly. "I was looking at our family album."

"Album" in the singular rather than plural, and Reid bet the images inside it didn't give rise to smiles and fond anecdotes, as his family's pictures did. He had a sudden vision of Mia sitting in the large, empty house and scrubbing away tears as she flipped through the pages of photos. Quinn had said how proud she was of the way Mia had stood up to Jay. He thought her solitary battle with the sadness that had marked so much of her life was equally impressive.

"Any word from Thomas?" Maybe her uncle had thought to ring her.

"No. He and Pascale were making their way directly to Corsica. He told me the cellphone connection would be spotty." She shrugged as if it didn't matter.

Her shoulders had been soft and surprisingly strong, he remembered. Like the rest of her. The hours working in the vineyard were to thank for those toned muscles. How much emotional pain had she endured so that she could handle her present sadness?

"I'm sorry," he said.

"Don't worry about it. It's fine."

No, damn it, it wasn't. He liked Thomas, but that didn't mean his friend wasn't being appallingly selfish right now. "Do you ever wonder about your father?"

For a second, there was silence. Under the weak bulb of the porch light, he could see the shadow that dimmed her eyes.

Feeling like an ass for having voiced the question, he opened his mouth to apologize again. She spoke first.

"Yeah, I used to wonder. I don't anymore. It doesn't help. And there's no point, since there's no way to find him. My mother was nomadic—a romanticized way of saying transient. She had no credit cards or bank account; her only ID was an expired California driver's license. When she drowned, she left behind three hundred dollars, her ID and my birth certificate, a shoe box with some photos in it, and me."

Now he felt like an even greater ass, because again he wanted—needed—to ask if she was okay when it was obvious she wasn't. There were lots of broken and jagged things in Mia's life. She dealt with them as best she could, but imagining they could be magically fixed or airbrushed away was just wishful thinking on his part.

"You haven't told me why you're here," she said.

"I wanted to make sure you locked your doors and the windows on the first floor. You'll do that, right?"

She nodded, her arms still wrapped about her middle. He read her body language. It screamed defensiveness. He hadn't missed the other not-so-subtle cue: She hadn't invited him inside. Talk about action speaking louder than words.

He knew better than to kiss her and attempt to stoke the fiery passion between them. But he could do something else.

He knew how to move quickly—quickly and smoothly. He closed the distance between them, cupped his hand beneath her chin, and molded his lips to hers before she could do more than blink. He kept the pressure light and allowed himself only a mere sampling of Mia, beguiling and unique, before he reluctantly released her.

Even that gentle kiss, meant to soothe and heal, had his libido lighting up like Times Square on New Year's

Eve. Too aroused to feel triumph at her stunned expression, he said huskily, "I'll see you tomorrow."

Taking the porch steps two at a time, he jogged into the enveloping darkness, away from the woman who was beginning to matter too much and in too many ways.

THE *SNIP, SNIP, snip* of her pruning shears was methodical, practiced. The thoughts inside Mia's head were not. There was, however, a pattern to the seeming chaos: The thoughts all eventually wended their way back to Reid.

They'd slept together. They'd fought. He'd fixed her driveway. They'd fought. They'd almost kissed. He'd taken the time to come and check on how she was doing. And then he'd kissed her, a sweet, enchanting kiss that had pierced her heart. A heart that was already far too vulnerable where he was concerned . . .

It was no wonder she was exhausted. Her emotions had been on an endless roller-coaster ride, careening from highs to lows and everywhere in between. But hadn't Reid always made her feel more than anyone else? The only difference now was that he'd given her a tantalizing taste of what it could be like if he ever really cared for her.

The sun had grown hot. Slipping the shears into the back of her jeans' pocket, she tugged off her baseball cap, mopped her brow, and picked up the jug of water she'd brought with her, taking several gulps. Though the ice inside had melted long ago, it still refreshed.

"Hello, Mia," Reid said from behind her.

She spun around. Couldn't there ever be a moment—just one—when this man saw her in a remotely attractive state? She didn't only have hat hair, she had *sweaty* hat hair. A voice reminded her that Reid hadn't seemed exactly repulsed by her when they'd had sex. Perhaps because she'd insisted they keep the lights off.

She jammed the cap back on her head. "Uh, hi. You're here." Great. Now she sounded like a dope. She pulled out her pruning shears and resumed pruning the lateral shoots, staring fixedly at the vine as if she'd never seen one before. She dropped the cuttings into the wheelbarrow with exaggerated care, all the while feeling his gaze on her.

And to think that two weeks ago he'd treated her as if she were the Invisible Woman—kind of like Sue Storm from the Fantastic Four—only not so fantastic.

"I thought maybe you'd be having lunch by now."

"I sent Paul and Roberto up, but I wanted to finish this row before I took a break." Lost in her thoughts of him, she'd lost track of time, too.

"Right. I'll give you a hand. Have you got another pair of pruners?"

She turned to stare at him, then quickly jerked her gaze back to the leafy canopy. "There's an extra pair in the canvas bag. Thomas always misplaces his."

Reid leaned over to rummage in the bag hanging from one of the wheelbarrow's handles. She tracked the play of his muscles beneath his gray T-shirt, and her mouth went dry all over again. "Do you know how to trim lateral shoots and pull leaves?" she asked.

He squeezed the shears in his hand, unlocking the safety catch. "Nope. But I'm betting you can teach me. I guess this will be a working meeting. Once I've got the hang of this trimming-and-pulling thing, we can move on to discussing what the winery needs. I have to be back by two o'clock to meet the vet who's checking a horse we're selling."

"Is that the horse Quinn told me about? The one you trained?"

"Yeah."

"And you're selling it to the man who supplied the gravel for the road?"

"Yeah. Howie likes our horses."

It was funny how he kept saying "we" and "our," even though Quinn had made it clear it was Reid who'd trained the horse and negotiated the sale. Mia had always viewed Reid as arrogant and cocky. But here he was, muting his horn rather than trumpeting it. It made him even more attractive to her.

This was getting dangerous.

What could she do, tell him she couldn't have a meeting about the winery because spending time with him only increased his irresistibility? How pathetic would that make her? And it would be beyond ridiculous to adopt her usual hostile attitude when here he was offering a hand with the pruning. She had to meet him halfway at the very least and match his cooperative tone. The trick would be to work with him and not let the pleasure she derived go to her head. Or her heart.

It took less than a minute for her to realize just how difficult it would be.

"Okay," she said. "So you see these leaves, how some of them are shading the grapes?" She pushed the leaves back to reveal the tight clusters hanging behind the green curtain. "We want to pull the leaves—not all but a number of them—so that more morning light and air reach the fruit. Watch what I do." Demonstrating, she snapped off the leaves that covered the grapes. "The *véraison*—when the grapes start to change color—is starting. You see that slight darkening there?" She touched the berries lightly with her fingers. "We want the sun to sweeten and ripen the fruit. Pulling leaves also allows the air to circulate around the bunches and prevents rot or mildew."

"But you'll let these other leaves remain?" He reached out to finger a leaf hanging near her wrist. His breath caressed her ear.

"Um . . ." She tried to remember what they were talking about. "Yes," she said, nodding and surreptitiously stepping to the side. "We want a dappled canopy, to give the grapes some light shade as the day progresses. Otherwise they run the risk of getting sunburned and too hot." And Reid was like her personal sun. She fought the need to fan herself.

"Okay. So am I doing this right?" He found an adjacent cluster of grapes also shaded by leaves, and Mia watched him break off leaf stems. He had beautiful hands. Dexterous and callused, they'd caressed her skin, her nipples, the sensitive flesh of her inner thighs, her straining clitoris. Those fingers had been inside her, sliding in and out.

"Is that how you want it, Mia?"

"Yes." Lord, she sounded as breathless as she'd been when those hands were working their magic on her. She admitted defeat. Another minute standing next to Reid, feeling his heat and watching the play of his muscles, and she would be whimpering with need. "But, you know, on second thought, it's getting kind of hot." And she prayed he'd think that was the reason for the quivery note in her voice. "Maybe we should have our meeting in the winery. I'll come back and finish the row after lunch."

He cocked his head. She could feel his eyes assessing her behind the dark-green lenses of his sunglasses.

"You sure?" he asked.

A flush stole over her cheeks. "Absolutely."

Lord, she only hoped she was.

* * *

It wasn't long before Reid concluded that Mia had hit upon the perfect torment. Standing next to her in the leafy aisle, he'd been assailed by colors, scents, and textures: the bright green of the densely planted grapes, the smell of the hot earth under the summer sun, the spring of the soft carpet of clover that lay between the trellised rows, the ribbed veins of the leaves, the smooth casing of the still unripened grapes, rich and vibrant. Yet compared to the woman standing next to him, they faded to a dull, blurry beige.

It was Mia, warm, glowing, and unconsciously sensuous, who dazzled, making him dizzy with need. He'd watched her fingers brush the leaves, skim over the clustered fruit, and he felt his body go hard. He'd caught her scent—a mix of warm woman, soap, and flowers—and seen how the sweat dampened her hair, causing the tendrils to curl even more wildly and cling to her neck, and he'd wanted to take her into his arms, lower her onto the ground, and make love to her under the brilliant noonday sun.

He was sure that she'd been as intensely aware of him. The blush coloring her cheeks, the trembling of her parted lips, and the hitch in her breathing were impossible to overlook.

But had she obligingly fallen into his waiting arms?

Nope.

She'd instead been Mia-like. Abruptly calling an end to any further pulling of the leaves, she'd marched with the grim determination of a soldier back up the path to the cool darkness of the winery, which, after being outdoors, felt like stepping into a freezer. But with the way his blood was pumping in his groin and his body was aching to touch hers, he could have made sex in a freezer work. Really, anyplace with a vertical or horizontal surface—a closet, a cave, the flatbed of her truck—would have worked.

Admittedly, it was hard to make love to a woman who was determined to keep her distance. What was he supposed to do? Lasso her again? Not his style. He had sex with women who *wanted* him.

He'd never bothered to pursue a woman who wasn't as eager as he. But never once in his life had he imagined he'd find a woman sending him the "stay back, way back" signals after he'd given her three orgasms.

Mia had always been different. Other women didn't drive him to distraction while seated at the opposite end of a work desk. Yet here he was thinking about circling around, lifting her sweet butt onto the scarred wood, sweeping the papers off, and lowering her down as his hands popped the metal button of her jeans. He wanted to taste her again.

Damn it, he could practically hear the physical awareness humming between them, the pluck of a tightly stretched string.

He didn't know whether to be annoyed or grateful that she was fighting her attraction with everything she had—yet another example of how thoroughly she was messing with his head.

There was a white legal pad and a pen in the middle of the desk. When he stretched across the pine slab to retrieve them, she stilled. He guessed she was holding her breath, waiting to see if his arm inched any closer.

He considered staying exactly where he was so he could watch her face turn bright red from the effort.

Tempting as it was, he shoved the childish impulse away. Grabbing the legal pad, he uncapped the pen. "Let's start with the physical improvements. What do you want in a tasting room?"

Her tongue swept over her lip. God, he wanted *his*

tongue there, running over the soft contour. How would she taste right now?

"At one point I designed one for Thomas."

"Go ahead, shoot."

"Well, there should be a bar. People like to chat up the pourer. It doesn't have to be too big, enough to accommodate six to eight people—"

"That sounds about right." He jotted it down. "Stools?"

"Not necessary. I don't want the space to get too cluttered."

He hid a smile. She really had thought about this.

"Where did you want to have the bar set up?" he asked.

"I thought we could use the area to the right of the front room. When the visitors stand there, they can see into the barrel room." She gestured at the thick thermal-glass panes enclosing the temperature-controlled barrel room.

He looked at the area and then drew a rough sketch on the paper. "Any tables at all?" he asked.

"I thought maybe four would be enough." As they'd talked, her voice had grown in confidence. "Again, it doesn't have to be fancy. We could stand some used oak barrels on end."

He considered the space, then marked down where four tables might fit. The idea was good. There'd be enough room to line the walls with wine racks and still maintain the airy, open feeling of the front room. What pleased Reid even more was how enthusiastic Mia had become in describing the tasting room. She'd even used "we" when discussing her plans. Did that mean she was accepting the idea of them as partners?

A test was in order, he decided. "And we could extend the space by creating a terrace on the other side of the French doors."

No frown, no instant smackdown at his presumption. Instead, she considered his idea, studied it with the care he'd given hers. "Yes, that would work. That would allow people to enjoy the wine when it's nice outside. The vineyard's easy to see from that vantage point."

"We can price wood versus wrought-iron furniture and decide which is the better buy," he said.

Again, she seemed more than happy to accept his suggestion. "There's only one problem. The ground outside the winery isn't very even. I'd worry about people tripping."

"That's an easy fix. I'll bring the tractor back and rake and level the ground, and then we can lay down some stone tiles. I know where we can get some ceramic or stone tiles at a good price—"

"From your gravel guy?" she asked.

He smiled. "No, someone else. We found a company outside Mendocino that did the pool area and all the walkways at the guest ranch. They're reasonable and do good work."

"If their work is good enough for Silver Creek Ranch, I think it'll probably be good enough for the Bodell Family Vineyard," she said wryly, adding, "The area doesn't need to be big."

"No, it doesn't. We can start out small and expand as the number of visitors grows. And since the weather's fine, the outdoor space can serve until the indoor tasting room's ready. The visitors will be able to enjoy the product and experience the beauty of this place—"

"You think the vineyard's beautiful?" She sounded genuinely surprised.

"Of course. Why wouldn't I?"

She shrugged. "Well, in comparison to your ranch, we're a little ramshackle, a little—"

"—different," he finished for her. "But no less beautiful, no less special."

Their eyes met, and a slow flush crept over her cheeks.

Ah, he thought happily. Progress. Definite progress.

THE SUN WAS sinking toward the horizon when Mia arrived at Silver Creek, her canvas bag clinking with the wine she'd selected for dinner with Quinn. It was the least she could do after being invited to dinner. It was precautionary, too, since Quinn couldn't identify a Chardonnay from a Riesling. Life was too short to drink the kind of wine that found its way into her kitchen. To be fair, though, Mia couldn't tell Quinn's goats apart, despite having been introduced to Henny, Alberta, Gertrude, and Maybelle a number of times.

Quinn had told her to come by the smallest of the enclosures, where she was feeding the shaggy tribe their dinner. There was lots of excited bleating and butting and stomping of cloven hooves as the goats went at the hay and pellets she placed in the suspended feeders.

Even with the din and commotion, Quinn noticed Mia hanging over the metal railing.

"Hi," she called. "Perfect timing. I'm just about finished with these rascals."

"No hurry." Mia slipped the canvas bag off her shoulder. "I brought you some wine."

"Good. My first thought was for us to go up to the restaurant for dinner and let you enjoy Jeff and Roo's magic, but the ranch is booked solid and, frankly, I'm all guested out—Jim and I led the afternoon trail ride, and I had a real motormouth in my group." She shook her head at the memory. "Luckily, I had a stroke of brilliance and asked Tess to cook. She's whipping something up and bringing it over to my place, so that my brothers can plan guy stuff with their buddy Brian for Ward and Tess's wedding."

"That's great. I like your sister-in-law-to-be."

"Yeah, I do, too. I also appreciate the fact that she's a way better cook than I am." Quinn scratched the pale-gray head of one of the goats. They were all the same creamy gray.

"Is that Maybelle?" Mia asked hopefully.

"Nope. She's over there, defoliating the blackberry bush." Quinn pointed to a very busy goat. "This is Gertrude. She likes an after-dinner scratch." Finished obliging Gertrude, Quinn opened the gate and joined Mia. She gave a sharp whistle through her teeth, and her black-and-tan sheltie, Sooner, appeared at her side.

"Home," Quinn said, and the dog took off at a brisk trot, leading the way past the PRIVATE ONLY sign and up the dirt road that led to the Knowleses' own quarters.

The cottage Quinn had moved into after college was a dollhouse version of her parents' place. Constructed of honey-brown timber and stone, it had two bedrooms, a living room with an open kitchen, and a small study. In the back was a fenced-in yard for dogs lucky enough to find their way into Quinn's care until she could place them in permanent homes. Inside was just as animal friendly. Cat trees stood in corners, and canvas drop cloths protected the sofa and chairs from muddy paws and sharp claws. The last time Mia visited, there'd been a rabbit living in the study.

Today, when Quinn led her into the mudroom and toed off her cowboy boots, setting them neatly beside five other pairs as well as some olive-green Wellies, Mia heard a screeching squawk and then "Out of my way, Pirate!"

"A new resident?" she inquired. "A boyfriend, perhaps?"

Quinn laughed. "That's a good one. No, that's Alfie, a blue-fronted Amazon parrot. My cat Pirate and he have a relationship. Go on and introduce yourself. I have to feed this lot." She gestured to the heavy-duty bins that were lined up against the other wall. Mia knew they were brimming with dog, cat, and other critter food. "Just keep your fingers away from Alfie's cage. He can be temperamental."

"Thanks for the warning." With the harvest approaching, she definitely needed all ten fingers.

Mia wandered into the study. A brilliant blue-and-green bird was in a six-foot cage, swinging from perch to perch and doing flips as he traveled through the air, all in an apparent attempt to impress Pirate, Quinn's one-eyed cat. Pirate was a cool customer. He sat on the corner of Quinn's desk, watching the bird's gymnastic feats, then raised a paw, licked it, and began to bathe himself.

Having lost his audience, Alfie shifted his attention to her. He jumped to the side of the cage. Wrapping his talons about it, he ran his curved beak over the wire. Mia wondered whether that helped sharpen it, the better to chomp silly people's fingers.

"He's something else, isn't he?" Tess said, entering the study and coming to stand next to her. "I'd only ever seen parrots in the zoo before I met Alfie."

"Oh, hi! I didn't hear you come in."

Tess grinned. "It'd be hard to hear a marching band when Alfie's putting on a show. Can you believe this house is even louder when it's at full occupancy? But the rabbit's healed and been released, and the opossum, too, thank goodness. Between you and me, I didn't really care for the opossum."

"That opossum was adorable, City Girl." Quinn entered the room, holding a measuring cup filled with raw vegetables—carrots and something paler—and a fistful of peanuts.

"You need to get out more, Quinn," Tess said, and crossed her arms. "Its tail looked way too much like a rat's. Actually, to be perfectly honest, I didn't like its face, either. It was freaky."

Quinn shook her head in despair, but any further discussion of the merits of opossums was prevented by Alfie. Turning his head to fix a beady eye on Quinn, he flapped his wings and shrieked even louder. Joy rendered him inarticulate.

Mia cupped her hands about her mouth and shouted to Tess, "I brought some of our Pinot for dinner."

With a grin, Tess gave her a thumbs-up and then signaled that the two of them should quit the study for the blessed quiet of the kitchen.

The dinner Tess provided was consumed with generous praise from Mia and Quinn. Very little was left of the tomato-and-onion frittata or the roasted zucchini, goat cheese, and pine nut salad. The first bottle of Pinot Mia brought was empty, and the three women were cheerfully working on the second while they savored the last bites of a peach crostata that Tess swore she'd made in less than a half hour. They'd taken the meal outside so that Sooner could gnaw a bone on the grass and Pirate could survey the world with his one eye.

Tess raised her glass and took a sip. "I'm loving your wine more and more, Mia."

"Thanks. It paired nicely with the food, didn't it?"

"It sure did. Reid mentioned he reserved a hundred cases of your latest vintage."

"He made Thomas's morning." Mia remembered her uncle's smile.

Tess pushed away her empty plate. "You know, I'm on Twitter a fair amount, for the ranch. I was thinking that maybe I could blast out some tweets about the winery and provide you with some promo."

"Wow. That would be wonderful. Reid said it was important to increase the winery's social-media presence. Thomas and I aren't all that into the Internet."

"That's okay, Mia." Quinn reached across the table and patted her arm. "Neither are any of us Knowleses. It's just one reason why we're so grateful to Tess. She doesn't mind whipping out her phone, snapping pics and videos, and sending messages across the cyber universe. She's freakin' excellent at it. She did most of the promo for the cowgirls' weekend. A ridiculous number of people are following her tweets and posts."

"Are you buttering me up, Quinn?" Tess asked.

Quinn held her hands up in a gesture of innocence. "I'm just giving praise where praise is due. I also appreciate the fact that you've put a smile on Ward's face. I like to see my brothers happy—even Reid."

For a second, both Quinn's and Tess's gazes fixed on Mia. Just before Mia's face went up in flames, Quinn reached forward and snagged the bottle to pour more wine into their glasses.

"But it's time you demonstrated your cowgirl chops, Tess," she continued. "How about we go riding tomorrow and you try a lope on for size?"

Tess rolled her eyes. "I knew you were saying all those nice things for a reason. I adore Brocco's trot, thank you very much. There is no need for me to try a lope on for size."

Quinn grinned. "We'll see. Mia, you should come riding, too."

"You know how to ride?" Tess asked her.

"Hardly. I'm not sure I can even manage a trot without bouncing out of the saddle."

"I knew I liked you for more than your wine." Tess raised her glass and took an appreciative sip. "I'm surrounded by champion riders, and none of them understand that I'm grateful to make it back to the barn in one piece. So you can come riding with me anytime—as long as you don't get it into your head that we have to start loping or barrel racing or acting in any way like cowgirls."

"You have my word," Mia said.

Tess smiled. "Good. Now, back to business. A website for the winery will help a lot—and I know from the meetings we've had that Reid knows what a site like yours will need, and he can find you a designer—but being able to send out a tweet about a special event is where Twitter really comes in handy. For instance, we have an event coming up later this month. I'll be tweeting lots about it."

"Are you talking about your artists' weekend?" Quinn asked.

"Yeah." To Mia, Tess explained, "Last February, we had a guest who wanted to sketch the newborn lambs. Her artwork was beautiful. Now Madlon Glenn—the guest—and I have become friendly. We cooked up this idea to hold an artists' retreat weekend devoted to capturing the different landscapes around Acacia."

Mia didn't hesitate. "Would you like them to come and sketch or paint our place?"

"Oh, that's a brilliant idea! Don't you agree, Quinn?"

"Brilliant and convenient. It'll mean we won't have to shuttle the guests too far. Bravo, you," Quinn said to Mia, raising her glass of wine and toasting her.

Tess was clearly taken with the idea. "I'd already thought of having sessions at Silver Lake and the forest preserve, as well as setting up the artists near the cattle and sheep pastures. Sheep and cattle are super picturesque, but the problem is, they *move*. And your goats, Quinn—forget about 'em."

Quinn smiled. "Mia's grapevines would be much better behaved, I'll grant you that."

"And the trellised rows of a vineyard are so pretty. Madlon and the instructors conducting the workshops will love the idea, I'm sure of it." Tess's dark eyes shone.

Mia felt her own excitement grow. The dinner had been fun, a sisterly camaraderie she didn't experience often. But even more, she was pleased to be able to suggest something that might benefit the guest ranch in return for all that Reid and his family—Tess included—were doing for the winery. "In the past, we commissioned an artist to paint a rendering of the vineyard for our wine labels, but she moved away. Maybe we could do something similar for your guests?"

"Oh my God, yes!" Tess exclaimed. "We could hold a contest. If you liked the artwork enough, you could ask the winner if she or he would be willing to have the picture made into a label for your next vintage—but only if you liked the image, Mia. No pressure."

"I think holding a contest could be really fun. The only hitch is that I don't know how much I'd be able to pay the winner," she said.

Tess waved off her concern. "I'm pretty sure that the thrill of having one's artwork chosen would be enough for most of these participants. You could offer a case of the wine, too. What do you think, Quinn?"

"I think you two are going to make Dad and Mom sleep easy."

"And Reid—do you think he'll be pleased?" The question was out of Mia's mouth before she could stop herself. Used to keeping all her thoughts of Reid locked away where no one could smile knowingly, it shocked her how easily the lock had sprung.

"Definitely. Cross-promotion is what great partnerships are all about," Quinn said. When Pirate jumped on her thighs, she caressed his black-and-white fur and he settled into a sphinxlike pose.

"It's just that Reid's doing a lot of hands-on stuff." As Mia's cheeks warmed at the memory of how very busy Reid's hands had been the other night, she hurried on. "He graded the driveway yesterday, and then this afternoon we went over my ideas for the winery. He said he can get some stone slabs for the visitors' patio at a good price. I feel like he's calling in favors left and right." Somehow she'd thought his involvement would be more removed, along the lines of developing a business plan.

Unfazed, Quinn shrugged. "That's the name of the game."

"Absolutely." Tess nodded in agreement. "I think this partnership is great for Reid. It's shaking things up for him and taking him out of his normal routine—out of his comfort zone."

"I wouldn't have thought Reid had a *discomfort* zone." Not once had Mia ever seen him struggle.

"Sure he does," Quinn said.

"Figuring out what gets your wine into as many glasses as possible will be a challenge, no doubt about it," Tess said. "But a good one," she added.

Quinn nodded in agreement. "It's all good, Mia. You'll see."

*   *   *

While she helped Quinn and Tess gather up the dishes and set the kitchen to rights—not a difficult job, since Tess had cooked everything at Ward's—Mia replayed the dinner conversation in her mind. She hoped Tess and Quinn's assurances were proved right.

She knew that she was being overanxious. Reid and his family would definitely be getting something out of the partnership—a chance to make a sizable profit. Somehow, though, she wanted the deal between their families to represent more than a dollar sign to Reid.

And wasn't that woefully naïve of her? a sharp voice questioned, as she said good night to Quinn and Tess and made her way to her truck.

The internal dialogue or, more precisely, lecture continued as she rolled down the darkened private road. She needed to be careful to avoid indulging in wild fantasies where Reid was concerned. Otherwise she'd run the risk of losing her sense of perspective all over again.

It was essential she remember the facts of the situation. They were involved in a business venture, not a romantic one. So while it was true that they'd succumbed to an impulsive round of sex, lots of people did that. Yes, the night spent in Reid's arms had been great for her—better even than her dreams. But there was a simple reason for that. The Mia Bodells of the world didn't often find the Reid Knowleses in their beds.

The mistake would be to believe their night together signified anything.

But what about the kiss he'd given her last night? It had been sweet and tender.

The rational voice inside her head was relentless. Why shouldn't he kiss her? He was a man who liked women and sex a lot. He was a sensualist.

Then he'd used the word "beautiful" today. . . .

Ah, now they'd come to the root of the problem. He'd been talking about the winery, *not* her, the sharp voice reminded.

But for Mia, hearing Reid utter that single word transported her into the rosy realm of the precious dreams she'd spun around him so long ago. Her girlish script had filled the pages of her diary with fantasies of his kisses and melting caresses. But more powerful than imagining the press of his lips against hers had been the story line she weaved, one where Reid assumed the role of the handsome prince encountering the plain and terribly lonely orphan girl. Descending from his noble steed, he swept her into his arms and whispered that she was beautiful.

Well, she simply had to remember that "beautiful" was a trigger word and to not begin spinning silly dreams again. Dreams that might be forgiven a lonely adolescent would be beyond foolish now.

It took awhile for Reid to realize his neck muscles had gone as rigid as steel rods and that his fingers were sore from drumming them impatiently on his thighs. He wasn't usually slow to notice things. The evening had started with the classic camaraderie Ward, Brian, and he had enjoyed ever since their high school days. That's when Brian and Ward's friendship was born, forged by blood and steel when a knife was thrust into Ward's ribs as he stepped in to save Brian from a gang of toughs.

Brian still treated Ward with a touch of hero worship, which Reid knew bugged Ward to no end, but now Bri had an additional reason to be in Ward's debt. This past June, Ward and Tess had pulled off an admittedly amazing wedding ceremony for Brian and his then girl-friend, Carrie.

Brian and Carrie were living in Boston. Thanks to the

genius of FaceTime, Brian's ugly mug grinned back at them from the laptop computer propped on Ward's wood-and-iron coffee table, and the exchange of BS and genial ribbing flowed as easily as ever. But there was something new to the mix: It was the rich dollop of happiness in their voices. It was as thick as whipped cream when they jawed about Ward and Tess's January wedding in New York.

Reid dropped his head against the back of the leather sofa and stared at the exposed timber beams of the living room's ceiling, impatiently waiting for them to move on.

They didn't. That's when he realized they were really *enjoying* talking about the guest count, about the church in Astoria, Queens, Tess's old neighborhood, and about the priest who would be performing the ceremony, a good guy who'd been a pillar of support to Tess's mother over the years.

The conversation improved when they discussed the restaurant where the wedding dinner would be held (Anna Vecchio's new trattoria in Brooklyn, of course), because Anna was a damned fine cook. But the topic they should have been focusing on—namely, which bars and clubs to hit on the night of Ward's bachelor party—was very much secondary. Ward didn't seem to care, either.

When the talk veered once again into Tess and Carrie Land, the answer finally flashed before Reid's eyes. *Love* was responsible for his brother's and their friend's happiness.

He told himself it wasn't envy that was making him so churlish. Considering how great a life he had, he'd have to be a real loser not to kick the green-eyed monster to the curb as soon as he felt it working on him. Why would he begrudge either Brian or Ward their bone-deep satisfaction? What worked for them didn't necessarily translate into a recipe for bliss for him.

Only yesterday he'd congratulated himself on his talent at avoiding relationships and emotional entanglements; they were too much heavy baggage for a man who preferred to travel light and fast. So what if Ward and Brian had found something special? His new preoccupation with seeing how often he could get Mia to smile was just about getting her into bed. It didn't mean he had to go down the road those guys had chosen.

He was safe.

To prove it, he decided he'd go over to Quinn's. Their dinner must be finished. He'd make sure Mia got home all right. Maybe they'd have sex, maybe they wouldn't. No biggie.

Okay, that was a lie, he admitted. Sex with Mia was definitely a biggie, and he wanted it again and again, until the explosive heat he felt when he touched her had cooled to a stale fizz.

Tuning back in to the conversation, he realized that Ward and Brian had moved on. The topic was the honeymoon itinerary. Hallefuckinlujah. Honeymoons and sex on the beach were way better than vows of eternal love. He cleared his throat.

"So, Bri," he said. "I'll be in touch with the final list of bars. The limo's set. And we're good to go on the other." The "other" being courtside seats to a Knicks–Lakers game. Reid made to rise from the sofa.

"You heading over to Quinn's? To take Mia home?" Ward asked.

Reid froze. How had Ward guessed? Reid didn't consider himself predictable. With a careless shrug, he said, "Yeah. The Jay situation still isn't resolved."

"It's time I hit the hay, anyway," Brian said. "Carrie wants to go running early tomorrow. Take care of yourselves. And, Reid, glad you have some months before the wedding. That shiner's scary-looking, dude." After telling Ward to give Tess a hug, Brian signed off.

Reid had just risen to his feet when Tess walked into the room. "Hi. Have you finished looking at videos of dancing girls jumping out of cakes?"

Ward stood and wrapped his arms about Tess, kissing her as if he hadn't seen her in days. "Not yet. Want to watch?"

"I've got something way better in mind."

Ward grinned.

Right, Reid thought, rolling his eyes. " 'Night, you two."

"Say hi to Mia," Ward offered distractedly.

"Oh, Mia's gone home," Tess said.

"What?"

"Don't worry," Tess said to him. "Quinn and Sooner went with her. Quinn convinced Mia that Sooner needed the exercise so she wouldn't think we're babysitting her. Oh, and Quinn told me she's found a couple of dogs that might suit Mia." She paused and looked up at Ward. "I really like Mia. What would you say to inviting her to the wedding?"

Ward took Tess's hand and, lifting it, grazed her knuckles with his lips. "I'd say you're wonderful and that you should invite anyone you want to our wedding."

"Even that mean old teacher you had in fifth grade?"

"Mrs. Radner? She was about a hundred years old back then, so I think I'm safe from the nightmare of her sour face staring at me from the pew. I'd much rather have Mia. Way prettier."

"She is. I'd kill for hair like that. But you know what I especially like about her? She seems to be the anti-Quinn. She's going to come riding with me, and neither of us is even going to *consider* loping."

Such was his brother's besottedness that he merely

grinned and murmured something that made Tess laugh and lean into him. Ward's hands slipped around her waist, pulling her even closer. They'd clearly forgotten his presence. With a shake of his head, Reid walked outside and then up the drive to his empty house.

Chapter
NINETEEN

MIA FOUGHT THE queasiness that assailed her at the prospect of meeting Jay. She'd be at The Drop, she reminded herself. Beau and Nell were friends. They and their staff would keep Jay in line. And what could Jay do, anyway? The contract between Thomas and the Knowleses had nothing to do with her. She was the manager of the vineyard and the winemaker, but when all was said and done, she was just an employee.

If he'd met with Don Polk, he knew this and recognized he wasn't going to be able to change the contract. She'd half-expected to hear his voice on the answering machine, saying he was heading back to L.A. or wherever he was living now. The absence of such a message confused her. What could he possibly want to discuss?

It was eight o'clock—still early at The Drop for many around Acacia who, like Mia, worked out of doors. A quick scan of the place told her that Jay hadn't arrived yet. No surprise there. He preferred others to wait for—and on—him.

Both Nell and Beau were working tonight. Nell, in the midst of wiping down a table, straightened.

"How are you, Mia? Holding up okay?" Nell, who'd grown up in Oregon before moving to Louisiana, didn't have Beau's thick-as-molasses drawl. She did, however, share her husband's eagle-eyed watchfulness. In her case, it made it easier to avoid hands unwise enough to attempt a grope and to alert Beau if any customers seated at the tables needed to be cut off and given a bracing cup of coffee and a ride home.

"Yeah, I'm okay. Though I may not be quite so cheerful in a few minutes. I'm meeting my cousin Jay here."

"Jay Bodell? Thomas's son? Don't think I've ever seen him."

"You wouldn't have. He'd already left Acacia by the time you and Beau opened the bar. But he seemed to know The Drop, so he must have passed it on one of his rare visits to Thomas."

"Well, it'll be interesting to meet another member of the family," Nell said. She gave the table she was cleaning one last swipe. "You're looking good, Mia. I like that skirt."

"Thanks." She'd decided to dress defensively in one of her nicer outfits—a white linen A-line skirt and a slate-blue knit top that she'd worn to her UC Davis graduation. She'd slipped the skirt on and had been pleasantly surprised to find it still fit. Maybe she could face Jay down and win this time.

It was an admittedly shallow thought, because of course she didn't equate her self-worth with her waist size, but there was no arguing that her self-confidence had spiked when she looked in the mirror.

Then the door to the bar opened. Jay walked in and Mia's stomach knotted unpleasantly. So much for self-confidence.

Nell must have been looking at her and caught her reaction. "I don't need to ask who that is," she said, and then glanced over to the entrance. "Funny, he doesn't look like Thomas."

"No, he doesn't."

Jay spotted Mia then, and the smirk she knew so well twisted his mouth.

"I guess you two will need a table," Nell said.

"Yes," Mia replied, with all the enthusiasm of someone about to sit across a very small table from a close relative who'd never made it a secret he despised her. "We'll take that one over there," she said, pointing to one close to the scraped plaster wall.

"Sure thing. I'll be by to take your orders in a few."

Mia had expected the meeting with Jay to be short and extremely unpleasant, something along the lines of him snarling and cursing and then storming out of the bar. Why it wasn't—not that any encounter with her cousin could ever truly be described as pleasant—remained a mystery. She'd read the contract that Thomas and Daniel and Adele Knowles had negotiated. While she wasn't a lawyer, it looked straightforward and, more important, airtight to her. The Knowleses had invested too large a sum for them to tolerate anything else. Moreover, Thomas's instructions for dividing the money they'd received were equally clear.

Thomas's accountant and lawyer, Don Polk, was a straitlaced guy. He'd always shaken his head when he came over to the winery and Thomas shamefacedly explained that Jay required yet another cash infusion. Mia could well imagine the man's quiet satisfaction at informing Jay that his favorite pipeline was closed out.

She was aware her thoughts were mean. Petty, even. But experience had left marks, and the ones involving Jay had been laced with acid, not only deep but corrosive.

It made her leery of his outward calm when he'd greeted her and followed her to the table she'd chosen. If she hadn't known him better, she'd have thought he might actually be looking forward to a pleasant chit-chat and that he wasn't seething with resentment at having his plans for a quick refill thwarted.

He didn't even give Nell his usual slime-bag leer when she appeared to take their orders.

"Nell, this is Thomas's son, Jay. Jay, this is Nell Duchamp. She and her husband, Beau, own The Drop," she said, in case he hadn't noticed that Nell had a huge "I'm taken" ring on her left hand and that Beau was watching them openly from behind the bar. Beau was not a man you wanted to come after you.

"Nice place you've got here, Nell." Jay leaned back in his chair as he let his gaze sweep over the interior. "I have some business interests in a few joints in L.A. If you're ever interested in selling, I could talk to my partners."

"That's mighty kind of you, but Beau and I are real happy here." Nell's easy tone didn't fool Mia. She was as possessive of her bar as Mia was of the vineyard. "What can I get you two?"

"A double whiskey and soda," Jay said immediately, without waiting for her.

"I'll have a glass of our Pinot, please."

"Coming right up."

Jay was content to wait to speak until Nell returned with their drinks. Perhaps he guessed that simply sitting opposite him would exact a toll on Mia's nerves.

He wrapped a meaty hand around his drink, his rings clinking against the glass. "Cheers, Mia." He took a long sip and then relaxed against the back of his chair, as if he wanted nothing more than to spend the next several hours enjoying her company.

There was no way she could continue with this fake-as-Cheez-Whiz situation. "I assume Don Polk answered all your questions satisfactorily," she said.

" 'Satisfactorily'?" He bared his capped teeth in a

smile. "Not by a long shot. I'm disappointed that Thomas didn't bother to consult me about whether the amount of money he allotted to me would be sufficient."

"And how much would have been appropriate?"

He shrugged and reached again for his drink. "I have a lot of deals in the works right now. One in particular requires a significant outlay of cash."

That was pretty much Jay's standard line. What he never mentioned was why none of his deals ever seemed to pan out, let alone make him money. Or maybe they did, and he turned around and blew every last cent.

"Still," he continued, as he put the glass down with a soft *thunk*, "it's useful to know exactly what the terms of the partnership are between the Knowleses and Thomas. They must have high hopes for the wine to have invested so much money."

"Our Pinot has always been delicious. As the vines mature, it's getting better and better."

"Ever the cheerleader. So how are the grapes looking this year?"

"The conditions have been good so far. The *véraison* has begun."

"And the wine aging in the barrels?" he asked.

Jay might be drinking whiskey and soda and living in L.A., but he'd grown up on the vineyard. He knew his way around a winery. Mia doubted his questions were moved by sentiment.

"Thomas was pleased with last year's harvest."

"So the Knowleses are onto something, huh? I bet they're thinking that if they can raise the vineyard's profile, it'll bring in easy dough." He smiled. Jay was smiling way too much for her comfort. "Listen, speaking of money, I need more than Thomas has deigned to give me. I'd speak to him myself, but I can't reach him on his cell and I don't even know if he understands how to work a computer."

She decided not to clue him in on Thomas and Pascale's romantic midnight Skype sessions. "He's due to return to Pascale's place soon," she replied. "You'll be able to reach him then."

"I have to let my associates know the money's a sure thing." There was an edge to his voice. "They might get impatient otherwise."

"What about the sum you just received?" she asked, keeping her voice even.

"I had expenses to cover." He leaned forward across the table, invading her space. "I live in L.A., not Hicksville."

"You mean it's gone?"

He shrugged. "Yeah, pretty much."

She tried not to show her shock. "How about getting a short-term bank loan? You'd be able to pay it off at the next fiscal quarter."

A muscle twitched in his cheek. "This isn't some pissant deal I've got in the works. I don't have time to draw up a business plan for a bank and then sit around waiting with my thumb up my ass while some dickhead loan manager decides to approve it. I've got to have the money soon or renege on the deal. My associates are not people you want to disappoint."

It was useless to ask why he'd entered into a business deal if he didn't have enough money. Jay's opinion of his canny intelligence when it came to his various ventures was unshakable. "Well, I don't know what else to suggest. I'm sorry."

His sigh was loud. "Yeah, me, too. It's a sweetheart of a deal. It could change things around for me, know what I mean?"

Right. She made a noise that Jay for some reason interpreted as sympathetic.

He took another sip of his drink. "Damn, I wish Dad had done the smart thing."

"The smart thing?" she echoed.

"Yeah." He nodded. "That he'd sold the vineyard."

Ice licked her insides. "Why would he sell it? He built it, planted each rootstock with Roberto and Paul, and designed the layout of the winery. He loves the vineyard."

"But now he's moved on. He won't be coming back here, not when he's got his Bergerac babe and a new terroir to love." He waited a beat, letting his words sink in. "But even though selling our place would bring in a serious chunk of change, he obviously doesn't feel it's an option. 'Cause if he sold, then he'd have to tell you to go live and work elsewhere, wouldn't he? And you'd be like a little lost lamb, wouldn't you?" Relentless, he fixed his gaze on her.

"I—" Swallowing, she tried again. "I don't think Thomas wants—"

He cut her off as if she hadn't uttered a syllable. "Lots of things would have been different if Dad and Mom hadn't taken you in. I'd probably be running the winery now. I'd be the one standing to rake in the profits from the partnership with the Knowleses."

She recognized the guilt trip he was laying on her. He was a master at manipulation. Even after all these years, she had few defenses against his stratagems. But in this case perhaps the reason she was so vulnerable was that he spoke the truth.

As if sensing her doubts, Jay leaned closer. It took all her willpower not to shrink back against the chair.

"So what about you helping me?" he asked.

"Me?"

"Yeah. It would make this whole situation a little more equitable, don't you think? You must have funds stashed away. It's not like there's anything to spend money on around here."

Dazed by his audacity, she stared.

"Come on, I know you. You must have a savings account."

She also had school loans to pay off. "Yes," she admitted. "But it's—"

"How much?" Jay demanded.

She opened her mouth, but another voice answered, in a slow drawl that did nothing to hide the steel force behind it. "Whatever it is, it's surely not enough to meet your needs. So I guess that means you're out of luck, right, Jay?"

Mia whipped her head around. With her attention fixed on Jay, watching him as one would a jackal, she'd lost track of the goings on in the bar. Reid must have spotted them and, as he approached, overheard the last snatches of her and Jay's conversation.

Relief washed over her. Belatedly, she realized how hard her heart had been pounding, and not in a good way but in a scary, slasher-movie way, during her exchange with Jay.

Reid came to a stop, standing by her chair. Drawing a shaky breath, she managed a quick smile as she dragged her hair back from her face. Though she'd twisted it into a knot at the nape of her neck, several coils had escaped.

Reid's eyes searched her face, as if unconvinced by her smile. The blue of his gaze was as intense as any laser. She had opened her mouth to utter something to reassure him, when Jay spoke.

"Hey, Reid! Long time no see, dude," he said, with a joviality that grated like fingernails down a chalkboard. "Mia and I were just catching up."

"So I heard."

Jay nodded energetically. "Fantastic news about our partnership, huh? Whoa, what happened to you?" He pointed to Reid's eye. "Some irate husband catch you and the wife fooling around?" He waggled his brows lewdly.

Reid ignored the comment. "I heard you saw Don Polk, so I know you're clear on the agreement between my family and Thomas. My official title in this partnership is administrative director of the winery. As such, I watch out for all the winery's interests—that includes the staff's. My advice to Mia would be to tell you to take a hike. There's no reason why she should give you even a penny of the money she's worked for."

The laid-back cowboy Mia had known for years was gone. In his place was a cold-as-ice businessman dealing with a crooked employee.

Jay's smile died. "If Mia wants to help me out of a little cash-flow problem I'm having, that's up to her, not you or anyone in your family."

The belligerent look on his face made her wonder whether he was going to lunge across the table at Reid. But he surprised her by abruptly throwing back his head and shouting with laughter.

"Aww, I get it now." Still chuckling, he wagged his finger between the two of them. "I got to admit, Reid, I wouldn't have thought she'd be the one you'd choose to do the nasty with, man. Wow, Mia, looks like *all* your dreams are coming true." He shook his head as if in admiration at her boundless good fortune. "I only wish mine could, too. This business deal could really change my life, kind of like it has yours. You know what I mean, cuz?"

With that, he shoved back his chair, the legs scraping loudly against the bar floor. "So, good luck with the harvest, guys. Hope it's bitchin'."

Unable to think what else to say, Mia managed a mumbled "Thanks."

"And if you decide to share some of the good fortune

you're enjoying with your closest relative, I'd appreciate it." To Reid, he gave a jerk of his head. "Later, man."

It was only after Jay had left that Mia realized he'd stiffed her for his whiskey. "A drop in the bucket," she muttered.

"What was that?" Reid asked, pulling out the chair next to her and folding his lean frame into it. She tried not to stare hungrily. Dressed in wheat-colored jeans and a gray T that hugged his chest and biceps, he looked divine, never mind that the skin around his eye was now dark lavender bordered by yellow-green.

"Nothing." As relieved as she'd been to see him, embarrassment had entered the mix. She was horrified that he'd witnessed Jay's selfish greed and general loutishness, and she was mortified that Jay had guessed she and Reid had slept together. Was it so obvious, her helpless attraction to Reid still stamped on her face?

It was bad enough that Jay could spot it, despite her attempts to keep her longing for Reid in check—what if Reid could see it, too?

She should thank him for delivering her from her cousin. "What are you doing here?" she asked instead.

"I heard something about Jay wanting to meet you. Couldn't imagine that was a good situation, so here I am, partner."

"Quinn told you, huh?" Sometimes she wished her friend didn't share quite so much with her family.

"She's got good people sense. Five minutes with Jay made her want to shower off the lingering stench."

She couldn't argue with that.

Nell came by their table. "Another glass of Pinot, Mia?"

"Yes, please." She definitely needed something to wash down the bitter taste left by her meeting with Jay.

"And you, Reid?"

"I'll have the Russian River IPA," he said, naming a local brewery.

When Nell returned with their drinks, Reid took a few gulps and set the glass down. "Mia."

"Yes?" She fiddled with her coaster.

He waited her out. Reluctantly, she met his gaze. "You're not going to fall for the garbage Jay was spouting, are you?"

"No, of course not."

Something in her tone must have given her away. He shook his head. "Come on, you of all people—"

"Exactly. I'm the one person who made it so Jay didn't get the attention he craved."

He shook his head. "That is total BS. I can't believe you're falling for the 'poor, pitiful Jay' crap—that if your mother hadn't died and Thomas and Ellen hadn't taken you in, he'd be a successful churchgoing pillar of the community, bowling with the guys on Tuesday nights and generally making Thomas strut with pride."

Mia rolled her eyes at the description. "Let's get a little real here. Jay feels I edged him out. He's always felt that way. Maybe it's not true, but he thinks it is."

"Sure, I can see that, because Thomas was such a cold and distant father, and Jay was such a mild-mannered kid," Reid shot back.

Reid was right about her cousin's personality, but Mia now understood the enormous pressure Thomas had felt whenever Jay approached him for money. Guilt certainly did a number on one's reasoning. She was actually considering emptying her savings account, if only to show him that she did care, that she did want him to find happiness and success.

Reid set down his half-empty beer. "What did he want the money for?"

"A business deal of some sort."

"Doubtless the deal of the century. Did he offer any details?"

"No, he didn't." Her tone was weary. "He only told me he needed the money soon and that it was a terrific—"

"—opportunity, the chance of a lifetime," Reid finished. "Don't fall for his scam, Mia."

Rather than answer directly, she picked up her glass and took a fortifying sip. It had a velvety smooth finish, and she liked its light note of licorice. The taste reminded her how hard Thomas and she had toiled to grow the grapes and to shape this wine. Jay had never professed the slightest interest in working alongside them.

"Mia?" Reid said again.

"Yes, I heard you." She sighed. "I won't do anything hasty, but if he calls—"

"Come on—you know as well as I do he will."

"Then I should at least find out what this business deal is about. It's possible it's legit." Hearing Reid, who had such a loving and supportive family, criticize Jay made Mia wish for the miraculous, that her cousin had finally changed his spots.

She heard him mutter something under his breath about eternally stubborn women and was about to offer a retort about obnoxiously high-handed cowboys, when a flash of canary yellow distracted her, the color extra bright against the bar's simple white walls.

Since Jay's departure, the evening crowd had trickled in and Beau had turned the volume on the sound system up several notches. Beau did love the Rolling Stones. Some couples had migrated to the dance floor, strutting their stuff to "Honky Tonk Women."

The bright canary yellow came closer. Now Mia could see who was wearing it. It was Maebeth Krohner.

She advanced with a swing of her hips that showed how determined she was to catch someone's attention.

No need to guess whose.

"Oh, boy," Mia said under her breath.

"What?"

"One of your fan-club members is coming over," she informed him, dredging up a cool smile. She hoped it wasn't going to hurt too much to watch Acacia's beloved Romeo in action.

Reid's eyes narrowed at her reference to his fan club. Then he spotted Maebeth, and a muscle jumped beneath his tanned cheek.

But that was his only reaction. It struck her again how good he was at hiding his thoughts. He could have been overjoyed, bored, or dreading the prospect of Maebeth batting her lashes at him and leaning over, the better for him to appreciate her cleavage.

Maebeth's emotions were unfortunately all too easy to read. She gasped in horror at Reid's bruise. "My God! I ran into Jay in the parking lot. The dope didn't even bother to mention you were sporting a shiner to end all shiners. Boy, that must have hurt." She leaned closer, clucking sympathetically.

Too bad Maebeth didn't really look like a big chicken, Mia thought. Or a canary on steroids.

"It's nothing," Reid said.

It was only because Mia was listening extra carefully that she caught the faint irritation in his voice. Maebeth missed it completely.

"I bet you got it wrestling a cow, right?"

His lips quirked as if suppressing a smile or, worse, a guffaw.

Threatened by a wave of humiliation, Mia made to rise from her chair and escape but was stopped. Reid's hand shot out, latching on to her arm. She glared at him and mutely tried to shake him off.

"No, it was a wildcat," he said, still holding on to her.

As if from a distance, she heard Maebeth say, "Holy crap, I heard they're around these parts."

Locked in their battle of wills, neither she nor Reid acknowledged her comment.

"I have to go." Mia spoke through molars clenched so tightly they hurt.

"I'll see you home." His voice, too, was tense and determined.

Mia and Maebeth responded simultaneously. "Not necessary" competed with "What? You're leaving already?"

" 'Fraid so. See you later, Maebeth." His hand still wrapped around Mia's arm, Reid rose to his feet, bringing her with him, and then led her away.

Chapter
TWENTY

"YOU ARE NOT driving me home. I've had all of one and a half glasses of wine," Mia hissed through gritted teeth after Reid tossed two twenties on the bar, waved a goodbye to Nell, and hauled her out the door to where her truck was parked.

"You're right; I'm only following you home. I need to make sure you're safe and sound."

Coming from Reid's lips, the words were swoon-worthy. She did her best to resist their lure and ignore how the rough timbre of his voice thrilled. "I don't need a bodyguard, for Pete's sake."

"Too bad. Get in, will you?" He gestured to the cab's interior.

With an aggrieved huff, she climbed in and started the engine. A second later, she saw a flash of light as Reid opened the door of his own truck. Then the twin beams of his headlights pierced the dark. When they circled toward her, she pulled out and hit the gas.

"It's nothing. Don't make this into more than it is." She repeated the words like a mantra on the drive back to the house, hoping they'd calm the racing of her heart, quiet the shallowness of her breathing, and stop the aching need spreading through her.

She really wanted him to go away, she decided as she scrambled out of the truck. Damn it, she thought, as the slamming of his door echoed hers. Maybe he'd get the message if she ignored him, and she scurried up the path toward the front porch steps on legs that felt far too rubbery. This time she couldn't blame the sensation on vodka.

It was all Reid.

He made her feel things she absolutely did not want to feel—at least not with him. With anyone else, she'd have some guarantee of safety, that a part of her heart would remain untouched.

Not with Reid.

Never with Reid.

He caught up to her, his feet hitting the porch steps in sync with hers. Reaching the top, she whirled to face him. "I'm here. Safe and sound. Now go away." She made a shooing gesture.

"You know, it's the craziest thing, but sometimes I get the impression you don't like me, which is funny, because I'm beginning to enjoy our post-Drop dates."

"This is not a date."

"Business hours are over, Mia. This is a date. Or would you prefer 'tryst'?"

Her heart banged so loudly she was sure he heard it.

"Neither. We're not dating—or anything else-ing. I wouldn't date you. We have nothing in common." She stopped before she began to babble.

"Sure we do." He plucked the key chain from her nerveless fingers. Inserting the house key into the lock, he turned it, and the soft *click* reminded her how easily he'd unlocked her desire. Did she have any defenses he couldn't breach?

"In fact," he continued, "I'd say we have a lot in common."

She tried to un-fry her brain. "Like what?"

"We're business partners, for one."

"Not my choice."

"We're neighbors."

"An accident of fate."

"Both of us love the land and love working it."

When she silently conceded the point, he flashed a smile. "And we can't overlook the fact that we're really good in bed together."

"We slept together? I can't remember."

He laughed softly. "I can. We men tend not to forget when our lovers come three times for us. And scream loudly each blessed time." His voice dropped even lower. "I'd like to give you four orgasms tonight."

Lover. Orgasm. Four. Dear God. A helpless whimper escaped her. It was as articulate a reply as she was likely to make.

He stepped forward, and she reeled as his body heat and scent enveloped her.

"But first, I'd like to kiss you." The words were a husky whisper.

She tried; she really tried to save herself. "You already have. Kissed me."

"Not the way I want to. Everywhere, and slowly. Inch by inch."

She swayed. "I—I don't think—"

"Don't think, Mia," he commanded as his arms stole about her. "Just feel."

This time, his movements were unhurried. He removed her clothes slowly, unfastening buttons, pushing the fabric off her body, and then pausing to let his gaze roam over her before following its meandering path with his hands and mouth.

It was unbearably erotic to be stripped with such care, to have his breath blow across her bared flesh as he whispered where he wanted to kiss her next.

The man really knew how to kiss.

There, in the quiet of her room, Reid made sensations explode inside her, as vivid as the morning sun lighting the world.

Her panties were all that remained. He slipped his thumbs beneath the elastic and, dropping to his knees, dragged the soft cotton down her legs. Continuing his sensual journey, he explored her navel with his mouth, his tongue dipping into the hollow. Her legs suddenly limp, she sank to the edge of the bed. He followed, blazing a trail over her hip bones with his tongue, the ends of his hair brushing her sensitive skin and awakening her every nerve until she trembled in mute supplication.

Reid sank back on his heels. He'd shed his clothes without ceremony. No need for any when what lay underneath was a masterpiece of muscle, sinew, and bronzed skin as well as blatant masculine power. His erection was a thing of glory. Yet despite being fully aroused, despite the fine sheen of sweat covering his pecs and darkening his gold-blond hair, Reid's focus was on her alone.

He shifted forward, his hands running up the inside of her thighs, each stroke bringing him closer and closer to where she longed for him most. When his fingers brushed her damp curls, she moaned, already so close.

He tilted his head and met her gaze. His eyes gleamed with a fierce passion. "You're so damned beautiful, Mia. Everything about you—the way you look, the way you feel, the way you taste, and, above all, the way you respond to me—drives me wild."

Her heart tripped and opened. Maybe they were just words to Reid. It was possible he'd profess something similar to some other woman at a future point. It didn't matter. Her heart was his now—if he chose to claim it.

"Keep looking at me, Mia. I want to watch your face, I want to hear you cry my name, I want to feel you shudder around me when you come."

His fingers had already found her. Nimbly they played, coaxing, strumming, and then sliding into her slick heat as she whimpered in pleasure.

His mouth joined in, met her heat with his, and drove her ever higher with flicks and lashes of his tongue. He made her writhe, made words tumble from her lips in a fevered rush. "I—oh, please, yes—oh!" Then his teeth grazed her. The sharp nip was followed by a slow sweep of his tongue. A second graze, another slow sweep, and the pleasure was more than she could bear. She screamed his name, her fingers digging into his hair, holding him to her as she arched and jerked, her orgasm rocking her body and soul.

He followed the frenzied movements of her hips, prolonging her climax, then let her drift back to earth with easy strokes and gentle, undemanding kisses. For a second she could only gaze at him dazedly, too wrung out to do more than luxuriate in the tiny aftershocks that continued inside her.

He was still kneeling between her open legs. Her gaze slid down the muscled ridges of his torso and encountered another very hard part of his body. Hard and eager. The sight of his arousal and the tension still gripping him banished her lethargy. She remembered the foil-wrapped condoms he'd dropped onto her bedside table and lunged for one, for the first time in her life truly feeling all that was sexy and powerful, when Reid laughed. The happiness in the sound filled the room and filled her.

With a smile that matched the joy in her heart, she scooted back across the mattress.

"Wouldn't the bed be more comfortable?" she asked, and grinned when he all but vaulted onto it. "Lie down. It's my turn to have fun."

He did as she requested. "I'm all for a girl having fun. Go wild, Mia."

Filled with hunger at the veritable banquet his body represented, she thought she might. Deciding the condom could wait, she dropped it beside her and reached for him. Her fingers skimmed his torso, tracing patterns along his chest and abdomen. Her eyes widened as his muscles quivered and jumped for her.

Lightly, she caressed the bulbous head of his penis. Triumph surged within her when it danced at her feathery touch. Wrapping her hand around him, she stroked him from velvety tip to thick root.

With her other hand, she cupped his balls and watched arousal stamp his cheeks and make his eyes glittery bright as she gently squeezed and fondled the warm sacs and then grazed them with her nails.

"Ah, Mia—"

Whatever he was about to say ended on a low hiss as she lowered her head. She kissed the tip of his penis, then opened her lips and drew him into her mouth. He tasted salty, with a touch of musk. The flavor made her head spin.

She savored him with slow licks and delicate nibbles, circling his throbbing length with her tongue and then scoring it lightly with her teeth. With each pass she took him deeper into her mouth.

"God, Mia, yes, just like that." His voice had gone rough with need, and she felt his hands fist in her hair. From the trembling that gripped him, she knew it was as much to anchor himself as it was to control her movements.

The groans and soft curses she wrung from him with each flick of her tongue, each slow suck of her lips, rekindled her own arousal until her core throbbed with an aching urgency to have him fill her. To be one with him.

But she wanted this first.

He was close—she knew it from the tightening of his balls when she caressed them, felt it when his hands dug deeper into her hair as his hips quickened their rhythm. With a guttural cry, he jerked and then stiffened, coming in a hot rush and an equally sweet groan.

Spent, he groaned again. "Sweet Jesus," he whispered, stunned stupefaction in his voice. Letting go of her hair, he grasped her arms and tugged so that she landed in a sprawl across him.

"Oof." With a smile, she kissed her way up his sweat-covered chest to the column of his neck, secretly gloating when her lips found his racing pulse.

"Just so you know," she said, dropping another kiss and then a deliberate lick along his bristled jaw, "you taste really good."

He cocked a brow, and his mouth curved in a slow grin. "That so? Coming from someone with as refined a palate as yours, that's some compliment."

"Mm-hmm, it is."

For a while they lay quietly, his fingers sifting through her hair, lifting it as if gauging its mass, letting it slide down to her shoulders and back, then stroking it to its twisting, curling ends.

Her fingers moved, too. At first they traced aimless circles across his ribs. Then, as her hunger reasserted itself, they traveled southward, with intent. When again his breath grew labored, his chest rising and falling heavily, when he stirred, thickening and lengthening to meet her questing fingers, she looked into his eyes and saw her need mirrored.

The neglected square foil was beside them. Grabbing it, she sat up, kneeling over him. He watched, waiting.

His willingness to follow where she led made happiness bubble inside her, as delicious as the pleasure he'd given her.

She tore it open. Condom in hand, she positioned it over him and smoothed it down as heat gathered inside her.

Her palms glided over the tops of his thighs, so muscular and sprinkled with light-brown hair. "Did I tell you I'm going riding soon with Tess and Quinn?"

A bright spark lit his gaze. "I heard something to that effect."

"I'm pretty rusty. I don't want to embarrass myself in front of them."

"You know," he said, as he reached around and palmed her rear, squeezing her cheeks gently before letting his fingers slide down to her slick opening, "I think I could help you with that."

"You could?"

"That's right." His smile was pure sin. "Now, why don't we start with the best way to mount. . . ."

Chapter TWENTY-ONE

SEX WAS SEX. That's how Reid had always thought about it. Physical, sweaty, and gloriously messy, at times awkward and occasionally mechanical—insert rod in slot and churn until done—but an act he rarely regretted. It was quite simply the best damned fun Reid could imagine with a naked or even partially naked woman. After all, it topped his personal list of pleasures.

He ran a hand down the length of Mia's back. She shifted, murmuring drowsily against his collarbone, and slipped back into sleep. Her boneless slumber was evidence of how much pleasure, how much damned fun, they'd wrung from each other. But sleep eluded him, his mind too busy grappling with what had happened.

Yeah, sex was a lot of great things. But that didn't mean Reid had ever considered it profound. Or even important. Or that he'd ever seriously believed the words "making love" related to what he did with the woman in his arms. "Faking love" was far more accurate.

This night with Mia changed that.

He was more than willing to admit that after interrupting her cousin's shakedown, he'd been gripped by another weird and alien protective urge. Actually, he'd felt not only protective but possessive. And proud, too, because from what he could tell, she'd been holding her own against Jay, an impressive feat considering how hard her cousin was pushing her emotional buttons.

After Jay had slithered off to whatever rock he currently lodged under, all Reid could think about was getting Mia in his arms. Bent on his goal, he'd hustled Mia out of The Drop in front of Maebeth Krohner.

Now Maebeth, who was a little too fond of gossip and a lot too determined to land a guy, would start putting one and one together, meaning that in a couple of hours all of Acacia would know his interest in Mia wasn't limited to figuring out how to peddle her fermented grape juice.

He'd known all this, yet it hadn't stopped him. He'd understood, too, that while the first time he'd escorted Mia home might have been written off as his watching out for a neighbor who'd over-sipped, this second instance would be interpreted differently.

From here on out they'd be viewed as a couple.

The speculation, the gossip, had neither mattered nor deterred him. And the lectures he'd given himself on the importance of keeping his distance from Mia? Every sentence, observation, carefully crafted justification and rationalization fell like a house of cards, scattered by the driving need to get Mia alone—and then get up close and personal with her.

Very personal.

It had started in the usual way. Hot, fun, and fiercely sexy. But then something had changed.

He'd been inside her. He stared up as she rode him, drinking in her beautiful rosy-tipped breasts and the curving line of her neck as she let her head drop back and arched on a wave of pleasure. Her lips had parted in a soft cry as she ground into him, making his blood surge and his brain fog. Where he gripped her hips, steadying her, the ends of her hair brushed his arms. The teasing contact, combined with the delicious clamp of her inner muscles around his cock, brought him perilously close to the edge. He clenched his jaw, fighting the need to wrest control, flip her onto her back, and drive into her, giving them both the sweet release that hovered so near.

Nothing, however, could stop his fingers from seeking the straining nub of her clitoris or stop triumph from roaring through him when her breath caught and she cried his name in astonishment, her body shaking from the force of her orgasm. Her core milked him, made his own body jerk as if jolted by a thousand watts of pleasure. He came, emptying himself into her, giving her everything.

His heart had been the last organ to recover. Even now it was pumping heavily in his chest. It felt different, too, filled with something new. He wasn't inclined to examine exactly what that something was, other than that it made him feel strangely humbled.

Then again, why should that be odd? Who wouldn't be humbled and, yes, shaken by the woman lying in his arms? He remembered the stunned awe in her eyes as her climax seized her and the tremulous smile she'd given him after she'd collapsed onto his sweat-slicked chest. Nor could he forget the sense of rightness that invaded his being when he folded his arms about her.

That's when he'd realized that his old vocabulary didn't cover what Mia and he had done together. This had been more than coitus, fornication, X-rated gymnastics, or, his favorite, a really good fuck.

With Mia, he'd done something that felt awfully like lovemaking.

But did that mean he'd fallen in love with Mia?

The very thought made his mouth go dry and caused

his already over-exercised heart to race. Jesus, he wasn't ready for that—for love. He knew he cared for her. He knew something funny had happened to him when he'd been deep inside her and that it was something he'd never felt for another woman—and thus no laughing matter. But love?

It occurred to him that he'd been careless. While he'd remembered to remove his watch to avoid any further entanglement, he hadn't taken the same precautions with his heart.

Maybe it was time to jump out of bed and make for the hills. Go while the getting was good.

Then again, maybe he was worrying over nothing more than a blip. As great, as sublime as he'd felt when Mia was wrapped around him and he was coming with a force that left him shaken, that didn't necessarily mean he'd gone and fallen in love. It wouldn't happen just like that, with the snap of fingers, because that would be precipitous—like jumping-off-a-cliff precipitous.

Insane.

And not necessary. Because Reid liked his life exactly the way it was.

Recalling that pertinent fact, he exhaled in relief. And when his breath sent one of her crazy curls floating upward to land lightly on his shoulder, he even managed a grin.

The solution was obvious. He needed to keep things between Mia and him as light as that wayward curl of hair. All things considered, it shouldn't be difficult to manage.

Decision made, he dropped a kiss on the tip of her stubborn nose and then another on her softly parted lips. Nope, he had nothing to worry about.

* * *

When Reid reopened his eyes, he noted three things in quick succession. First, Mia hadn't budged from her angled sprawl across his torso, and that was good, very good. Second, the sky had lightened. Not so good. It was time to get to work. He wasn't leading a trail ride this morning, but there was still plenty on his to-do list. He, Ward, Pete Williams, their foreman, and Carlos, one of the ranch hands, were going to check the cattle in the upper pastures. Third, someone was banging on the front door. Annoying as hell. Though the sun was up, it was way too early for social calls.

Mia raised her head and blinked at him. "What's going on?"

She looked adorable, with her hair sticking out all over the place and a confused frown furrowing her brow.

"Not a damned clue," he said, lifting her off his chest and swinging his legs over the side of the bed. He stood and grabbed his pants, shoved his feet into them, and zipped the fly. "Stay here. I'll go shut the idiot up." Afterward he'd sprint back upstairs and wake her up properly.

"No, wait!"

But he was already jogging down the hallway and then taking the stairs two at a time.

The pounding on the door continued.

He opened it with a snarling demand of "What the hell," only to give an exasperated shake of his head. "I should have guessed. Don't you have a trail ride to lead?"

"Nope," Quinn said breezily. "Mom volunteered to take my place when I told her what I had planned for Mia this morning. She approved wholeheartedly." She grinned at his naked torso. "Something tells me she'll be real happy about this turn of events—"

He crossed his arms. "Which, unless you have a death wish, you are not going to share with her."

"Come on. As if she hasn't figured it out. You know, she's moved on to Tom Jones tunes."

"Tom Jones?" This was not good. Soon she'd be singing Celine Dion. "Listen, don't encourage her. I don't want Mom to start planning my wedding—"

"Quinn? What are you doing here?" Mia said.

He and his sister turned. Mia was standing on the last step. She'd obviously leapt out of bed right after him and yanked on a pair of jeans and a shirt. From her carefully blank expression, he got the bad feeling she'd overheard his and Quinn's exchange.

But before he could even begin to formulate a sane explanation for his mother's nutty ambition to see her three children married and making babies, Quinn brushed by him.

"Hey, Mia," she said. "Glad to see you're up. You had breakfast yet?"

"Uh, no—"

"No worries, we can grab a coffee from Spillin' the Beans and still make it on time."

Mia felt as if her brain had been chopped into quarters, with each part in fierce competition. One was still reliving the hours of pleasure Reid had given her. Another was trying to remember whether she'd actually made a date with Quinn. She was pretty sure she hadn't. The third part was struggling to hide her embarrassment over Quinn's finding Reid and her. It kind of amazed her that Quinn seemed so unfazed by the situation, as if it were all perfectly normal. Then again, Quinn didn't always react as expected. And the remaining segment of her brain? It was on repeat, blasting Reid's words: *I don't want Mom to start planning my wedding. . . .*

Of course he didn't. Last night might have been the stuff of dreams for her, but that didn't mean she was expecting him to go down on bended knee. For Pete's sake, she wasn't sure they would even be spending another night together—as far as she could tell, the two times Reid and she had ended up in bed had been fueled by impulse, an immediate and unstoppable need. Perhaps last night had been enough for him and now he was ready to move on to his next conquest.

The thought was like an icicle stabbing her heart.

Luckily, Quinn's presence provided a distraction.

"Make it where on time?" Mia asked.

"I'm helping out at the animal shelter this morning," Quinn replied. "I thought you might enjoy the chance to get away for a few hours and come with me. Once the harvest starts, there won't be many breaks for you, right?"

A mild understatement. She and the crew would be working nonstop to pick, sort, de-stem, and crush the grapes at their peak ripeness. "We won't be gone more than a couple of hours?" she asked.

"Tops," Quinn said with a nod. "I promised I'd pick zucchini blossoms for Jeff. He's planning a special appetizer for the guests tonight. So, you game?"

Mia suddenly realized that she was being offered the perfect means of avoiding any awkward morning-after conversation with Reid. "Just give me a few minutes to wash up, deal with my hair, and put on a pair of shoes. And I need to write notes to Paul and Roberto and Leo and Johnny—oh, and Vincent needs his kibble." She turned, intending to dash into the kitchen.

That's as far as she got.

Reid caught her, looping his bare arm about her waist. "Just a second," he said. "Quinn, go be useful and feed Vincent breakfast."

"Sure thing." Raising her voice, she called, "Vincent! Chow time!" and headed down the hall to the kitchen.

Reid hadn't removed his arm. The heat from his body had transferred directly to her cheeks. Darn, it looked like she hadn't escaped the awkwardness of listening to his explanations and excuses.

"Come over here." He pulled her into the living room and dropped onto one of the faded floral armchairs. She landed in his lap.

When she opened her mouth in an embarrassed protest, he kissed her. For a long time.

Raising his head at last, he gave her a lopsided grin. "Morning, Mia."

She pursed her lips. "Good morning, Reid."

"Man, I love it when you go all prim and proper on me. Listen, last night—"

Dread flooded her. Here comes the "it was great but I'm not ready for a commitment" speech, she told herself. "Yes, it was fun. I had a good time. Thanks so much." She made to slide off.

"Oh, no, you don't." He drew her back against his chest. "It was fun. I had a good time, too." He pushed her hair aside and nuzzled her neck. Shivers skipped down her spine. "I want to see you again."

"Again?" she asked warily, even as her heart lifted, helium-light.

"Yeah." He pressed a kiss against her jaw. Who knew she had so many nerve endings there—he did, obviously. "I like this thing between us. It's good. Don't you agree?"

"I suppose you mean this 'thing,'" she said. And despite her better judgment she squirmed, rubbing against his very obvious "thing."

For a second he went still. She didn't know why. From shock, perhaps. Then she felt his lips curve against her skin as he kissed the spot just below her ear. "I'm glad you noticed." His quiet laughter fanned her damp skin. "So why don't we just see where this takes us? Okay?"

She was pretty sure that was Reid-speak for "I like having sex with you, but I'm not into commitment." Could she handle that? She'd have to. Although she knew that in the end she'd likely watch him walk away, calling it quits was beyond her. She wanted to hoard the joy he gave her like a miser with his gold until the day he said goodbye.

"How about it, Mia? Does being with me work for you?" His teeth closed about her earlobe, nipping lightly. "Say yes," he whispered, and then flicked his tongue over the sensitive spot.

"Yes," she moaned.

"Smart girl." He cupped her chin and brought his mouth to hers, slipping his tongue inside and thrusting slowly until she was gripping his bare shoulders and returning his kiss, rubbing her tongue against his.

A shout interrupted them. "Time's up, Reid. Let her go."

He ignored his sister and continued to kiss Mia, releasing her only when they were both breathing heavily. "I'll come by later."

"Okay," she managed to whisper.

"Okay, then." He raised a hand to stroke her hair and then pushed a lock behind her ear, grinning boyishly when it sprang free. "You've got the most amazing hair."

She attempted to smooth it. "Yes, so I've been told. Jungle vines, right?"

His grin widened. "Absolutely."

"You know, flattery might get you somewhere," she told him as she slipped off his lap.

"That so?" he asked, his eyes sparkling with amusement. "Do me a favor and don't let Quinn bring too many animals home. You're one of the few people she might listen to."

"A tall order, but I'll try."

He rose, too. "Thanks. And, Mia?"

"Yeah?"

"I'll be thinking of you. A lot."

By some miracle she managed to stay on her feet. "That works."

"Best part? It's true."

The trip to the rescue shelter took less than twenty minutes even with a lightning stop to pick up a triple skim latte for her and a double espresso for Quinn, who was hard-core when it came to her caffeine fix. While Mia sipped her coffee in an attempt to reenergize her system after a night of shattering pleasure, Quinn downed hers in four quick gulps, scrolled through her iPod's playlist until she found the one she was looking for, and gunned the truck's engine. Los Lobos's *How Will the Wolf Survive?* filled the truck's interior.

Five rockin' songs later, Quinn pulled into a parking lot in front of a nondescript one-story building that had a wooden sign with a dog running and a cat licking its paw and the words MENDOCINO COUNTY ANIMAL RESCUE painted between them.

The bells attached to the front door chimed as it opened, which set off a round of frenzied barking from somewhere in the building. The noise didn't seem to disturb the dark-haired woman sitting behind the counter, a cellphone pressed to her ear while she jotted something on a pad. She glanced up, saw Quinn, smiled, and waved her through. Quinn made a beeline for the door to the woman's right.

Mia followed, sparing a glance at the colorful array of collars and leashes hanging in rows and at the metal shelves filled with cat and dog beds in a variety of sizes and materials, feeding dishes, and cans and bags of pet food. Two large baskets held plush toys and balls.

They walked down a short hallway lined with pictures of cats and dogs with their smiling new owners.

"Nice place," Mia said.

"Purgatory, actually. Lorelei and Marsha try their hardest for the animals—that was Lorelei behind the desk. Marsha's the director. She's probably doing rounds." Quinn pushed a door and the barking erupted again.

"Pipe down, everyone. Quinn's here now," said a woman in faded jeans, a plaid shirt with rolled up sleeves, and beat-up running shoes, her attire as comfortable as her weathered face and short-cropped gray hair. "Hey, Quinn, glad you're here." She turned to Mia. "You must be Mia. I'm Marsha. Thanks for spending the morning with this pack. A lot of our regular volunteers are on vacation."

"I'm glad Quinn asked me to come along. It's a great thing you do."

Marsha smiled wearily. "We try. But when times are hard and money's tight, pets are often the first to suffer. We're seeing too many given up."

The dogs had calmed as Quinn began going from crate to crate, giving a scratch and a hello in her low-pitched voice.

Not sure what she was supposed to do, Mia looked around the brightly lit room. Far too many of the steel cages were occupied with dogs of every shape and size. One immediately caught her attention. She didn't know why—perhaps it was because it was the biggest dog there, perhaps because it was looking at her rather than tracking Quinn's movements. When their gazes met, it gave a single, loud bark. Its tail thwacked the sides of the crate.

The dog barked again. Its massive body shivered

with excitement, making its shaggy white-and-brown-splotched coat ripple.

Quinn noticed—Mia swore she noticed everything in an animal. "He likes you."

"What makes you say that? Maybe he just wants out of the crate."

"For sure. But he's talking to you about it, not to Marsha or me, two humans he knows far better. For some reason it's you Bruno wants to spring him."

"Bruno? That's his name?"

Marsha walked by with a terrier of some sort. It was straining on the leash. She made it sit. "Yup. We decided 'Bruno' suited him, and he seems to agree. He was left tied to a door overnight. He was a real mess, half-starved and dehydrated. He quaked with fear when I approached, but he never growled or bared his teeth once."

"What an awful story." Mia swore that when she looked over at Bruno he cocked his head as if listening. Then he gave another bark, his eyes on her the entire time.

"All the dogs and cats who end up here have heart-breaking stories, but, yeah, Bruno's is pretty sad. I can't understand how humans can be so fucking cruel—pardon my language—to neglect the animals in their care."

"Forgiven. I'd be swearing, too, if I had to face this every day."

Marsha grinned. "We're going to have to sign you up for regular visits. By the way, I agree with Quinn: Bruno does seem to like you. Why don't you take him outside to the exercise yard? This is his regular play group that we're bringing out."

"Me?"

"Sure. He's been here two weeks, so he knows the routine. And he's been a perfect gentleman with every volunteer. Haven't you, Bruno?" Marsha addressed him affectionately before continuing. "He's young—I'd say two at most—but he understands 'sit' and 'down.' We've been teaching him 'wait.' The collar and leash we use for him are there." She pointed to the right of the crate. "Don't worry, Quinn will supervise your every move."

Mia picked up the collar and leash and got a woof of encouragement for her effort. She eyed Bruno through the metal grate. She liked dogs. Thomas and Ellen had one—a dachshund named Cork—but he'd died when Mia was still little. Other than patting Quinn's dog, Sooner, and the ones she encountered in town, Mia didn't have a lot of adult experience with them.

"Tell him to sit and wait before you open the crate door," Quinn suggested. "And don't make it into a question—it's a firm command."

"Sit, Bruno."

Bruno sat.

Stunned, Mia looked over at Quinn, who grinned. Then she looked back at Bruno, who grinned even wider, showing lots of teeth and an impossibly long tongue. "Wait," she said, waiting herself before opening the latch.

Only his white tail with its brown tip moved, sweeping the bottom of the crate.

She reached inside and put the nylon collar around his massive neck and fastened it, noting as she did the unbelievable silkiness of his coat. The leash was already attached to the collar.

"Tell him 'good boy' and 'okay'—that's his release from 'wait.' You can follow me and Lucky here, who's not nearly as well behaved."

Indeed, Mia felt ridiculously proud of Bruno as they walked behind Quinn and a madly baying beagle, which grew only more berserk as they entered the fenced enclosure.

Quinn had Lucky sit and then unleashed him. He took off, barking at everything he saw. "Marsha's going to have to find Lucky a human who's deaf as a post and lives far from any neighbors," she said. "It's your turn now. Use the same commands with him as before."

Mia followed suit and with a smile watched Bruno bound off happily to say hi to the other dogs, pee, and then recommence the meet and greet. "Why has no one adopted Bruno? He's a nice dog."

Marsha answered the question. "He's big. Even out in the country here, people are generally looking for smaller dogs, sixty to seventy pounds, max. Bruno puts away a serious amount of kibble, and that cuts into people's budgets. And he sheds. A lot. He's got an incredibly thick coat, which has to be brushed regularly. Not many people want to deal with it."

She knew the trials of having too much hair. But Bruno's coat was beautiful. Taking care of it wouldn't be that hard.

Finished playing, the dog came trotting back to the center of the enclosure, where the women stood. Mia had expected that Bruno would do the dog thing and sniff the humans and then race back to his four-legged friends. Instead, he made straight for her and sat down next to her, so that his body brushed her pant leg. His white head, framed by matching brown ears, reached her hip.

She looked down in bemusement and stroked his forehead lightly. He looked up adoringly. His brown eyes, which had a touch of caramel in them, seemed so soulful.

Okay, she was in serious trouble here. "Quinn, why don't you take Bruno? He's really great."

"He is, no doubt about it. But I can't make the commitment to foster a dog until I place Alfie in a good home. That may take a while, since he's a pretty special parrot. And if I adopt another dog it has to be a herder, a second lieutenant to Sooner. Whatever wonderful cocktail Bruno is—"

"What would you say he is?" Mia interrupted. "I've never seen a dog that looks anything like him."

"Off the top of my head?" Quinn stepped back to study him.

"I'd say he's got Saint Bernard, golden retriever, and setter in him. What do you think, Marsha?"

Marsha pressed her index finger to her lips as she considered. "Yeah, he could have Saint Bernard in him. Or maybe a Great Pyrenees came along. The rest of his ancestry could range from a collie to a hound breed."

Listening to them, it struck Mia that Bruno had even more unknowns in his family tree than she did—and look how spectacular he was.

Marsha was still speaking. "But Quinn's right: Even if Bruno does have some collie or sheepdog in him, he's not wired or built for rounding up sheep or stubborn cattle."

"Bruno's a people dog. Aren't you, big guy?" Quinn asked, affection in her voice.

The dog thumped his tail.

"How about you, Mia?"

Still pondering the mysteries of parentage, she gave a start. "Me? What do you mean?"

"You could take Bruno home."

"Oh, I couldn't adopt—" Her words were cut short by Bruno. He shifted, extending his front paws to lie down in front of her. With a deep sigh that had his ribs heaving, he settled his chin over her shoes, and she felt the warm weight of him through the canvas of her sneakers.

Quinn laughed. "He's got some smooth moves, doesn't he?"

"Yes, he does." Mia smiled wryly.

And, like that, she was a goner.

Two hours later, Bruno sat wedged between Quinn and her. His new extra-large bed, his food and water bowls, and a thirty-pound bag of dog food that Quinn and Marsha had recommended were stacked in the flatbed of the truck. Mia was still dazed by how fast she'd fallen for the massive canine and how quickly he'd become hers. She was excited and more than a little terrified.

Bruno, however, was taking it all in stride. He seemed perfectly content to gaze through the windshield and watch the road. Every so often he'd turn his head and give Mia's jaw a sloppy sweep of his tongue as if to reassure her.

"Hey, Quinn?"

"Yeah?"

"Do you suppose it's because I look like Bruno's previous owner?" she asked, after he'd bathed the side of her face once again.

"Why he chose you, you mean? Could be," Quinn said with a shrug. "Although if I had to lay a wager, I'd say he simply likes you. In case you haven't figured it out, Mia, you're kind of amazing. Dogs sense goodness in people." She shot Mia a grin. "But judging from what I saw earlier this morning, it ain't just overgrown hairy dogs who are attracted to you."

Mia fiddled with the end of Bruno's brand-new red nylon leash. It matched his collar, which already had a metal tag with her name and number fixed to it. The rescue shelter had a machine that engraved them. She'd chosen one in the shape of a large bone. "Quinn," she began, her voice tentative. "Are you okay with, you know, Reid and me?"

"You're kidding, right?" she laughed. "I'm really happy for you guys."

"Even after what I said about him?"

"What was that?" Quinn frowned. Then her brow cleared and she laughed again. "Oh, yeah, you mean the great chocolate theory, the one where Reid lives a chocoholic's dream, devouring dessert carts filled with éclairs and fudge brownies and then walking away in search of the next dessert tray?"

"I believe my view was slightly more nuanced than that," she said, fighting a smile.

Quinn snorted. "Not much. If you recall, I blew some major elephant-sized holes in your argument. I'm just glad that whatever ideas you had about Reid, they didn't stop you from getting together with him."

"Your brother can be pretty persuasive." And happened to be one of the sexiest men alive.

Quinn's smile was full of pride. "Yeah, he's got a way about him." She was silent for a minute, braking and then turning left onto Bartlett Road. "But, Mia," she continued, her voice now serious. "Even though he may be treating you like the most mind-blowingly decadent brownie ever baked, don't go deciding that's all there is to him. I don't want to see him hurt."

"I won't hurt him, Quinn." An easy promise to make. Because if anyone was vulnerable to heartbreak, it was she, not Reid.

SHE HAD A new dog; she had a vineyard filled with ripening purple fruit and the promise of a terrific harvest; she had a lover whose gaze seared, whose touch melted, and whose kiss transported her. These were the ingredients to a happiness the likes of which Mia had never known.

Two weeks had floated by with the ease of a puffy cloud drifting across a cerulean sky. Every so often Mia would bring her fingers to her forearm and give herself a hard pinch. Weird but necessary. Amazingly, the pinch didn't cause her world to darken with sadness. Worry and insecurity didn't loom threateningly on the horizon. And the reason for Mia's continued internal sunshine? The man kneeling on the grass next to an ecstatic, tongue-lolling Bruno.

Reid had arrived a few hours ago with another of Daniel's mammoth tractors to level the ground outside the winery. The company Reid had told her about would be coming tomorrow to lay the stone slabs. The chairs and tables were due to be delivered next week.

So many of her dreams were coming together, and every day she grew more excited and optimistic.

Again, it was thanks to Reid.

She knew that, without him, she'd have been lying wide-eyed in bed in the wee hours of the morning, plagued by visions of torrential rains flooding the vineyard, turning her perfect grapes into water balloons. Before any nightmare could ensnare Mia, Reid's arms unerringly found her, pulling her into the solid warmth of his muscled body and lending her his quiet strength.

Instinctively, her eyes sought him out. He was still busy bonding with Bruno, scratching the dog's belly. And Bruno, on his back, his front legs folded, his hind legs splayed, his long tail swishing rhythmically in the grass, was shameless in his plea that Reid continue his efforts into the next decade.

As Mia had quickly discovered, in Bruno's world only one thing topped having his tummy scratched, and that was having it filled with food. He was a walking vacuum cleaner.

Mia watched them in quiet bafflement. How had these two males become so central to her life? She didn't know which was more improbable, that Reid, the womanizing cowboy who'd previously only looked through her, now seemed the person who saw and understood her better than anyone else, or that an oversize white-and-brown mutt had snuck into her heart with little more than a bark and an adoring doggie grin?

Reid must have felt the weight of her gaze, Bruno too lost in the pleasure of a good belly rub to notice. He looked up with a grin. "What?"

Reid's hair had grown even shaggier, its gold-streaked ends brushing the neck of his white T-shirt. The short sleeves exposed tanned skin and roped muscles. Watching them flex as Reid stroked Bruno's silky fur, Mia felt a hot twitchy awareness spread low inside her. If he were to touch her like that right now, she'd be as shameless and greedy as her dog.

"Earth to Mia," he said.

"Oh!" she exclaimed, and blushed, unsure how long she'd been staring at him. "I was just wondering how I ended up with a dog," she said, voicing only part of her thoughts. "Your sister pulled a fast one on me, inviting me to the shelter."

"Yeah, Quinn's devious. Always has a trick up her sleeve. She gets it from our mother."

"Adele? No, your mom's sweet. She was humming Celine Dion yesterday when she came down to the corral. She showed me how to bridle Glory before Tess, Quinn, and I went riding." Mia thought Reid paled at the mention of Celine Dion, but she chalked it up as a typical male response to the singer. "But maybe you were in on the plot to turn me into a dog owner. After all, didn't you tell me to keep my eye on Quinn and make sure she didn't come home with a new cat to accompany Pirate on mousing expeditions or another dog for Sooner to boss around? I'm sure my own guard would have been up otherwise."

"No, the credit goes to Quinn alone. She's into equal opportunity—she wants everyone to adopt animals. But the way she tells it, she didn't have to do any kind of slick maneuvering. Bruno adopted you." Giving the dog a final pat, he straightened.

Recognizing that the belly massage was at an end, Bruno clambered to his paws, shook himself, gave his signature *woof,* and then went into what Mia had decided was his crazy-puppy-dog mode, racing about in tight circles. The performance lasted all of ten seconds. Then he came over to stand by Mia, his plumy tail wagging and his wide grin telegraphing how pleased he was with himself, with her, with Reid, and with the world.

Impossible not to share in his happiness.

"So, the grapes look good?" Reid asked, taking her hand as they walked up the path to the winery. Bruno already knew the route and ambled alongside them.

"The grapes look good."

"How good?"

Her lips twitched. "Roberto and Paul are quite pleased."

"And Ms. Bodell?" he continued as his thumb stroked the inside of her wrist. "Is she equally pleased with her inspection?"

" 'Guardedly optimistic' would be a more accurate description."

He laughed. "Coming from you, who defines perfectionism in all things vino, this is cause for celebration."

Fighting a smile, she shook her head. "No celebration until the grapes are harvested, de-stemmed, and fermenting in the tanks. I'm superstitious."

They'd reached the winery. Mia's steps slowed as she saw the neatly graded rectangle. "Oh! You did such a nice job."

"Mm-hmm. And I expect payment for my efforts." The husky timbre of his voice was like a caress.

She rose up on her toes and kissed him, slipping her tongue into his mouth to dance slowly with his.

With a groan, he pulled her flush against him and slanted his mouth, deepening the kiss.

When at last they broke apart, she smiled into the sparkling blue of his gaze. "Thank you for prepping the patio area, Reid."

His grin was crooked. "Kiss me like that again, and I'll prep a football stadium or two."

"I'll keep that in mind," she said. Lord, this man was good for her ego. He made her feel so powerful and sexy. Impulsively, she kissed him again, a light, teasing nibble of lips that ended in a peal of laughter when he tightened his hold about her waist and lifted her, spinning in a circle.

She was still laughing when he brought her feet back to earth. "Hey, you know what?"

"What?" he asked.

"We could hold weddings here."

"Weddings?" From the look on his face, she might as well have said "torture sessions."

"Weddings," she repeated, her tone turning dry as dust. "For instance, if you had guests who wanted to be married in a vineyard, you could suggest our place as a possible venue. I realize it's not as fancy as many Napa vineyards, but—"

"Not everyone's into the Napa scene," he finished for her. "I'll speak to the powers that be about it. Tess broke our lousy track record for hosting weddings at the ranch when she planned Brian Nash's—you might remember him from high school—to his girlfriend, Carrie Greer. I guess that means we'll be booking more of them."

She had to give Reid credit. He'd recovered quickly, even pretending enthusiasm for her idea. She shrugged. "It was just a thought. Having the visiting artists come and sketch and paint here got me thinking about other events that could benefit both our businesses."

"It's a good idea. Really. Like I said, I'll talk to the others. And don't stop brainstorming about what other special events we can offer to promote the vineyard. You're good at it." He lowered his mouth to kiss her.

The distraction almost worked.

But Mia couldn't help recalling her conversation with Quinn and Tess at dinner when she'd doubted Reid had a discomfort zone.

Lo and behold, she'd found it. The "W" word was it. So weddings—and, by extension, marriage—made him twitchy. She had a hunch he'd break out in hives if she were to utter the "L" word.

It shouldn't come as a surprise. After all, she'd been the one to formulate the famous chocolate theory. She'd also overheard him warning Quinn not to encourage

Adele in any wedding planning for him. And what was the word he'd used to describe what was between them? A "thing"—not a relationship, not an affair, not even a fling. How many different ways did she need to understand that he was commitment-averse?

The sex between them was obviously exceptional. The man was a master at giving her earth-shattering orgasms. Could she blame him simply because being with him meant more to her than physical bliss?

She knew he liked her and that she mattered to him. Was it right to demand more? Was it fair to expect him to give her his heart just because he had hers?

Maybe not, but love wasn't fair. She longed to hear him say the words. She needed them to free her own. Although she'd come a good way in beating back her insecurities, she couldn't pretend they hadn't left their mark. As full as her heart was, she couldn't bring herself to voice the wonder of her feelings—not if it meant exposing herself to the crushing blow when Reid couldn't respond in kind. The awkward smile, the hemming and hawing, would devastate. She would once more be the lonely, pathetic girl who had dreamed too big.

Reid's mouth was still on hers, kissing her with devastating thoroughness. His hands roved, shifting to the small of her back, massaging it and then moving down to cup her rear and bring her into perfect alignment with his erection. At the contact, her own desire spread like flames licking dry kindling.

Lord, he was so very good at this. The thought was tinged with sadness.

At last he raised his head a fraction. "So what's on the agenda now, or is my favorite vintner's work done for the day?" he asked. His eyes glittered with a light she'd come to know well.

She forced her sadness away, banished the worry that

the intense chemistry between them might be all he really wanted from her. She made herself focus on the relationship they *did* have: business.

"Actually, Johnny, Leo, and I are taste checking the barrels. Do you want to join us?" She had asked the guys to run the routine lab tests on the aging wine, but it was time to also perform a sensory test. She needed to know the wine as well as Thomas had.

He nodded. "Yeah, I'd like that."

She took his hand. "Come on, then."

Christ, he'd come close to blowing it, Reid thought, as they walked in to the winery. Thanks to Tess and Ward, the word "wedding" had been bandied about constantly. Yesterday his brother and fiancée had made a date to meet with the priest who'd be marrying them in New York. For some mysterious reason, that had sent his mother into preparation overdrive. Convinced that Reid's shoulders had broadened since he last wore his tuxedo, she'd badgered him into trying it on.

Damned if she wasn't right. His thighs were more muscled, too. He supposed he should be thankful she hadn't harped on that. But the end result was that he'd had to pick out a tux from the styles Tess had selected. Luckily, she had good taste. The tuxes were all black, the lapels not over-wide, the shirts plain, and the bow ties and cummerbunds unadorned.

His role as best man had required Reid to call Brian and Greg Ralston, who would be serving as Ward's groomsmen, and make sure they were okay with his selection.

By his tally that had brought the "wedding" word count far too high. It buzzed about like an annoying fly that wouldn't die. But he couldn't lay the blame for his clumsy reaction solely on Ward and Tess. It was partly his fault. He'd been steeped in Mia and not thinking clearly.

When she'd glowed with pleasure at the neatly raked area for her future patio and then thanked him with one of her sweet and unbelievably hot kisses, he'd responded as always: with a pounding heart and piercing need.

Then, with no warning, she'd begun talking about how they might hold special events—*weddings*—at the vineyard. With the word still hovering in the air, he'd been slammed with a vision of Mia in a long white wedding gown, her head crowned by a simple ringlet, her amazing hair flowing free about her shoulders, her smile radiant as she approached her fiancé—who just happened to bear a striking resemblance to him.

It was like being sucker punched, a feeling Reid didn't care for.

He'd already acknowledged that Mia was special and that she'd made him feel something no other woman had. And the past two weeks had been great, no doubt about it. But marriage? A covenant meant to last forever? That was a hell of a scary vision.

So, yeah, he'd flinched. It was normal to recoil at the prospect of losing one's freedom. Some guys would have jumped right out of their skin. The only reason his reaction bothered him was the suspicion that Mia, whose clear gaze saw far too much, had identified what spooked him.

Yet she hadn't called him on it.

As he held open the door to the winery for Mia and Bruno, he wondered why she hadn't spoken up. She'd never hesitated to point out his weaknesses before.

None of the answers that came to mind were particularly flattering. But that didn't mean he was going to broach the topic of what they meant to each other or where they where headed. Not until he had to. Not until he'd figured it out.

Besides, he'd always held to the belief that actions spoke louder than words. In that respect, he'd proved himself beyond a doubt.

So Reid quit wondering why she hadn't gotten bent out of shape or shown him how irritated she was by sticking her pretty nose in the air, as the Mia of old would have done, and focused instead on the fact that she'd invited him to taste the wine aging in the barrels. Including him must mean things were basically copacetic.

After the heat of the late August afternoon, the winery was refreshingly cool and, as usual, spick-and-span, the floors clean enough to eat off. The large steel fermenting tanks that stood in the processing area to his right, which soon would be filled with crushed Pinot Noir grapes, were equally spotless. The Bodells were meticulous about the equipment. One of Leo and Johnny's most time-consuming jobs was keeping it all clean and sanitary. Reid had often entered the building and found them using the ozone machine on the tanks and barrels or scrubbing and hosing down the equipment and valves, the rinse water flowing into the channel-like drain that ran the entire length of the processing room's concrete floor.

They crossed the open area in the front of the winery where Mia wanted to set up a tasting room. A wall of thermal glass divided the space. On the other side was the "cave"—the wine cellar—where large French oak barrels lay in neat rows.

Leo and Johnny were inside the cellar, waiting for them. Spying Mia and him, they waved.

Mia pointed to a large dog bed. "Go lie down, Bruno," she said. The number of beds for Bruno had multiplied since Mia brought home her very lucky dog.

Bruno ambled over and stepped on it. He circled four

times, then sank down onto the corduroy-covered foam and began to gnaw one of the dozen nylon bones Mia had purchased along with a miscellany of toys.

"Good boy," Mia said with a smile.

Bruno looked up, thumped his tail, and went back to gnawing. Reid was pretty sure the dog knew exactly how good he had it with Mia. He hadn't gotten Quinn to admit it, but he was certain she'd scoured the rescue shelters to find Mia a perfect match. Already Mia loved the dog as if he were her baby.

She was going to be a terrific mother.

Whoa, where the hell was he getting these thoughts? They did *not* belong in his head.

Making sure none of his bizarre preoccupations showed in his expression, he greeted Mia's cellar assistants. "Afternoon, Leo, Johnny."

"Hey, Reid, you here to give your senses a treat?" Johnny asked. A cart was at the ready. It held wineglasses and a bunch of "thieves"—turkey-baster-like tubes used to siphon the wine out of the barrel's bunghole. Using a thief prevented air from entering the barrel and oxidizing the wine.

"That's the plan," he said.

"Sweet." Leo nodded his bandanna-wrapped head amiably. "We're all set, Mia. I'll just grab a few more glasses for Reid."

Reid was glad that Leo and Johnny had accepted his presence, though it had to be said that they were pretty mellow dudes, relaxed about everything—except when it came to the art of winemaking. But Paul and Roberto, older and gruffer, who'd worked the vineyard for far longer, seemed to be coming around, too. All four doubtless appreciated that Reid wasn't stupid enough to try to tell them how to grow grapes or make wine. He only wanted to help them sell it.

That he'd repaired the road and saved their cars' suspension and Leo's bike tires helped.

Leo returned with more glasses and set them on the cart. "Here we go."

"Thanks, Leo." Mia smiled. "Shall we begin, gentlemen?"

There were all sorts of barrel tastings. Reid had been to a number, had even sampled aging wine with Thomas in this very cellar. Today's tasting was different. Mia wasn't just working. She was donning the mantle of winemaker. Like everything that happened in the vineyard, this would now be her domain. Hers would be the final decision in the handling of each barrel's contents. And in two to three weeks, depending on the weather and how quickly her grapes ripened, she'd be running the harvest, overseeing every aspect of the process.

Apart from being astonished at Thomas's gushing over his new love, Pascale, and being vastly irritated with his friend for giving Mia so little warning about his intention to decamp to France, Reid hadn't given much thought to Thomas's decision in terms of the timing of his departure.

Watching Mia move from barrel to barrel, Reid now believed he understood what had been hidden behind Thomas's seeming self-absorption. Despite all appearances, he'd orchestrated his departure carefully to ease Mia into her new role as winemaker.

Sampling the barrels offered a snapshot of how the wine was developing, so the vintner could then decide how best to shape it—whether to rack it again, blend its contents with other barrels, or let it develop on its own with no further adjustments. Thomas knew Mia well. He'd have recognized that if he left Mia the job of taste testing the young wine, she'd become excited about this final but important stage in shaping it. And while she was tasting this vintage, discovering its flavors and strengths, she would already be envisioning possibilities for the grapes she and her crew would be harvesting in a couple of weeks' time.

Reid realized he was witnessing a special moment: This afternoon Mia was coming into her own as a vintner. It was fascinating to watch her apply her formidable knowledge as she held the glass to the light to evaluate its clarity and color, swirled the ruby contents to allow it to aerate, and lowered her nose deep into the bowl to inhale its bouquet.

And then she sipped, that first taste telling her volumes.

When Reid sampled wine, he could kind of, sort of, talk about its characteristics, identify some of its flavors, and make a pronouncement about its finish.

When Mia tasted a young, unformed wine, it was a whole different story. She could see its future, predict what it would look, taste, and feel like in five years' time. Her skills didn't end there. She could also recall with stunning clarity the taste of a specific barrel, even after sampling several others, and know which barrels would blend well together and which should be left to mature on their own.

It was great to see her channel her understanding of the grape and decide what combination of notes would make a really special Pinot that reflected its origin.

But for Reid, there was an added kick in watching her.

He saw her innate sensuality, recognized it from their lovemaking, when she set her senses free to savor and delight in the taste and texture of him, to absorb him deep into her body until they became one.

It occurred to him while he took his own sip of the

young wine—very fruity and rich in tannins—that Mia was like the finest vintage, full of notes and subtleties, strong and complex. Haunting. Unique.

Yeah, she was amazing. She was also gloriously, won-drously sexy.

THE AFTERNOON'S SAMPLING was over. Mia had helped Leo and Johnny wash and rinse the glasses and thieves while Reid took Bruno outside for a quick walk so the canine could sniff and mark his favorite bushes, a job he took very seriously.

The cellar put to rights, they went outside. Reid was lobbing a ball for Bruno. When Bruno saw Mia, he came over and dropped the ball at her feet. She picked up the slimy thing and tossed it. It didn't go very far, barely past the neatly raked rectangle that marked where the terrace would go.

Leo and Johnny laughed at her attempt.

"Hate to break it to you, Mia, but you can't throw a ball worth spit," Johnny said with a grin.

"That's all right. Bruno doesn't mind. See?" she said as the dog trotted back, dropped the ball, and gave her hand an encouraging lick.

Leo finished stowing his bike on the rack attached to Johnny's Subaru. They were off to a barbecue at Echo Vineyards, a small farm that produced Sauvignon Blanc and Gavi.

"You want to come along, Mia? It should be a fun crowd, lots of wine folk," Leo told her.

"Reid should come hang, too. You know the Koenigs' place, don't you?" Johnny asked him.

Reid nodded. Bending over, he gave Bruno a pat on the shoulder. "Thanks for the invitation, but I'll leave the decision up to Mia. She's the one who's been working this afternoon."

Mia cast him a grateful look. It was nice that Johnny and Leo had accepted her—and Reid—into their group, but now that the tasting was over, she just wanted to relax. "If it's okay, I'll take a rain check. I'm still unwilling to leave Bruno alone for too long. Send the Koenigs my best."

"Sure thing. So when do you want to sample the remaining barrels? Tomorrow?" Johnny asked.

Mia nodded. They'd tasted fifteen of thirty barrels. More, and her impressions of the young wine would have lost the necessary definition and become muddied. "Yes, let's plan on finishing up tomorrow afternoon, so we can decide which blocks to blend when it comes time to rack the wine."

"Some of those barrels were damned close to awesome, right?" Leo said.

"Yeah, they were," she replied, exchanging a smile with her assistants. Wow, she thought, as realization struck. At some point this afternoon she'd truly begun to consider Johnny and Leo as her crew rather than Thomas's.

With a wave goodbye, Johnny and Leo climbed into the car and drove off.

"They're nice guys," Mia said, after the bumper-sticker-covered car had disappeared down the drive.

"They are. And, man, do they love the wine they're helping you make."

"True," she said with a laugh, adding, "and they're actually smart. I like how Leo thinks about a wine. He gets it. Thomas picked well." She gave a small sigh.

Reid's hearing was too sharp. "What?" he asked, and he turned to face her. "What are you thinking?"

"Oh, it's, well . . ." She gave a shrug, unsure whether she could explain it to him. "The vintage we tasted today—it's young and has a lot of growing up to do. But, Reid, it's *good*. I think Thomas hit another one out of the park."

"Yeah, even with the tannins I sensed that—in my very inexpert way." He smiled. "So why the sigh, Mia? Where's the problem in this picture?"

"The problem is, I wonder if I can make a wine that comes even close to any of our previous vintages." She sighed again, no longer able to hide her anxiety. "It's not guaranteed."

"Where would the fun be in a guarantee? You might as well be making Twinkies, then."

"Twinkies?" She raised her brow.

"An extreme example of relentless sameness, of scary uniformity. You know even better than I that wine should never be like that. Hell, not even meat loaf should taste the same every time you make it."

She smiled. "Okay, I'll grant you that point. But then there's the question of money."

"Money?"

"Uh-huh." She nodded. "Need I remind you that your family has invested a substantial amount of it, in the belief that I can produce a wine that's as good as what we tasted today or as the one that you went and bought a hundred cases of before it was even bottled? Crappy wine doesn't move."

"Well, I seem to remember from the talk you gave our cowgirl guests that the most important ingredient in making great wine is the quality of the grape—"

"My God, you were actually paying attention?"

"Brat," he said, and swatted her rear, making her laugh. "May I continue?"

"Please."

"By your own admission, this year's harvest stands to be excellent—"

"I believe I merely said I was optimistic—guardedly so."

"Right, which translates into 'excellent' by anyone else's standard. So if the weather holds, you're on your way to crafting a superior wine. The money will come."

She looked at him. "That was neatly argued," she said, and smiled in spite of her worry.

He stepped closer and cupped her chin. "You're going to make great wine, Mia. I saw it today." He kissed her lightly. And again, lingering longer, this time molding his lips to hers. "I liked watching you work today."

Like champagne, his kiss fuzzied her brain. "Really?"

At her dazed tone, amusement danced in his eyes. "Really."

Having him tease her only made her feel as if she were floating higher. "I don't see why you would. My work isn't very interesting to observe. It's not like when you're cutting cattle with Sirrus and the two of you won't let a thousand-plus-pound steer even contemplate a step in the wrong direction, or when you're breaking one of the young horses—"

"Uh, Mia," he interrupted. "We prefer to use the term 'gentling' to 'breaking.'"

"Oh! Right, sorry. Now that I think about it, I can't imagine anyone at Silver Creek ever trying to *break* a horse," she said. "But to continue, and though it pains me to admit it, even when you're horseless and just tossing a lasso, you're pretty awesome. Very watchable."

"Now, those are words I never thought I'd hear." A grin stretched his tan face and made the corners of his eyes crinkle.

"Don't be so modest."

"And you should be prouder." He raised his finger and lightly traced her brow. "Thomas would have loved seeing you test the wine today. He'd have been as impressed as I was. You should call him."

"I'm not sure that's a good idea." She stepped back and began to walk toward the house, Bruno ambling beside her. She dug her fingers into the thick ruff of his neck.

Reid's long legs kept stride. "He's back in France now, isn't he?"

"Yes. If I understood the dates right, he returned last week. But he hasn't called, so . . ."

"He'll want to hear from you, Mia."

She bit her lip and kept her gaze fixed on the house.

"I was thinking about him earlier while we were sampling the barrels. It occurred to me that his departure might not have been as impulsive as it appeared."

"Perhaps. It doesn't matter," she said with a small shrug. It still hurt to recall the days leading up to his rushed and distracted goodbye at the airport.

"It does matter, Mia. Think about it. Thomas only left for Europe once he was fairly confident that this year's grapes were coming along as you all hoped. He also waited until the vineyard's latest vintage was safely bottled. I bet he timed it all so that you could have a chance to find your footing before the craziness of the harvest."

It was possible Reid was right. "I miss him so much," she blurted, unable to keep the words back, knowing he could hear the pain in them.

"Of course you do. So call him already, damn it. He's your family."

Her throat worked as she swallowed a boulder-like lump.

"Come on, Mia. Give the guy a break. Nobody's perfect. He may not have handled leaving here well, but I'm sure he was trying to do the right thing."

With a loud sniff, she pulled herself together. "Okay," she said with a wobbly smile. "I'll call him." She checked her watch to calculate the time difference. "And you're right. He'll want to hear how things are going."

"You want me to take off?"

"No—no! He'd love to talk to you, too."

"All right." He nodded agreeably. "Why don't we do this? You get his number. I'll open some wine and scrounge up something for us to eat. I'm bloody starving. I'll also feed your hairy beasts. Then if Thomas wants to regale me with tales of the Aegean or life in Bergerac, I'll get on the phone."

The *"Allô, oui?"* that came across the line in a near shout was classic Thomas. Hearing his voice made her heart squeeze with gladness.

"Thomas? It's me."

"Mia, my love! You've called! How are you getting on? Has Vincent been taking good care of you? Tell me everything."

And there it was, their connection reestablished. They fell into the easy back and forth of decades: him quizzing her on what the weather had been like, how the grapes were tasting and looking in the different blocks, and when she anticipated the harvest would begin; her hearing about the wonders of grilled sardines and black olives and feta and that the terroir in Pascale's vineyard was different and exciting to work with. Thomas was worried about the recent rains, however. This last week had been full of them, and the downpour had been heavy. More storms were predicted.

They were still talking when Reid returned to the

porch with a platter of cheese, some sliced salami, cherry tomatoes, and thick slices of seeded bread—roughly the entire contents of Mia's pantry and refrigerator. He'd also brought a bottle of Cabernet and two glasses.

He raised his brows inquiringly. She couldn't help but smile. With a superior grin, he motioned for her to rise. Then he sat down in her chair, pulled her into his lap, and began to entertain himself by toying with the ends of her hair as Thomas chatted in her ear.

"And how's that rascal Reid? Is he proving his weight in gold?" he asked.

As heat crawled over her cheeks at the thought of all the ways in which Reid had obligingly proved himself, the rascal in question tugged her hair to the side so he could plant a kiss against her neck.

"Oh, yes, he's been quite helpful." She cleared her throat in an effort to sound less like Minnie Mouse. "We're setting up an outside tasting area to the right of the winery. Reid found a company to lay stone slabs for us. They're coming tomorrow. Actually, Thomas, Reid's right here. He sampled the barrels with Johnny and Leo and me today. Do you want to speak to him?"

"Of course! Pass the phone to the boy. And, Mia, next time you call, I want us to Skype—you do know how, don't you?—I want to see that beautiful face. I miss it."

"I miss yours, too, Thomas. Um, here's Reid." Passing him the phone, she slipped off his lap and went to sit on the top step of the porch, where she could toss one of Bruno's toys for him and still catch most of what Reid was saying.

"Hey, Thomas . . . Yeah, it's good to hear yours, too. Things are good. . . . Yeah, I'd say she's pleased with the young wine. To quote the lady, she thinks you hit another one out of the park. . . . No, they'll taste the remaining barrels tomorrow. . . . Sure we will. . . . How's she looking?" Reid paused.

Feeling his gaze upon her, Mia turned her head and met it.

"I'd say she's looking real well. Tanner. I think she forgot to wear her hat last week. Some new freckles have sprung up across her nose." When she scowled, he answered her with a teasing grin and continued his conversation. "Yeah, she does. I'm a little worried she's getting too scrawny. I went into the kitchen just now, and there wasn't enough to feed a mouse. . . . Mm-hmm, I'll do that. And did she tell you about Bruno, her dog? He's a big, hairy mutt she adopted. Follows her around everywhere. You'll get a look at his ugly mug when you guys Skype. . . . Yeah, the family is fine, thanks. Busy. We're bringing artists over here to sketch the vineyard. . . . No, it was Mia's idea. That's right, Mia's doing a great job—just as you predicted. And Pascale—things are good between you? . . . Glad to hear it. . . . Same goes, old man. Call whenever you can. . . . I will," he said, and with a laugh he clicked off the phone.

Mia tossed Bruno's rope toy and watched him galumph across the lawn for it. Picking it up in his mouth, he shook it as if it were a snake before trotting back and dropping the vanquished rope at her feet. "Thomas sounded happy, didn't he?" she said, not turning around.

"He did. He misses you, though. You caught that, right?"

She heard Reid rise to his feet. "Reid?"

"Yeah?"

"Thank you," she whispered, blinking her tears away.

"You're welcome. Here." He handed her a slice of cheddar and a hunk of the seeded bread. "Eat this."

"So I can regain all the weight I've apparently lost," she said with a sniff.

"Yup. You're wasting away."

"Tell that to my jeans." She took a bite of the bread and cheese. "I can't believe you shared that hogwash with Thomas."

He dropped down next to her on the step. "He wants to know that kind of stuff. Like I said, he's family."

"The best kind," she agreed. "Oh, cripes, I forgot to tell him about Jay."

"Why should you? Since he's not the best kind."

"Not by any stretch of the imagination," she agreed drily. "But Thomas would probably want to know that he paid a visit. I wonder if Jay has tried to contact Thomas."

"Unlikely. Jay's doubtless figured out he's tapped that source dry." He turned to look at her. "Mia, don't even start feeling guilty. I told you what Grant found out about Jay's business interests."

"I remember." She sighed inwardly. According to the Knowleses' head of security, Jay and his associates owned a string of super-sleazy strip joints. Grant Hayes's contacts had also discovered that Jay was in hock up to his eyeballs. He'd been losing big time at the tables recently—which explained where Thomas's money had gone. "No, I'm not feeling guilty," she said.

"That's a relief. The guy's worse than a hustler, Mia. He'd steal the collection money in church." He thumped her casually on the back as she choked on a mouthful of bread and cheese. "Luckily, I think he's understood he won't be able to play you, either."

She gave a final cough. "No, he won't."

"Good. Let's stop talking about Jay. It puts me off my feed." He stood, and she saw him grab the wine and glasses as well as a black-and-gray-striped blanket she didn't recognize.

"Where'd you get that?"

"My truck. I keep a spare saddle blanket in case I need to bring an injured animal home to Quinn. Come on. Let's take the rest of the food and have a picnic on the lawn. We can watch the sunset."

Chapter TWENTY-FOUR

THEY FINISHED THE picnic food in short order. Only the wine remained. They drank it slowly, watching the sun settle lightly on the distant mountains while magenta streaks crossed the deepening sky.

"A good day," Reid observed idly. He was lying on his side, propped up by his elbow. He held his wineglass in his other hand.

"Mm-hmm." And much of it was due to him, Mia thought. It had done her so much good to talk to Thomas. His voice had soothed like a balm. And if Reid hadn't gently bullied her into making the call, she'd have stalled, cutting off her nose to spite her face. Had she ever bothered to see the deep well of kindness, of generosity, in him before? No, and the realization shamed her. No matter what happened between them or how this "thing" they were in ended, she hoped she'd never lose sight of what he'd done for her.

She felt the weight of his gaze on her. How incredible that he'd noticed the newly sprouted freckles across the bridge of her nose and cheeks, there because she'd forgotten to wear her hat one day last week. He was more observant than any man she knew. No wonder she was helplessly in love with him.

"So what do you think of the wine?"

His question brought her up short.

"The wine?" she repeated.

"I chose it because I thought it would be different from your Pinot. But there's something about it." He paused, frowning as he considered. "No, I can't put my finger on it."

She glanced at him curiously, then raised the glass. She dipped her nose into the bowl and inhaled the wine's bouquet. Taking a slow sip, she let it speak to her and then let her mouth "chew" it for a better feel. She swallowed. "A solid Napa Cab," she said. "I like its depth. It's got some nice notes of cherry, pepper, and licorice, and just a tease of eucalyptus. It's a powerful wine without being obnoxious."

He laughed softly. "Ah, the 'tease of eucalyptus'— that's what slipped by me. Did you know that when you study a wine you angle your head slightly? Sometimes you bite your lower lip—a light scrape of your teeth. Did you realize that?"

"Um, no." She fought not to bite her lip.

"When you bring the glass to your lips and let the wine flow into your mouth, and you hold it there, I like to think about all you're feeling, all you're sensing."

She shifted and cleared her throat. "Reid, are you trying to seduce me?"

His smile made her body heat up several degrees. "Oh, most definitely."

"Oh." Wow, did he really think he needed to? She was already melting.

"I was hoping you'd take off your shirt."

Instinctively, she glanced about.

"Everyone's gone home for the day," he said, guessing the reason. "It's just us and Bruno."

"We'd be giving Bruno quite an eyeful—"

"Bruno's witnessed some of the worst man does. I

doubt anything we do will faze him. Lose the shirt, Mia."

Thank God it was a scoop-necked T. She couldn't have handled buttons with his glittering gaze searing her. She dragged the shirt up, exposing skin that tingled and burned.

"Mm-hmm. A purple lace bra. Did you choose it because you knew you were going to be sampling the grape today?"

"No." She swallowed. "I chose it because of you. I thought you might like it."

His blue eyes turned silver as desire flared in them. In a voice now sandpapery-rough, he answered, "I do, but not as much as what's beneath it."

This time she took the initiative. Her hands went to the catch between her breasts. She unhooked it, paused, and slowly peeled the fabric away. Her breasts felt heavy; her nipples were already puckered and aching for his touch. For his taste.

"Exquisite."

Reid hadn't moved from his lounging pose. His eyes were hooded now, giving him an almost sleepy air. But behind the heavy lids, his gaze devoured.

Around them the air thickened, charged with desire. A muscle twitched beneath his cheek.

"The rest needs to go, too," he said.

Her eyebrows rose. "Does it?" She took a deep breath and released it, aware of how it made her chest rise and fall and how he tracked the movement.

His laughter was warm with appreciation. "You've become a tease. Damn, you're beautiful."

She bit her lip to contain her smile. Lowering her gaze, she let it land on the unmistakable bulge pressing against the fly of his jeans. "Speaking of beautiful bodies, will that make an appearance?"

"Rest assured." And the bulge grew bigger.

Their eyes met and her smile broke free. How delicious that seduction was a two-way street, she thought.

Emboldened, her fingers traced a lazy path down her torso, stopping when she reached the metal button of her jeans. She freed it and then tugged the zipper down, revealing the matching purple fabric of her bikini bottoms.

"My compliments on the lingerie of the day. But, again, it can't compare to what's underneath."

She grasped the waistband of her jeans to drag them over her hips, then paused. "Show me something."

He sat up. His shirt flew through the air.

She laughed in delight.

He was gorgeous. A perfect specimen of male beauty, possessing just the right combination of hewn muscle and bone, the whole kissed by the sun and sprinkled with light-brown hair. And here he was, whipping off his clothes like a horny teenager desperate to get naked with her. How could she not love him?

"Your turn, Mia," he prompted, grinning.

She shook her head. "Oh, I need a little more incentive than that."

"You drive a hard bargain, lady." With quick, efficient movements, he unbuckled his belt, unzipped his jeans, and shucked them, shedding his underwear, too.

He wasn't just gorgeous. He was awesome.

"You're very good for my self-esteem," she said faintly. His erection never failed to impress.

"Sweetheart, I'm willing to be very good for whatever you need."

"Really?" She licked her upper lip.

His penis lengthened.

Incentive enough. Matching his previous pace, she yanked off her jeans but slowed as she worked her panties down, uncovering her triangle of brown curls, then rolling the panties down her legs. Her heartbeat was pounding in her ears by the time she flicked her wrist, tossing them aside.

His chest was heaving. "God, Mia," he said hoarsely, and then swallowed visibly. "Okay, listen."

"I'm all ears."

"Thankfully a couple of other things besides."

"You noticed."

"I'm nothing if not observant. I need you to lie back and lift your arms over your head."

The movement made her back arch, thrusting her breasts toward the sky. Impossibly, her nipples drew even tighter, into twin points of need.

"Oh, yeah. Stay just like that. You know, don't you, that you drive me out of my mind?"

"Reid." She moaned his name in invitation.

"Right here." He swung a muscled leg over and straddled her hips. At the contact, she bucked, her heat meeting his hard length, her gasp mingling with his groan.

"Witch." He groaned again. Squeezing her with his horseman's thighs, he said, "Hold still. I'm about to conduct a very delicate operation, and it requires total concentration. I can't have you distracting me."

"And the nature of this procedure?" Blatantly ignoring his command, she arched her hips again.

He hissed a breath. "Dual nature, actually. It's clear I need to hone my Cab-tasting skills. I thought I might also catalog the flavors to be discovered in the lush peaks and valleys of Mia Bodell." With a wicked grin, he leaned over and plucked his wineglass off the blanket. It was still full.

"So, are you ready?"

She managed an "mm-hmm." Then her breath caught, lodging in her throat, as she watched him dip his finger into the glass and bring the moistened tip to her breast. At the touch, her breath escaped on a ragged moan.

To the sound of her soft pants, he painted her flesh. And then licked it clean, naming honey, vanilla, and cinnamon as he went. With every damp drag of his callused finger, with every lap of his tongue, she heaved and writhed.

Her nipples begged for his touch. He obliged, drawing a tiny circle with his finger over the aching tip, and she cried out as heat pooled deep and low, making her throb. He glanced up from his handiwork. At the look on his face, her toes curled into the wool saddle blanket.

Slowly, he lowered his mouth and drew her nipple deep inside. He suckled until she was writhing against his erection, opening her legs to let him feel the dampness between her thighs.

He released her nipple, only to latch on hungrily to its twin, feasting with his tongue and nipping with his teeth. She arched off the blanket, offering him more.

"Honey and salt, mint and rose."

Relentless, he continued at his task, licking the wet trails covering her, naming flavors as he consumed her. She lost track of them, lost track of everything but the cool glide of wine over her body, the fiery lashes of his tongue, the press of his rock-hard length against her aching center. With every breath, she absorbed the scent of him. Leather, horse, sweat, citrus, and man mingled with the warm earth beneath her. She let it fill her, let it enter her heart and flood her veins, until he was in every cell of her being.

He'd reached her navel. This time he didn't dip his finger into the glass but, with the seriousness of a scientist, poured a slow trickle of the cool liquid into the shallow indentation. Her body convulsed with shudders as his tongue dipped into the pool and lapped it in lazy circles.

Panicked by the wave of pleasure bearing down on her, she cried, "Oh my God, Reid. Please, I'm so close."

"The best is yet to come."

Had she not been on the brink of madness, everything inside her straining wildly, she might have laughed.

"I can taste nutmeg and musk. You're addictive, Mia. I can't get enough of you. But I want the sweetest taste of all, the one that haunts me. Will you give it to me?" he asked, already shifting lower and settling between thighs that quivered in welcome. "No wine this time. I want the pure, unadulterated taste of you. It puts any vintage to shame." He spread her legs wider still. "God, you're a vision," he whispered hoarsely.

His lips closed over her, and she screamed from the exquisite rush of pleasure that swept through her. Arching into the magic of his mouth, she shared her passion, her essence, and her endless desire for him.

Rising to his knees, Reid lifted her legs and, wrapping them about him, entered her in a single powerful thrust. Joined, he held himself deep inside as she trembled about him. With infinite care, he drank the tears that slipped from her eyes.

Their hands linked, they began to move. Alternately guiding and urging each other, together they found joy in the gathering darkness.

IT WAS ALL fun and games until somebody lost their heart. And Reid knew his was long and irretrievably gone. Lost forever to Mia on the night of their impromptu picnic, when she'd taken him into her body, and her sweet cry had called to his heart and then captured it.

"Forever" was a damned scary word for a guy who'd always lived in the here and now. He was still coming to grips with the notion. But it was getting harder and harder to imagine a future without her. It was that simple.

A sudden flash of russet caught his attention. Sirrus spotted the steer, too, and Reid only had to close his legs and move his hand slightly forward on Sirrus's neck, and the gelding surged toward the runaway.

Reid angled his body forward as his horse ate up the distance. Then they were upon him. It didn't take long for the bovine to understand that Sirrus could anticipate his every turn and feint and wasn't afraid to gallop right next to his massive body, so close that Reid's chaps brushed the dark-red hide. Nor did Sirrus hesitate to dash in front of the steer, cutting off his getaway route. Spooked, the beast gave up his attempt and, braying angrily, ran back to the slow-moving herd. Sirrus and Reid resumed their position on its right flank.

The sound of a hundred cattle pounding the earth with their hooves, their snorts and bellows combining with the men's shouts and whistles and the yips of the two cattle dogs, made it almost impossible for Reid to hear his own thoughts.

It was why he was more than happy to be out here in the company of Ward and their dad, their foreman, Pete, and two of their wranglers, Frank and Jim. They were rounding up the selected steers to take them to the lower pasture, where they would graze until it was time to send them to market.

Ordinarily, Quinn would have joined them—she and Domino loved the work—but she and Rick, another ranch hand, had taken Mia and Tess for a trail ride, along with some of the artist guests who'd arrived earlier in the day.

The official start of the artists' weekend was this evening. Tomorrow the participants would divide into groups, some painting views of the ranch, some heading over to Mia's to test their talent at capturing the vineyard's terrain, and some setting up their easels on the banks of Silver Lake.

The same steer as before cut loose, but this time he avoided Sirrus, running toward Rio, Ward's gelding, instead. But Rio wasn't tolerating any renegade cows, either, and the gelding made quick work of returning the steer to the herd.

Reid felt a flash of sympathy for the persistent beast. He understood the animal's innate desire for freedom. Unfortunately, the steer didn't stand a chance against their experienced cow horses.

Just as his heart didn't stand a chance against Mia.

For all Reid's professed need for independence, his heart craved Mia, in all her sweet-tart complexity, more. Even the prerogative to bed another woman—or a dozen—had lost its piquancy. Compared to Mia, anyone else would be a watered-down imitation.

They'd covered about four miles of the ranch's rolling meadows when Reid spied in the distance the last gate, which would bring them to the lower pasture. He drew his lips back and whistled, piercing the noise. The others raised their hands, signaling they'd heard, and he and Sirrus galloped ahead. The gate needed to be opened and secured far in advance, so the mass of bodies would continue to move forward. If the cattle were given a chance to stop, more of them might entertain the notion to head for higher ground.

Once he'd opened and secured the wide metal gate to the wood-and-wire fence so it wouldn't accidentally swing and spook the herd, Reid loped back, positioning Sirrus where the gelding could block any bovines that didn't feel inclined to pass through to the adjacent fields.

Fortunately, the herd was accustomed to being guided through the various gates on the property, and while the pace slowed as the formation funneled like cars on a highway with a lane closure, none balked.

His father, astride Kane, his big chestnut gelding, had moved closer to Reid, the two of them now taking up the rear along with Bo and Hank, Pete's border collies.

"They're looking good, these steers. We'll drop hay down nonetheless to make sure we don't overgraze the pasture and that their weight is maintained," Daniel said. Decades of ranching had given him a keen sense for how much grazing a pasture could tolerate. In addition to raising certified organic and grass-fed Angus beef, the Knowleses also practiced sustainable farming. Reid shared his father's pride in their careful stewardship of the land.

"I'll let Pete know to drop bales," Reid said, as the last of the herd passed through the opening. Already the steers in front had begun to disperse. Their heads down and their broomlike tails swishing, they set to grazing on the two-hundred-acre pasture.

Reid guided Sirrus over to the fence. Using his legs to direct the gelding, he grabbed hold of the gate, swung it shut, and latched it.

His father had waited for him. Sirrus and Kane trotted side by side, Kane's coppery neck bobbing in unison with Sirrus's dapple-gray one.

"Glad to see your eye's all cleared up," Daniel said.

"Yup."

"Everything's working out okay with Mia? Todd Wilkins lay down the slabs for you?"

"He did a great job. It looks sharp with the tables and chairs. Thanks for suggesting we piggyback on one of the ranch's orders." They'd gotten a steep discount. Mia had been pleased, so he'd been doubly happy.

"Your mom's idea. Mia's a nice young woman."

His dad wasn't nearly as skilled at fishing as his mom.

"Yup. Mia's going to plant some pink roses in the ground after the harvest."

"And the harvest? She said the grapes will be ready for picking next week, right?"

"Yeah. She wants them to hang on the vine a little longer. The weather's promising to hold."

"She's got her crew in place?"

"Yeah. Paul and Roberto's wives will be there, as well as some of the cousins. They're all experienced pickers and have worked the vineyard before."

"Good. If she needs extra hands—"

"I'll let you know, Dad."

"Good, good." Daniel paused. "Your mom and I are pleased at how things seem to be moving in the right direction over at the vineyard. But, well, like I said before, it'd be nice not to have this deal bleed money."

"I don't think you need to worry," Reid said. "The

harvest is looking good, the wine aging in the barrels shows real promise, and I tasted the wine Thomas and Mia just bottled. It's excellent."

"That's right—you pre-ordered a hundred cases. Thomas certainly knows how to make wine. You're confident Mia's got the touch?"

He grinned. "Dad, we're talking Mia, okay?"

Daniel smiled and the lines around his blue eyes deepened. "Good point."

"You know, she's the one who thought of holding events at the vineyard. I floated the idea past Jeff. He got jazzed, to put it mildly. He immediately began to rattle off special pairing menus that we could plan throughout the year to showcase the wine's versatility and the local produce. And I don't need to tell you how Tess reacted to the suggestion of holding weddings there. Phil even jumped on the bandwagon." Phil Onofrie handled reservations and helped with marketing and publicity. A techno geek, he was on occasion a bit of a prick, given more to grousing than to enthusiasm. It had surprised the hell out of Reid when he'd volunteered to get Mia's website up and running.

"Just checking." Daniel reached out and slapped Reid's shoulder. "I'm real happy for you, son. Mia's not like the other women, is she?"

"No, she's not," Reid replied, conceding that perhaps his father was better at fishing for information than he'd suspected.

When Reid spotted Mia among the group of trail riders returning to the corral, he'd already untacked Sirrus, sponged him off with cool water, fed him a carrot from Quinn's secret stash, and turned him out with his best buddies, Forster and Ziggy.

Mia was riding better, he noted. She sat straighter

and more balanced in the saddle, and her grip on the reins was light, her right hand relaxed and resting on her thigh. He watched her body shift, following Glory's rolling walk. Nice, very nice. Good thing he'd taken the time to give her all those private riding lessons. A cocky smile split his face.

"Hey," he said as he approached her, when the horses had come to a halt by the barn closest to the corral. "How'd Glory go for you?" He waved to Al and Mel—ranch hands who'd come over to help the riders dismount and to unsaddle the horses—to let them know he'd take care of Mia and Glory.

"He was great. I can't believe he's only been here for five months. He seems to have the trails memorized."

"He'd been an experienced trail horse before Quinn adopted him. But she took him out herself in the beginning to make sure he was dependable and rock solid. He's been a great addition. Here, let me help you dismount."

"Oh, I've got it."

"Come on, are you really going to deprive me of a chance to put my hands on you?"

She blushed. "I'm awfully sweaty."

"That's okay. So am I."

"Well, then." She flashed a grin and swung her leg over the saddle. Glory wasn't a big horse. He stood about 15.2 hands. As Reid wrapped his hands about Mia's waist, eyeing the delicious curves of her ass and getting all sorts of ideas for what he'd like to do later with her—perhaps in the shower, or over the arm of a sofa—he wished the horse were at least 17.1.

He leaned in a fraction so her body rubbed his as he guided her down. Even this light contact sent a charge directly to his groin. When Mia's feet reached the ground, Reid couldn't resist ducking his head, dodging the brim of the straw cowboy hat Quinn had given her, and kissing her neck. Opening his mouth, he scraped his teeth over the delicate skin, scoring it lightly, and then licking it all better.

Yeah, she tasted salty. He'd like to make her saltier still and deliciously wet. Reluctantly, he stepped back. It wouldn't be good to get carried away and start doing things that too many people might witness—his family, in particular. They had enough ideas about how deeply Mia and he were involved.

"Mia, Reid, how nice to see you two together."

Busted, he thought, as he turned around and faced his mother. It occurred to him it was why he enjoyed being at the vineyard with Mia so much. He loved his family, but they were always around here. "Hi, Mom," he said evenly.

Mia had spun around hastily, and he bet she was thanking Quinn for the hat she wore. He knew exactly what color pink her cheeks must be right now. He'd have given her braided ponytail a teasing tug if his mother's eyes weren't trained on them.

"Hi, Adele," Mia said politely. "That's such a nice outfit."

His mother was in hostess mode, dressed in a lavender-blue blouse, a necklace made of chunky dark-blue beads, and a straight skirt. The skirt ended mid-calf, allowing her cowboy boots' stitching to be revealed.

"Thank you, dear. And you're looking more and more beautiful. Riding obviously suits you. You had fun?"

Reid bit the inside of his lip to keep from laughing at his mother's comment about how riding suited Mia. Of course, he agreed wholeheartedly. And Mia did look radiant.

"Oh! Yes—yes!" Mia stammered, her voice pitched high from self-consciousness. "It was great! I was just telling Reid how nice Glory is. Tess and I rode next to each other, so we got to chat. And I met some of your guests—Tess introduced me."

"Madlon Glenn arrived just awhile ago with her husband, Kirk. She's the one who sparked Tess's imagination for the artists' weekend. Madlon says the instructors holding the workshops are thrilled at the prospect of using the vineyard. Apparently all those rows of vines are great for perspective. We're so grateful you're letting us use the property."

"But of course," Mia said. "Thanks to you, I'll even have a place for the artists to sit."

Listening, Reid had the feeling that his mother might go on for another couple of hours and that by the end of her and Mia's chat she'd have nailed down a wedding date and begun discussing what style of wedding gown would best suit Mia's voluptuous body.

Damn it, he refused to be rushed. There was no point in taking the next step until the harvest was over and the grapes were fermenting in the tanks. Mia would be working insane hours until then. He needed those weeks to figure out how to plan his proposal and convince Mia that she wanted to spend the rest of her life with him.

She was happy, he knew, so it should be a simple thing to pull off. Yet the idea made him nervous. Tense.

Perhaps that's why his tone came off sharper than normal when he spoke, why he cut off his mother, who was in the midst of talking about some planters she could give Mia to decorate the terrace until she had time to plant the roses. "Sorry to interrupt, Mom, but Glory needs to be put away. Come on, Mia. I'll show you how to sponge-bathe him."

His mother's smile was unfazed. "Of course, dear." Addressing Mia again, she said, "Would you like to stay for dinner afterward?"

"We have previous plans." At least he did. And they didn't include anyone but Mia and him.

A flicker of annoyance flashed in his mother's blue gaze. Damn if it didn't make him feel guilty. But silently he stared her down.

He felt Mia's gaze shift between them. "Thank you for the invitation, Adele, but I should get back. I've left Bruno at home for longer than I like. And I need to make sure everything is neat and tidy for our visiting artists tomorrow."

"Well, perhaps you'll come to the dinner tomorrow night, then."

"I'd like that," Mia said.

His mother's answering smile was warm and, Reid thought, triumphant.

She really needed a new hobby.

Once Reid had removed Glory's saddle and bridle and draped the saddle blanket on top of the railing to air-dry, he showed Mia how to sponge the gelding off and then how to wield the metal scraper so his coat would dry faster. He talked about how important it was to check that a horse's chest was cool to the touch before turning it out or putting it back in a stall.

They led Glory to the corral, where Reid told Mia to position herself by the side of the horse's head when she unbuckled his halter and to take a step back as she removed it and turned him loose—always a good precaution when dealing with a strange horse.

He even got a laugh out of her when Glory wheeled about, trotted to the center of the corral, sank to his knees, and proceeded to give himself a dirt bath, his hooves pawing the air as he rubbed his back, withers, and rump.

"I feel almost as dirty as Glory, and I didn't even have

to get down and roll on the ground," she said, a smile in her voice.

He tipped the brim of her hat up. "I have a solution for that. How about we go spring Bruno and take a shower? Because I'm a nice guy, I'll even sponge you off."

It was only because he'd pushed her hat back that he caught her wistful expression. Then it was gone.

"Sure. That sounds nice."

Nice? He intended to make their evening together a hell of a lot more than that.

Chapter TWENTY-SIX

IT WAS A strange and novel experience to see the vine-yard temporarily overtaken by people who wielded paintbrushes and pencils rather than pruning shears and wire ties and who had no connection to wine-making. Though a number of the ranch's art-loving guests had mentioned that they'd like to buy a few bottles of the winery's Pinot Noir as souvenirs of the landscape they were attempting to capture on canvas and paper, which was gratifying and went some way toward alleviating the headache pounding Mia's temples.

She hadn't slept well, plagued by confusing dreams. Their origins were easily identifiable. The approaching harvest and all it would require of her were making her stressed. Her relationship with Reid—or lack of it—was making her emotions seesaw and her stomach clench. Sometimes she was convinced he felt something for her; other times she despaired of his ever wanting more than friendly bouts of hot sex with her.

His attitude yesterday at the ranch conformed exactly to the frustrating pattern. His lightning-fast nixing of his mother's invitation to stay over for dinner made it transparently clear that he didn't want Mia crossing the lines he'd drawn in their relationship. Apart from her trail rides at the ranch, Mia was never invited over. And that hurt, because of course the ranch represented so much of who Reid truly was.

But how could she argue or even broach the topic of whether he was interested only in screwing around when he was so generous with what he *was* willing to share?

He never failed to help her at the vineyard; he listened to her ideas and did his best to implement them; he got along with her crew and respected their work. And she'd have to be insane to find fault with how he treated her body. He gave and gave, bringing her hours of pleasure.

And whenever Mia did go for a ride at the ranch, Reid either made the time to accompany her or was there to send her off or greet her upon her return. He invariably took the time to teach her something about the horse she'd ridden. She loved that.

She loved so much about him.

But she felt stuck in a weird place, where she had to reconcile being worshipped by a warm and indulgent lover with being held at a painful distance when it came to sharing his life. No matter how she looked at it, she couldn't find a satisfactory explanation, except that maybe she'd been right: She was the chocolate of the day.

The realization made the extraordinary blue sky darken to gunmetal gray and her head continue its vicious pounding.

Mia had spent the morning walking the aisles with Paul, moving from block to block, sampling the grapes by taste and also by conducting a Brix test to determine the sugar content. They needed to know which blocks were ripening fastest, as they'd be the first to be harvested. Bruno had come along, too, but leashed, to prevent him from wandering off and greeting every artist and sniffing every pencil box and palette.

At break time, she and Bruno walked back up to the house. When Reid had driven over this morning in one of the two vans full of artists, he'd also delivered baskets of granola scones, peach muffins, and baby quiches, which Roo Rodgers had baked for the guests to enjoy when they were finished painting and drawing.

She set the baskets out now, along with pitchers of lemon and mint-sprigged ice water, on two of the tables gracing her new patio.

The noise of a vehicle rolling up the drive had her looking up with a smile. No matter how confused she was about Reid, when he was near, happiness outweighed all else.

Her smile died when, instead of white van, she saw a silver BMW roll to a stop. Dread invaded when Jay climbed out of the car.

He was dressed in a black shirt that was unbuttoned too low and fit too snugly, white jeans, and black driving mocs. His skin looked like polished leather.

As he approached, his sweeping gaze took in the new patio, the tables and chairs, as well as the food-laden baskets and pitchers and glasses she'd set out. Then he looked at her and, unconsciously, her hand tightened around Bruno's leash.

A fierce growl erupted from Bruno. She glanced down at him in surprise. The dog had shown nothing but outsize affection toward every human he'd encountered since she'd adopted him.

Jay halted. "What the fuck is that?" he demanded, jerking his chin at Bruno, who looked even bigger with his hackles up.

"This is my dog, Bruno. He's very protective of me." Mia didn't know if this was actually the case, but he'd obviously sensed her tension and responded to it. "Sit,

Bruno," she said, patting the dome of his head when he obeyed immediately. If she'd been alone, she'd have dropped to her knees and hugged him for stopping Jay in his tracks.

"And what's all this?" He waved his hand.

"It's a tasting area for the visitors. We're going to put one inside the winery, too."

"Getting real swank around here with your new partners, huh?"

She kept her voice even. "Most wineries have tasting rooms. We've just never been able to allocate funds for one."

"And who are those people camped out on the edge of the vineyard?"

"Guests of the ranch. They're sketching and painting the scene."

"Well, la-di-fucking-da," he said with a sneer. "So you haven't only gotten cozy with Reid. You're busy sucking up to the whole family, aren't you, cuz?"

"Why are you here?" She wanted Jay gone before the ranch's guests came up for their refreshments. She wanted him long gone before Reid or any Knowles appeared.

"I came about the money. I still need it, Mia."

"You'll have to wait until the next quarter for your payment, because I don't have any to give you."

"Oh, but you can get some. You see, I'm just not cool with having to wait for my cut. I've been thinking that all you need to do to help me out is to ask the Knowleses for an advance on your share of the profits. They'll do it. They like you, and they're rolling in the dough."

"I wouldn't dream of asking them. Besides, there's no way to estimate what the profits will be."

"Don't give me that bullshit. I grew up on this fucking vineyard. The weather's been great. It'll be a good harvest."

"Maybe, but I still won't ask them." She straightened her spine and eyed him with cold distaste. "The Knowleses made a deal with Thomas and have been incredibly helpful to me. I'm not going to turn around and ask them for money to fund your so-called clubs."

His sneer disappeared. Now his expression was even more repellent. "Listen to Saint Mia. Funny, you pretending to be holier than thou, when your mother was a whore, a drugged-out whore. Even funnier, when you're spreading your legs for Reid." He laughed. "Of course, that's a dream come true for you, isn't it? You've been wanting to spread your legs for him ever since you figured out what was between his. Bet you can't get enough of his dick."

"You're disgusting." She held her arms tightly against her sides to hide the tremors racking her.

"Ooh, that hurts," he said, jutting his lower lip out as if he might cry. "So what, you think Reid's actually going to marry someone like you, someone whose mother fucked anyone who looked at her? Get real. He's screwing you because he can. You're a convenient lay, nothing more, Mia."

"Get out of here, Jay, or I'll let my dog loose on you."

"I'm going, but you're going to regret not helping me, Mia."

❧

Reid had intended to be at the vineyard while the artists were sketching, but Mel, who helped tend the flock, had come upon twenty of their Lincoln sheep with pink eye. The infected sheep needed to be separated from the flock and quickly treated to prevent the disease—as contagious in ruminants as in humans—from spreading and perhaps affecting the dairy goats, as well.

Sooner made quick work of rounding up the affected sheep and herding them into the barn and then into the

pens. The more-painstaking labor involved cleaning the
inflamed eyes and applying ointment to them.

By the time Reid and Mel had finished and washed
carefully with a disinfectant soap, it was already close
to when he should be driving one of the vans over to
pick up the artists.

They were milling around the new patio when he
parked the van behind the one Estelle Vargas had
driven. Estelle worked the front desk, but, like most of
Silver Creek's staff, she was always ready to lend a hand
with whatever needed doing—chauffeuring guests included.

"They don't look like they're in any hurry to leave,"
Reid said as they crossed the courtyard.

"It's real pretty here," Estelle said.

"It is," he agreed. "Have you met Mia?"

"No, not yet. I've heard Tess and Adele mention her a
lot, though."

"Come on, I'll introduce you."

Something was wrong, Reid realized. To her credit,
Mia was doing her best to pretend otherwise. She was
nodding and keeping a smile on her face as an earnest
white-haired man in wire-rim glasses told her about a
series of portraits he'd done of butchers in his home-
town in North Dakota. He'd painted some standing
proudly behind the glass cases with the different cuts of
meats piled in the foreground; others he'd depicted
wielding cleavers over a carcass. He loved all the rich
reds he could use in the composition. He wasn't so sure
the greens of Mia's vineyard would have the same visual
impact—not that they weren't beautiful. Maybe he
could paint her portrait.

Thinking perhaps that Mia's tense stance had something to do with the man's enthusiasm for certain paint-

ing subjects, Reid stepped forward. "Excuse me, Mia."
He glanced at the older man's name tag: JOE KREANY.
Since some of the artists had come from as far away as
North Carolina, they all wore them. "I wanted to make
sure Mr. Kreany has had a chance to enjoy Roo's baked
goods." He smiled at the man. "You must have worked
up an appetite this morning."

"They do look tasty, don't they?" With a nod, Joe
Kreany wandered off to the table that had a basket
brimming with scones and muffins.

Reid looked back at Mia. "Hi."

She managed a brighter smile for him, but it failed to
dispel the tension in her body.

"Mia, I wanted to introduce you to Estelle Vargas."

Mia said hello and nodded in recognition when Reid
added that she was married to Carlos, one of the wranglers.

"Can I offer you anything, Estelle? A glass of lemon
water? A quiche? There's enough food here for an
army," Mia said.

"It'll get eaten, don't worry. We'll leave some for you
and your staff and bring the rest down to the barns.
Carlos and Jim—do you know him? He's tall, thin as
a toothpick, and has ginger hair—they live for Roo's
baking." Glancing around, Estelle spotted Bruno lying
placidly on his dog bed, his chin resting on a red fuzzy
toy while he watched the humans eating and chattering.
"Hey, what a great dog. Mind if I pet him?"

"Of course not."

Reid noted that Mia watched as Estelle bent over
Bruno and let him sniff her hand before stroking his
massive head. The dog thumped his tail enthusiastically
and promptly rolled over onto his back for a belly rub.

Mia's shoulders relaxed slightly. But now that he was
standing close, Reid saw just how pale she was, as if
she'd been thoroughly spooked. He couldn't understand

why. Other than Mr. Kreany and his blood-soaked slabs of meat, these people seemed a benign lot. He'd have thought she'd be pleased that they'd clearly enjoyed their morning at the vineyard.

"Are you okay?" He raised his hand to stroke her cheek and frowned in surprise when she flinched and took a step back.

"I have a headache."

"Oh, I thought maybe you'd seen a ghost." The joke, admittedly weak, fell flat. She didn't even attempt a smile.

"No, no ghost," she said, her voice mixed with irritation and a shot of something else he couldn't quite pin down. It worried him, which had the effect of sending a jolt of annoyance through him.

"Sorry. A lame attempt at humor. Listen, you don't have to stick around."

"Where am I supposed to go? This is my home."

Whoa. He took a breath. "What I meant was, I can take care of this." He checked his watch. "Estelle and I'll give them fifteen more minutes here to enjoy Roo's food. Why don't you go lie down?"

She shook her head. "I can't. The de-stemmer needs to be cleaned, the valves on the tanks checked, and then there's all the other equipment for the harvest we need to get ready."

Somehow he knew it wouldn't be wise to suggest that a short nap might make the work go better. "Okay, how about this? We ditch the dinner tonight. I'll come over here instead and cook for you. If that doesn't restore you, I have a few tried-and-true techniques—"

"No—no, thanks. I think I want to be alone tonight."

He raked a hand through his hair. Jesus, she was in a hell of a mood. "Mia, you should—"

"Actually, I'm thinking maybe it's time to bring this

thing between us to an end. I don't really see it going anywhere, do you?"

The air flew from his lungs. Reeling, he looked around, trying to get his bearings. The amateur artists were standing around in their comfortable cottons, sensible shoes, and floppy hats or baseball caps, wiping crumbs from their mouths and sipping water as they discussed shadows, light, and horizon lines. The picture of sanity. But Mia and what she'd just said? Insane.

"Are you serious?"

He saw her throat work. How many times had he kissed that slender column or run his mouth down its length to feel the pounding of her pulse—and know he was the reason it raced?

"Why wouldn't I be serious?" she asked flatly. Coldly.

Anger colored his hurt. "A hell of a place and time to dump me, Mia."

She raised her chin. "I didn't realize there was ever a good time to be dumped. Besides, I'm not sure it's dumping if we never had a relationship, is it? I'm just putting an end to the 'thing,' to the sex, which is all this was for you, right?"

He looked at her, anger, hurt, and a terrible sense of betrayal churning inside him. He wanted to grab her by the shoulders and yell at her for stomping all over his heart. "Yeah, sex was pretty much all it was."

She went a shade paler. One of the artist guests here could probably have named that particular shade of white. Reid only knew it made the green and brown in her wide eyes even more vibrant.

He hated himself for having retaliated to her stupid question by saying something even stupider and, worse, patently untrue. What he hated most of all was that she believed it.

"Well, no hard feelings, then," she said tightly.

And he damned her for rallying and looking at him as

if he were a stranger. He wanted her to be as wrecked as he was, so he could put his arms around her and say he was sorry.

"I'm sure this won't affect our business relationship. I know how important that is to you and your family," she said.

He cocked his head. "You know, in all the years I've known you, I never took you for a bitch. I guess I wasn't paying attention."

That struck the mark, he thought, seeing the sudden sheen in her eyes. But then she whirled around and hurried over to where her dog lay. Crouching, she exchanged a few words with Estelle and then unhooked the leash she'd looped around a post. Mia led him away, disappearing into the winery.

He stared after her with eyes that burned.

Christ, what the hell had just happened? How had everything between them blown up with the force of a megaton bomb?

Estelle appeared at his side. "You think the guests are ready to leave yet?"

"I don't know about them, but I sure am."

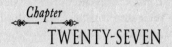

"Reid, darling!"

Stoically, he turned, his grip light on Bilbao's reins, and waited for his mother to catch up.

"I thought you'd be over at the vineyard."

"No, I'm riding Bilbao for Ward. He was checking the remainder of the flock for any more sheep that might have come down with pink eye, so he didn't have time today." He welcomed the ride. The young gelding would require all his concentration.

"So is Mia coming over on her own? You two haven't forgotten about the barbecue—"

"Mia's not coming. She's not feeling well."

"Oh, I'm sorry. Maybe you should—"

"Let it go, Mom, will you? Mia and I are over. And now I'd like it if you quit trying to matchmake. It's time to stop meddling."

A single blond eyebrow rose. "Meddling? How have I meddled, Reid?"

"You've pushed Mia and me together at every opportunity." And, damn it, he'd known the results would be disastrous.

"Excuse me. All I did—with your father and Thomas's wholehearted agreement—was ask you if you'd be willing to handle the marketing end of the winery, since you've done much the same for us." She paused. "But I'm very sorry to hear you and Mia have fought—"

His free hand fisted against the suede of his chaps. "We haven't fought. She ended it, civilly and coldly. And, yeah, you did meddle, constantly inviting her to dinner—"

"Really, Reid," his mother interrupted. "I had a very good reason to invite Mia over. I wanted to let her know how much we appreciated the hard work she's doing to make the winery a success. Thomas had Ellen and then Mia to rely on as backup. Mia's bearing the brunt of the work and responsibility alone. It seems to me she deserves to know that we recognize that and care about her. Inviting her to dinner is an easy—an obvious—way to demonstrate it." Her blue gaze pierced him. "I wonder, Reid, whether the real reason you're upset with me is that you neglected to do that simple thing yourself."

"Damned if I did."

"Did you let her know how you truly felt about her, how much you cared?"

When Reid didn't respond, Adele gave a small yet audible sigh and left.

He climbed into the saddle, an amazing feat, since his mother's words had made him feel like he was five years old again.

To his frustration, Reid soon discovered that finding a way to tell Mia how he felt wasn't easily accomplished. Part of the blame lay with him, he admitted grudgingly. He'd done a good bit of self-sabotaging over the weekend, spending it sulking, licking the wounds she'd inflicted with such stunning force, and growling at anyone who so much as looked at him.

But the next week taught him that even had he been

ready to face a second trampling of his heart, Mia wasn't willing to get within three feet of him. He'd never realized how nimble she was, assuming, conceitedly, that it was he who was the master at evasion.

When he did manage to occupy the same space as Mia, her vineyard crew and cellar assistants were always about. With the harvest scheduled to begin that week, their presence was wholly justified—and thoroughly frustrating.

Even more daunting than Mia's avoidance of him or the omnipresence of her staff was the careful politeness she displayed toward him whenever he addressed her. It was most effective, an impenetrable wall that loomed higher with every one of her guarded utterances.

God, he missed his tart and prickly Mia. Missed the exhilaration of matching wits with her, missed the sweet happiness of gliding into the silken heat of her body and feeling as if he was finally whole.

He ached for what he'd lost and prayed he'd get the chance to regain it.

The sun shone in Acacia, California, and misery reigned for Reid Knowles.

Mia welcomed the first day of the harvest with an enthusiasm that bordered on manic. The reason for her desperation had little to do with her desire to prove her talents as a winemaker. It was that the harvest would usher in eighteen-hour workdays. Thus a respite. Soon she'd be unable to think of anything but the grapes, the tons upon tons of grapes that required picking. Soon she'd be too busy to do anything other than concentrate on simply staying upright on her feet. Soon she'd be too consumed by the harvest's myriad demands to feel the pain of her broken heart and to pine for Reid. She'd be too damned tired to run to him and beg that he take her in his arms.

If she worked hard enough, ceaselessly enough, she might be able to blot out the horror and clammy fear that had seized her when she'd listened to Jay and his talk of revenge. His words had hurtled her back in time, reviving her insecurities and self-doubts. Too vulnerable, she'd succumbed to their insidious hold.

Would she have been capable of rallying and beating them back? She didn't know. Because any glimmer of hope in her breast was extinguished when Reid echoed her worst fears.

She loved him still and knew there would never be another love for her like Reid. But there was only heartache in loving him. That had always been the case for her, even as a foolish and lonely teen. So she embraced the backbreaking, mind-numbing work of the harvest. With her pruning shears, she cut the brown woody stems, dropped the black-purple fruit into the bin by her feet, and moved on to the next cluster, making her way down the fruit-laden row. The hours blurred, one into the next.

At night her tired brain offered an endless loop of the day. She dreamed of vines, of sturdy plastic bins piled high with pungent grapes. She dreamed of arm and back muscles strained from lifting the laden bins onto the flatbed of her truck. She even felt the heat of the sun penetrating her hat and shirt and heard the buzzing of bees searching out the sugar-laden fruit. And then she'd catch his low-pitched drawl, so beguiling, and she'd know it would haunt her forever.

Given the demands of the harvest, she should have been able to at least block Reid from her consciousness if not her dreams. But she'd never been able to ignore him. He'd always loomed larger, shone brighter, than anyone else.

Now he disarmed her with his helpfulness. When one of the crew needed a break, he took up the pruners, removing grapes and dropping them in the bin. He arranged for Jeff and Roo to supply lunches for the entire staff, delivering the food himself. When Mia's flatbed reached full capacity, he offered to drive it to the winery's processing area, so that Leo and Johnny, along with members of Roberto's family, could pick over the grapes.

She knew he did these things primarily to protect his family's interest in the winery. It was also the way the Knowleses did things. A good deal of Silver Creek Ranch's success lay in the fact that its diverse staff was treated and paid well. But when Reid snapped on Bruno's leash and took him for a walk, as if he knew that Mia would be too tired to provide one herself, a bittersweet yearning filled her.

"We did it, huh, Mia?" Paul said. He had an arm crossed in front of his chest and was rubbing his heavily muscled shoulder through the thin cotton of his shirt.

"Yeah, we did it." Her gaze swept the group. "I want to thank you—thank you all. The grapes look beautiful, and we beat the rains." Her voice shook from emotion and exhaustion.

They were all—she, Paul, Roberto, their wives, Anita and Sue, along with six members of Roberto's extended family—in various stages of dishevelment. Sweat and dirt streaked their clothes. Grape juice colored their hands, Johnny's and Leo's the most purple-stained of all. They stood in an open circle in the processing room, stiff and hollow-eyed but satisfied—giddy, even.

The grapes were in. This year's harvest had yielded twenty tons. After weighing the grapes, the crew had picked over them by hand, discarding the bits of yellowish leaves that had accidentally found their way into the bins and removing any green stems. The unwanted material would be used as compost along with the must—the remains of the grape skins and seeds—once the wine was fermented and pressed. Mia had instructed her crew to leave some of the grape clusters whole and attached to their woody stems. They would add flavor to the wine.

Mia had decided that only a quarter of the mountain of grapes would be crushed, and then only lightly. The rest would go into the tanks as whole berries. She wanted her vintage handled as gently as possible, letting the flavor of the Pinot come forth in its purest form.

The mix now sat in the gleaming vats where the cold soak and fermentation would take place.

"Yeah, we did it," she repeated, marveling. "I think this is going to be a great year for our Pinot."

Around her, everyone seconded the prediction and, going further, foresaw high scores and glowing write-ups.

From their lips to Bacchus's ears, she thought, borrowing one of Thomas's favorite expressions.

Before they could disperse to their homes, showers, sofas, and televised baseball games—or, in her case, a bowl of cereal and bed—Mia distributed the envelopes. She'd sat up the previous night, writing out everyone's paycheck. No one should have to wait to be paid after the arduous workdays each had put in. Smiles broke out as the checks were accepted and pocketed.

She felt the pull of Reid's gaze. Unable to resist, her eyes met his.

He was as coated in dirt as the rest of them, and a heavy stubble covered his cheeks. She knew exactly what that five-o'clock shadow felt like against her palm, the delicious scratch of it against the underside of her breast, the inside of her thigh. He'd never looked handsomer to her. Swallowing a lump of longing, she looked away, keeping her eyes fixed on a distant spot even as Reid spoke.

"I'd like to invite you all to the ranch this Sunday night for a barbecue. There'll be good food, dancing, beer, and, best of all, the Bodell Family Vineyard's 2010 Pinot."

A cheerful chorus of "Sounds great!" greeted Reid's invitation.

"Feel free to bring your family and friends; the more the merrier. Just let Mia know so we have an approximate head count," he told them.

With calls of thanks and goodbye to both Mia and Reid, her crew trickled out of the winery.

"See you *mañana*," Leo said to her. Of Mia's core staff, only Johnny and Leo would arrive early tomorrow, to monitor the fermenting juice and punch the cap.

"Great. I'll bring you and Johnny breakfast," she promised. She'd have to run to the general store and pick something up—maybe blueberry muffins from the luncheonette, in Thomas's honor.

"You rock, Mia," Johnny said. "Come on, Leo, we'll stick your bike in the back of my car. You're likely to end up in a ditch otherwise."

"Thanks, dude. Things do seem a tad hazy around the edges."

"Purple haze, huh?"

"You got it."

Their laughter followed them out.

Only Reid remained.

"Thank you, Reid, for inviting them all to the ranch," she said. "That was very kind of you." The three days of grape picking and sorting suddenly hit her. She was so tired she could barely stand. She locked her knees in an attempt to hide it. Far more difficult to conceal was her nervousness at being alone with him. Please, please leave, she begged silently.

"They worked damned hard. They should have a night of celebration. And we'll invite some others, like Beau and Nell and our staff. You'll come, too?"

It was the last place she wanted to be. She needed distance and time. Then maybe her heart would no longer feel ripped to shreds anytime Reid was near. Who was she kidding? She could go to the ends of the earth. An eternity could pass, and she'd still ache for him. But it would be awkward for her crew if she hid away here. And she owed the Knowleses so much.

"Yes. Thank you. And thank you for everything you did this week. I really appreciate it."

He made some kind of noise. Perhaps he cursed.

Could this get any more awkward? She felt as if her bones were going to crack from holding herself so stiffly.

"So the wine will ferment now."

"Yes, we'll begin to punch the cap tomorrow, so that the skins can mix with the juice—once a day in the beginning, then twice, and then three times a day once the juice begins to ferment. Punching the cap and running the tests is work, but it's a lot more controlled than the harvest, where it's often a race to get the grapes—" She broke off, and a flush stole over her cheeks. She was so nervous she was babbling, telling Reid what he already knew. He'd visited their winery during the fermentation process, had even climbed up on the catwalk with Thomas so he could punch down the skins himself.

"You'll be able to rest now," he said.

"Yes." She ran her fingers through her hair, encountered a massive snarl, and winced inwardly. She imagined she looked as if she'd been electrocuted.

From the corner of her eye, she saw him move toward the door. *Thank God.*

He pulled it open, only to stop. "Mia, I need to apologize for what I said to you the other day. I didn't mean it. I was angry and hurt. I lashed out."

She lowered her head, squeezing her eyes shut. "Thank you."

"I also wanted to say that I'm damned proud of you." The door shut quietly behind him.

Alone, Mia pressed the heels of her hands to her eyes, barricading her tears.

AFTER BEING IMMERSED in the demands of the harvest, Mia felt as if months rather than days had passed since she'd last been in the general store.

It was early. She glanced at the luncheonette as she passed and saw Maebeth and Nancy tending to the customers hunched over the counter, intent on eating their eggs and pouring coffee into their systems before they headed off to work. No one was talking much.

The bank was still closed. The metal grille at the post office's counter was pulled down as well, though Mia saw the postmistress, Arlene, moving behind the grate.

Her neglected mailbox was crammed. She needed both hands to pull the mail, flyers, and catalogs out of the narrow space. She began to sort the mail, dumping the junk into the recycling bin, sticking the bills under her arm.

Nestled between two business letters was a postcard showing an unbelievably picturesque harbor with fishing boats bobbing on a bright-blue sea. She smiled and flipped it over. *Mia, darling, having a wonderful time in the Greek Isles. The retsina is undrinkable, of course, but the weather's perfect for ouzo. Love, Thomas.*

She would call him later today and let him know how well the harvest had gone. He'd be so happy he might not even ask after Reid.

The next piece of mail was an even greater surprise. The heavy, cream-colored envelope was addressed to her in a flowing script. Puzzled, she turned it over to read the return address: *Mr. and Mrs. Francis Casari, Queens, New York.* She opened it slowly. Tess and Ward had invited her to their wedding.

She was touched that they had thought to include her. But how could she possibly accept? It would be awkward, to say the least. It would also be the worst sort of torture. By January, Reid would have found someone new.

Carefully, she reinserted the invitation and the additional cards in the envelope and tucked it under her arm just as Quinn rounded the opposite end of the mailboxes. Quinn had a catalog she was flipping through as she walked. She looked up, saw Mia, and her expression emptied. "Hey."

"Hey," Mia replied. Hesitation crept into her voice as she asked, "How are you?"

"Fine." Her expression remained blank.

Okay, so Quinn knew Reid and she were no longer seeing each other. It was equally easy to guess whose side Quinn had chosen. Panicked at the thought that she'd lost not only Reid but the closest friend she had, Mia reached out and touched her arm.

"Quinn, please don't be—"

"Mad? Royally pissed at you? Sorry, no can do, Mia. Do you have any idea how much you've hurt my brother? I thought you of all people would know to be careful with someone's heart."

Quinn's words found their mark. Determined to defend herself, Mia said, "I'm not going to discuss why your brother and I ended things, but I will tell you that I never had his heart."

Quinn shook her head. "God, if you'd only stop being so friggin' blind for two seconds. Now, if you'll excuse me." She turned and strode out of the building, her bootheels ringing.

Acutely aware that the early-morning crowd had overheard the exchange, Mia wished she could flee the premises, too. But she hadn't gotten Johnny and Leo their promised breakfast. No matter what Quinn thought, she really did like to keep her word.

She stepped up to the luncheonette's register and tried to ignore the curious looks cast her way.

Maebeth walked over. "Morning, Mia," she greeted her. "So Quinn's pretty upset with you, huh?"

It would have been too much to expect Maebeth to remain silent about a public confrontation. Wholly unexpected was the sympathy Mia read in her expression.

Her own features crumpled. "Yeah, she's pretty upset." Her breath hitched. "Can I have two blueberry muffins and two egg sandwiches on sesame seed bagels, please?"

"Sure thing," Maebeth said, handing Mia a napkin to wipe the tears that had begun to fall. "Take a seat while you wait. There's always a lull right about now."

"Thanks," Mia whispered, and slid onto the round stool. She sat with her elbows propped on the counter and her hands fisted on either side of her face as the tears continued.

Maebeth slid a glass of water under her nose. "Haven't seen Reid around much lately, so we didn't know you guys had split. It's over?"

For once Mia didn't think that Maebeth was calculating how this might affect her own chances in snaring Reid. She nodded jerkily and drank half the water. With a sniff and a dab of her eyes, she looked up.

Maebeth was studying her. "You have it bad for him, don'tcha?"

"Yeah. I always have."

"Really?" Maebeth cocked her head. "You mean, like, forever—ever since high school?"

"Yes." She nodded glumly. "Even before then. He's just always been the one, you know."

"Dang, I always thought you were protesting a shade too loudly and all. But that's a long time to want someone." Her voice held a note of admiration.

"I know." She drew a shaky breath. How strange that, of all the people she knew, it was to Maebeth she was confessing her long-held secret.

"Wow. That's, like, epic." Maebeth fell silent, perhaps out of words to describe Mia's condition. The quiet lasted the time it took for her to put the muffins in a bag. "Well, all I can say is that I'm with Quinn on this one. I think Reid's pretty into you. We all noticed it the night that guy at The Drop was hitting on you."

Mia could hardly remember his name. Will Somethingorother. Reid eclipsed him—any man—for her.

"That's what I told Jay," Maebeth continued, setting the bag next to Mia's elbow. "Not that he listened."

Her stomach roiled at the mention of her cousin. "Jay? You talked to him about Reid and me?"

"It wasn't like I started it. We ran into each other in the parking lot. I was gonna ask him about life in L.A. He must be doing all right to judge by that Beemer. But he immediately started dissing you both—saying that you must've thrown yourself at Reid and how this time he'd decided to take you up on the chance for an easy lay." She snorted. "Jay really hasn't taken a good look at Reid, has he? He can get *any* woman."

Mia smiled weakly. "Jay's too busy trying to catch a glimpse of his own reflection to see anyone else."

"Yeah, he's a real ass. He has some nerve coming back to Acacia and trashing you and Reid. I guess I was willing to write off how he behaved in high school, because, heck, we were all dumb jerks in one way or another. But we're not teenagers anymore. There's no call for that nastiness. For some reason Jay's still stuck in a rut. I would have told him how pathetic that was, except I knew I'd be wasting my breath. Again."

Lou called out the order for two egg sandwiches. "That's yours," Maebeth said, and went over to the grill. She returned with them wrapped in foil. "Here you go."

"Thanks, Maebeth."

"Sure. That'll be twelve dollars and fifty-nine cents with the tax."

Mia dug out her money and handed it over. "Actually, I meant thanks for everything."

"Well, I figure I have to encourage love wherever I see it. It's the karma thing—what goes around comes around, and all that. Besides, I knew it would never work between Reid and me." She leaned across the counter and her voice dropped to a whisper. "I'm fated to be with a Leo."

Reid draped the saddle blanket over Sheikh. The Arabian cross was the last to be tacked for the morning ride. Sixteen guests had signed up for the outing—not a large group—so Reid had told Rick that Quinn and he would lead the trail ride on their own. This would allow Rick to help Pete and Ward trim the sheep's hooves; for the wrangler, rounding up and tackling sheep was more fun than leading greenhorns along trails.

Generally, Silver Creek's guests were a good bunch, far less obnoxious and needy than most. But the summer had been long. Burnout on the part of the wranglers happened—there was only so much small talk they could take.

Reid was happy to be going on the ride. There'd be just enough chitchat and monitoring of how the guests were handling their mounts to distract him from thinking about Mia.

'Cause saddling a horse certainly wasn't cutting it.

He kept remembering how she'd looked in the processing room yesterday afternoon: tense and miserable at the prospect of spending even two minutes alone with him. The image weighed heavily on him.

Reid lowered the saddle and adjusted it, moving it a little farther down Sheikh's withers, and then bent to fasten the cinch. The gelding liked to suck air when he felt the strap tightening around his belly, so Reid always took the process in stages. Their horses worked hard for them. Important to keep them happy and willing.

Mia hadn't simply appeared stressed and unhappy. She'd also been disheveled and bleary-eyed with exhaustion. He'd never wanted her more, the urge to take care of her as powerful as anything he'd ever felt.

And she wouldn't let him.

Reid had no problem figuring out the best way to handle a fifteen-year-old gelding with a dished profile and wide-set eyes. Yet he was stymied when it came to approaching a beautiful and sensitive woman whom he'd hurt with his careless words and his selfishness.

He didn't know whether his apology had done anything to heal her. To judge by the tension in the air—as thick as the scent of several tons of crushed grapes—he'd have said not, not in this lifetime. But he couldn't give up. Somehow he had to show Mia that she could trust him with her heart and convince her that she had his.

He'd slipped the headstall of Sheikh's bridle past his pointed ears when Quinn appeared. She was carrying two cups of coffee. She balanced one on the top of the wooden post. "That's for you," she said. "You finished saddling the horses already?"

"Not that many to groom. I even got Domino ready for you."

"Thanks. You could have left a few for me." She put her own coffee cup on the ground and slipped her chaps off her shoulder to buckle them about her hips.

"The riders should begin wandering down in fifteen minutes. Besides, I'm a nice guy."

"Not so sure about that." Quinn picked up her coffee, took a slug, and gave him the evil eye. "Not after I ran into Mia looking like a lost soul, which annoys me, since I spent a lot of time defending your character to her and telling her what a great guy you were. Did you really have to go and prove you're just another dumb set of XY chromosomes?"

"Where was she?"

"At the post office." Coffee finished, Quinn lowered her head and ran the zipper down the fringed legs of her chaps. Her long ponytail whipped through the air when she straightened. "You are planning to fix this mess, right, so I don't have to go on pretending solidarity with my utterly worthless brother?"

"Do you know I sometimes contemplate what life would be like without an annoying little sister?"

She snorted. "Terminally boring, that's what. Are you going to answer the question?"

"I'm trying to make it right, damn it. I've invited her and her crew over here for a barbecue tomorrow night."

"It's a pretty sad state of affairs when a man has to pin his hopes on a roast pig. Still, I guess it's a decent plan. You can feed her as you grovel. Oh, and here's a tip: You might mention that you're not a big chocolate lover."

"What?"

But his sister sauntered away to welcome the first of the guests who'd signed up for the trail ride without bothering to explain what the hell she was talking about. Women, he thought, shaking his head.

Chapter
TWENTY-NINE

MIA HAD PLACED her computer on the living room coffee table and angled the screen so the camera would include Bruno as they sat together on the floor.

Bruno and she were having their first Skype session with Thomas.

"Dear God, Mia, you've finally found a creature with more hair than you!" Thomas exclaimed with a delighted laugh when he got his first glimpse of the dog. "He's gorgeous. And his name's Bruno?"

"Yes, and he's wonderful, so well behaved and very respectful of Vincent. I'm sorry I couldn't convince Vincent to sit beside us."

"That's all right. It would have been beneath his dignity, I'm sure. Give him a kiss for me, though. Now tell me all about the harvest."

While Mia was doubtful that Reid and she had any kind of future, her outlook on the harvest and the grapes fermenting in the tanks was increasingly hopeful.

She smiled into the camera. "Well, the last two weeks were perfect. Warm and dry without being scorching—"

"And here it's been dismally wet," Thomas interjected. "So, perfect weather. And the gang was all there to help bring in the grapes?"

"Yes, they worked so hard. It wasn't the same without you, though, Thomas."

He waved her comment aside. "And Reid? He was helpful?"

"Oh, yes." She kept her smile firmly in place. "He brought food and lent a hand wherever it was needed. He even took pictures. We're going to post them on the website. A kind of photo-essay."

"Going high tech on me, darling," he teased. "That's great. Are the Knowleses aware the harvest was a good one?"

Relieved that he hadn't continued to question her about Reid, she nodded enthusiastically, her hair brushing Bruno's ear. "It'd be hard not to. Every winegrower in Northern California is thanking Demeter and Dionysus."

"Mia, I can't tell you what a relief that is. So you'll do a press of the grapes?" he asked, referring to the process of separating the juice from the skins, seeds, and stems.

"A light one. I think by early next week it should be ready."

"Good, good. Pascale and I have delayed our harvest until the day after tomorrow, to give the grapes a chance to dry, but the front just isn't moving." Thomas gave what she recognized as a Gallic shrug. "We'll see. This may be yet another year where Californian wines beat out French ones."

"If anyone can make good wine from so-so grapes, it's you, Thomas. Remember 2009?"

He gave an agonized groan. "A terrible year! I'm happy that fortune's smiled on you, Mia. I'm counting on you making something truly special for us all to enjoy."

"Don't jinx me," she said with a laugh.

"I wouldn't dream of it. And we'll see some money soon, when the cases, of our 2012 vintage hit the shelves."

"Yes—did I tell you that Phil Onofrie, who's designing our website, is including a page where visitors can shop for our wines?"

"Even better news. France isn't cheap, Mia," he said, and a frown marred his face.

His mention of money triggered thoughts of Jay. She hadn't seen her cousin again—thank God. She assumed it meant he'd realized she wasn't going to cave in to his demands or threats and had returned to L.A. But perhaps he'd practiced his tried-and-true form of emotional blackmail on his father.

"Thomas, has Jay contacted you?"

He looked taken aback by the question. "No, he hasn't. And a good thing, too, since I don't have a euro to spare. Why?"

"I was just wondering." It was kind of incredible, but maybe Jay had finally realized he could no longer sucker them.

"Did he contact you?"

"Oh, you know," she said, digging her fingers into the thick coat covering Bruno's neck. "He came by and—"

"—wanted money." Thomas shook his head in disgust.

She shrugged. "Well, yes, but Reid made it clear no one was going to be transferring funds to his account."

"Good for Reid. I'm glad he stood up to Jay. That boy burns through money like there's no tomorrow."

Mia couldn't bring herself to tell Thomas what Reid had discovered about Jay's strip clubs and gambling habits. His profligacy was distressing enough, and quaint by comparison.

Thomas was still speaking, now busy praising the

elder Knowleses. "I should have approached Daniel and Adele long ago about entering into a partnership."

"They've been really great. I'll forward you copies of their guests' artwork when Tess sends them. And did I tell you they invited the entire crew to a barbecue?"

"A barbecue? When is it?"

"Tomorrow night."

"Give them my best. You know, I'm glad this has been a good harvest, not just for you and me, sweetheart, but for them, too. Have fun at the ranch, Mia. You deserve it."

"I'll try," she said, hoping the computer screen wouldn't reveal how overbright her smile was.

The weather had held for the barbecue the following night. Mia heard the cheerful mix of music and laughter as she circled the main lodge to where the rear patio was located. She'd come alone. Johnny was bringing his girlfriend, Dana, and was also driving Leo and Fran. Even for a short drive, five in the car would have been tight. But the real reason Mia declined Johnny's offer was that, by driving herself, she could then make a discreet and early departure. She didn't know how long she could last in Reid's presence or pretend to be oblivious to the waves of hostility coming off Quinn.

The Knowleses had done it up right. Mexican tin-star lanterns were strung over the expansive patio. They cast gem-colored patterns on the clothes of the mingling guests. The mouthwatering scent of roasting pork filled the air, and Mia knew the long tables positioned at the other end of the patio would be covered with equally delicious dishes. Jeff and Roo didn't do food in a halfhearted way. Already, Mia saw guests helping themselves to chips and guacamole and nibbling on grilled shrimp.

For a few seconds she lingered on the perimeter. She'd spotted Reid immediately, of course. Her gaze seemed to find him no matter how large the crowd. He was dressed in a bluish-lavender shirt. She could only imagine how stunning it would make his eyes look up close, and she renewed her vow to keep her distance.

For all Quinn's anger on her brother's behalf and Maebeth's pronouncements, Mia still didn't believe that Reid loved her.

He was standing with Clinton Stiles. Clint owned a tack shop outside Acacia. She watched him nod at something Clint said. Realizing she could stare at the gold glints in Reid's hair for half the night, she stepped out of his angle of vision before he could catch her.

Most of her crew had arrived and was already socializing with the other guests: ranch hands and Silver Creek staff and Acacia locals. Among them were Beau and Nell Duchamp. They were talking to Roo Rodgers. Mia knew Beau wanted to visit Australia and so was probably pumping the pastry chef for travel tips about her native country.

The Knowleses were interspersed among the guests. Quinn was chatting with her friend Jim, a ranch hand, and Lexi Carter, a high school student who helped Quinn with her goats and the vegetable garden that supplied the guest ranch's kitchen with much of its produce. For the first time ever, Mia gave her friend a wide berth.

Adele was talking to Clover Stiles, Clinton's sister. Clover owned a wool shop in Acacia. One of her sources was the Knowleses' sheep; she used their wool to weave blankets and knit clothing that she then sold in town and at fairs up and down the coast. The crowd shifted, and Mia saw Ava Day and Naomi Blaine walk up to Adele and Clover. Ava owned the beauty salon in town, and Naomi was a yoga instructor. Like Clover, they had ties to the ranch, offering spa services and yoga classes on weekends and holidays.

Seeing these women together, it struck Mia how varied the Knowleses' interests and connections to the community were. It amazed her that she'd become part of this network.

Wanting to say hello to her hostess, she made her way toward the group.

"Mia, welcome," Adele said with a smile.

"Hi, Adele, this is a wonderful party. Everything looks so pretty. Thank you for including me and my crew—and all their friends and family."

"The more the merrier. It's nice to have an end-of-the-season barbecue just for us working folk, isn't it? We've all had a long summer."

"So true," Ava Day said. "How are you, Mia? I've heard the harvest was a good one this year."

Mia nodded. "Yeah, we were lucky with the weather. Now that the crop's in, maybe I can deal with my hair."

"You're not thinking of cutting it, are you? It's glorious," said Clover, who wore her bright-blond hair cropped close to her head.

"You're only saying that because you're partial to long-haired sheep, Clover," she said with a smile.

"Clover's right, Mia. Most women would kill to have hair with half the body yours has," Ava said. "But make an appointment and we'll see what we can do to tame it a tiny bit."

"Thanks. I'll give you a call once the wine's been transferred to the barrels. Right now we're still in the careful-tending stage."

"Speaking of wine, Mia, can I get you something to drink?" Adele asked.

Mia smiled and shook her head. "I'll wait a little. I should go and say hello to Daniel. I spoke to Thomas today. He sends his best to you both. His thanks, as well."

"We haven't done anything," Adele said. "It's been all you and Reid."

An ice age couldn't have stopped her cheeks from warming. "Well, yes, Reid's been great—"

"Hi, Mia," Reid said.

She turned. "Hi." She cleared her throat. "I was just telling everyone how helpful you've been."

"I like your dress. You look beautiful."

"Oh! Thank you," she stammered. Of course she'd agonized over her choice. In the end she'd decided on a blue floral-print jersey that crossed in the front and had a floaty kind of skirt. Mia had always felt that too much of her stuck out whenever she'd worn it previously. But something had changed. It seemed to hang differently. Maybe she truly had lost weight. She suspected that any weight loss was caused less by her grim morning yogurts than by Reid's fiery lovemaking, a calorie burner if there ever was one.

Abruptly realizing that the four women standing next to her were beaming as their gazes flitted between Reid and her, Mia felt the flush on her cheeks travel south. Half her body was probably bright red. So attractive.

"Actually, Adele, I think I will get that drink now," Mia said.

"I'll come with you. Excuse us," Reid said.

"Of course." The Mexican lanterns made Adele's blue eyes twinkle brightly.

The food had been delicious; she was sure of it. But since Reid had stayed by her side throughout the dinner, she could have been eating straw for all she knew. He didn't crowd her; he didn't monopolize the conversation; he didn't stare fixedly at her. He was simply there and being his casual, charming self, conversing easily with whatever person or couple joined them. Since a good number of the guests were her employees or, in the case of Nell and Beau, friends, they were never alone.

But to Mia, they might as well have been. Being near him made her feel as if she were fourteen again and filled with helpless yearning.

She thought dessert—the earliest moment when she could legitimately steal away—would never come. Finally, Jeff Sullivan and his waitstaff—with Tess, Quinn, Ward, and Reid chipping in—cleared their plates and the serving dishes, and Roo's dazzling creations appeared. Mia saw platters being passed by Roo and her assistants, offering up miniature tarts and what looked like fruit ices, but mainly there was chocolate: decadent brownies, and pots of Mexican chocolate pudding, and chocolate truffles.

"Roo's riffing on chocolate tonight," Beau observed.

"She's been experimenting with some new recipes and tweaking old ones," Reid said, having rejoined them.

"You won't hear me complaining." Nell sniffed the air. "I swear I can smell the truffles from here. How about you, Mia?"

She could smell only Reid when she inhaled. Citrus, soap, and man. "I'm afraid I'm going to have to skip dessert tonight. I need to get home. Bruno," she said by way of explanation. She'd been monitoring her crew. They were having a fine time. No one would miss her.

She turned to Reid. "Will you thank your parents for me?"

"Certainly. I'll accompany you home."

"Oh, no." She shook her head. "Really, that's not necessary."

"I'll see you home safely."

"But . . . but . . ." she scrambled for something that would keep him at the party. "Dessert's starting."

"Strangely enough, I've never really been that into chocolate."

Reid had his hands balled into tight fists and shoved deep into his pockets. It was the only way to resist the urge to haul Mia into his arms or even to reach out and caress the bare skin of her arm with his fingertips. It wasn't just the setting—her porch, her fumbling with her keys—that triggered memories of their first mind-blowing kisses and what they'd led to. He'd been fighting the need to wrap his arms about her, breathe her in, and taste her from the moment she arrived at the party. Actually, long before that.

He'd told Quinn the truth. He was trying to figure out how to make things right between Mia and him. He'd obviously screwed up. Mia believed that he was into her only for the sex, and damned if he hadn't been stupid enough to let her think that.

This time he wanted to leave her in no doubt that she was being wooed. He was going to do it carefully and thoroughly. Very thoroughly. She deserved roses and champagne and romantic dinners. Unleashing his desperate need and pouncing on her was not the way to begin his do-over.

She finally got the door unlocked, and Reid heard a heavy scrabbling of nails on wood, then a joyous *woof* as Bruno rushed out to greet Mia. Then, after receiving a hug and a "Hey there, Bruno," from her, the dog went over to him, circling while his tail thumped Reid's legs.

Reid had just removed his hand from his pocket to stroke the dog when Bruno bounded down the stairs, racing for the nearest bush.

"It's a good thing I came home early," Mia said.

"Yeah." He shoved his hand back into his pocket and took a breath. "I miss you, Mia."

The silence seemed to last an eternity.

"I miss you, too."

He exhaled in an unsteady rush and nodded. "I'd like to ask you out."

"Out?"

"On a date." Another eon passed. Tension squeezed his gut as he waited.

"I—I don't know if I should."

"Dinner, Mia. Just dinner. I'd like another chance with you. Please."

"I—okay," she whispered.

He nodded, happy and nearly weak-kneed that he'd gotten her to agree to that much. "Good night, Mia. Don't forget to lock up." He forced himself down the porch steps and strode quickly to his truck, before his feet turned around of their own volition and brought him back to where he most wanted to be.

Mia was in a state of shock and unexpected, bubbling gladness. He wanted a date with her. A second chance. Could it mean that he actually did want something more than convenient, next-door sex with her?

Slowly she became aware of her surroundings. She was standing on the porch, hugging her middle, a goofy smile lifting her cheeks, and she was cold. There was a nip to the night air. And for some reason her dog was still rooting around in the bushes.

She frowned. "Bruno!" she called. "Bruno, come on inside now."

Nothing. Usually only a second or two would pass before he'd bound toward her, more than happy to obey. She peered into the darkness and made out his white hindquarters. They were sticking out of the overgrown aucuba bush she hadn't had time to prune. Her voice was sharper this time. "Bruno, come here!"

The seriousness in her tone must have registered. He scuttled backward out of the bush, shook himself, and trotted over, licking his lips as he did.

"Sit, Bruno," she said when he reached her.

He sat and gave his muzzle another long swipe.

She was pretty sure he was looking guilty.

"What did you get into?" she asked.

He thumped his tail, his brown eyes shining.

"Forget it," she said with a sigh. "I don't want to know. Come on, it's time for your bedtime treat—not that you deserve it, you hound dog."

SHE WAS AWAKENED by a single sharp bark and then a piteous whine. Her feet were over the edge of the bed and moving toward her bedroom door before the second whine reached her.

The hall light was illuminated. She hurried down the short passage to the stairs and gave a cry at what she saw on the landing: Bruno, collapsed on his side, breathing heavily. He didn't so much as raise his head as she barreled down the stairs.

"Bruno," she whispered as she reached him. His eyes were fixed straight ahead and his ribs heaved dramatically as he panted. Beneath her palm, his heart raced. "Oh God. Hang on, Bruno, please. I'll get help for you." Turning, she sprinted up the stairs for her phone.

He answered as she was hurrying back down the hall to Bruno. "Yeah?"

"Reid, can you come right away? I need you."

"Mia?"

"Yes. It's Bruno. He's sick. Really sick. I can't lift him into the truck."

"I'll be right there." He hung up.

Reid had arrived at her house within minutes, bringing with him the striped wool blanket they'd picnicked on. The grim expression on his face when he'd looked at Bruno made Mia's heartbeat stutter in fear. Placing the blanket next to Bruno, he'd managed to shift him until he lay on top of it. Scooping the dog into his arms, Reid carried him outside. A Jeep—Mia recognized it as Ward's—was idling outside, the back door to the cargo area open so the interior was illuminated.

Mia was so grateful he'd anticipated the need for a car large enough to accommodate Bruno. Trying to slide her dog onto the front seat of either Reid's or her truck would have wasted precious time and possibly hurt him more.

While waiting for Reid to arrive, Mia had looked up the name of the closest emergency animal hospital that was open twenty-four hours. It turned out Reid had, too, with a quick call to Quinn. According to Quinn, it was the best in the area.

The seven-mile trip felt ten times the length, with Bruno's labored breathing the only sound except for Mia's murmured chant of "Don't die. Please don't die."

Once there, Reid jumped out of the car and ran around to the back, then lifted Bruno, cradling him in his arms.

Mia followed them into the animal hospital, clutching her bag and Bruno's records from the shelter and his latest trip to the vet. She'd pulled a sweater on over the T-shirt she slept in and dragged on the first pair of jeans she'd found hanging in her closet.

The brightly lit waiting room was empty save for a couple who sat next to each other, a small animal carrier resting by the man's feet. Their faces were etched with the same lines of fear Mia knew marked her own.

A young man in blue scrubs was behind the counter.

He looked up from the computer as Mia and Reid hurried toward him, Mia already speaking.

"It's my dog. There's something terribly wrong with him. He's trembling and not responding."

The young man looked at Bruno's head, which hung listlessly. Drool was running out the side of his muzzle. "Come with me," he said, rising from his chair. "We'll get him in an exam room and I'll take your information there. The doctor's with another patient right now, but it should only be a few minutes more."

It was difficult to judge how much time elapsed after the vet tech left. Reid and she sat on the exam room's floor, Bruno between them, the harsh rise and fall of his chest faster than the second hand of a watch. He remained unresponsive.

Mia couldn't speak, could only stroke her dog's silken head and will the tremors that racked his body to cease.

The door opened and a woman in a white doctor's coat entered. She was accompanied by a man in scrubs. "Hi, I'm Cat Lundquist, and this is my assistant, Ted Block."

Hurriedly, Mia introduced herself, adding, "And this is my friend Reid Knowles."

"Any relation to Quinn Knowles?"

He nodded. "My sister."

"We're fans of hers here at the hospital," Dr. Lundquist said, as she knelt down beside them. "And this is Bruno?"

"Yes. I've had him almost a month now." And she loved him as if they'd been together for years. "I got him from the county rescue shelter."

Dr. Lundquist nodded. "Tell me how long he's been like this."

"About an hour—though maybe more. He was fine when I went to bed. That must have been around eleven o'clock—"

The vet checked her watch. "So, four hours ago he was fine."

"Yes. Bruno woke me up with a bark. Then he began to whine. He's never done that before. I went downstairs and he was just lying there. His breathing was off—like this—and he couldn't get up."

As Mia spoke, Dr. Lundquist was running her hands over Bruno, opening his clenched mouth, looking at his gums and his tongue, sniffing his breath, lifting his large ears and examining their insides. Then she moved to his eyes, drawing back the lids. Before she lowered his head, she quietly asked her assistant to slip a towel beneath Bruno's head so he wouldn't be lying in a pool of saliva.

She shifted, moving to his belly, her hands gently probing. "Was Bruno behaving differently at any point today? Was he lethargic?"

"No, he was his normal self. We went for a long walk together this afternoon. He had a great time."

The vet gave an abstracted nod. Inserting the tips of her stethoscope into her ears, she placed the chest piece against Bruno's heaving ribs. Mia waited while she moved it from point to point across his stomach.

Sitting back on her heels, Dr. Lundquist took off the stethoscope. "Has he eaten anything unusual today or yesterday?"

"No—" Mia paused, remembering. "He did spend some time under a bush tonight. He didn't listen to my command to come for a few minutes. And when he did come, I saw him lick his lips. But I don't think he was under there for very long."

"What kind of bush was it?"

"An aucuba," Mia said.

"Good for you for knowing." Dr. Lundquist withdrew a thermometer from her jacket pocket. "I'm going to take his temperature and draw some blood before we take him back with us."

"Dr. Lundquist, do you have any idea what's the matter with him?"

"My guess is that he's eaten something toxic." Kneeling over Bruno's prone form, she slipped the thermometer under his tail and held it there. "Do you have any poisonous products—antifreeze, fertilizer, pesticides, rodent poison—around your house?"

"No." Mia shook her head, confused and horrified at the notion that Bruno could have eaten any of the things just listed. "I have a vineyard—we don't use pesticides or fertilizers on the grapes. And I have a cat that prowls for any mice or chipmunks. I'd never use a poison to eliminate them."

"You mentioned him nosing around a bush. It's possible that whatever was lying under there—a dead animal, for instance—could have been poisoned. If Bruno ingested it, the chemicals would then begin to attack Bruno's system, too." She removed the thermometer. "One hundred and four degrees."

"Is that bad?"

"It's high." Her grim tone indicated just how high. "Ted, can you pass me the syringe, please?"

With the same efficiency she'd shown throughout, Dr. Lundquist drew two vials of blood, capped them and the syringe, handed them to her assistant, and sat back on her heels again.

"This is what I'd like to do. We're going to take Bruno back into the surgery, where we'll collect a urine sample from him. Then we'll perform a lavage to flush out his stomach—I think that's a safer course of action than inducing vomiting, since I don't know exactly what he's ingested. Certain chemicals can cause additional damage to an animal when they're being regurgitated. If it's poison, my worry is that he's bleeding internally. So, in addition to the lavage, I'm going to start him on an intravenous drip. With a fever this high, we need to keep him hydrated. The IV will also allow me to administer other drugs as quickly as possible once we have the lab results for his blood and urine."

"Okay—thank you." Mia nodded dazedly. How could her dog, who only a few hours ago had been running and leaping so happily, so healthily, now be so sick? "Will he be all right?"

"I hope so. It's good you didn't delay in getting him here."

Dr. Lundquist's assistant left the room, returning a few seconds later with another scrub-uniformed man.

Reid spoke for the first time since introducing himself. "Mia, we need to get out of the way so they can carry Bruno into the surgery."

She realized she'd been staring down at Bruno and stroking his head, willing that spark of canine joy to return to his fixed, vacant gaze.

"Oh, yes, of course." As Mia scrambled to her feet, Reid rose, too.

Carefully, the two assistants wrapped their arms about Bruno's prone form, lifted him, and carried him into the adjacent room.

She pressed a fist to her mouth and swallowed back a sob.

Dr. Lundquist turned to her. "It shouldn't be too long before I have a better sense of what's going on with Bruno and his chances for a recovery."

Mia nodded tightly. "Thank you."

* * *

Quinn was in the waiting room. She stood when they entered, walked up to Mia, and gave her a fierce hug. "Are you okay?"

"Yes." She would not cry, she told herself. "Thanks for coming, Quinn."

"Of course. How's Bruno?"

She had to press her lips together for a second before answering. "They're running tests and hooking him up to an IV." The breath she took made her shoulders jerk. "Dr. Lundquist thinks he's eaten something poisonous. She mentioned internal bleeding."

"Shit," Quinn muttered. Mia saw her exchange a look with her brother.

"Dr. Lundquist said it was good Mia got him here so quickly. And he's a strong dog." Reid's voice was steady and firm.

"That's right. He is strong," Quinn said with a nod. "I've brought lots of animals to Cat Lundquist, Mia. She's good and totally dedicated. She'll do everything she can for him."

It wasn't long before Dr. Lundquist came out. She looked pleased though unsurprised to see Quinn sitting beside Mia. Quinn had obviously made other trips to the veterinary hospital at close to four o'clock in the morning.

As she approached Mia, Dr. Lundquist's expression grew serious. "From our analysis of the lab tests, we've concluded that Bruno did consume rat poison, somehow, somewhere. What we still don't know, however, is how much he ingested. From his symptoms, my guess is several ounces."

Reid's arm slipped around Mia's waist, holding her steady.

"We've given him K1, a coagulant, to try to stop the

internal hemorrhaging," Dr. Lundquist continued. "His fever has gone up, despite the IV drip. We'll be monitoring his condition closely to address any other symptoms that might present themselves."

"And what might they be?"

Dr. Lundquist's mouth flattened into a grim line. "My biggest concern is kidney failure. It can have a domino effect. We also have to get the bleeding stopped. The thing to remember is that there are some factors in Bruno's favor. He's a big, strong dog, and he's young, too. Those things might help him pull through. I'll be in touch later with an update on his condition."

Neither Reid nor Mia spoke on the way back, but every few minutes he reached over to touch her lightly on her knee or arm. With no one on the roads, the trip was short. Reid pulled into her drive and the headlights cut through the dark, sunrise still an hour away. By the back of the house, he braked to a stop.

Unutterably weary, Mia lifted her head from where it had rested against the window as her fingers felt for the door latch.

"Mia, you didn't leave the winery's lights on, did you?"

An instant and awful premonition seized her. "Oh my God!" she cried. "No! No!"

She shoved the car door open, jumped out, and raced into the building.

THE OVERWHELMING ODOR of fermented grape juice assaulted Mia before she even reached the processing room. She could hear the noise, too, of cascading liquid. Yanking open the door, she was met by a dark blood-red sea. It rushed past her, soaking her shoes and calves.

"Jesus! What the hell!" Reid yelled as the wine hit him, too.

She didn't stop but made straight for the nearest tank. From behind her came the splash of Reid running to the one next to hers to shut off its tap, as well. Then, like her, he raced to the tank farther on.

Oh God, there was so much wine—thousands of gallons sloshing in the processing room and now streaming into the front of the winery. She couldn't even guess how many more gallons had already escaped down the floor drains.

Frantically, she and Reid ran to the two remaining tanks, shutting off the flow with an anguished jerk of wrists. Then there was only the sound of their harsh breathing, the slap of liquid hitting the walls, the awful gurgling of the drains.

"The cellar—my God, Mia." Reid's shout bounced off the walls as he sprinted out of the processing room.

Mia closed her eyes, her shoulders slumped in defeat. She didn't need to race into the cellar. She knew what they would find: barrels rolled, bungholes unstoppered—and more senseless, stupid wreckage.

The smell of wine had never sickened her before. Of course, what assailed her wasn't merely the odor from the spillage. What overpowered was the stench of wanton, vindictive destruction. Only ruin could satisfy Jay's thirst for revenge, his festering hate.

She was still standing by the steel tank when Reid returned. His face told what she'd already known.

"It's all gone."

Mia closed her eyes and nodded.

She heard the splash of his steps as he walked over to her. Silently, he wrapped his arms about her. For a few precious seconds she let her head rest against his shoulder, and then she straightened and looked around her, assessing the devastation. By now the level of the wine had receded. It lapped the tops of their shoes.

How quickly it had all disappeared, she thought absently. Everything destroyed.

"We need to call the police, Mia."

"Yes."

He took her hand and led her outside and into the dark.

"Here, sit." Reid pulled out one of the patio chairs and pressed on her shoulder until her legs folded. "I'll be right back."

She leaned back in the chair and let her head fall, staring up at the moonless, starless sky. This was when the tears should come. But she couldn't cry, since she could no longer feel. Jay had sworn she'd regret refusing him the money. How naïve, how endlessly stupid of her to think he wouldn't follow through on his favorite kind of promise.

It was all over, everything she'd worked for and dreamed of for the winery.

She wondered whether Jay had realized that his act of vengeance would also destroy any chance of a future with Reid. Probably. He was clever that way.

There'd be no date with Reid. There'd be no anything with Reid. And no matter how much she'd longed to have the chance to tell him she loved him, the words would remain locked in her heart forever.

The Knowleses had given so much to Thomas and her. Now their investment had literally gone down the drain. Mia couldn't expect them to funnel more money into a business that had taken such a devastating hit. She wouldn't burden Reid with her love when his family would be taking the necessary steps to dissolve the agreement they'd made with Thomas.

"Here." He'd approached quietly. He was carrying a blanket, the same one in which he'd wrapped Bruno.

That was when the pain sliced through her numbness, the prospect of how close she was to losing Bruno too awful to bear. Tears slid down her cheeks and she accepted the blanket, pulling it close about her, comforted when she caught the scent of her dog. She sent a prayer to the heavens that at least Bruno might survive this night.

Officers from the Mendocino County Sheriff's Department arrived in two patrol cars. One of them, who introduced himself as Lieutenant Nick Armstrong, came over to where Mia sat wrapped in the wool blanket and asked whether she and Reid could answer some questions for him.

She nodded. "Of course. Would you like to sit down, Lieutenant Armstrong?"

He settled himself opposite Reid and Mia. "Ms. Bodell, this is your winery?"

She shook her head. "No, the property belongs to my uncle, Thomas Bodell. He's moved to France, and I'm running the winery and vineyard for him."

He wrote down the date when Thomas had left and asked for his contact information. Mia said she had it in the house and could give it to him. Then, because she could guess what his next question would be, she gave him the names of her crew as well as those of Roberto and Paul's extended family who'd worked during the harvest.

"And, Mr. Knowles, are you a friend of Miss Bodell's?"

"Yes," Reid replied.

"And a business partner," Mia told him. "Reid's family entered into a business deal with my uncle. Reid is in charge of marketing for the winery and is its administrative director."

"And so you and Mr. Knowles were away from the winery until approximately four A.M.?"

She clutched the blanket more tightly around her. "No, that's not quite right. I went out earlier this evening, at seven o'clock, to a barbecue at the Knowleses'—where all my harvest crew was also invited—and returned at about ten-thirty P.M. Then my dog became very sick late in the night. I called Reid, and he helped me bring Bruno to the emergency animal hospital. That must have been at about three A.M. After that I lost track of time."

"I remember glancing at the clock on the dashboard as we drove through Acacia on the way back to Mia's. It read four twenty-five A.M.," Reid told him.

"So no one was here for approximately an hour, maybe a little more. And the winery? Do you keep it locked?" Armstrong asked.

Mia squeezed her eyes shut as regret washed over her. "No," she said, with a shake of her head. "We never have. As you can see, Lieutenant, we're not a big operation. Before we entered into a partnership with the Knowleses, we didn't even have this patio area for visitors."

"I understand," he said. "But it means that anyone who wanted to could simply open the door to the winery and walk right in."

"But who would?" Reid asked. "Mia's got a great crew. They're loyal to her and immensely proud of this place. She's well liked in the community and respected by the other vintners. I can understand someone stealing cases of wine, but this kind of vandalism here in Acacia in a small boutique vineyard makes no sense." Anger hardened his voice.

Knowing what was coming, she lowered her gaze to her lap.

"Ms. Bodell? Do you have any idea who might be behind this?"

"Yes," she said quietly.

"Jesus, Mia, who?" Then, as he made the connection himself, Reid let out a string of curses.

There was no use pretending the ugliness didn't exist, so Mia continued. "I have my suspicions, Lieutenant Armstrong. But I'm assuming this person is smart enough not to have left any obvious clues, so it will be my word against his." Another instance of the past repeating itself. Whenever Jay had stolen or broken one of her favorite possessions, he'd always had a fabricated explanation at the ready.

"We have fairly sophisticated tools at our disposal, Ms. Bodell."

God, she prayed their tools worked. "I think my cousin, Jay Bodell, was behind tonight's destruction." There, she'd said it, and, yes, accusing Jay of committing such a vile act against his own family was every bit as repugnant as she'd imagined.

In a toneless voice, she offered Armstrong what little she knew of Jay's particulars. He'd been living in L.A. for the past eight years. No, she had no address for him, only a cell number. She'd get it for him when she retrieved Thomas's information.

"And what makes you believe your cousin would want to sabotage the winery?"

She looked at Nick Armstrong. She guessed he was in his late thirties and more the CrossFit type than the donut-munching brand of law enforcer. She imagined he had a nice family, not one where a rebellious daughter ran away from rigidly conservative and disapproving parents, nor one in which a toddler was orphaned when her mother drowned following a night of wild partying, leaving her child with nothing—not even the name of her father. Armstrong probably didn't have cousins who despised him with frightening virulence.

An all-too-familiar self-consciousness had her shifting restlessly in the chair. The still-wet fabric of her burgundy-soaked jeans rubbed her calves. A cold reminder of all that had been lost, it prodded her into speech. "Jay was angry when I refused to give him additional money—"

"I was there when he tried to shake her down," Reid interjected. "So you have a witness, Lieutenant. I told Jay he could forget about getting any money other than the lump sum he'd already received."

"That was the first time he approached me about giving him money," Mia told Armstrong.

"Wait." Reid's surprise was plain. "You mean Jay came to see you again, Mia? When was this?"

"He showed up at the vineyard a couple weeks after we met at The Drop." From the expression on Reid's face, Mia knew he had more questions, but she returned her attention to the officer. "He noticed all the recent improvements that had been done around here and asked questions about the harvest. Then the talk turned to money. I again refused to give him any or to ask the Knowleses for an advance. I told him that he would have to wait until the next quarter to receive his percentage of the profits—"

"Sorry to interrupt, but I'm not sure I understand this part. Mr. Knowles mentioned something similar," Armstrong said. "Am I right in thinking that your cousin was due to receive another sum based on the winery's profits?"

Mia nodded. "Yes, that's right. The contract that the Knowleses and my uncle negotiated gives him ten percent."

"Then why would he destroy the product?"

She looked at him steadily. "I know. It doesn't make sense. Ordinarily, Jay is very consistent when it comes to acting in his self-interest. But before he left that day, he promised I'd regret not giving him the money he wanted. I'd say he achieved his aim."

"Excuse me, Lieutenant." Another officer had approached their table.

"Yes?" Armstrong said.

"There's something I'd like to show you, Lieutenant."

He nodded to the officer and then said to them, "If you'll excuse me a minute."

When the officers had moved out of earshot, Reid turned to her. "Mia."

She looked at him, and another piece of her heart broke. An orange-yellow band lined the horizon to the east and offered just enough light to detail his haggard features and his own disheveled and wine-stained clothes.

He'd done so much for her tonight.

"Mia," he said again. "When Jay came here, it was

the day the artists were sketching the vineyard—the day you broke up with me—wasn't it?"

"Yes."

At her answer, an expression she'd never seen before settled over his features. He looked . . . dangerous. "Damn it, Mia. You could have told me." He stood, tension radiating in every line of his body.

"Reid?"

His eyes glittered with emotion, but his voice was controlled. He was holding his anger in check. "I need to speak to Armstrong. You should go in and change so you don't catch a chill."

He was furious with her, yet still he thought of her welfare. She watched him go with an aching regret.

It was over.

MIA DIDN'T GET the chance to change into dry clothes. Before she could will her stiff limbs to move, Leo and Johnny appeared, and shortly after them came Paul and Roberto. Their arrival marked the beginning of the day's tears. They started to flow as she explained the presence of the patrol cars and what had happened to the wine these four men had helped make and of which they were so proud. Their tears joined her own.

"And Thomas? Does he know yet, Mia?" Roberto asked, and swiped a flannel sleeve across his eyes. He'd worked for Thomas the longest of any of them. All of a sudden he looked every day of his sixty-five years.

"No, not yet. I told Lieutenant Armstrong I'd get his number, so I'll try him now. Do you want to speak to him?"

As one, they nodded, demonstrating their willingness to give their employer and friend the comfort he would need. She'd never appreciated her crew more than in that moment.

As she left the group, her eyes searched for Reid. He was standing by one of the areas that was cordoned off with yellow police tape, deep in conversation with Lieutenant Armstrong. Just then she saw him gesture toward the house. At what and why, her tired brain couldn't fathom. She saw Armstrong nod and then turn to one of his subordinates.

She went in the back door and reemerged with the telephone numbers and her cellphone, which she'd forgotten on the kitchen counter when she'd hurried out after Reid and Bruno the night before. She needed it with her not only to speak to Thomas but also to answer when Dr. Lundquist called with an update on Bruno's condition.

Shutting the door behind her, she turned and saw a navy-blue-and-gray-uniformed officer walking toward the front of the house. Reid accompanied him.

What were they doing or hoping to find over there? she wondered.

For a moment she considered following them, but then she remembered Reid's fierce anger. He wouldn't want to have anything to do with her now. She should respect that.

Her crew had drifted closer to where the officers were conducting their search. It was just as well. She needed to be alone when she delivered the news to Thomas.

Wearily, she sat down on one of the patio chairs and punched in the country code and then the number Thomas had given her. She had no idea what time it was in France. Calculating the time difference was beyond her abilities right now.

He picked up on the third ring. *"Allô?"*

"Thomas, it's me." She forced the words out before her courage could fail her. "I have bad news. Terrible news. And I'm so very sorry."

Across the vast distance that separated them, she heard the shock in Thomas's voice as he began to pose questions while carefully skirting the one Mia dreaded. She suspected he'd already guessed the identity of the culprit; he knew Jay. But it was far better for officials to deliver the news—should they ever find sufficient proof.

Her heart was already heavy enough. She couldn't be the one to accuse her cousin to his father.

"Mia, is there any way to save what's in the tanks?" he asked, his voice thin with strain.

She dug deep for a trace of optimism to inject into her own. "I honestly don't know. Reid and I haven't been back inside since we called the sheriff. The winery's cordoned off until the officers have finished searching for evidence. We're all—Leo, Johnny, Paul, Roberto, and I—waiting for Lieutenant Armstrong, the officer in charge, to give us the green light. Even then, we'll have to leave what's in the tanks until the insurance rep has come—"

"Of course. He'll need to see how great the loss was. I understand," he finished, sounding infinitely weary. "But after the insurance agent has gathered what he needs for his report, will you see whether there's enough to do a press?"

"Of course." Thomas must know as well as she that the tanks' contents were most likely unsalvageable. Undrinkable. But if he wanted her to try to make wine out of it, that's what she'd do.

The conversation didn't last long. Too many topics—whether they'd have enough money to continue paying the crew, and whether Johnny and Leo would even wish to remain when there was no wine to tend and bring along—were shrouded in uncertainty.

With a choked goodbye and the promise of news as soon as she had any, Mia signaled to Roberto and passed him the phone.

At nine o'clock, the representative from the insurance company came to inspect the damage to the building and calculate the loss they'd sustained. A futile endeavor. Numbers might be crunched and figures arrived at, but Mia knew they were meaningless. What had been destroyed here was more than just dollars. It was her crew's livelihood. It was her identity. And her heart.

Soon after, Adele and Daniel arrived. Their presence made Mia long for the numbness that had engulfed her earlier. Daniel's tanned face was set in severe lines, and Adele's blue eyes lacked their usual sparkle.

"We're devastated by what's happened, Mia," Adele said.

"I know you are. Thank you," she said quietly.

"We'll call Thomas later to discuss where we go from here," Daniel said.

Mia knew the answer to that. Donald Polk's office, where the Knowleses would seek to end the partnership, was the obvious destination.

"Of course," she said, and bit her lower lip to stop its trembling.

"Have you seen Reid, Mia?"

"No." She shook her head. "He left in Ward's Jeep about twenty minutes ago. I don't know where he went." She'd been on the phone with Thomas when she spotted Reid rounding the corner of the house with the officer. They went over to Lieutenant Armstrong and exchanged a few words with him. Then he'd jumped into the Jeep and driven off—where to, she had no idea.

"He'll be back soon," Adele said gently.

Of course he would. He was too responsible to leave for long in a crisis. But his absence served to highlight a hard truth: It showed how much she'd come to count on his steady support and his seemingly endless strength.

She would have to learn to do without them, as well.

Unable to trust her voice, she nodded tightly.

With a small, sad smile, Adele held out her arms. Mia stepped into them and sobbed.

* * *

She'd managed to get her tears under control when she heard a vehicle roll up the drive. She turned, thinking—hoping—it was Reid. Instead, Quinn climbed down from her truck. She made straight for Mia and gave her a fierce hug.

"You've had ten hours of utter hell, haven't you?" she asked, stepping back.

"Yes. Yes, I have," Mia admitted quietly.

"The second we got the news, Roo and Jeff whipped up some food for you, your crew, and the officers. They wanted to do something—anything. There are bean-and-butternut-squash quesadillas and breakfast burritos and corn muffins. And coffee."

"Wow," she said, too weary to smile. "Thank you."

"I can't imagine you feel like eating, but you need to. Maybe this will reinvigorate your appetite: While Roo and Jeff were cooking, I drove over to the animal hospital. Bruno's hanging in there, Mia. He's still really weak but his condition appears to have stabilized. Cat Lundquist wants to keep him under her observation until he's out of the woods, though."

With a cry of gladness, Mia threw her arms about her. "Thank you, Quinn. I so needed to hear this."

Quinn hugged her back. "I know you did. I'm sorry for all that you're going through, Mia."

"What's with the hug fest?" Reid asked.

Quinn and she broke apart and Mia turned to Reid, wiping her eyes as she did. "Quinn went to the animal hospital. Bruno's hanging in there."

His smile temporarily banished the harsh lines stamping his face. "That's good news. Really good news."

She nodded. "Yes. Where did you go off to just now?" she asked.

"I was checking something out for Armstrong."

"Oh. I see." She knew she'd have to get used to it, but it hurt that he wasn't forthcoming.

Before she could muster the courage to ask what he'd been checking, he spoke. "I need to touch base with him. Quinn, take care of her, okay?"

She nodded. "Sure thing. Come on, Mia, let's get some food and coffee in you. It'll work wonders."

The officers and the insurance agent had gone, leaving the Knowleses to enter the vandalized winery with Mia and her crew. It was a silent and bleak tour; the scent that lingered in the air told the story. That, and the dark stain that ringed the interior walls of the processing room, marking exactly how high the flood of wine had reached.

The cellar was as heartbreaking a sight. Hacked at by a criminal hand, the stoppers littering the floor had then drifted like flotsam when the barrels were rolled, their contents dumped.

Mia had attended funerals that were cheerier. But "funereal" was the only way to describe how it felt as Adele, Daniel, and Quinn shook her staff's hands and offered her grim hugs before departing.

Reid remained to take up one of the mops alongside Johnny and Leo; Mia, Paul, and Roberto armed themselves with sponges and hoses. The five of them set to work. It took two hours of continuous scrubbing, hosing, and mopping before the winery looked as it had before the night's destruction.

With a glaring difference: The cellar was empty. And Mia, Leo, and Johnny had checked the six tanks. At most, a tenth of the fermented wine remained.

"I can't believe this," Leo said. His usual mellow vibe had disappeared hours ago. "There's hardly enough to take a bath in."

"The amount is irrelevant. I told Thomas we'd press whatever remained," Mia said.

"Then a press is what we damned well will do," Johnny said, his voice as determined as his expression. "They better catch the motherfucker that did this, though," he added.

"They will," Reid said. "He's not going to get away with it." Like Mia, he'd taken care not to mention Jay's name to her crew at any point. Turning to her, he continued, "I have to tend to some stuff at the ranch. I'll be by tomorrow."

"Okay," she said, refusing to break down and ask him to stay. "Thank you, Reid. Thank you for everything. I don't know what I would have done without you."

He gave her a long, inscrutable look. "You still don't get it, do you?" he said, and he shook his head. "Don't work too much longer. You've already put in a fifteen-hour day."

Leo had been right. The amount of wine pressed was pitifully small, enough to fill only three barrels. The men were as silent exiting the winery as they'd been entering it.

After Paul and Roberto drove off, Mia turned to Leo and Johnny. "Guys, I want to thank you. This has been without question the worst day of my life. I don't know what I would have done without your support."

"Hell, Mia, you know we love this place—the terroir and the grapes—and the way you and Thomas respect Pinot Noir," Leo said.

"Yeah, so don't even think about telling us that we should go off and find jobs at some other winery," Johnny added.

She sighed and mustered a small smile. "You knew

that was coming, huh? I could call Andrew Schroeder at Crescent Ridge. It's a good vineyard. They try to be true to the grape. I know they'd be happy to add you to their cellar crew—" She stopped, because Johnny was shaking his head.

"Mia, we don't want to leave. Now more than ever, this winery is what we care about," he said. "We're not going to let this keep us down."

"Hell no," Leo agreed. "Those barrels are going to be the best damned wine the three of us can make."

"Okay, then. But—"

"No buts," Johnny interrupted.

"*Mañana,* Mia," Leo said, with some of his old cheer.

"Sleep in, at least," Mia told them. "We all need it."

"We'll take that into consideration." Leo swung his leg over his bike.

Mᴵᴬ sʜᴏᴡᴇʀᴇᴅ, sᴛᴀɴᴅɪɴɢ under the hot stream until the water ran cold, which actually felt good. It rejuvenated her enough that, once she'd toweled off, she was able to drag some clothes on and braid her hair into a ponytail before grabbing her keys and heading out to her truck.

Unsurprisingly, the animal hospital was more crowded at this hour. Waiting next to their owners was a quivering spaniel, some kind of terrier breed that Quinn could surely have identified, and two cat carriers. Deep, growling meows emanated from one of them.

Mia went to the front desk. A different assistant was behind it.

"I'm Mia Bodell. I'm Bruno's owner. Dr. Lundquist said I could come and see him."

"Oh, yes. Just follow me and we'll put you in an exam room. He's able to walk a bit."

She'd settled herself in a plastic chair and had finished reading all the charts and animal posters hanging on the wall when the door opened. Bruno stumbled woozily toward her. Mia slid off her chair and opened her arms. He walked up to her, put his muzzle on her shoulder, and then sank down with a groan, too weak to stand any longer.

"We removed the IV about an hour ago. That's why his leg is bandaged," the vet assistant said, pointing to the gauze. Around the gauze was a larger square of shaved fur.

"He doesn't need the intravenous medication?" she asked, running her hands over Bruno's large body. Less than twenty-four hours had passed, yet he seemed so much thinner. And now that his head had found her lap, he hardly moved.

"The medication he needs, K1, can be administered in pill form—he'll be on it for some time—and Dr. Lundquist would like to see how he does off the IV, if his vital signs hold steady."

Mia nodded in understanding. "And if he does okay, can I bring him home tomorrow?"

"I'm sure that's what Dr. Lundquist hopes."

"Good," Mia whispered, stroking Bruno's domed head.

"I'll let you and Bruno comfort each other. Just knock on the door to the surgery room when you need to leave and I'll take him back to his bed," the assistant said.

"I will. Thank you."

When the door closed with a soft *click,* she leaned over him and buried her face in the silky ruff of his neck. "Oh, Bruno, stay strong for me, buddy."

Reid was in Grant Hayes's office. Of the back offices in the main lodge, Grant's was located closest to the reservations desk. Problems with guests didn't arise all that often, but when they did, it helped for Grant to be on the spot as quickly as possible.

Reid had showered and shaved and downed two cups

of coffee in the kitchen with Roo and Jeff and their sous-chefs and staff before meeting with Grant. He was feeling slightly more human-like, if still as pissed off as ever.

"So far, Armstrong and his men haven't been able to locate Jay. They're not sure he's still in the area. In L.A. he'll have dozens of ratholes he can go to ground in," Reid said.

"But you're not convinced he's left." Grant posed it as a statement rather than a question.

"That's right, I'm not. Jay's always been the kind of guy who gets off seeing firsthand the damage and pain he's caused. The temptation to witness how badly he's hurt Mia would be irresistible." The anger simmering inside him began to boil once more.

"As you requested, I've got the entrance to Ms. Bodell's vineyard covered. My men have Jay Bodell's description and the color, make, and model of his car. They'll be watching for any other unknown vehicles that turn in to her road, in the event he's ditched his car."

"I doubt he'll have done that. Quinn told me it was a BMW. It would hurt him to give up a slick set of wheels." Unfortunately for Jay, Reid was going to make sure he felt a whole lot of hurt, and very soon.

After Jay was caught, then Reid would confront Mia about what had happened to them. "Confront" wasn't quite the right word, but he couldn't think of another one right now. He was hurting and tired, not the state of mind he wanted to be in when trying to reason with the woman who had his heart and didn't seem to realize it.

And if he felt exhausted and bruised emotionally, Mia was all that, and raised to the power of three. He'd kept an eye on her all day, worried she would collapse under the force of the calamities she'd been dealt. She hadn't.

She was a hell of a lot stronger than he'd ever imagined. He wanted to tell her that—and a hundred other things besides.

"I'll ask the men on watch to alert both of us the minute they see anything," Grant said.

"Good. I appreciate your help in this." He rose and noticed a list of names on Grant's desk. A number of them were crossed out, some in red ink, some in blue. "What's that?" he asked, pointing to the sheet of paper.

"Pete Williams sent me a list of people who've shown an interest in working here as wranglers. I've crossed out some who didn't meet our qualifications. Mrs. Knowles has nixed a number, as well. Sometimes it's difficult to figure out what her criteria are, but she's a smart woman. I trust she'll choose the right person for the job."

The comment had Reid wondering exactly what his mother was looking for in the applicants' profiles, but before he could ask Grant, a knock sounded.

"Come in," Grant called.

Reid's father stuck his head inside the office. "Sorry to interrupt."

"That's okay, Dad," Reid said. "Grant and I were just going over the security surveillance for the vineyard until Jay Bodell is caught."

"So the sheriff's department hasn't tracked him down?"

"Apparently not."

Daniel looked as if he wanted to punch something— or someone. Reid recognized the emotion all too well.

"What can I do for you, Mr. Knowles?" Ex-army, Grant was more formal than most of the staff, many of whom were on a first-name basis with their employers.

"Actually, Grant, I was looking for Reid. If I could have a word?"

"Sure." To Grant, Reid said, "Thanks again. Let's stay in contact."

"Understood."

Reid followed his father down the carpeted hall to his office. His mother had decorated all the rooms in the main lodge—public and private. Here she'd hung enlarged photographs of the ranch as it had evolved over the decades.

The space suited his father, but Daniel used it only for business meetings. He far preferred to be down at the corrals or out in the pastures, either astride Kane or perched on one of his tractors.

Reid dropped into the chair opposite his father's. "What's up, Dad?"

"Hell of a day." His father rubbed the side of his face wearily.

"Yeah. Unbelievable."

"Reid, I was just on the phone with Thomas. He's real worried. He's lost two years of revenue. That's a devastating hit for him to absorb under any circumstance."

"I know. It's going to be a rough ride."

"Yeah, and that scares him. The money he took for himself may not cover his needs, even when the 2012 Pinot hits the market. He's not sure he'll be able to pay the staff to keep the winery going. Land prices have started to rise again. He's thinking he'll have to sell."

"Oh Christ. Mia . . ." Reid tried to picture that piece of land without Mia working it. He couldn't. It was as inconceivable as his family no longer raising their horses, cattle, and sheep on Silver Creek's acres. "Thomas can't sell the place off. Mia would be devastated if she had to leave. She should have the chance to prove what she can do with those grapes and that land."

"I know, son. So what do you propose we do?"

It was suddenly clear. The challenge he'd been looking for: This was it. He'd found a challenge that, if he was very lucky, could last a lifetime, one where the rewards would mean so much more than adding zeroes to the balance in a bank account.

He leaned forward.

OLD HABITS DID indeed die hard. Mia had given herself the same advice she'd offered to Leo and Johnny, but, despite falling into her bed and into a dreamless sleep upon returning home the previous night, she'd awakened with the sun.

And now she had to face the void that was her life. Three lonely barrels lying in the cellar were her only chance to nurse the young wine to maturity. It would be one thing if the wine had undergone all the steps in the fermenting process without a glitch. But the contents of those three barrels had been compromised. She really didn't know if it could come close to expressing the subtlety of the grape and its place of origin.

Many people didn't understand the passion that drove a vintner. When Mia tried to explain it, the best she could do was compare it to the obsession that drove artists: the thrill of the painter whose composition captured a previously unrecognized truth using only color and line; the joy of the poet in the distilled purity of expression; the power of the opera singer who attained and held the perfect note.

Setbacks occurred in every life. It was the hatred behind this loss—Jay's corrosive malice—that threatened to paralyze Mia.

She knew she couldn't let it. After her shower, she went downstairs to feed Vincent and herself. There was still the vineyard to tend, and though the pace of the work would be slower, the vines and the rows of earth still required her care.

She brought her coffee cup out onto the porch so that Vincent could sit with her and swish his tail imperially and track the birds that were crisscrossing the lightening sky. She hunched her shoulders against the bite of the wind and the gnawing ache in her heart. She missed Reid so.

Here was another thing she couldn't allow Jay to destroy. Or, rather, attempt to destroy again. It didn't matter whether Reid loved her in return or if they ever got back together—Mia was realistic enough to know how unlikely a prospect that was after everything that had happened.

But love was a gift, and Reid deserved to be given what she'd been keeping locked away in her heart. She had to stop holding the best part of herself back. If she succumbed to fear, then Jay had succeeded once again in diminishing her.

The question was how to tell Reid she loved him and then be strong enough to let him go, however painful that would be. She would simply have to find a way.

At peace with her decision, she carried her coffee cup back to the kitchen and filled a thermos with the remains of the pot to take with her into the vineyard. In the mudroom she grabbed her canvas carryall with her tools and put the thermos in it. She was grateful there was still work to be done in the vineyard, vines to be readied for the winter months. Otherwise she'd go crazy thinking about all the things she couldn't do in the winery.

She stepped out the back door and was distracted by the sight of Vincent running with his tail straight up and puffed. "What spooked you, Vincent?" she asked.

He offered no clue but raced toward the other side of the house. Thinking to follow him and make sure he was okay, she turned, only to spin around when a hated voice reached her.

"Guess the kitty doesn't like me much."

She stared in shocked disbelief. Jay was leaning against the side of his car, his arms folded casually, one leg crossed over the other.

"What are you doing here?" she demanded, silently damning herself for having again forgotten her cellphone in the kitchen.

"Thought I'd check up on my little cuz before I split this burg."

"You won't get very far. The police are looking for you."

He scrunched his face in a mockery of concern. "The police? What do they want with me?"

"To find out where you were the night before last. But you and I know the answer to that already. You were here, emptying the tanks and the barrels."

He bared his teeth. "Oh, but you're mistaken. I wasn't anywhere near here. I have a real hot lady who will vouch for me. Glo kept me up all night."

Of course he had an alibi. She could see the satisfaction oozing from his large pores. "Why'd you do it, Jay?" she asked. "You wanted money, but then you went and flushed hundreds of thousands of dollars down the drain. You won't see a cent now—not ever."

"So you're saying it's all gone, huh? Well, ain't that a shame? Your friends the Knowleses have lost quite a few of their pennies. I suppose they'll pull out now. Ooh, I guess that means your boyfriend will, too. You'll miss that, won't you?" He tilted his head, studying her with his cold gaze. "Aww, what's the matter, Mia?" And then he laughed. Hard. "Oh my God, you really did think he'd marry you!"

"Get out of here, Jay."

"Happy to. Course, you'll be packing your bags soon enough, since the only way Thomas'll be able to get the money he needs out of this place will be to unload it."

The words were yet another verbal punch. "He won't." It was what Don Polk would advise, but she'd die before she admitted as much to Jay.

"You're such a fool," he said. Then, abruptly, he made a show of looking around. "Hey, where's that fearsome dog of yours? Napping?"

"He got sick. I had to take him to the animal hospital."

"Your poor doggie-woggie had a little tummy trouble?"

Everything inside her went still. "I didn't say Bruno had anything wrong with his stomach."

He gave a careless shrug. "Didn't you?"

"No, I didn't, you sick bastard." Suddenly it all made sense. Twisted, perverted sense. "You poisoned my dog, didn't you?" Rabid rage propelling her, she launched herself without warning, charging and swinging her canvas bag with all her might. It struck his face with a resounding *whack*.

If only it had been filled with bricks rather than pruning shears, wire, and a metal thermos.

Still, she felt a vicious satisfaction as he bellowed in pain.

Then Jay shook his head, like a boxer in the ring. He looked at her, eyes narrowed with the promise of violence, and raised his fist as he advanced. "You fucking whore—"

She braced herself for the blow.

It never came. Instead, she heard the sudden pounding of the earth. Then a whistling *whoosh* cut the air, and Jay cried out in surprise as his upraised arm was caught in a loop of rope. A loop that closed with a rough jerk. Thrown off balance, Jay stumbled and fell.

For a second he lay on the ground as if stunned. Then he raised his head and stared at Reid astride Sirrus. "What the fuck are you doing?" he yelled, his free hand scrabbling to untie the lasso.

Reid backed Sirrus up a few quick steps, so the rope tightened and Jay was dragged on his belly. He screamed.

"First lesson, Jay. You put your hand anywhere near that rope, and Sirrus is going to move and you're going to go for a little ride. Second lesson, you scream and you're going to spook Sirrus. He may take off really fast."

"You son of a bitch," he panted. "Let me go."

"Then again, maybe I should just let Sirrus have a nice run. He's feeling feisty with this cooler weather. I'd be fine with giving you a tour of our ranch, all two thousand acres of it. Course, you'd be dead by the end of it." He shrugged his shoulders. "You know, it's funny. I'm not into violence, but I'm totally cool with killing you, Jay. To tell you the truth, I really want to, for what you did to Mia."

"She's a goddamned lying bitch—" Jay's curse ended on a high-pitched howl, as Sirrus moved into an elegant sidestepping trot, his dark-gray legs crisscrossing.

"Stop! Fuck, stop!" Jay was crying now. Dirt mixed with his agonized tears.

Reining Sirrus to a halt, Reid continued in the same conversational tone. "Here's lesson number three. You say another word about Mia, and I won't stop Sirrus until there's no blood left in your carcass."

"Fuck you, you can't kill me."

"Oh, it'd be easy. So easy," Reid contradicted with a

smile. "I can think of any number of places where I could dump your body—what remained of it—and nobody, I mean nobody, would ever find it. But you know what? I kind of like the idea of you rotting in prison better. You're going to be there for a long time, you slimy fuck."

"I'll get you for this."

"I'd like you to try."

For the first time, Reid looked over at Mia. "Hey, Mia, sweetheart."

Her heart leapt at the smile—a real smile—that curved his lips. "Hi, Reid. I'm so happy to see you and Sirrus."

"We were just passing by. Arrived in time to see you belt Jay with your tool bag. Nice job. You feel like giving Nick Armstrong a call?"

"I think I would. My cell's in the kitchen, though."

"Use mine. Here, catch," he said, giving the phone an easy toss. "Scroll through the recent calls. Armstrong's is the second one."

"The cops will let me go. They don't have jack shit on me." In panic and fright, Jay fumbled with the knot around his wrist. To no avail. Sirrus merely skipped a few steps sideways. Jay shrieked as he was towed along. Sirrus ignored him, as did Mia and Reid.

When he finally brought Sirrus to a stop, Reid stared down at Jay's panting form and shook his head. "You never were very smart, were you? You, know, we really don't like litterbugs around here—especially the jerks who toss plastic nonbiodegradable bags on our roads. If you'd used the trash cans in town, I might not have found the d-CON and the package of hamburger. And damned if the bag didn't have the store's name on it, as did the sticker on the ground beef. Ever hear of video surveillance cameras, dickhead? Every grocery chain has them."

Jay gave a forced laugh. "That's pissant stuff. So I made a boo-boo and a little d-CON got into the treat I was giving the dog. No prosecutor can make the charges stick."

"You keep telling yourself that," Reid said easily. "I'll let Lieutenant Armstrong fill you in on the evidence his team found in the winery. So glad you brought your car, too. You get out those wine stains? They can be such a bitch."

Mia cleared her throat as Nick Armstrong's voice sounded in her ear. "Hello, Lieutenant? My cousin Jay came to pay an unfriendly visit. Yes, he's waiting for you here."

The patrol cars' sirens didn't spook Sirrus. If Lieutenant Armstrong and his men were surprised to find Jay lassoed by the wrist and looking considerably worse for wear, they didn't show it. Reid's simple explanation of "He tried to hit Mia" was sufficient for all concerned.

Jay was read his Miranda rights and led away to one of the patrol cars, handcuffs now manacling both wrists.

Looping his lariat so it lay next to his saddle horn, Reid dismounted and made straight for Mia. He kissed her hard.

"You okay?" he whispered, cradling her face in his hands.

"Yes." She nodded. "I'm so glad you stopped Jay for me, Reid."

The lines bracketing his mouth deepened. "It's something I should have done twelve years ago," he replied. "We both hurt you back then. I can't tell you how sorry I am. I should have beat the crap out of him—or tried to—for taking your diary. I've felt so damned guilty for slinking off to the showers while he read from—"

"You weren't there—in the locker room?"

He shook his head. "No. I didn't like to be anywhere near Jay. But that's no excuse, and I should have done a better job apologizing about it. But I was embarrassed and couldn't figure out how to apologize *and* get you to agree to go on a date."

"A date? With you?" she said in disbelief.

His smile was crooked. "See? Not so easy."

"Reid, I—" but her sentence was left unfinished when Lieutenant Armstrong approached.

"We'll be taking your cousin in now, Miss Bodell. There'll probably be some follow-up questions we'll need to ask you and Mr. Knowles."

"I understand. And thank you for coming so quickly."

"We were already on our way. Mr. Knowles's head of security called as soon as they spotted your cousin's car heading your way on Bartlett Road. A tow truck will be along to impound the vehicle. We'll run tests on it."

"I'm sure you'll find traces of wine in the interior. There's no way Jay could have emptied the barrels and opened the tanks without getting soaked," Reid said.

"That's the hope. And we've sent the grocery bag to the lab. Thanks for contacting the vet who treated Miss Bodell's dog and having her send us the lab analyses. The more charges we can pin on him—"

"—the better," Reid finished with a nod. He stuck out his hand. Armstrong shook it and then Mia's.

"I hope your vineyard can recover from this loss, Miss Bodell," he said.

"Thank you, Lieutenant."

Reid and Sirrus stood beside her as the patrol cars backed up, turned around, and headed down the drive. "Come sit down on the porch, Mia, so I can tie Sirrus and he can nibble on your grass."

Rounding the house, they reached the porch. Reid looped his rope around the top rail and then knotted Sirrus's reins so they wouldn't drag on the ground.

The gelding happily set to grazing.

"I wish I had an entire field of clover and timothy for Sirrus. Or at least a bag of carrots."

"We'll raid Quinn's stash later, don't you worry."

"He was magnificent. You were, too, Reid."

"We're a family that protects our own. You're mine, Mia." He clasped her chin and brought his lips to hers, kissing her lingeringly. "I love you."

"Oh, Reid." She looked up at him. "I love you, too. I have for so long. It's just that I've been scared of admitting my feelings. And then Jay—"

"Jay was the reason you told me it was over between us, wasn't he?"

She could see the hurt in his eyes. "Yes. He's always been really good at preying on my fears and insecurities and the stupid garbage I've carried around inside me for years. On that day of the artists' weekend, he did it again, making me think that you could never love me, because of my background—"

"Mia, for all I care you could be Queen Elizabeth's grand-niece."

"Unlikely." Mia smiled sadly. "It's hard not having an identity, the way others do, the way you do, Reid, with a family that's loving and supportive. Jay always knew how to twist that particular knife in his attacks against me. Then, after the winery, when we lost so much, I convinced myself that if I told you I loved you, it would sound as if I was trying to tie you to me. I couldn't bear the thought of taking more from you when you'd already done and given me so much."

He caught her hand and laced his fingers with hers. "It wasn't you who took, Mia. It was Jay. He tried to poison you with his words as surely as he poisoned

Bruno and destroyed the wine you and Thomas made. He wanted to destroy everything you cared about."

"I know." Mia nodded. "This morning I woke up and realized I couldn't let him or my fears control me anymore. I was going to find a way to tell you how much you mean to me"—rising on her toes, she pressed her lips to his—"which is everything."

With a ragged groan, Reid wrapped his arms about her, pulling her close and deepening the kiss. "I've missed you so much," he whispered. "You're mine forever, Mia. Tell me I'm yours."

Tears slipped down her face as she replied, "Yes, yes. Always."

"Marry me, Mia. The vows say 'for richer, for poorer, in sickness and in health.' Judging from what we've been through in the past forty-eight hours, I'd say we can weather anything. We'll figure out a way to save the winery, too."

"Jay thought Thomas would sell the winery. I bet he even thought he'd be able to persuade Thomas to hand over a share after the sale went through."

"The bastard. We'll talk to Thomas. I have some ideas that will allow us to keep the winery and give Thomas enough to live his life with Pascale. We can discuss them later, after we've gone and picked up Bruno."

"I want him back home so much," she murmured. "He was so weak yesterday."

"We'll make him better. And we'll make this winery one of the best."

"Oh, Reid. I was so afraid I'd lost you—"

"Never fear that."

And when he touched his lips to hers, Mia tasted something infinitely sweet and rare: She tasted love.

ACKNOWLEDGMENTS

IN MATTERS OF wine I am woefully ignorant. Like my character Quinn Knowles, I frequently buy a wine based on how pretty its label is. Fortunately I have friends who are far more discriminating and who helped me when it came to writing about winemaking. My thanks go to Carolyn Swayze and Howard Benedict for their careful reading and corrections concerning all things wine-related, and to John Hoskins, Master of Wine, who recounted hair-raising stories of sabotage perpetrated in wineries. Should any wine connoisseurs find inaccuracies in my descriptions, the mistakes are mine alone.

Brave indeed are those willing to read a first draft of mine. As ever, my thanks go to Marilyn Brant, my critique partner, for her comments on the manuscript and her unfailing encouragement. To Sally Zierler, friend and fellow dog-lover, my gratitude for her insights when I was consumed by doubts.

I consider myself endlessly lucky to have the friendship and support of the brilliant team of editors and publishers at Random House. My deepest thanks go to Linda Marrow, Gina Wachtel, and Junessa Villoria. I am indebted to Janet Wygal and her sharp-eyed copyeditors who caught more errors than I will ever admit to making. And to Lynn Andreozzi, my thanks and admiration for the amazing covers she has designed for the Silver Creek series.

No acknowledgment would be complete without mentioning my family's support and patience—even when I'm at my most doubt-riddled and preoccupied. I love you. To Charles, forever.

Read on for a sneak peek of the next book in
Laura Moore's Silver Creek series

ONCE TOUCHED

WHEN QUINN KNOWLES needed to talk, she turned to
her goats.

Human beings were all right to talk to now and again.
But her friends and family were unsuitable for the present topic, for the simple reason that they were part of
the problem.

"Okay, so I admit it's not exactly fair to call love a
problem," she said. Shifting on her perch on the goat
pen's top railing, she leaned forward to scratch Hennie's
furry chin. "And I know you've all been feeling the love
big time with Romeo—" Last week, Quinn had driven
her four does, Hennie, Alberta, Gertrude, and Maybelle, for their annual tryst with Romeo, a fine and
randy buck who stood stud at a Sonoma farm. They'd
returned yesterday, mellow as warm cream.

"—But for me, it's all a bit much. These days I feel
like I can't take two steps without tripping over some
blissed-out pair." When Maybelle gave a bleat that
sounded suspiciously like a laugh, Quinn looked at her
sternly. "I'm not exaggerating. The situation is seriously
annoying."

In reply, Maybelle stuck her nose in the feeder and
withdrew a mouthful of timothy hay.

The couples who stayed at her family's guest ranch

were a given and thus exempt. Silver Creek Ranch, located on two thousand secluded acres in a bucolic Northern California setting, encouraged amorous play. The guest ranch's menus offered delicious food to set the mood. And the cabins, stocked with luxury comforts—cloud soft beds, organically combed cotton bed linens, and bathtubs big enough to accommodate two—provided the sensual nest where guests could relax, indulge, and, in the true spirit of Marvin Gaye, get it on.

It would be one thing if the hum of love and romance were confined to strangers passing through the guest ranch. But that wasn't the case. Thanks to her family, the love vibe was closing in on Quinn and only increasing in volume and intensity.

"I tell you, it's spooky as all get out," she confided in Albertina who was nibbling on Gertrude's neck in some communal morning grooming.

Her oldest brother, Ward, was engaged to be married, his and Tess's wedding scheduled for January, a mere three months away. Quinn preferred not to think about how fast the date was approaching. She was fairly sure she was allergic to weddings and that no EpiPen would alleviate her reaction.

Reid, her other brother—her better and wiser by four years as he liked to claim—had also succumbed to love. He and Mia Bodell, their neighbor and one of Quinn's good friends, had announced their engagement last night at Sunday dinner. Mia had looked beautiful, radiant with happiness, and Reid couldn't stop grinning. Quinn's mother—equestrian by vocation, hotelier by profession, and matchmaker by some twisted impulse—had wept tears of joy and bone-deep satisfaction. Her two sons were destined for a happy-ever-after with great women.

Of course, Quinn was thrilled for the four of them.

But just because she was happy for her brothers and friends didn't mean she wanted to keep running into the lovers with their lips locked and their hands clutching and stroking, or to listen to their besotted cooing.

Even her parents, who were certainly old enough to know better and had been married for thirty years and counting, were afflicted, infected, behaving like newly-weds.

Whatever was going around the Knowles family, Quinn had no intention of succumbing. The whole point of being a twenty-four-year-old woman in the twenty-first century was that she could be single and totally absorbed in her own thing. She had neither time nor desire to deal with guys with all their neediness and expectations.

But now Quinn was the last progeny standing. She couldn't avoid the sneaking suspicion that her mother was at it again, the compulsive matchmaking business. Couldn't the woman leave well enough alone? It was embarrassing. Uncomfortable, too.

It wasn't that she had anything against love. Love beat in her breast just like in any other reasonably well-adjusted and decent human being's. She adored her friends and family—maybe her mother a little less on this chilly November morning, but Quinn planned on at least ten more years of freedom before tying herself down. She had too much to accomplish to have a man hanging around and slowing her down. End of story.

The question was how to outwit a mother who was as wily as they came.

"So, any suggestions, ladies?"

"You often talk to your goats, Quinn?" Josh Yates, the new ranch hand asked.

She started, nearly falling off the rail and onto Hennie. She clutched the metal bar, which felt cold after stroking her nanny goat's light gray coat.

Just then she noticed that Hennie's ears were sticking straight out and her almond-shaped eyes were closed. She doubted that the rollicking sex fest Hennie and the other does had enjoyed during their visit with Romeo was solely to blame for the animal's present stupor. Nope, she'd gone and talked her favorite goat to sleep.

Swinging her legs over the rail, she jumped down to the ground next to Josh Yates and brushed off the back of her jeans, refusing to feel self-conscious about either her goat-talking habits or her appearance.

After all, Josh Yates was unwittingly part of Quinn's current dilemma. The cowboy had arrived three weeks ago, hired by her parents to help with the fall sale of the cattle and to take up the slack when Ward's wedding and honeymoon came around.

Josh's presence was also a boon to her. It would allow Quinn to avoid having to witness the steers being herded and loaded into the trucks and then hauled away to the market to be sold and processed. It didn't matter how humanely and painlessly the animals' lives ended—the sight of the russet and black Angus steer entering the trucks tormented her.

Quinn was happy to work on the guest ranch in practically all capacities—waiting tables, leading trail rides, herding the sheep and cattle, helping train the horses, tending the dairy goats, planting the kitchen's vegetable garden, heck, even helping out with wedding events—but she couldn't willingly participate in the slaughter of the cattle.

That her family cared enough to hire an extra ranch hand so that she could go off and be distracted from her horror and guilt was just one more reason she loved them. They understood and accepted her limitations.

And her gratitude extended to Josh.

But did her parents really need to hire a wrangler who was jaw-droppingly good looking? Quinn usually couldn't care less about a guy's looks, but Josh was just a bit too dreamy with his thick, curling blond hair, caramel brown eyes, engaging smile, and square, cleft chin. He was tall and leanly muscled, too. His good looks made Quinn wonder whether her mother had asked all the job applicants to include a headshot with their résumé.

She really was fine with the hire. She liked the ranch hands who worked for her family. They were like extra brothers and uncles. Josh Yates was no different. . . .

Except that her mother was dangling him as bait.

"I was just catching up with the girls," Quinn said. "Hey, is that for me?" she asked, eyeing the second cup of coffee in his hand. "Or did you have a really late night?"

"Well," he drew the word out as if he enjoyed the feel of his rich drawl in his mouth. "It's true I accompanied Jim to The Drop last night. Shot a couple rounds of pool with two ladies—" he paused, searching his memory. "Nancy and Maebeth—"

"Regulars," Quinn provided. "They work at the Luncheonette."

"That's right," he said, nodding. "Fun place. Fun ladies. It would have been even more fun if you'd been there, Quinn. And yeah, the coffee's for you. I remembered you take it black." Josh's quick, bracket-shaped grin appeared, it and his flattery as easy as everything else he did.

Unnerved as she was at the prospect of a too-good-looking cowboy bothering to bring her a cup of coffee, let alone indulging in an early morning flirtation, she nonetheless accepted the ceramic mug. Quinn was not the type of woman to turn down caffeine.

"Thanks." Together they began walking toward the horse barn. Keeping her tone light, she continued. "So, you're coffee-ing me up, huh? What's the angle?"

"Waylon's thrown a shoe. I was wondering whether you'd let me ride Domino today until the farrier can get here."

She shook her head in mock despair. "That kind of bribe should have been accompanied by a pecan and pumpkin muffin at least. I mean, you're an okay rider and all, but Domino, he's—"

"Special. Royalty. A prince."

"Well, yeah." His Texas twang and the dimple in his chin were awfully cute, but it was his excellent eye in judging horses that was damned near irresistible. "He's all that and more. So you're leading the guests on the morning ride?" Josh had been here only a couple of weeks and Pete Williams, the ranch's foreman, was already letting him lead trail rides, an embossed stamp of approval in case there were any doubts about how well Josh was fitting in. The safety of Silver Creek's guests was paramount.

"It's a small group, only six riders. Afterward Pete wants me to ride the fence line."

She nodded. There'd been more coyote sightings in the area. Any gap in the wood-and-wire fence that encircled Silver Creek's two thousand acres could leave the sheep exposed. The cattle were less vulnerable. By now even the calves born in the spring were large enough to fend for themselves. "Well, I have to be at the staff meeting, so—"

"Yeah, Pete mentioned that."

She raised her brow.

His grin was unabashed. "I thought you'd be happy knowing Domino was enjoying the morning while you're stuck sitting inside talking business."

She couldn't help but laugh. "Neatly planned."

Josh tipped his cowboy hat in acknowledgment. "Planning's important. I like to get what I want."

Quinn was okay with that—she liked getting her way,

too. Josh could make plans all day long if that's what he wanted, just as long as he didn't include her in his list. Cleft chin, Texas twang, and appreciation for fine horseflesh notwithstanding.

And when a little voice teased that if Quinn kept rejecting every man she met, she'd end up being the oldest virgin in California, she stubbornly ignored it.